Praise for Sara Richardson

"With wit and warmth, Sara Richardson creates heartfelt stories you can't put down."

—Lori Foster, *New York Times* bestselling author

"Sara Richardson writes unputdownable, unforgettable stories from the heart."

—Jill Shalvis, *New York Times* bestselling author

"Sara [Richardson] brings real feelings to every scene she writes."

—Carolyn Brown, *New York Times* bestselling author

HOME FOR THE HOLIDAYS

"Fill your favorite mug with hot chocolate and whipped cream as you savor this wonderful holiday story of family reunited and dreams finally fulfilled. I loved it!"

—Sherryl Woods, #1 *New York Times* bestselling author

"You'll want to stay home for the holidays with this satisfying Christmas read."

—Sheila Roberts, *USA Today* bestselling author

ONE NIGHT WITH A COWBOY

"Richardson has a gift for creating empathetic characters and charming small-town settings, and her taut plotting and sparkling prose keep the pages turning. This appealing love story is sure to please."

—*Publishers Weekly*

FIRST KISS WITH A COWBOY

"The pace is fast, the setting's charming, and the love scenes are delicious. Fans of cowboy romance are sure to be captivated."

—*Publishers Weekly*, Starred Review

A COWBOY FOR CHRISTMAS

"Tight plotting and a sweet surprise ending make for a delightful Christmas treat. Readers will be sad to see the series end."

—*Publishers Weekly*

COLORADO COWBOY

"Readers who love tear-jerking small-town romances with minimal sex scenes and maximum emotional intimacy will quickly devour this charming installment."

—*Publishers Weekly*

RENEGADE COWBOY

"Top Pick! An amazing story about finding a second chance to be with the one that you love." —Harlequin Junkie

"A beautifully honest and heartwarming tale about forgiveness and growing up that will win the hearts of fans and new-comers alike." —*RT Book Reviews*

HOMETOWN COWBOY

"Filled with humor, heart, and love, this page-turner is one wild ride."

—Jennifer Ryan, *New York Times* bestselling author

NO BETTER MAN

"Charming, witty, and fun. There's no better read. I enjoyed every word!"

—Debbie Macomber, #1 *New York Times* bestselling author

The Summer Sisters

The Summer Sisters

SARA RICHARDSON

FOREVER

New York   Boston

Forever
Hachette Book Group
1290 Avenue of the Americas, New York, NY 10104
read-forever.com
twitter.com/readforeverpub

First Edition: July 2021

Forever is an imprint of Grand Central Publishing. The Forever name and logo are trademarks of Hachette Book Group, Inc.

The publisher is not responsible for websites (or their content) that are not owned by the publisher.

Library of Congress Cataloging-in-Publication Data
Names: Richardson, Sara (Romance fiction writer), author.
Title: The summer sisters / Sara Richardson.
Description: First edition. | New York : Forever, 2021. | Series: Juniper Springs ; 1 | Summary: "The Buchanan sisters share everything – even ownership of their beloved Juniper Inn. But their mother and Aunt Sassy won't even stay in the same state, and no one knows the story behind the sisters' decades-long feud. When youngest sister, Rose, plans the inn's grand reopening for the same weekend as Sassy's 70th birthday's party, a family reunion seems unavoidable. Only Rose needs help from a certain handsome, if surly, hardware store owner to pull off an extravagant celebration. The sparks between them are undeniable, but Rose can't help suspecting he's hiding something from her ... After a heartbreaking end to her marriage, Dahlia Buchanan and her kids have built a new life in Colorado. She's started flirting with the town doctor, but how does she know she's ready to open her heart again? When her youngest daughter cleverly maneuvers her to Juniper Springs on her estranged sister's birthday, Lillian Buchanan has no choice but to finally face her once-beloved sibling. But some wounds are just too deep to heal. And what will her daughters do when the family secrets she's tried so hard to hide come flooding into the open?"– Provided by publisher.
Identifiers: LCCN 2021006604 | ISBN 9781538718254 (trade paperback) | ISBN 9781538718247 (ebook)
Subjects: LCSH: Domestic fiction.
Classification: LCC PS3618.I3452 S86 2021 | DDC 813/.6—dc23
LC record available at https://lccn.loc.gov/2021006604

ISBNs: 978-1-5387-1825-4 (trade paperback), 978-1-5387-1824-7 (ebook)

Printed in the United States of America

LSC-C

Printing 1, 2021

To my wonderful editor Amy Pierpont

It's a joy working with you!

Chapter One

Rose

D on't do this to me, Tony." Rose Buchanan popped out of her chair and stepped around the antique desk that was three sizes too big for her cramped office, ready to fall on her knees and beg if she had to. "Please. Don't walk away. We can work this out. I know we can." Desperation flared in her chest, nearly squeezing out a panicked squeak. They *had* to work this out. She couldn't lose him…

"Not this time." Tony held his ground, arms crossed so tightly over his barrel chest that the shoulder seams of his plaid shirt separated. He widened his boots into a stubborn cowboy's stance. "I told you, Rose. One more surprise and I'm outta here." The man's gray-green eyes had always had their own weather system, and right now they were downright stormy. "It's too much. I'm done."

"You can't be done." She cast a fleeting glance at the door. Six months ago, she might've had too much Southern pride to block him from leaving, but trying to renovate an old run-down resort in the Colorado mountains had shaken the decorum clean out of her.

Tony might be twenty years older than her. He might be gruff and moody. He might wear his jeans low enough to make you avert your eyes whenever he bent over, but he was still the contractor of her dreams, and she wasn't about to let him walk out that door.

"I'll double your pay." She imagined her eyes were bulging as big as his were right now. *Double his pay?* Ha! Apparently, old habits die hard. That was something she would've said in her past life.

Back in Savannah, she could've tripled his pay without the subtle eye twitch she was experiencing now. Back in Savannah, she wouldn't be two months behind on a renovation project that might break her. Back in Savannah, she'd likely be spending her entire summer hanging out by the country club pool, sipping on sweet tea while she gossiped with other high-society wives.

But she'd walked away from that life. She'd walked away from her future as Gregory Cunningham's wife so she could transform Aunt Sassy's quaint Juniper Inn into a mountain resort that actually made money instead of literally flushing it down a toilet with faulty plumbing.

Since the renovation on the Juniper Inn's cabins had started, they had encountered every setback in the book—unstable foundations, rotted pipes, defective wiring. And now—the final straw for Tony—a leak in the roof of the cabin they'd finished working on two days ago.

Sweet Lord, this place had better make money soon, or both she and her sister Dahlia would have to resort to panning for gold in the river outside.

Rose peered up at Tony's face. His frown had definitely

started to budge. Money had a way of talking, but she couldn't back up the promise. "What I meant to say was, I will pay you and your crew a generous bonus when this project is done." That was the other thing renovating a mountain inn had done for her—it had made her an expert in backpedaling. She had yet to make one dime on this place, but she'd nearly spent their entire rehab budget already, and her sister was a single mom with two mouths to feed. There were others to consider too. Her other sister Magnolia and brother-in-law Eric had invested. And Colt, the man her aunt had helped raise since he was a teenager. They'd all put her in charge of this project. If she failed, she would let them all down. "We can negotiate a percentage based on the reservations that come in next month." She couldn't pay Tony more money until they *made* more money.

"This project will never be done," Tony informed her. He could obviously read between the lines of her amended offer. "You'd be better off selling it right now, Rosie. The place is so old you're gonna keep havin' one issue after another. The land would be worth a whole lotta money."

"I can't sell." That was the bottom line. She'd given up everything for this. So had her sister. Dahlia had moved her two children from Minnesota to help Rose manage the place. And what would Colt think if she gave up? When she'd first met him last Christmas, the man had treated her like she didn't belong in Juniper Springs. He'd thought she was flighty and capricious. But spring had been lonely around here with Dally back in Minnesota, and Rose had found herself talking to the man more and more—seeking him out for his opinion on this design for the Mistletoe Cabin and that design on the Gingerbread

Cabin. Before Colt left to accompany Sassy on her trip, she'd promised he would return to a beautiful new resort that was ready to open. She couldn't let him down. "I'm *not* selling."

"Well then, you're gonna hafta find another contractor." Tony took a lumbering step in the direction of the door. "I'm already behind on three other projects because of this disaster. I can't keep putting off my other clients." He made it out the door in two fast steps. "See ya later, Rose."

"Wait!" She fled after him, stumbling through the living room of her aunt's house, and finally caught up to him on the expansive front porch. "Just give me one more week. You can send some of the crew over to the other jobs, and I'll pitch in on the roof work."

That stopped the man midstride. He shifted to face her, amusement written all over his face. "*You?* Rose Buchanan is going to climb herself up onto a ladder and repair a roof?" He eyed her white eyelet capri pants and the Jimmy Choo wedge sandals she wore on her feet.

Was it her fault she hadn't found the time or money to invest in a new, mountain-appropriate summer wardrobe?

"Yes." Rose set her chin. "I will personally climb up on that ladder and repair the roof myself." She straightened her backbone and met his eyes with a look that dared him to laugh like he obviously wanted to. Gumption might be all she had left of her Southern roots, but that was all she needed to save the Juniper Inn. Okay, well, gumption and maybe a few miracles.

"One week," she repeated. They had to have the cabins done by then anyway. Next week, they were supposed to welcome their first guests with a grand reopening celebration that would also coincide with Aunt Sassy's seventieth birthday.

The Cleary family had been coming to the Juniper Inn for three generations before the place had fallen into disrepair, and the family had wanted to be the first to stay at the new and improved resort, so they had rented out the cabins for their children and grandchildren, and there would even be a few great grandchildren.

Everything was set. Deposits for the cabins were already made—that was the only thing keeping them afloat right now. She wouldn't be able to pay back the money, even if they weren't able to open their doors in time.

The familiar stress knot pulled tighter in her stomach. "Seven days. That's all I'm asking. You tell me what to do, and I'll do it." She would roll in a mud puddle like a hog in her white capris if that's what it took.

"Fine." The word came out in a thundering sigh. Tony pointed a stubby finger at her. "Seven days. That's it. And half my crew is going to start on the upgrades to the town hall, so you'd best be ready to work hard."

"I'm ready." She'd been working hard ever since she'd returned to Juniper Springs last Christmas. This would only add a little more grit and grime to her daily routine.

"And do yourself a favor," Tony added, trudging down the porch steps. "Get a pair of jeans. None of them fancy things with the glitter or whatever the hell they put on them, either. A pair of real jeans."

"Will do," Rose called cheerfully to his retreating back. She held her smile in place until Tony drove away in a cloud of dust, and then she let her posture wilt. For her, gumption tended to come in waves, and this one had quickly receded.

Leaning her forearms against the porch railing, she drew

in a deep breath while she gazed out at the land that had provided a backdrop for her most cherished memories. There was no place in the whole world quite like the Juniper Inn. The facilities themselves weren't much to look at—though Tony and his crew had managed to spruce up the log exteriors of each of the eight small cabins scattered around the property. But it was the clusters of aspen and juniper trees, the sparkling pond down at the bottom of the hill, and the glimpses of the mountain peaks still dusted with snow even in July that made this place special.

She and her sisters, Dahlia and Magnolia, had grown up coming here in the summers and then again for long trips at Christmas, before their mother had a falling-out with Aunt Sassy. After that, the sisters hadn't spoken to their aunt in nearly eighteen years. Then out of the blue, Sassy had invited the three of them to spend Christmas here last year, and they'd all jumped at the invitation. It's like Sassy had known—the sisters needed an escape; they needed the Juniper Inn.

Rose had been as shocked as her sisters when Sassy told them she wanted to give them the resort. At first, she had assumed they'd simply have to sell it. But the more time she'd spent here, the more she'd wandered the land and laughed with her sisters and sipped hot cocoa from the same mugs as she had when she was young, the more she'd realized how deeply this place was a part of her—more a part of her than any home she'd ever lived in. She couldn't imagine being anywhere else.

But her brain cells must've been compromised by the high-altitude air, because sitting by the pool in Savannah was sounding a lot better than experiencing failure after failure at the moment.

A distinctive *woof!* sounded from the woods on the other side of the pond and brought a smile back to Rose's face. She watched her fluffy white rescue dog Marigold bound up the hill—all clumsy paws and disheveled fur and sloppy grin coming straight for her.

Rose braced herself for impact. She hadn't quite figured out how to stop her dog from putting her paws on people's shoulders and giving their faces a good lick to greet them properly. She had to admit she hadn't tried too hard. Even when the dog had muddy paws, there was nothing better than big ol' hug from Marigold.

Her dog licked her cheek about twenty times while Rose laughed. "I just saw you a half hour ago, you know." But that didn't matter to Mari. She was always this happy to be reunited, whether it had been ten minutes or four hours.

"Okay, okay." Rose gently nudged the dog down. "I see you've been digging in the mud again." Which meant she now had one paw print on each shoulder.

The dog peered up at her with a guilty grin, and Rose couldn't scold her. "How do you always know to come running just when I need you the most?" She scratched behind the dog's ears. There'd been a time Rose had been terrified of dogs, but last Christmas Marigold had wandered onto the property and into her heart. Maybe Marigold was what had started the avalanche of changes in her life in the first place. "Change is good," she told the dog. "But it's also hard and painful and terrifying." Especially when she was trying to figure out who she was in the midst of this new life she found herself in.

The dog's ears perked as though she sensed something. Rose heard it too: a car making its way down the drive.

Her sister's Subaru rounded the bend, and Marigold took off again, heading to greet Dahlia, Maya, and Ollie—the sweetest nine-year-old niece and five-year-old nephew in the whole world. Not that she was biased.

Her sister got out of the car and hugged Marigold. Even though she'd only been in town about a month, Dahlia already looked the part of the elegant mountain inn owner, wearing a pair of sensible dark jeans and a blue T-shirt with exactly the right amount of lace trim. Her shoulder-length strawberry-blond hair had lightened over the summer, and her blue eyes seemed to shine a little brighter than Rose had remembered seeing them in a long time.

"My turn," Ollie called, even though the dog was almost as big as he was.

"Auntie Rose!" Maya beelined straight up the porch steps. "Do you like my new cowgirl boots? I bought them with my own money." Her niece lifted her foot off the ground and showed off all angles of the impractical red leather boots, the little fashionista. She was a girl after Rose's own heart.

"I love them. Do they happen to have any in my size?"

Dahlia laughed as she made her way up the steps behind her daughter. "I'm pretty sure you already have a pair of red cowgirl boots in that massive closet of yours."

"The stitching is different. I like yours better." Rose planted a kiss on her niece's cheek and winked at her sister. Dally had always had a much more practical sense of style. Maybe it came with being the oldest of three sisters. She'd always been like another mother to Rose, for better or worse.

Most days Rose envied her sister's analytical and industrious approach to life. She used to want to be just like her older sister. If she was more like Dahlia, maybe the Juniper Inn project wouldn't be over budget and still nowhere near finished. Rose hadn't wanted to bother her sister with the details while she was in the process of moving and settling in, so she'd kept her updates generic, but she wasn't sure how much longer she could protect Dally from the truth.

"I'm guessing neither of you will be wearing red cowboy boots come October when the snow is flying." Her sister wore a playful frown. "But there was no convincing this one to get the sensible snow boots."

"They were so ugly," Maya lamented, every bit as dramatic as Rose would've been back in the day. "They looked like something you would wear to outer space."

"I wanna go to outer space!" Ollie chimed in from where he was throwing a stick for Marigold. "That would be awesome."

"You can't go to outer space, silly," Maya insisted in her big-sister-knows-all tone. Rose had heard that same melody many a time growing up. She might be a fashionista, but Maya still had traces of Dally's practicality.

"I don't know." Rose smiled at Ollie, unwilling to let his sister dim his creativity. "I'll bet you could find a way to get to outer space someday." Even if it was only in his imagination. "But first, why don't you two go into the kitchen and help yourself to some muffins?" So she could talk to Dally about more pressing matters.

Ollie dropped the stick on the ground, his mouth pulled into a grimace. "Where did you get the muffins?" he asked as though he was afraid she'd made them again.

"I'll have you know that I picked them up from the Sweet

Tooth Bakery earlier this morning." Rose had permanently given up on baking after Maya and Ollie had nearly broken their teeth on her last round of muffins. Her middle sister, Magnolia, was the baker in the family, but Mags lived down in Florida, where she was currently basking in the glow of her two-week-old son. Hopefully Mags and her husband, Eric, would make it up for Sassy's celebration, but they hadn't committed yet.

"I want a chocolate chip one!" Ollie sprinted up the steps as though trying to beat his sister through the door.

"No, I want the chocolate chip!" Maya scampered in after him.

"They're all chocolate chip," Rose called behind them. Chocolate chip was her favorite too.

"What's wrong?" Dally asked the second the children's voices faded.

Rose scratched behind Marigold's scruffy ears while she contemplated her answer.

"Nothing's *wrong*, per se." Ever since they'd been little, Dally had always been the responsible one. She'd taken care of details and organization while Rose had let her right-dominant brain run wild. She hated that she was seen as the capricious one in the family, and she still wanted to prove this whole endeavor hadn't been a terrible idea. "Tony needs to finish up the job within a week so he can move on to other jobs." She could sugarcoat the truth with the best of them. "So we only have seven days to finish all the repairs."

"That shouldn't be a problem." Dally seemed to shrug it off. Probably because Rose hadn't told her about the latest roof leak on the cabin that was supposed to be done.

"It's kind of a bummer since we'd hoped to have everything done before Sassy got back, but we'll figure it out," her sister went on.

"We can still have everything done before she gets back," Rose said quickly. The work *had* to be done. That was part of the surprise birthday party slash grand reopening of the Juniper Inn.

Dahlia reached down to pet Marigold. "You think we can have everything done by this afternoon?"

The stress-induced eye twitch she'd had earlier when she was discussing the money with Tony returned. "What do you mean, this afternoon?"

"Didn't you see Sassy's text this morning?" Dally pulled her phone out of her pocket and held it out so she could read. "She and Colt are coming home early."

Colt was coming back early? Her heart rate spiked, but she couldn't tell if it was anticipation or panic. Lately, she'd found herself thinking about him, looking back at the pictures he'd texted her from his travels. The images of him smiling and laughing and standing on the edges of cliffs had made her see him in a different light. He seemed so carefree and happy, it had made her smile too. When he left, she hadn't realized she would miss him, but she had. She'd found herself picking up her phone to call and ask him if he could come over to help her pick out windows or tile or stain for the wood floors. For weeks, all she'd wanted was to see him, but now that he was coming home early she didn't feel prepared.

Rose's eyes glazed over, blurring the words on Dally's phone. "I didn't see any text." She'd been too busy trying to retain their contractor so they could finish this project.

"Hi, you two," her sister read. "Wanted to let you know we're flying in today. I miss my mountains and my girls, so we're coming home early."

"Why would they come home early from an amazing vacation?" Rose would give anything to take a vacation right now. Especially if it meant she could take a break from worrying about the inn.

Her aunt and Colt had spent the last two months visiting some of the places on Sassy's bucket list—Alaska, the Grand Canyon, New York City, Nova Scotia. It had been the perfect way to get the woman out of their hair while they revamped the cabins and planned her surprise party.

"I don't know..." Dally looked around at the mountains surrounding them. "It's pretty gorgeous here. I could kind of see why she would miss home."

"Alaska's beautiful. Nova Scotia too. The Grand Canyon? Amazing." She didn't mean to sound so grumbly, but... "How are we supposed to keep the grand reopening celebration a surprise while she's here?" And how was she supposed to hide the lack of progress on the inn from Colt? He would probably take one look at their current situation and go right back to thinking she didn't belong here.

"We can distract her." Dahlia shifted into administrator mode. "I can help out more now that things are settling. I put the kids in a day camp program so they can meet some friends before school starts. That means I'll have a lot more free time."

"That would be great, actually." Some of the weight Rose had been carrying around on her shoulders seemed to fall away. "If you're going to help out, you might want to wear jeans." She would spare Dally the rest of the details until she showed up tomorrow and they had to repair a roof.

"Okay. I'll come by first thing tomorrow after I drop off the kids." Her sister glanced at her watch. "Right now we have to head to the doctor."

"Ohhhh. The doctor, huh?" Rose batted her eyelashes like a Southern belle. Last winter, Dahlia had made a special connection with the town's lone MD, but lately Rose couldn't get her sister to say anything about what was going on between her and the good doctor. "How is Ike, anyway?"

Dally avoided looking her in the eyes. "I don't know, honestly. Things have been so busy since the move, we haven't seen much of each other."

Rose doubted that was from Ike's lack of trying. The man had been quite taken with her sister when they'd been visiting last Christmas, but she'd seen the hesitation in Dahlia since she'd moved here from Minnesota. It was like Dally never wanted to talk about him. "Well, maybe you should ask him out when you see him today. You know I'm happy to babysit anytime." She wouldn't allow her sister to use the kids an excuse.

"Maybe. We'll see." Her sister employed the same noncommittal tone she used whenever Ollie asked if he could swim across the pond. "We have to get over there." As if hoping to avoid further discussion, Dally poked her head inside the house and called for the kids.

They both came bounding out, still munching on their muffins.

"Bye, Auntie Rose." Ollie hugged her and then wrapped his arms around Marigold, who happily licked the crumbs off his face. "Thanks for the muffins."

"They're the best," Maya added, following her brother down the steps.

"Glad you liked them." She followed them to the car, still watching Dally. All of a sudden, her sister seemed flustered...nervous. "You two will have to come for a sleepover soon." She couldn't help but wonder how the kids would be with roof repairs. They might be looking at an all-hands-on-deck approach for the next week.

"Yes!" Ollie climbed into the backseat. "We could have a campout under the stars!"

"We'll see," Rose said, borrowing her sister's favorite tactic. Camping out wasn't really her thing unless there was a memory foam mattress and full bathroom involved. But again, let the kid dream.

"I'll be back tomorrow." Dahlia still wasn't looking directly at her. Since Rose had brought up Ike, there had been a distinct change in her sister's demeanor. What was that all about?

Chapter Two

Dahlia

M om, the speed limit is thirty." Maya peered at the speedometer from the backseat, a frown of disapproval furrowing her pink sparkly lips. "You're *barely* going twenty."

"Am I?" Dahlia blinked the numbers on the dashboard back into focus. "It's safer to go slower on Main Street." Safer, and it would take them longer to reach Ike's office. She wasn't sure she was prepared to see the man.

Last Christmas, while she'd been staying at the Juniper Inn, Ike had reawakened every desire her divorce had suppressed, bringing romance back into her life. He'd made her dinner and had kissed her and had helped her see herself in a different light—as someone who could be desirable and fun. They'd stayed in touch through the spring, talking on the phone late into the night at least once a week. But now that she was back in Juniper Springs for good, she couldn't seem to get up the courage to face him again. When she told Rose they hadn't seen much of each other, what she really meant was they hadn't seen each other at all.

Dahlia rolled to a stop and waved a group of pedestrians across the street.

"Go as slow as you want," Ollie grumbled. "I don't wanna get any shots."

"You don't have to get shots today. This is just a quick physical for your day camp." Usually she didn't wait until the day before a camp started to get the kids' physicals done, but nothing in her life was usual at the moment. Maybe that's why she kept responding to Ike's phone messages with quick texts. *Sorry, things are crazy! Gotta get the kids to bed! Making dinner, will try to call you later! Painting Ollie's room right now. Let's talk tomorrow!* They hadn't been lies, but she'd definitely used the heck out of every excuse she could find to avoid connecting with him.

The truth was, she didn't know how to do this—how to be a mom and also date someone and maybe even fall in love again. After her husband had left her for another woman two years ago, she'd have been fine taking an oath of celibacy, keeping both her heart and her body safely isolated.

She hadn't planned on the spark of attraction that had blindsided her when she'd met Ike last December. She hadn't planned on going on dates with him or kissing him the way she had in front of his fireplace those few times. She hadn't planned to take over ownership of her aunt's inn and move her kids across three states to start a whole new life…

Maya sighed loudly. "I don't see why we have to go to a stupid day camp anyway."

"You'll love it," Dahlia assured her. "You'll get to meet a lot of the kids who will be in school with you this fall." This transition hadn't been easy for any of them, but Maya seemed to be taking it the hardest.

"I'd rather be at my old school. I knew everyone there. I

had a lot of friends." Maya turned her head away to stare out the window, her shoulders slumped.

Dahlia let her daughter pout. She got it. She'd pouted a couple of times this week herself. Change was hard and scary and frustrating. Since the divorce, her life had been nothing but change. She couldn't blame Maya for wanting familiarity and stability. She knew how hard it was to open your heart to new things.

"I think Juniper Springs is the coolest place ever!" Ollie had his face pressed against the glass of the window. "I mean look at those mountains! They're huge! I can't wait to climb one. Can we climb one, Mom?"

Dahlia peered past the brick façades lining friendly Main Street and took in the view of the rocky cliffs that seemed to disappear into the sky. "We'll see." They were wild, those mountains. Unpredictable and bigger than she could even fathom. But there was also something exhilarating about them. Something strangely alluring.

"I'll bet Dr. Ike knows how to climb a mountain." Ollie kicked the back of her seat in obvious excitement. "I'm gonna ask him if he'll teach me."

Dahlia held her breath, feeling a warm blush seep into her cheeks. The kids knew of Ike. They'd met him briefly last Christmas, and she'd referred to him as her friend, but they didn't know how hearing his name made her heart pound or how the memory of kissing him drove a surge of warmth from her chest to her toes.

"Why would Dr. Ike take you mountain climbing?" Maya demanded. "He probably has his own kids." She turned her head to Dahlia as though looking for confirmation.

"He doesn't have kids, actually." Hopefully her children thought the breathlessness in her tone came from the high altitude. "He doesn't have a family."

"He's not married?" Maya seemed to recalibrate her stare, looking intently at Dahlia's face.

She focused extra hard on parking the car as far away as she could get from the doors that led into Ike's office. "Nope. He's not married."

"Perfect!" Ollie exclaimed. "Then he'll have all the time in the world to help me climb a mountain."

"Well, I don't know about that." Dahlia cut the engine and withdrew the keys from the ignition, holding them tightly in her fist. "He's still a very busy man, being the only doctor in town."

"It doesn't hurt to ask," her son told her, using the exact words she'd said to him on more than one occasion.

"You can't ask the doctor to help you climb a mountain." Maya rolled her eyes, even though Dahlia often told her they'd get stuck like that. "We hardly know him, right, Mom?"

"Oh. Uh." Actually, she knew him pretty well, but she couldn't necessarily explain that to her children. "We should get in there. We're five minutes late as it is."

From the outside, Ike's office looked like any other small-scale medical facility—a nondescript square brick building with dark tinted windows. But when you walked inside and entered the waiting room, it seemed you were walking into a whole other world.

"Wow!" Ollie exclaimed. "This is the coolest place I've ever seen."

"Is this a doctor's office or a library?" Maya asked, her eyes wide with awe.

Dahlia smiled. It did bear a resemblance to their library back home in Minnesota. It seemed every time she walked in here there was more for her to see. One corner of the room was decorated in a space theme, with colorful planets hanging down from the ceiling and black wallpaper with flickering stars. Another corner had a jungle theme, complete with large trees and stuffed monkeys hanging from their branches. The waiting room only proved Ike wasn't your average brilliant doctor. He was also creative and…whimsical. Maybe that's what she liked best about him. She'd never had one creative bone in her body, but Ike inspired her.

Today the waiting room sat empty, except for Mrs. Miller sitting behind the reception desk. The kids didn't seem to notice her, though. They took off for the jungle first, admiring the stuffed animals perched in the trees.

"Good morning." Dahlia greeted Mrs. Miller with a smile that hopefully hid her nerves. "We have an appointment for Ollie and Maya today."

"Of course." Mrs. Miller tapped on the keyboard in front of her. "Ike is running a little bit late today, but you can see Dr. Jolly if you'd like to."

"Dr. Jolly?" She hadn't realized Ike had invited a partner to join his practice. Dahlia glanced to where her kids were now looking through the space magazines in the opposite corner of the room. They still had quite a few errands to run, going to the store to pick up some supplies for camp and then also running to the grocery store before they went home for the night. "Do you know how long Ike will be?"

"He should be here in about twenty minutes." Mrs. Miller shook her head with an affectionate smile. "That man drove all the way to Salida to visit one of his patients who had a baby last week."

"That doesn't surprise me at all." Ike was always doing things like that for people. He wasn't only a doctor to most of his patients. He was also their friend. He was kind and open and generous with his time.

Why was she avoiding him again?

"Mom! Check out this awesome spaceship." Ollie zoomed the spaceship through the air, running toward her with a giant grin on his face. "I knew Ike was cool, but I didn't realize he loved outer space like I do."

Yes, her son and Dr. Ike had a lot in common. So why did she find it so hard to bring him into their lives?

The door opened beyond the reception counter, and Grumpy walked out into the waiting room, accompanied by a woman clad in scrubs.

Dahlia waved at the man. He owned the only coffee shop in Juniper Springs, so she tried to stay on Grumpy's good side. Not that she knew she was succeeding. He was always… well…Grumpy. But was that a smile on the man's face?

"Thanks, Doc." Grumpy actually shook the scrub-clad woman's hand. "Glad to know the burn isn't too serious."

Dahlia couldn't seem to take her eyes off the woman she presumed must be Dr. Jolly. She had to be younger than Dahlia by at least a couple of years, judging from the lack of wrinkles around her eyes. And she was gorgeous. Her black hair was pulled loosely back, and there wasn't one imperfection on her dark skin. Even her brown eyes seemed to sparkle when she smiled. The woman standing next to Grumpy wasn't exactly what she'd picture for someone with the name Jolly. For some reason, she'd assumed the doctor would look like Santa Claus...

"It's no problem at all, Grumpy." The woman paused by the reception counter. "Keep an eye on the dressing, and don't forget to apply the cream. If you have any problems at all, give me a call."

"Will do!"

Dahlia watched in shock as Grumpy gave the doctor a cheerful wave on his way out the door.

There was something she never thought she'd see— Grumpy smiling and waving in the same day.

"Hi there." Dr. Jolly turned her attention to Ollie, who was still holding the spaceship in his hand. "Isn't that the coolest rocket you've ever seen?"

"Yes!" Her son showed the doctor how all of the doors opened, while the woman oohed and aahed.

"Watch how fast he can fly." Ollie raced around the room again.

"That is the fastest rocket I've ever seen." The doctor winked at Dahlia. "I'm Dr. Jolly, by the way. I don't think we've met."

"No. We haven't." She shook the woman's hand. "I'm Dahlia. And you just met my son Ollie. Maya is sitting over there." She pointed to where her daughter had curled up on a small sofa in the jungle area with a book.

"It's wonderful to meet you all." Dr. Jolly offered her a sincere smile. "Are you here for an appointment?"

"They were supposed to see Ike," Mrs. Miller offered. "But I told them you'd be happy to take the appointments since he's running late."

"I would love to, but it's totally up to you." The doctor walked behind the counter and jotted something on the chart that was sitting there. "I completely understand if the children are more comfortable seeing Ike."

"You can be my doctor." Ollie zoomed back to the woman. "Especially if I can bring this spaceship into the room with me."

Ha. Her son had always been the great negotiator.

"Fine by me." Dr. Jolly looked at Dahlia as though she wanted to make sure it was fine by her too.

It should be, but she'd prepared herself to see Ike. "I'm not—"

The door across the room flew open and Ike breezed through, his white lab coat fluttering behind him. "Sorry I'm so late."

"Ike! Ike!" Ollie ran to meet the man, waving the spaceship in the air. "I found this over on the shelf. It's amazing."

"It's pretty cool, isn't it?" Ike took a knee in front of Ollie and started to tell her son about how he'd gotten the spaceship from the NASA center in Atlanta, but Dahlia couldn't hear much past the gentle swooshing in her ears.

The sight of the man made her blood run faster and warmer. It didn't matter what he was wearing, Ike always had that handsome mountain man vibe going on. The summer sun had turned his hair into a brownish blondish color that made him look both outdoorsy and carefree. Maybe that was why she'd been so drawn to him.

When she was with Ike she felt carefree too.

"Since the doc is back in the house, I'll let him take your appointment." Dr. Jolly gathered up a file folder and held it against her chest.

Did Dahlia imagine the way that she looked at Ike? The woman's eyes seem to linger on him a bit too long.

The man finished his conversation with Ollie and hurried to the counter. "If you guys would rather see Dr. Jolly, I'm okay with it." His eyes were friendly, but Dahlia could feel a yawning distance between the two of them. That was her fault. Her silence and avoidance had carved out a chasm between them. "No, no. That's okay. We...um...were planning to see you anyway."

"Sure. Yeah. We'll get you back in a few minutes." Ike slipped behind the desk and pulled a wrapped muffin out of his bag and handed it to Dr. Jolly. "I stopped by that coffee shop you love."

"You always seem to know just what I need." The woman peered up at him from underneath her long, lush eyelashes, her smile softening into something more than appreciation.

Dahlia had to look away.

"This is my absolute favorite flavor." Dr. Jolly unwrapped the muffin and offered it to Dahlia. "Do you want to try a bite before I dig in?"

"No, thanks." Normally she didn't turn down chocolate, no matter what the circumstances, but right now confusion clouded her judgment. Maybe she'd misunderstood his regular phone calls as interest. Maybe he'd already given up on her.

She wouldn't know until she asked. Dahlia held on to her fragile smile. "Can I talk to you for a minute?"

"Of course." He waved her to the door. "Mrs. Miller can get the kids situated in the exam room. We can talk in my office."

Dahlia followed him down the short hall past the exam rooms, the sinking feeling in her stomach growing with each step. Dr. Jolly seemed to be exactly the type of woman Ike should be with—beautiful, vivacious, genuine. Not to mention she probably hadn't kept him at arm's length like Dahlia had.

"What's up?" Ike left the door open and sat behind his desk, unpacking a laptop from his bag.

She hadn't exactly planned what to say. The awkward silence blared in her ears. "I didn't know you'd hired someone." She meant to say the words casually, but a squeak slipped through at the end of the sentence.

"Business has nearly doubled since I opened the clinic." Ike gestured for her to sit across from him. "Nikita is a friend of a friend. Top of her class in med school. And she's great with people. I couldn't pass up the chance to hire her."

"No. Definitely not." He didn't make it sound like they were anything other than professional colleagues. Yet as Dahlia lowered into the chair, she found it difficult to look into his eyes. Every kiss they shared seemed to flash through her memory.

Their Christmas romance had reminded her there was more to life than PTA meetings and errands and kids' sports and school functions. But, after she had gone back home to Minnesota, she'd forgotten. The details and responsibilities of everyday life had consumed her again, and now she'd brought all of those things back with her to Juniper Springs. "I'm sorry I haven't been returning your calls." The apology sounded feeble even to her.

Ike didn't seem to find it difficult to look into her eyes.

His steady gaze held hers. "Don't worry about it. You have a lot going on right now. I know how overwhelming it is to move states."

Dahlia nodded but couldn't help but feel something had changed between them. "Well maybe—"

A nurse poked his head into the room. "I've got Ollie and Maya all checked in. They're in exam room two when you're ready."

"Perfect." Ike stood and wrapped his stethoscope around his neck.

It seemed they were done with their conversation.

"How are the kids doing anyway?" he asked leading her into the hall.

She couldn't lie to him. "It's been a transition, that's for sure. They've had their moments." There'd been some complaining and some crying. The changes seemed to have made both Maya and Ollie act out by bickering more than usual. "But they really seem to love it here. Especially when we visit the Juniper Inn."

There was something magical about the place. Her aunt's old resort seemed to have the power to change people and circumstances. Dahlia only hoped it could change her by helping her open her heart a little bit more.

Her stomach knotted the way it always did when she had to grasp for courage. Just outside of exam room two, she reached for Ike's shoulder in a silent request for him to pause.

He turned, catching her in his captivating, clear-eyed gaze.

"I really would like to see you soon," she murmured so the kids wouldn't hear. "Once I get them more settled and into a routine, things will be a little easier." Once Maya and Ollie were settled she would feel more settled too.

Ike was quiet a few seconds while he seemed to study her. "I'd like to see you too," he finally said. "Just let me know when you're ready."

That was the problem. She didn't know what ready was supposed to look like.

Chapter Three

Sassy

There was one magic hour in the mountains.

One hour in the early afternoon when the glow hit the landscape just right—lighting the trees from above, intensifying every color, from the greens of the foliage to the grays of the granite peaks to the unfathomable hues of the royal sky. Sassy's eyes drank in the scene framed in the windshield in front of her, and all at once something inside—that restlessness she'd begun to feel on her extended vacation—started to settle.

She was home.

It was only fitting that Colt would drive her back to this place during the magic hour. The mountains had always been home, though she hadn't known it until she'd moved to Juniper Springs, Colorado, when she was only eighteen. Sassy had arrived at her aunt and uncle's Juniper Inn on a summer day much like this one, both her heart and her spirit broken.

Back then, the mountains had terrified her. They were massive and imposing—a barricade keeping her from what she wanted most in the world...to know love. True love. Deep love. The kind of love that both hurt and healed.

Now, more than fifty years later, the immensity of the peaks in front of her—the sheer impenetrability—was what she loved best about those mountains. They were bigger than her, bigger than almost anything in the whole world—rock solid and strong. And she was a part of them as much as they were a part of her.

"Still feel like you made the right decision cutting the trip short?" Colt glanced over at her, concern etching itself into his brow the same way it used to for his father.

Oh, she'd loved his father. And she could see so much of Robert in this boy she'd helped to raise. Even though she'd never married his father, she considered Colt her flesh and blood, her son. And they'd spent the better part of the last two months solidifying their bond when he'd accompanied her on the quest to see the sights she and his father had always dreamed of visiting together. Before her beloved Robert had passed away.

Sassy kept her gaze on those mountains, tears adding to the pressure building behind her eyes. "I made the right decision cutting the trip short." Another headache was coming on, but she couldn't seem to close her eyes—to shut out the view—to fend off the gnawing pain. She hadn't told Colt about the headaches, which now seemed to come every day.

At first she hadn't thought much of them, what with the travel fatigue and the flying and the constant changes in climate they'd experienced. But now that they'd become part of her daily routine, she couldn't stop thinking about them. Maybe because she'd watched her uncle die of a brain tumor. He'd only been fifty-eight when he'd passed—nearly twelve years younger than she was now. So she couldn't ignore the headaches. As much as she'd like to.

Slowly, steadily, they had moved past an inconvenient annoyance to a reminder she wasn't invincible. She wouldn't live forever.

"You want to head straight back to the inn?" Colt asked, slowing his truck on the hairpin curve as they came down the west side of the pass.

"No." Sassy loved this part of the drive, where the road tilted and bent with the contours of the mountain until you were nestled safely into the Juniper Springs valley. "Let's make a stop in town." She knew Colt had worried about being away from his hardware store for so long. And it didn't matter what impressive city she'd found herself in— Vancouver, Seattle, New York, Chicago, Washington, DC— none of them had given her the sense of awe she found so easily in her little town.

It had been wonderful to travel, to experience new places, all with their own unique cultures, but she missed her people. She missed her place. She hadn't realized how much her community was a part of her identity until she'd left it behind.

"Town it is." Colt made the right turn off the main highway to head that direction.

Sassy watched for each landmark as they neared Juniper Springs. The single cottonwood in the valley's farm pasture. The tree had been only a sapling the year she'd moved here. Now the branches plumed high into the air, providing shade for the herd of Jersey cows munching on the green grass below.

Then there were the ruins from the old homesteading cabins perched atop a swell of cleared land at the base of Castle Peak. The structures had been built in the late 1800s, but time and weather had reduced them to simple shells that evoked a simpler past. "Time passes much too fast." She hadn't meant to say the thought out loud. It just sort of tumbled out, a melancholy observation.

"It sure does." Colt seemed to take in the view. "It feels like we only left town yesterday."

"Mm-hmm," Sassy murmured, though time flying by on the trip wasn't what she'd meant. She swore, the older she got, the closer her memories seemed. "It feels like only yesterday we were hiking up to Castle Falls with your father." She and Robert would hold hands, and Colt would run up ahead, swinging his stick like a sword to fend off imaginary predators. Colt had been so much freer back then. After his father had gone to prison, he'd become gruff and distant, having few relationships with anyone besides her.

"Dad always loved Castle Falls." Before this trip, the man rarely indulged her attempts to meander down memory lane, but something in Colt had changed over the last two months, and she'd seen glimpses of her boy again.

They rolled past the acreages on the outside of town— modest homes set on sprawling lots with goats and chickens roaming the land.

"Thank you for coming on this trip with me," she murmured, trying to battle the headache with a soft tone. "I wouldn't have enjoyed traveling nearly as much if you hadn't been there." She had said as much to him many times over the course of their adventure, every time he'd carried her luggage or made their reservations for various meals and sightseeing excursions.

She knew he'd been worried about her traveling alone.

That's the only reason he'd agreed to find someone to mind his hardware store—so he could keep an eye on her. And she appreciated it.

"I had a great time too." Colt rolled to a stop at the only light in town, waiting to turn left on Main Street. "In fact, after this, I'd like to hit the road more. Maybe even live somewhere else for a while."

Sassy had to let that statement sit. Colt had nothing tying him down—other than the store, which could easily be managed. No matter that she would miss him, that she would miss still having a part of Robert with her. No matter that with two of her nieces moving to town to take over the inn, she'd finally felt like she had the family she'd always dreamed of surrounding her.

She waited to speak until she was sure her voice wouldn't wobble. "That would be exciting. You deserve to have an adventure." He'd been working hard almost his whole life. "I think you should do it." The pressure behind her eyes turned into a dull throbbing. The headache was starting to gain ground. Sassy took a long drink from her water bottle, willing it simply to be dehydration and the elevation gain.

"You all right?" Colt had been asking her that more often over the last several weeks, as though he could tell something wasn't quite right. And just like she did every time, Sassy put him at ease. "I have a small headache. I haven't been drinking enough water, but a walk around town will do me good."

The man quirked his lips into a skeptical expression, but he turned into the heart of Juniper Springs anyway.

This. This is what she'd been missing. Sassy inhaled deeply as if she could pull the peace and friendliness of this place right into her lungs. In contrast to the rest of the world, the town hadn't changed all that much since she'd first walked these cobblestone sidewalks. The square brick buildings held all kinds of different stores—there was Grumpy's coffee shop and Patty's antique store, and Leon's handmade jewelry gallery, and Nora's quilting and fabric boutique.

Striped awnings stretched over the large storefront windows, providing shade for people to linger and chat as they window-shopped their way down the street. In true Juniper Springs fashion, summer seemed to make the town shine brighter. A good portion of the annual budget went to beautifying the whole downtown area with wildflower gardens and flower pots bursting with colorful annuals. Hand-carved benches were placed strategically where people could sit and rest and visit.

The sidewalks were always busier near the end of the summer season, as though people wanted to get one last look at paradise before they went back to their busy lives.

Colt pulled the truck into a parking spot in front of his hardware store and cut the engine. "Well, at least it's still standing."

"Of course it's still standing." The man Colt had hired to manage the store was a retired carpenter who'd worked on half the buildings in this town. "Adam is perfectly capable," she reminded him, climbing out of the truck with her bag and a wince. The sudden movement accentuated the headache and brought on a dizzy spell.

"Adam is perfectly capable," Colt repeated as if trying to convince himself. He walked around the front of the truck to stand by her. "You want to meet back here in an hour so we can head to the inn?"

"Sounds perfect," she said with a bright smile and did her best to stand straight without leaning against the truck. If Colt noticed anything amiss, he'd likely take her straight to Dr. Ike's office, and she wasn't ready for all that mess. She wasn't ready for tests and speculation and more tests. She most definitely wasn't ready to hear a diagnosis. She took another long drink of water and waved him away. "Good luck at the store. See you in a bit."

Colt seemed to watch her walk as she passed him by, but Sassy lived up to her name and kept her shoulders proudly straight and a smirk on her lips. Even if she did have something terribly wrong with her, she wasn't going to let people make a fuss.

Shoving the strap of her travel purse higher up on her shoulder, she marched down the sidewalk, working out the kinks in her lower back and legs. It did help to be outside, to feel the warm sun on her face, to breathe in the clean mountain air. As soon as she was out of Colt's line of vision, she paused and dug around in her purse until she found the over-the-counter headache medicine, quickly popping the pills and washing them down with another long drink of water before anyone could see.

Most times, the medicine didn't take away the headache, but it made it more bearable.

"Sassy?" Peg Conway waved at her from across the street. "It *is* you! You're back!"

Lord have mercy. Sassy looked to her left and then to her right, but it was too late. She had no place to hide, and the woman had already stopped traffic to make a beeline across the street.

"We weren't expecting you back in town for another month." Peg ripped off her bedazzled sunglasses and seemed to inspect her with narrowed brown eyes. "What's wrong? What happened? Are you pale? You look pale."

"I'm not pale," she corrected patiently. "I'm Irish." Peg, on the other hand, had ancestors from Greece, and the woman earned a golden sun-kissed appearance every summer.

"Well, thank the good Lord you're back early." The woman prodded her underneath the antique emporium's awning as though she worried someone would see the two of them talking in broad daylight. Even if someone did see them, they likely wouldn't believe their eyes given the way she and Peg used to bicker when they'd both been on the town council two years ago. Peg and Harold owned the bank in town and somehow believed that qualified them to run things the way they saw fit.

Money or no money, Sassy had never had a problem standing up to them.

"You're not going to *believe* what's happened."

That happened to be Peg's favorite line. While her husband held the role as president of the bank, his wife had earned the title of queen gossiper in town.

"Mayor Lund up and quit!" The woman didn't wait for a response. "She walked out of the office two days ago without even bothering to give two weeks' notice." Peg gave a good look around as though this news hadn't already traveled within a hundred-mile radius of where they stood.

Ha. By now, even the moose in the woods likely knew about the mayor's untimely departure. Especially with Peg on the loose.

"Rumor has it she met someone online." The woman's whisper somehow seemed louder than her speaking voice.

"Well, good for her." Lord knew poor Mayor Lund wasn't going to meet someone in this town. Sassy could attest to the fact that there weren't any eligible bachelors over the age of fifty. Mayor Lund was only a few years younger than her and had gone through a terrible divorce a few years back. She deserved to be happy.

"It's not good for *us*." Peg went into full argument mode, one hip kicked out, arms crossed like she was standing behind her head councilwoman podium at the town hall. "Not at all. I'm sure you've heard Ned Pearson passed away..."

Sassy hadn't heard boo while she'd been on vacation, but that likely wouldn't matter. The more she spoke, the longer this conversation would go on, and Peg wasn't helping her headache any.

"Ned was going to leave that nice plot of land he owned next to the museum to the town trust." The woman's eyes widened and narrowed with the different inflections in her tone, adding dramatics to the bits of gossip. "We were going to create a community garden there, but instead that horrible Graham Wright talked poor old Ned into leaving the land to the museum instead."

That she could believe. Graham had moved to town six years ago to take over as the president of the Juniper Springs Geology Museum. From the start he'd been more concerned about preserving the building and grounds than he had about making the museum a fun and educational gathering place for tourists and the town. She'd even heard he'd kicked someone out for touching the glass on a display case. Needless to say, museum attendance had dropped nearly in half.

"Mayor Lund was going to challenge the will and get that land back for the town," Peg continued, uttering a humorless laugh. "Obviously that's not going to happen. So we need an interim mayor to continue this battle. And you're the perfect one for the job."

Those words thrust Sassy into sudden clarity. *"Me?"* She couldn't have heard right. "Why me?" Peg had hardly agreed with anything she'd said back when they'd served on the town council. They'd argued on just about every issue—from the budget to the town's goals to the community growth and infrastructure. "Why can't *you* be the mayor?" Peg wanted to be the one pulling the strings anyway. Wasn't that why she'd spent the last ten years serving on the city council in the first place? Well, that and the woman was bored.

A lengthy aggravated sigh made it obvious Peg had considered the possibility. "It's no secret that my…um…*charitable* involvement in the town hasn't been well received by everyone."

Or by anyone, really. But there were certain ways small towns like this one worked. Harold had amassed enough wealth to make sure he could contribute to all of the various causes in Juniper Springs—the Rotary Club, the schools, the youth baseball and soccer teams, the community improvement programs. While no one particularly liked Harold and Peg, most everyone in town was also afraid to lose funding and donations for one program or another. Everyone except for Sassy, that was.

"I know we haven't always seen eye to eye on things."

Sassy snorted a little. She couldn't help it. Didn't this beat all? Peg begging her to be in charge?

"But think about it, Sassy." The woman's face broke into an encouraging smile. "You would be the perfect mayor. Everyone here loves you. You have no conflicts of interest, and you've always wanted the best for this town. This is your chance to really contribute. On an interim basis, of course."

All true. And yet... "You can't just make me the mayor. There has to be an election, a process—"

"I can make you *interim* mayor," Peg interrupted. "I can call an emergency session early this evening, and the council won't hesitate to approve you." She pulled her phone out of her sleek leather purse and started to tap on the screen, already setting her agenda in motion. "This is the perfect next step for you anyway. Now that you've given up the inn, what were you planning to do with your life?"

That was the question. The one she hadn't been able to answer for herself for the last two months. She'd enjoyed the traveling, the new experiences, the food, but being gone so long only proved she wasn't meant to be a professional tourist. She thrived with connections, community, family, and now that Rose and Dahlia and her sweet great-niece and great-nephew were here, this was the only place she wanted to be.

She might be turning seventy. She might be facing a health struggle. But she still had something to offer the world.

"The meeting is on the calendar." Peg dropped her phone back into her bag and raised her eyebrows hopefully. "You don't have to make a long-term commitment if you don't want to. I'll set up an election later this fall. I *promise*."

Mayor Sassy. Madam Mayor Sassy. It did have kind of a nice ring to it. She could do this. She could champion a community garden in her beloved hometown and leave her mark on this place for future generations to come.

Peg clasped her hands in front of her chest, her face flushing as though she was holding her breath. "What do you think?"

"I think I'd best go home and unpack my suitcases." She'd been home all of one hour and she was about to become the new mayor of Juniper Springs.

Chapter Four

Rose

How hard could it be to fix a tiny leak in the roof?

Rose stared up at the ladder she'd leaned against the side of the Mistletoe Cabin and tried to decide the best way to get her supplies to the top. There were the extra shingles she'd found in the garage. And then the roofing cement the online video had recommended.

Thankfully, she'd located a pair of old jeans in one of the boxes her aunt had stored in the attic. They happened to be men's Levi's, and the waist was about four sizes too big, but she'd managed to secure them in place with a leather belt that certainly did not match her beat-up tennis shoes. But who cared what she looked like. She had a job to do.

And, actually, men's jeans weren't half bad. This style had all kinds of pockets where she'd stored her tools—a hammer, a box of roofing nails, a small crowbar. Now she just had to lug all this stuff up there without losing her balance.

Marigold barked out her encouragement from a few feet away.

"Believe me, I wish you could come up with me too." When

she'd first gotten the idea in her head to fix the leaky roof before Tony showed up tomorrow morning, it had seemed pretty simple. The online video had shown a step-by-step tutorial of a lumberjack-type guy replacing a few compromised shingles, but he'd likely had a whole crew helping him set up before filming.

"I don't need a whole crew." She was a mountain girl now, damn it. There was no reason to waste Tony's time with a minor leak when they had much bigger things to tackle tomorrow.

That in mind, Rose secured the shopping bag with the shingles and cement onto her arm and then began the climb up the ladder one rung at a time, the hammer and crowbar in her pockets weighing her down.

At least it was a nice day. The sun sat directly overhead, giving a metallic sheen to the blue sky. A light breeze trembled through the aspen leaves surrounding the cabin, making her comfortable in the sweatshirt she'd worn to protect her arms from getting scratched.

"Woof!" Marigold put both paws on the highest rung she could reach and whined.

"I know, girl." Rose took the dog almost everywhere she went these days. "You can spot me from the ground." Thankfully the Mistletoe Cabin was only one story, so even if something did go wrong, she wouldn't have that far to fall.

Eyes straight ahead. No falling. Rose made it to the top with only a slight quiver in her knees and carefully pulled herself onto the roof on all fours, heaving the bag next to her.

"Okay, first things first." She awkwardly shifted to her butt and started to organize the supplies, lining up the new shingles and setting the plastic bucket of cement to the side.

She had identified the general area of the leak from analyzing the water damage on the cabin's ceiling, and now she could see where a few of the shingles had curled and separated— likely thanks to the windstorm they'd had a while back.

The roofs on the cabins had been one thing she'd thought they wouldn't have to worry about, since Sassy had them all replaced six years ago. Rose should've known better. There wasn't one thing she hadn't had to worry about around here. But it was worth it.

She lifted her head to scan the property she now owned with her sisters…and with Colt. Four equal shares to keep her aunt's legacy in the family.

She'd spent summers swimming and canoeing in the glistening pond, the sun warming her skin. She and Dahlia and Magnolia wandered in and around the trees, making up stories about a fairyland they had yet to find. And now it was up to her to bring the magic back to this place. To give her niece and nephew, and countless other kids who would come visit with their families, a place to play and dream and create and get away from the screens that always seemed to be positioned firmly in front of their faces.

Leave it to her to turn roofing into a global quest for the greater good. Rose shimmied the hammer and crowbar out of her pockets. She'd never used a crowbar before, but how difficult could it be?

First step? Remove the damaged shingles. She went to work, prying and pulling against them with the bar. Yes! One came loose and popped off, flipping onto her leg. See? She could totally do this.

Rose picked up the shingle to move it aside, but it stuck to her fingers. Wow, that glue made a mess. She carefully secured the crowbar under her arm while she tried to detach the shingle from her skin. "Ow." It stung exactly like ripping off a Band-Aid. The shingle fell to her lap, landing sticky side down, and attached itself to her jeans. Of course.

Rose went to pull it away and lost the crowbar in the process. The tool rolled down to the edge of the roof and landed in the gutter with a clang.

Somewhere below, Marigold barked.

"I'm good," she called to calm her dog. "Everything's fine." Now she knew why her father had hated home improvement projects so much. They never seemed to go smoothly, no matter how much you prepared.

"No problem." Rose turned onto her knees, the rogue shingle still sticking to her leg, and gingerly made her way to her feet, carefully standing up. She'd have to ease down the roof a few feet and get the crow—

The sound of wood cracking stopped her cold. What the—

Craaaack! The roof under her left foot gave way, and her whole leg plunged through the wood up to her mid-thigh.

"Ah!" She steadied both hands against the shingles around her, trying not to move, trying not to even breathe, in case the whole roof caved in.

Marigold went crazy. Rose could see her now, running in desperate circles while she yipped and barked.

Yes, it was time to panic. She had neglected to bring her phone up with her because she hadn't wanted to drop it. And she was pretty sure she wouldn't get her leg out of the ceiling without some serious help. She could scream, but with the nearest neighbors over a half mile away, they weren't likely to hear her.

Great. Just great. It appeared the water damage up here

may have been a bit more serious than she'd originally anticipated. Tony was going to love this.

"It's okay, Mari," she called down to her dog. "I'll be okay." The roof, however, would not be. Somehow, she had to get out of here without doing more damage.

Rose eased her upper body forward, trying to army-crawl her way out, but her leg wouldn't budge.

The boards beneath her groaned.

Nope. That was it. She wasn't going to move another inch. She rested her forehead on her arm, fighting back tears. All she'd wanted to do was fix a couple of broken shingles, and now she would likely have to have Tony replace the whole roof, not to mention re-drywall the ceiling inside.

"Woof! Woof!" Marigold's bark suddenly had a happy lilt.

Rose lifted her head and held her breath so she could listen. A car. The very distinct hum of an engine slowly grew louder.

"Help!" She propped herself up on her elbows and tried to get a view of the driveway. "I'm stuck! Somebody please help!" Oh, please let it be Dahlia. Or she'd even take Tony at this point...though he would likely quit on the spot if he saw her right now.

Straining her neck to lift her head higher, she finally got a glimpse of the car. Or, rather, the truck.

Colt's truck.

Rose let her forehead fall back to her arm with a groan. What impeccable timing. When she'd seen Colt and her aunt off, his exact words had been, "I can't wait to see what you do with the place." He'd actually shown confidence in her. Now he was about to find her with her leg stuck in the roof.

The engine noise died and doors slammed. Marigold was

practically singing now, serenading Sassy and Colt with one of her howling welcome home ballads.

Rose lifted her head again. She had no choice. It wasn't like she could hide up here forever.

Down below, both Colt and Sassy were greeting the dog. She'd best get this over with before they walked away and couldn't hear her.

"Welcome home!" Rose yelled to get their attention.

Everything seemed to silence. She could imagine the two of them trading confused frowns. "Rose?" Sassy called, probably looking around the land.

She sighed, the humiliation already traveling up her neck and making its way to her face. "Up here!"

"Up where?" Colt asked.

Why oh why did all of her most embarrassing moments seem to happen with that man as her audience? Like last Christmas, when she'd first come to town and had face-planted in the snow right in front of him? Or when she'd been trying to help him hang up the Christmas lights and a stray dog—who she now knew and loved—had come tearing out of the woods, causing Rose to freeze in panic on that very ladder right there?

Speaking of the ladder, the top of it started to wiggle.

"I'm coming up," Colt announced.

She braced herself, trying to find a posture that would help her maintain an air of capability when she saw him. But there was no bracing her heart. It seemed to lift at the sound of his voice, lift and then dive and then roll...

"Rose?" Colt appeared at the top of the ladder. His dark hair had grown a little longer, fringing the tops of his ears. The shadow on his jaw suggested he hadn't shaved for a good few days, but it fit him, that scruff. It looked good. *He* looked good.

"Hi there." She smiled as though her cheeks weren't burning up. "I seem to have a little problem."

"Yeah." Shock registered in his wide eyes. "Are you hurt?"

"No, no." She laughed a little to ease the pressure in her chest. "But my leg does seem to be stuck in the roof." As if he couldn't see that fact for himself.

"Okay." He didn't move, but his eyes darted around, and Rose had gotten to know him well enough to know he was formulating a plan. Colt wasn't much of a talker—which might be another reason she worried about annoying him sometimes—but he was a man of action.

"I'm not sure how stable the rest of this area is." He crawled fully onto the roof, seeming to test each move before he made it. "So we're gonna have to move slowly and carefully."

"Good idea." As if she hadn't been doing that before she fell through. He probably thought she'd been tap-dancing up here.

Colt made it about a foot in front of her on his knees and then extended his hands. "Hold on to me, and we'll ease you out of there little by little."

"Is everything okay up there?" Sassy called. Thankfully, her aunt didn't seem too eager to climb the ladder.

"Everything's great now," Rose assured her. At least she had backup. "We'll be right down." Her aunt didn't need to know the full extent of the damage they were dealing with.

Colt's large hands seemed to swallow hers up, but they were surprisingly warm and gentle as he carefully tugged and coaxed her body away from the hole in the roof. She shimmied her leg free and then rolled onto her back, staring at the sky.

"You sure you're not hurt?" The man sat next to her, looking her over as though he wasn't convinced.

"I'm sure." She may have earned a few scrapes on her leg, but nothing serious, thanks to the jeans.

"What's going on, you two?" Sassy's voice sounded closer. "Do I need to come up there?"

"No." She and Colt said it at the same time, and despite the throb of embarrassment in her heart, she smiled at him.

He smiled back, causing her heart to break out into another gymnastics routine. What was the matter with her? This was Colt.

"We're coming down now." Rose quickly sat up and inched her way to the ladder. "I'll get the supplies later," she mumbled, withdrawing the crowbar from the gutter and setting it aside before she started the climb down.

To Colt's credit, he didn't ask any questions or demand an explanation for why she was on the roof in the first place. He simply hovered behind her, waiting until she'd made it to the ground before climbing down himself.

"There's my girl." The second she turned to face her aunt, Sassy wrapped her in one of those calming, world-righting hugs. "Oh, I missed you."

"I missed you too." A sheen of tears blurred her eyes again. She couldn't help it. With Dahlia consumed by moving and settling in, these last two months she'd been on her own, more or less, and she hadn't realized how lonely it had been until Sassy hugged her.

"Aren't you a sight?" Her aunt pulled back and seemed to admire the jeans with amusement flickering in her eyes. "You're looking more and more like a mountain girl every day."

Ha! If only her aunt could've seen her yesterday in her white designer capris. Sassy would've given her the same look Tony had. "I hope you don't mind that I borrowed these old jeans."

"Of course not. This place belongs to you. Use anything you like." Her aunt beamed that typical joyous smile, but something on her face made Rose study her closer. Her red hair looked perfectly styled, and her lipstick was firmly intact like always, but Sassy's eyes didn't seem as bright. Maybe it was simply all the traveling she'd done. "Welcome home. I'll bet you're exhausted."

Her aunt brushed the words off with a shrug. "Who has time to be tired?" She panned her gaze around to the different cabins. "This place looks amazing, Rose. Simply amazing!"

Rose held a death grip on her smile and avoided Colt's lingering glance. "It does, doesn't it? Tony and his team have done a great job." No matter that they were way behind schedule for the grand reopening celebration. No matter that there was a brand-new hole in the roof of the cabin they stood beside. "We still have some work to do." She'd added on a couple more hours with the repair debacle.

"I'm sure everything will turn out perfectly." Her aunt squeezed both of her hands. "What were you doing up on the roof anyway?"

"Oh, you know…" She snuck a peek at Colt. His lips had folded as though he was trying—unsuccessfully—to hide a grin. "Just some minor repairs on the shingles." Or major structural damage to the roof.

"You're a marvel, my dear." Sassy hugged her again. "I'm proud of you. I can't imagine how hard you've been working."

Not hard enough, Rose wanted to tell her.

"Why don't you go inside and make some tea?" Colt suggested, gently directing her aunt toward the main house. "I'll help Rose finish up out here, and then I'll bring in your luggage and we'll join you."

"What a great idea." Her aunt traipsed across the driveway. "It's hard to find good tea at the airport. It's terribly weak and bland." She continued to discuss good tea with herself all the way until she disappeared into the house.

"Those are my pants." Colt posted his hands on his hips and gave her an amused look that made her feel young and defensive. No matter what, the man always seemed to draw a reaction out of her.

"You want them back?" Rose started to undo her belt in a fit of righteous indignation.

Colt threw back his head and laughed, shocking her hands to stillness. He never laughed that easily. Or that loudly and carefree. She watched him with her jaw hinged open.

"What?" he asked, the smile on his face hardly fading.

She couldn't answer him. While she'd noticed a subtle difference in her aunt—a tiredness, maybe—the differences in Colt were much more obvious. Before he'd left on that trip, he'd typically held his face in a pensive expression, as though he was always analyzing everything. Now, though, he had no lines of contemplation in his forehead. His broad cheeks were relaxed and tanned. And that smile. Crooked and easy. It had the power to change his eyes.

"You can keep the pants, Rose," he said. "They look good on you."

"*Right.*" She finally found her voice again, lacing it with a good dose of sarcasm. "Well, you know, I was really hoping I could try out for the roofers pageant next year."

Colt laughed again. Not *at* her, but *because* of her. Not because he thought she was silly but because he seemed to actually think she was funny. Her heart lightened and she laughed too. It felt good to laugh.

Colt edged closer to her, and yes even the man's eyes seemed different than they had only a couple of months ago. "I wasn't thrilled when Sassy said she wanted to cut the trip short because she was homesick. But I'm glad we did. I missed you."

Her heart did that little dropping trick again. "You missed me? Wh-wh-why?" Why was she finding it so hard to talk all of a sudden?

"What do you mean, why?" He laughed again. "There's never a dull moment when you're around. You always liven things up."

Was he complimenting her? She couldn't quite tell. Who the hell was this laid-back man, and what had he done with serious Colt?

"How are things really going around here?" he asked as if the two of them were in cahoots.

"Wh-why do you ask?" She really had to stop this stammering thing. It was just…this was all so weird. Colt smiling and laughing. Colt making her heart do little flips.

The man called her out with a deadpan expression. "You were on the roof. You. On the roof. By yourself."

Yes, she realized now that had been a bad idea. But she couldn't admit to him that things weren't exactly going according to plan. They'd entrusted her with overseeing this project—he and Dally and Mags. They'd all had other things going on. And she wouldn't let them down. She would figure this out. "There was a small leak, some damaged shingles," she said as though it was no big deal. "We're on a tight timeline to finish up before the Clearys get here next week. Tony's got a lot going on, so I figured I would try to help. That's all." "Try" being the operative word.

Colt graciously didn't mention that she'd made the roof leak about ten times worse.

"I can fix the roof." Preferably before Tony showed up tomorrow. "It'll be fine." She had to say it out loud to convince herself.

Colt must've detected a wobble in her tone because he gave her shoulder a pat. "I've got a ton of experience roofing. I can help you out."

"You don't have to." The words came automatically but there was absolutely no conviction behind them. Dear God, what she really wanted to do was throw her arms around the man in a sloppy hug.

But Colt likely hadn't changed *that* much. Traveling probably hadn't increased his threshold for spontaneous hugs.

"I want to help." He turned and headed for his truck. "Go have tea with Sassy. I'll grab some supplies and be back soon. We'll have that roof fixed before dark."

Emotion surged through her, hot and fast and unexpected. She'd missed having help, having someone to lean on. "Right. Okay. Will do."

Rose watched him get into his truck and drive away, making sure the dust had cleared before the tears started to fall. With Colt and Sassy home, she wasn't alone anymore.

Chapter Five

Sassy

W ell, well, well...It had been quite a while since she'd worn this getup.

Sassy admired the matching skirt and blazer she'd managed to get herself into *and* button up—which was the real miracle. This outfit wasn't your average boring old suit. No siree. She preferred hot pink to sensible black, naturally, and both the skirt and the jacket had a ruffle at the hem for good measure.

This had been her town council suit once upon a time, back when she'd been a bit thinner. Now she happened to be older and wiser instead, which meant she wasn't going to do this mayoring thing on Peg's terms. It would be on *her* terms, thank you very much, and she most assuredly wasn't going to let a museum president bully the town into giving up on the community garden.

A clamoring downstairs made her rush to reapply her lipstick. That would be Dahlia and the kids, no doubt about it. She'd recognize Ollie and Maya's giggles from a mile away. Quickly, Sassy shoved her feet into her patent pink Mary

Janes and hurried out of her bedroom to meet her great-niece and great-nephew in the kitchen.

"Auntie Sassy!" Ollie flew across the room and threw his arms around her waist, hugging her every bit as fiercely as she hugged him back.

Maya joined them there right in front of the refrigerator, completing a little circle. She'd only met these two last Christmas, but they were already like the grandchildren she'd always dreamed of having. Seeing the children made her think of her sister. Their real grandmother. She'd been thinking of Lillian more often since she'd started getting the headaches. Her sister had shut her out, but she might not have much more time to make amends.

She released the children and glanced at Dally. "Have you heard much from your mother?" she asked casually. "I thought she might come out for a visit after you moved." Hope of reconciling with her sister was the only thing that seemed to grow stronger instead of weaker as she aged. Now that they shared a family again, Lillian would have to come for a visit sometime.

"Oh." Her niece seemed to look for an escape. They all seemed to walk on eggshells when it came to Sassy's ruined relationship with their mother. "Um. Yes. We've talked with her some." She found a watering can on the shelf near the door and filled it up in the sink. "It sounds like she's doing great. She's super busy. She'll come sometime, I'm sure." Her niece started to water the plants on the windowsill, quickly putting an end to the conversation.

Knowing when to let things lie, Sassy turned her attention back to the children. "My, you two grew tall while I was gone." She could nearly rest her chin on Ollie's head now.

"I think you've grown taller too." The boy peered up at her, scrunching up one side of his mouth as though he was trying really hard to measure her.

"She hasn't grown taller," Maya corrected. "Grown-ups don't get taller, isn't that right, Mom?"

Dahlia finished watering the plants. That girl was always doing something helpful.

"Grown-ups *usually* don't get taller." Dahlia took her turn for a hug. "Maybe she looks different because of the amazing suit. Where are you going, all snazzed up?"

"I have a meeting in town." She'd already decided not to say too much about her new role until the council had made it official.

"Hot pink is my favorite color." Maya snuck a few jellybeans from the candy jar next to the coffeepot.

"Ah, yes." Sassy made it her business to know these things. "Well, I brought home some gifts for you both in all shades of your favorite colors. But you'll have to wait until I unpack to get them." What fun she'd had collecting T-shirts and trinkets to bring home to her family. Her family! Not so long ago, Colt had been the only real family connection she'd had.

"Woo-hoo! I love surprises!" Ollie shoved a handful of jellybeans into his mouth, earning a look of disapproval from his mother.

"What?" The boy shot them both a colorful grin. "Dr. Ike said I'm super-duper healthy when we saw him today."

"Dr. Ike?" Sassy gave Dahlia her full attention. No surprise that her niece's cheeks had a lovely rosy glow. "You saw Dr. Ike today, did you?" She'd wondered how much Dally had seen of the good doctor while she'd been gone.

"Yes, and we saw Dr. Jolly too," Maya informed her. Her great-niece went on to report all about their respective visits, but Sassy kept watching Dahlia. "Who's Dr. Jolly?"

Her niece wouldn't meet her eyes. "That's Ike's new partner."

"She's real pretty," Maya added. "Like supermodel pretty."

Was she now? "I didn't realize Ike was looking to hire anyone." She had been gone for two months, but that was big news. Surprisingly, Dahlia hadn't mentioned it in one of their phone conversations.

"Um, yeah." Dally busied herself with refilling the candy jar using the surplus of jellybeans Sassy kept in the cabinet. It looked like Rose had kept the tradition alive.

That was it? Her niece wasn't going to give her more information? "Well, is she nice?" Why did Dally suddenly seem to want to clam up?

"She's super-duper nice," Ollie supplied. "Dr. Ike brought her a coffee, and she was *really* nice to him."

"Is that so?" Well, that was certainly an interesting tidbit. Last she knew, Ike and Dahlia were being really nice to each other. But, now that she thought about it, her niece hadn't mentioned the doctor once when Sassy had talked to her on the phone. At first she'd thought her niece was being private about their budding relationship, but now she might have to dig deeper.

"Dr. Jolly seems great." Dally's smile had tightened. "We can't wait for dinner so we can hear all about your trip."

The change in subject just about gave Sassy vertigo again. But that's how it was with her niece. Dally wouldn't want to talk about Ike now. Especially not in front of her children.

"Yes, Colt and I have so many pictures to share with you." If he and Rose ever came down from the roof, that was.

Those two had gone back up there after a quick cup of tea and had been working on some project up there all afternoon. She peeked out the window at the Mistletoe Cabin further on down the hill. It looked like the two of them were taking a break from whatever it was they were working on, sitting side by side while they chatted. They'd been chatting every time she'd peeked out at them.

And her dear Colt was not much of a chatter.

After the rocky start Rose and Colt had last Christmas, it was nice to see them getting along. "I should be back from my meeting in an hour, and then we'll get our family dinner started." It would be the perfect opportunity to announce her new job, as long as the council approved her.

Nerves rolled through her stomach, making her feel like she was back on one of those airplanes. She hadn't even been this anxious about the takeoff and landing during her trips.

"I'll work on dinner while you're gone," Dally offered. Her niece liked to keep as busy as Sassy kept herself.

"We can help." Maya pulled Sassy's favorite apron off a hook behind the door. "Can I wear this?"

"Be my guest." She planted a kiss on Maya's forehead, and then on Ollie's. Sweet little cherubs. How had she ever survived without them in her life?

And how much more time would she get to spend with them?

The headache that had accompanied her home had released its grip with the help of those over-the-counter meds, but she could never seem to predict when it would come back. Not tonight. She couldn't let anything ruin tonight. "I'll hurry home as soon as I can," she promised.

"Have fun." Dahlia quirked her lips. "Must be an important meeting, huh?"

"We'll see." Sassy bustled to the door and escaped before they could ask more questions. Maybe she should've told them now, but there was a chance Peg's harebrained idea might not go through. Maybe someone else on the council would want to step in and take the job.

She got into her car and started the engine. Maybe this was crazy. She was about to turn seventy years old, for goodness' sake. Was this really the time to be launching a new career in politics? She'd always been active in the town's decision-making processes but had never been able to stick to one side or another when it came to her convictions. She'd rather put humans over politics, and there were plenty of people who wouldn't take kindly to that approach.

Nerves bunched her stomach again as she steered the car down the driveway and rolled to a stop in front of the Mistle-toe Cabin, where she could see Rose and Colt. Why, wouldn't they make a handsome couple? If Colt hadn't set his heart on leaving town.

Rose waved. Whatever they were doing up there, her niece sure seemed to be enjoying herself. That smile nearly stretched from one ear to the other.

Sassy buzzed down her window. "I'll be home soon, and we're having a family dinner tonight," she called.

"Sounds great!" Rose set down the hammer she'd been holding. A hammer? She never thought she'd see the day when her designer-shoe-loving niece would be sitting atop a roof with a hammer in her hand. But there you had it. Since she'd shown up at the Juniper Inn last Christmas, Rose had completely reinvented herself. And wasn't that what life was all about? The reinventing? Reimagining your dreams? Redefining your goals?

Before these girls had come back into her life, Sassy had been stuck. The resort had become too much for her to keep up all by her lonesome, and truthfully, she'd lost her passion for running the place, especially with the decline in customers, who'd started to opt for luxury vacations instead of trips to a rustic mountain inn.

But Rose and Dally and sweet Magnolia with her excitement for motherhood had inspired her. She didn't know how much time she had left. No one could know. But even at this age, she had something to offer. She wasn't obsolete.

Sassy followed the speed limit signs all through town like a good mayor would. She parked at the back end of the town hall lot. The two-story painted brick Italianate structure had been there since 1883, when the town was founded. She'd always thought it was the prettiest building in Juniper Springs, with the carved stonework lining its windowsills, lintels, and the pediment above the bracketed cornice at the roofline.

Peg stood in the doorway, waving frantically. Sassy checked the clock on the dashboard. She was fifteen minutes early.

By the time she'd climbed out of the car, the woman had made it to the middle of the parking lot.

"Graham is here!" After once being distant and combative, the woman now cozied right up to her as though they'd been best friends for years. "He came to observe the meeting. What should we do?"

Sassy marched to the building in her steadiest gait. "Let him watch the meeting." He'd find out she was mayor soon anyway. "We have nothing to hide. I'm sure he's well aware the town wants that land."

"Well, yes. Mayor Lund sent the museum a letter a couple weeks back." Peg hurried to keep up with her. "She was trying to settle this amicably, but Mr. Wright wouldn't hear of it."

"He hasn't talked to me yet." She'd never actually had a real conversation with the man, but she'd talked to plenty of people who had. "I'm not worried." First things first, she needed the vote.

She rushed up the steps with Peg at her heels and held the door open for the woman. "Everyone else will be here?"

"They're already here," she said. "And they're ready to confirm you as the best choice for our new mayor. The council is absolutely thrilled you're up for it."

Sassy hoped she was up for it. A familiar pressure had started to build in her temples, a sure sign that the headache was coming for her. "All right, then. Let's get this going."

Windows lit up the hallway with patches of bright sunshine, making the plush red carpet look softer. They passed the framed pictures depicting the town's history and went straight into the meeting room, where the council members were already seated at the head table—Raymond Sneed, the town's lone real estate mogul; Tyra Blair, the owner of the Juniper Springs Hair Salon and Spa; Christine Hodgins, the town dentist; and Arnie Felker, the retired elementary school principal. These were all people she knew—Tyra had been doing her hair for years. She and Arnie and Christine had played bridge together. And Raymond's mother had been a good friend before she'd passed away last year. They all liked her, and yet the sight of them sitting there set her nerves to buzzing again.

"Welcome, Sassy! It seems you got back at the right time." Tyra gave her a wink.

"I don't suppose you'd be up for a bridge game tomorrow night, would you?" Arnie asked hopefully.

"I'm in!" Christine squinted at her phone screen. "I could do seven o'clock."

"Oh. Sure. Yes. Bridge would be lovely." Sassy started to relax until she caught a glimpse of Graham Wright, who sat in the first row of chairs that faced the table. Council meetings were open to the public, but he was the lone observer.

Everything about the man seemed to be in direct opposition of her. He wore a light gray button-up shirt with dark gray pants. Even his short, well-kept hair seemed to match those same grayish tones.

Sassy hoped her hot-pink suit didn't blind him.

"Let's call this meeting to order." Peg settled into her chair at the center of the long table. "Sassy, you can have a seat right over there." She pointed to the row across from where the museum president sat.

This should be interesting. Sassy took her place, greeting the expressionless man with a wide smile. "Mr. Wright," she said politely as she made herself comfortable a few feet away.

"Ms. McGrath." His voice seemed as monotone as his outfit.

Peg cleared her throat a couple of times. "I officially call this emergency meeting of the town council to order." She slipped on a pair of bifocals. "Christine will be recording our notes so we can make them public."

"You bet I will." The woman held up a pen and notepad. No technology for her.

"Fabulous. We'll make this brief." Peg shifted her attention back to the paper in front of her. "According to the town by-laws, if the current mayor vacates the position and there is no time to run an election, the town council has the authority to approve an interim candidate." She stopped reading and slipped off the bifocals, focusing her serious gaze on Sassy. "Ms. McGrath has graciously agreed to step into this role in our time of need. All in favor of approving Sassy McGrath as our interim mayor, please say aye."

A chorus of enthusiastic ayes went around the table, finishing with Peg.

Christine furiously scribbled on her notepad, likely capturing the unanimous vote.

"Wonderful." Peg seemed to hesitate and then frowned at Mr. Wright. "We now have to ask if there are any objections from the…um…spectators. Or, rather, specta*tor*."

Wait…they did? Peg hadn't mentioned that earlier. Sassy turned to face the man, who had risen from his seat like he was about to make a speech.

Here we go.

"I am just wondering what Ms. McGrath's qualifications are to be mayor." His voice carried. He had a nice voice, she'd give him that. Very authoritative.

"I'm sorry?" Peg's glare seemed to send a warning, but it didn't deter Mr. Wright. He faced Sassy directly, completely ignoring the head councilwoman.

"I'm assuming you have qualifications to be in a position of leadership?"

For the first time, Sassy noticed his eyes didn't seem to fit his sourpuss expression. They were a deep brown. Very warm.

"Running a town takes certain skills," he went on when she said nothing. "Like running a museum. You have to manage a budget. Abide by certain processes and procedures. Do you have any experience in these areas?"

The pressure in her temples turned into a throb, but her anger chased the headache away. Sassy stood too, though she had to be a good foot shorter than him. "I'll have you know, I ran an inn for over thirty-five years." She stepped nearly toe-to-toe with the man. "I managed a budget. I followed processes and procedures. And you know what else I did? I *welcomed* people to our town." She'd made it her life's work to be a good hostess. To give people a refuge. That mattered more to her than any budget ever would.

She waited until he looked *at* her instead of *through* her. "What about you, Mr. Wright? How welcome do people feel at your museum?"

Surprise tinged his eyes, but for the most part his expression didn't change. "I know what you're doing," the man said instead of answering her question. "And I will tell you right now...Ned wanted the land to go to the museum. He was very specific in his will. Going against his wishes will cost this town a great deal of time and money. And you will still lose."

Oh, heavens. He was right. Sassy hadn't thought about how much money it would cost the town to get caught up in some legal battle for a plot of land.

"That is a risk we're willing to take," Peg answered for

Sassy. "Ned had always talked about leaving that plot of land to the town trust."

"He had a change of heart. He was passionate about geology, and we are considering using the land to expand the museum if we can secure the proper funding." Graham still seemed to be addressing Sassy as though he wanted to convince her. "I will do everything in my power to protect that land." The words walked a fine line between a promise and a threat.

"And I will do everything in my power to help this town," Sassy told him.

That was what she'd always done, and she wasn't going to stop now.

Chapter Six

Dahlia

H ot plate! Comin' through!" Ollie carefully carried the casserole dish from the oven to the opposite countertop where Dahlia had set a trivet, his hands clad in oven mitts two sizes too big. "Come on, people, let's serve it up. We don't want this food dying on the pass."

Dahlia laughed. She wasn't going to mention names, but someone had been watching too much Food Network lately. Both of her children had always loved to be in the kitchen with her, measuring and stirring, and, yes, licking the spoon after she made cookies, but lately Ollie had turned into quite the little kitchen boss.

"Looks good, chef." She leaned in to peer over his shoulder. In terms of making a family dinner, they hadn't found much to work with in the refrigerator. Rose didn't exactly cook often, but Dahlia had managed to scrape together a decent salad, and after rifling through the freezer, she'd found enough chicken to make a casserole with cheese and broccoli.

"Good?" Her son shook his head. "It looks *amazing*! Because I made it!"

"I helped too." Maya sat at the kitchen table leafing through an outdated American Girl catalog she'd found in the living room.

"It was a team effort," Dahlia said before the exchange snowballed into a fight. "And Sassy is going to love dinner." Where was her aunt, anyway? She'd been gone for nearly two hours, after telling them she'd be right back.

"I don't know about everyone else, but I'm starving." Ollie removed the oven mitts.

"Then how about you set the table?" She handed him a stack of plates. "And Maya, you can fill glasses with lemonade."

"Okay." Her daughter folded over another page in the doll catalog—likely to the tune of five hundred dollars.

While the children worked to get the table set, Dahlia washed the few dishes in the sink so Rose or Sassy wouldn't have to do them later. Her sister had been up on that roof with Colt all afternoon. She had to be exhausted.

Leaning forward, she glanced out the window. Speak of the devil. Those two were walking up the hill toward the house right now. "Better set an extra plate for Colt."

"I like Colt." Her son pushed the step stool to the cabinet and found another dish. "He's nice."

"He is nice." Dahlia liked him too, though she was still getting to know him. He'd been a hero for accompanying their aunt on her extended trip.

The door opened and her sister breezed through with Colt only a few steps behind. "Mmmm, something smells delicious." Despite being out and doing manual labor all day, her sister didn't seem the least bit worn.

"You look dirty, Aunt Rose." Ollie still hadn't mastered

the art of filtering his observations. "You'd better wash up before dinner."

Rose laughed and fluffed his hair. "I've been out working, kid. I know how to fix a roof now."

Dahlia caught the neon smile her sister shot at Colt and had to clamp her lips so her jaw wouldn't hit the ground. Out of the three of them, Rose had always been the most concerned about her looks—especially when in the company of the opposite sex. Her younger sister had a flair for fashion and design. That's why it was so weird looking at her now— in those baggy jeans and a tattered sweatshirt. Rose did indeed have dirt smudges on her face and clothes...but she'd never looked happier.

"You should've seen me up there, Ollie," her sister bragged. "I hammered in nails, I sawed, I cemented."

"And I sat there sunbathing," Colt quipped, making Maya giggle.

Rose draped her arm across Colt's shoulders. "He helped *a little.*"

"A little?" Colt gently elbowed her sister. "Who had to pull you *out* of the roof earlier?"

Dahlia couldn't tear her blatant stare away from the exchange. Were those two actually flirting? When had she stepped into an alternate universe?

"You were stuck in the roof?" Ollie forgot about his table-setting duties and stood on a chair so he was eye level with Colt. "And you *saved* her?"

The man happily launched into the story of how Rose had stepped through a soft spot in the Mistletoe Cabin's roof and had both kids in hysterics.

"Ha-ha." Rose came over to where Dahlia stood and stole a tomato out of the salad bowl.

Dahlia simply stared at her sister. She hardly recognized the woman.

"What?"

Before Dahlia could demand to know what this tough-chick imposter had done with her sister, another commotion started at the other side of the house. The front door banged open and Sassy's voice floated down the hallway.

Who was she talking to?

"Yes! We can finally eat dinner!" Ollie tore out of the kitchen and disappeared around the corner. "Hey, Ike's here!"

Ike? Dahlia fumbled with the dish towel she'd been holding. She didn't have time to take off the apron she was wearing or check her hair before the man walked into the kitchen behind Ollie and Sassy.

"I brought Ike and cake." Her aunt set a decadent-looking chocolate cake at the center of the table. The kids crowded in, studying the frosted flowers, but Dahlia stared at Ike. He'd changed out of his work clothes and was now wearing shorts and a casual green polo shirt that enhanced the color of his eyes.

"Hey, Dally."

Rose nudged her. Right. She had to speak.

"Hi." She quickly untied her apron and pulled it off over her head so she could escape his gaze. "I hope everyone's hungry." She hung the apron behind the door. "We should go ahead and eat. The food's been ready for a while now. Don't want it to get cold."

Now Rose was the one staring at her. But Dahlia ignored

her sister's questioning gaze. "That cake looks delicious. What's the occasion?" she asked her aunt, hurrying to get salt and pepper on the table. What could she say? When she got nervous, she went into hyperdrive.

"It's a very special occasion. I have an announcement." Sassy directed them all to sit, and wouldn't you know it, by the time Dahlia had retrieved the butter from the fridge, the only seat left was next to Ike.

"What is it, Aunt Sassy?" Maya kept staring at the cake the way Dahlia imagined she was staring at Ike. Hopefully her kids wouldn't pick up on her attraction to him. What would they think if they found out she and Ike had been more than friends?

"You're looking at the new mayor of Juniper Springs."

Sassy's announcement temporarily dislodged the worry from her heart. "Mayor?"

"Wow." Rose shared a wide-eyed look with Dahlia.

Colt laughed. "We got home all of eight hours ago, and you're already the mayor?"

"That means you're in charge of the whole town!" Ollie's eyes were nearly as big as the rims of his glasses. "We can make up whatever new holidays we want! We should have a Star Wars Day!"

"There's an idea." Sassy filled her glass with lemonade and passed the pitcher to Colt. "I'll take it to the council."

Was her aunt being serious? Sassy obviously had a love for this town, so her being mayor made sense, but she hadn't wanted to be tied down anymore. "I don't understand. How did all of this come about?" To Dahlia, the whole thing sounded like one big complication.

"It's a long story." And Sassy didn't seem in a hurry to tell it.

"I'm sure it has something to do with Peg." Ike leaned closer to Dahlia. "She's head of the town council and is always furthering her own agenda." The man's smile nearly melted her kneecaps. He did have such wonderfully skilled and seductive lips.

"It's true." Sassy dropped some salad on her plate and passed the bowl to Dahlia. "Peg did ask me to step in to fill Mayor Lund's shoes, but it's for a good cause."

"Star Wars Day would be a good cause," Ollie insisted, helping himself to a whole pile of casserole. Dahlia gave him a look to remind him to save some for everyone else.

"I could get on board with a Star Wars Day." Ike high-fived the boy. "In fact, I was Darth Vader for Halloween last year."

"He was," Sassy confirmed. "He wore the costume to the office and everything. I happened to get my flu shot that day, and Ike about scared the bejesus out of me."

"Cool." Ollie peered up at the man with awe. "What're you gonna be for Halloween this year?"

Ike raised his eyebrows mysteriously. "I guess you'll have to wait and see."

Dahlia's heart clenched as she watched him interact with her son. With her ex working in London this year, the children were both missing their dad. FaceTime just wasn't the same as being together. She snuck a peek at Maya, who stared at Ike too, but with a totally different expression. Her daughter's lips were pursed tightly together in disapproval.

"What's that smell?" Across the table, Rose crinkled her nose. "Is something burning?"

"The rolls!" Dahlia hopped up from her seat. "I completely forgot about them!" The timer had gone off just before Ike walked in, but taking them out the of the oven had slipped her mind. She opened the oven door, and sure enough, those babies were charred.

"Oh no." Ollie rushed to her side and peeked in over her shoulder. "They're ruined. We worked hard on those."

If by working hard, he meant pulling them out of the freezer and putting them on a cookie sheet, then yes, he was right.

"Sorry, everyone." She slipped on the oven mitts Ollie had left on the counter and pulled out the cookie sheet. At least they weren't smoking too badly.

"It's no problem." Ike stood to open the kitchen window over the sink. "Bread is just empty carbs anyway."

"Well, I like bread." The sass in Maya's tone caused Dahlia to whirl. The rolls slid off the tray and bounced across the floor.

"Oh no." She stashed the cookie sheet on the counter and snatched the basket she was going to put them in before kneeling to collect the buns. It wouldn't be a family dinner without a game of chase the rolls.

"Here, let me help." Sassy joined her on the floor, quickly picking up the warm bread and tossing it into the basket while Ike picked up the rolls that had somehow made it to the other side of the room and tossed them in the trash.

"Thanks." If Dahlia's cheeks got any hotter, they'd probably spontaneously combust. She scrambled to her feet.

Sassy moved like she was going to stand, too, but stopped suddenly. Still crouched, her aunt squeezed her eyes shut and gasped.

"What is it?" Dahlia let the rolls fall back to the floor, her heart racing.

"Sassy?" Ike was already at her aunt's side, offering his arm to support her.

"I'm fine, I'm fine." The words might've been more convincing if they weren't breathless. "I stood too fast, that's all it is."

Ike helped her settle back into the chair, and then he knelt in front of her. "What happened? Did you get dizzy? Were you in pain?"

"Stop worrying." Sassy patted his cheek. "I've had a little headache today, that's all. This old girl needs to get used to the altitude again."

The man didn't look convinced—and neither was Dahlia. She glanced at her sister to get a read on what Rose thought.

"Maybe you should drink some water," Rose suggested. She hurried to the sink and filled up a glass.

"Yes, that's all I need," their aunt agreed. "I might be a bit dehydrated after so much traveling." She sipped from the glass Rose handed her and set it down. "Now let's finish our dinner and have some cake. After that, I think I'll go lie down and take a nap."

Throughout the rest of their meal, Dahlia kept a close eye on her aunt. Something wasn't right, she was sure of it, and she could see the concern simmering in Ike's eyes too. Colt and Sassy entertained them with tales from their travels, but Dahlia caught her aunt massaging her temples a couple of times as though she was in pain.

Maya and Ollie rushed everyone through dinner and ate their cake in record time, but Sassy didn't want any dessert.

"I'm going to unpack and get to sleep early." Her aunt pressed both of her hands into the table as she stood. "That way I can find all the treasures I brought you two kiddos and give them to you first thing tomorrow."

"Okay." Thankfully Ollie didn't bellyache about not getting his surprises tonight. He gave Sassy a hug, and then Maya took her turn.

"Let me know if you need anything," Dahlia told her aunt on her way out of the kitchen.

"Don't be silly. I'll be fine." Sassy squeezed her hand, but even that didn't reassure Dahlia.

"Hey kids, why don't you walk Marigold down to the pond and throw a stick for her?" Rose opened the door to let the dog in. After Mari had cleared the table more than once when they'd turned their backs, she wasn't allowed in the kitchen while they ate anymore.

"Yes!" Maya hugged the dog. "Wanna go for a walk, girl?"

Ollie had already made it halfway out the door. "Let's go find a stick."

The dog bounded out after them, yipping with pure joy.

After they left, Dahlia finally let her worry show. She, Ike, Colt, and Rose still sat at the table finishing their cake.

"It's not normal for Sassy to get dizzy." She set down her fork. "I've never seen that happen before." Her aunt had always been so lively and energetic.

Rose cut herself another small sliver of the dessert. "It *could* be the altitude. She was traveling all over the country up until this morning."

Her aunt had also lived in Colorado for more than fifty years and had never had issues with the altitude before. "But it could be something else too." She looked at Colt. "Did you notice anything off when you were on the trip?"

He thought for a moment. "She seemed tired sometimes, I guess. Maybe she didn't have as much energy." The man shook his head. "But then other times she had more energy than me."

Her sister nodded. "Sassy looked a little tired when I first saw her again, but she did just get home from a long trip today." Rose turned to Ike. "What do you think? Should we be concerned?"

"Traveling can be exhausting." He finished his cake and pushed away his plate. "And dehydration makes you much more susceptible to altitude sickness." Even with those facts, there were still questions in his tone. "I think we should probably all keep an eye on her. Maybe it's nothing, but it doesn't hurt to pay attention. You three spend the most time with her. You'll be able to tell if something's off."

"We'll do our best." But with Sassy's new career launching, Dahlia didn't know how much they'd see her.

"I'll encourage her to come in for a checkup too." Ike laughed. "Not sure if that'll do any good. She pretty much stops by once a year for her annual physical, and that's about it."

"We can all encourage her." Colt stacked everyone's plates and carted them to the sink. "But we all know Sassy won't go in unless she wants to."

That's what had her so worried. Dahlia got up to help Colt with the dishes, but Ike laid a gentle hand on her shoulder. "You two sit. Let us take care of the cleanup."

Dahlia paused before answering so he wouldn't take his

hand away. Oh, she'd missed his touch. She hadn't realized how much she'd missed the feel of his hand until right now. It made her warm all over. Warm and hopeful and hungry for something other than chocolate cake.

He walked to the sink, taking her gaze with him. While they worked on the dishes, he and Colt talked about the whale-watching excursion Sassy and Colt had gone on in Alaska.

"What's going on?" Rose mouthed, nodding toward Ike's back.

Dahlia shook her head. They were not doing this now. "How's the roof looking?" she asked instead.

"It's looking good." Her sister got a mischievous gleam in her eyes that Dahlia recognized all too well. "But I left something up there." Her sister popped out of her chair. "Colt, can you help me grab it?"

Dahlia stood too. "What thing did you leave up on the roof?" She was onto Rose. Her sister was never subtle.

"That tool. Remember Colt?" She grinned at the man. "That one tool I forgot to grab?" Her eyes were so wide and cajoling even Ollie would've picked up on her motivation to leave Dahlia alone with Ike.

"Ohhhhh." Colt nodded slowly and stashed the last glass into the dishwasher. "Right, the *tool.* We should get that tool off the roof before we forget."

"Yes, we should." Rose winked at Dahlia and traipsed out the door with Colt not far behind.

Well, great. That left her alone with Ike, and there weren't even any dirty dishes left that she could use as a distraction.

"I hope it's okay that I came for dinner." He wiped his hands on a towel and leaned back against the cabinet.

The uncertainty in his guarded posture tugged at her heart. She hadn't meant to make him feel unwelcome. "I'm glad you came." It wasn't Ike's fault she didn't know how to introduce the idea of her dating to her children. Her ex had had no problem introducing them to the woman he'd started dating after the divorce.

Maya hadn't seemed to hold Jeff to the same standards she held Dahlia to though. "I miss seeing you." Dahlia missed kissing Ike. She missed sitting on his couch wrapped in his arms in front of a fire while they watched the snow fall. God, that seemed like a lifetime ago.

"I miss seeing you too."

He stayed where he was, but Dahlia found it difficult to keep her distance. She moved within a foot of him but didn't trust herself to go any closer. "I've been overwhelmed." She hadn't even admitted that to herself.

"That's completely understandable." He closed the distance between them, his eyes genuine. "I know your kids need all of your attention right now. I know they've been through a lot. You can have as much space as you need to settle in, Dahlia. I don't want you to step into a relationship before you feel ready."

Some moments she felt ready. Very ready. Like this moment. When he stood so close to her, and the hard pounding of her heart made her feel more alive. "I *want* to be ready," she half whispered, bringing her hands to his broad shoulders. She wanted to skip forward six months to when there wasn't so much change and to when things with Maya weren't so hard. "I want—"

The sound of the front door opening cut her off.

"Yoo-hoo! Anyone home?"

Dahlia froze where she was, her hands still on Ike's shoulders. No. No way. Not now…

Ike's brow wrinkled in a question, but the back door crashed open before he said anything.

Rose stumbled through out of breath. "Mom's here," she hissed.

"Yeah." Dahlia backed away from Ike. "I heard."

"Girls?" Their mother's voice had gotten closer.

"What is she doing here?" Rose paced across the kitchen. "Colt saw a car service drop her off and left. I don't blame him—"

"There you are. I knew you were home." Lillian Buchanan paraded into the kitchen, her silk pashmina flowing behind her. "And Ike! How wonderful to see you again."

"Nice to see you as well, Ms. Buchanan," he said politely and he grabbed a rag and started to wipe up the table, obviously giving the three of them space.

Dahlia immediately stepped between the two of them before her mother could question him about their current relationship status. Her mom had briefly met Ike last Christmas when she'd ambushed them to try to convince Rose to go home to her fiancé, but Dahlia purposely hadn't told her they'd kept in touch. "Wow, this is a surprise. What're you doing here, Mom?"

"I decided I would come for the grand reopening after all." She slipped her arm around Rose, who visibly stiffened.

While Dahlia and Magnolia had both moved away and started new lives outside of Savannah, Rose had stayed in the city where they'd grown up. After their father had passed away a few years back, her sister had taken the brunt of their mother's social climbing and constant meddling up until she'd moved to Colorado.

"I've missed my girls." Their mother planted a kiss on Rose's cheek. "And since Sassy is off galivanting around the country, I figured it would be fine for me to stay."

That was the other thing about their mother. She certainly knew how to hold a grudge. She hadn't spoken to Sassy in almost twenty years.

"You can't stay at the inn." Panic raised Rose's voice. "The cabins aren't ready yet..."

"Well, then I'll stay in the house. With you." Her mother gave her sister a squeeze, and Dally cringed for her. That would be a disaster. Especially with Sassy now home. Besides that, Rose had moved into the camping trailer they'd renovated for the summer.

"There are plenty of extra rooms here, right?"

"Well, sure, but..." Rose shot Dahlia a desperate look.

"Why don't you stay with us, Mom?" The invitation came out automatically. She'd always been the one to save the day.

"Really?" Rose didn't try to hide her shock.

"Yeah." Dahlia kept a sigh trapped. Just what she needed. One more thing keeping her from spending any time with Ike. "Then you could spend more time with the kids. We have an extra bedroom. There's plenty of room."

"I suppose that would work." She sent her sweetest smile in Ike's direction. "As long as you don't mind."

"Oh." The poor man stood up straighter. "No. Um. Not at all—"

"Ike doesn't live with us, Mother." And now, with her mother in town, he'd probably want to stay far, far away.

Chapter Seven

Rose

Y ou're telling me *you* fixed this?" Tony inspected the drywall repair on the Mistletoe Cabin's ceiling, his narrowed eyes obviously searching for imperfections.

He wouldn't find any. She and Colt had worked on the roof and ceiling all day, and in the course of working with him, she'd learned Colt was something of a perfectionist. "I fixed it with Colt's help." Okay, so maybe it had been the other way around, but Tony didn't need to know that. "What do you think?"

Tony climbed down off the stepladder, still a suspicious slant to his eyes. "I think Colt does good work, and maybe I need to hire him to be part of my crew."

"Hey." She pretended to be offended but couldn't hold back a laugh. "What about me? I do good work too." She'd done a lot of the grunt work, once Colt had shown her how. He'd been extremely patient with her, explaining everything they needed to do and then showing her the right technique before letting her try it herself. She'd had no idea it would be so empowering to use tools.

Tony eyed her with amusement. "You're also the one who put the hole in the roof in the first place."

He had a point. "Well, it's fixed up now. That's what matters." Thankfully. They could at least check one cabin off their never-ending list. "We should probably go over the schedule for the rest of the week."

Tony grunted an acknowledgment as he folded up his stepladder. "We need to finish up the kitchen installs in the Sugar Plum, Gingerbread, and Silver Bells Cabins."

"Right." She recorded the notes in her book. "And all that's left in the Reindeer, Candy Cane, and Holly Cabins are the trim and doors."

"That's it, huh?" She might've missed the sarcasm if it hadn't been for the man's exaggerated frown.

"Colt said he would be happy to help with whatever we need." There went that subtle trilling in her chest again. It was wonderful to have the man home. Not only for his knowledge and expertise with the remodel, but...Well, she probably shouldn't go there. Colt shouldn't be making anything inside of her trill. She shouldn't have let herself study his sturdy jawline or look so deeply into his eyes or brush his hand with hers yesterday either.

"We could use his help, that's for sure." Tony opened the door, and they stepped out onto the Mistletoe Cabin's front porch.

"No problem," she assured him. "He said he would stop by after he spent some time at the store this morning." She whistled and clapped her hands at Marigold, who had found a nice pile of deer poop to roll in. "Come on, girl. I just gave you a bath two days ago."

The dog had the decency to let her ears droop with a guilty look and wagged her tail.

Shaking her head, Rose turned back to Tony. "What can I do to help out this morning?"

There went that little sarcastic rumple of his lips again. "You can wait until Colt gets here and team up with him again."

"Fine." She could take a hint. "I have plenty to keep me busy." She had to take inventory on the rest of the furniture sitting in the barn and make sure they had everything they needed once they were ready to move things back into the cabins. Then she would check in on their reservation system to see if they had any new bookings—

Her phone started to blare Dahlia's ringtone. Oh thank God. She'd tried to call her sister twice this morning to see how it was going with their mother. She shouldn't have let Dahlia take on Lillian, but she'd panicked last night. She wanted nothing more than her aunt and her mom to reconcile, but this would take some serious finesse, and it would not happen with the two of them living in the same house.

Right now, Rose didn't even want Lillian to know Sassy was in town.

She walked away from Tony, tsking at Marigold, who was now eating the deer poop. Seriously. Dogs were disgusting sometimes.

When she'd made it out of earshot, she answered the phone on speaker. "Hey."

"I need backup," Dally barked. "We're at Grumpy's. Get down here now."

The line clicked.

All right then. That answered how things were going with Lillian. "Hey, Tony," Rose called. "I have to run into town real quick. Be right back."

Marigold heard the word *town* and hotfooted it to Rose's truck as though she didn't want to be left behind.

Tony simply waved her away, probably relieved she wouldn't be around to put any more holes in anything.

By the time Rose made it to her truck, Marigold had already jumped in through the open window. "Okay, you can come. But don't you dare lick my face after eating deer poop." She scooted in next to her dog and fired up the engine.

The whole way to town, Marigold stuck her head out the window, ears flapping while she greeted everyone she saw with a happy bark.

Rose found a parking spot two doors down from Grumpy's and hurried along the sidewalk, admonishing her dog to behave.

Marigold sprawled herself out under the awning's wonderful shade while Rose ducked inside. She spotted Lillian at the ordering counter right away.

"This is an outrage," her mother was saying. "I've never been treated so poorly in any establishment. I'm going to give you a one-star review online."

Grumpy stood behind the old-school cash register with his arms crossed. "Go ahead, lady. Make sure to mention in there that you were acting crazier than a bag of cats."

"A bag of cats?" Lillian stomped her foot. "How dare you!"

That was Rose's cue. "Hey, Mom." She rushed to the counter and gave Grumpy her most atoning smile. "What seems to be the problem?" And where the hell had Dahlia gone?

"I'll tell you the problem." Her mother glared at Grumpy. "All I did was ask for a splash of almond milk in my Americano—"

"Don't got almond milk," the man interrupted. "You know that full well, Rosie."

"Of course I know that." She also knew that no one dared to ask Grumpy for any alternative milks—ever. He was a heavy cream guy through and through and didn't believe in using that fake crap. His words, not hers. "But my mom doesn't know that," she said sweetly.

His frown only deepened. "She wanted me to walk to the market and get some." Grumpy's voice always edged toward a growl, but now it got downright snarly.

"Almond milk is much healthier." Lillian posted her hands on her hips, a sure sign that an impassioned monologue was inevitable. "Have you checked the fat content of cream lately?" she asked Grumpy. "What about the cholesterol? That stuff will kill you!"

"Lady, I've been drinking cream since I was a boy, and I still have the heart of a moose." Grumpy leaned an elbow into the counter as though daring her to argue. "Now do you want the splash of cream or not? 'Cause I got other customers. And they ain't annoying."

Her mother's face turned the same shade of red as it used to when Rose would say something to embarrass her.

"No cream," Rose said before Lillian lost it. "We'll just wait down there at the pickup area." She dragged her mother to the end of the counter.

"That man is awful," Lillian huffed. "How he stays in business is beyond me."

"To be fair, the café is called Grumpy's." The man gave people fair warning before they walked in. "Besides, he's a staple in Juniper Springs. Maybe he's a little rough around the edges, but I know for a fact he gives free coffee to our police force and firefighters, and he takes all the leftover baked goods down to the assisted living facility the next town over every other day. So he has a good heart." Not that her mother had ever paid too much attention to what hid beneath a person's surface.

"Well, I've never been talked to like that as a paying customer." Her mother directed her glare to the man behind the counter. "And look at this place. It's absolutely filthy."

Rose ignored her mother's complaints. She'd gotten used to doing that over the years. All Lillian had to do was take a look around to realize they weren't in some upscale restaurant in Savannah. Grumpy had antlers on the walls, for crying out loud. And the tables were made from logs the man had found himself. "Where'd Dally go, anyway?" Hopefully their mother hadn't driven her sister outside the state lines.

"She went to the bathroom." Lillian threw up her hands. "She walked away and let that man attack me. Can you believe that?"

"Kind of?" Rose wouldn't mind escaping either. She loved her mother. But the woman did stick out like a turd in a punchbowl around these parts. It wasn't only her hoity-toity attitude, either. The few other patrons sitting in the coffee shop all wore jeans and different varieties of T-shirts. No one here cared about impressing anyone else. Then there was Lillian Buchanan—dressed head to toe in rayon and silk.

"Americano," Grumpy mumbled as he slid the to-go cup in front of her mother.

"Thanks, Grumpy! We appreciate it." Rose snatched up the cup and used it to lure her mother out of the coffee shop.

The second they stepped outside, Marigold jolted to her feet and trotted over to greet them. The poor dog couldn't seem to take the hint that Lillian didn't want anything to do with her. Mari rubbed up against her mother's pants and licked her hand.

Rose decided not to mention her dog's little deer poop indulgence earlier.

"Are you ever going to teach this dog some manners?" Her mother dug a wet wipe out of her purse and cleaned her hands.

Rose shrugged. "She likes you." What were manners when it came to love?

"Did you solve the great almond milk crisis?" Dahlia walked over from the bakery next door and got a hearty greeting from Marigold too.

"It was a simple request." Their mother set her coffee on a nearby table and pulled a lipstick out of her purse. "I don't see why the man couldn't have walked across the street to the market. There were no customers in line behind me. And I told him I would pay more."

Rose didn't tell her mother that throwing money around wouldn't get her very far here. "So how was last night?" She noticed some dark circles under Dally's eyes.

"It was fine." Her sister kept that tight, guarded expression firmly in place.

Their mother's headshake contradicted her sister's answer. "We had to do quite a bit of work on the guest room before I was comfortable sleeping in there."

Rose had nearly forgotten how patronizing her mother could be sometimes.

"The sheets were so old they were positively stiff," Lillian went on, as if she didn't notice Dally's expression darkening. Rose definitely did.

"But thankfully I packed my own bedding, so we were able to swap out the linens."

"Thankfully," Dahlia muttered.

I owe you, Rose mouthed to her sister so her mother couldn't see. She hadn't meant to pile more stress on Dally when she was still getting settled and obviously still trying to figure out things with Ike. "Hey, while we're out and about, we should take Mom to that little boutique down the street."

Knowing her mother, she would spend hours checking out the couture clothing and accessories. They didn't have to mention it was all secondhand.

"Good idea." Dahlia started to walk onward without waiting for them.

Marigold fell in line with Rose. It still amazed her that the dog had never needed a leash. She simply followed along like one of the girls.

"I'm surprised a town this size would have a high-end boutique." Lillian seemed to scan the streets. She likely saw Juniper Springs very differently than Rose did. There were no grand buildings, no fancy restaurants, and very few expensive cars cruising the roadways. Things here were tidy and functional. And the charm came in the small details—the flower pots bursting with colorful annuals that hung from iron lampposts, the full water bowls outside of nearly every shop storefront for the many dogs that accompanied the owners downtown, the various benches where people could sit and linger, visiting with their neighbors.

It was funny, last year when she'd shown up here, Rose had stuck out as obviously as her mom did now. But in eight short months, she'd fit here better than she'd fit anywhere in her life.

"Here we are." Dally paused outside of the So Chic Boutique.

Thankfully, there was a display of purses in the window that caught their mother's eye right away. "Is that a Jimmy Choo?" Lillian practically broke down the door getting into the shop while Rose and her sister lingered outside.

"I'm sorry." Rose hugged Dally. "I didn't mean to make your life harder right now."

"It's not your fault." A hint of her sister's real smile came back. "I'm the one who offered my guest room." She laughed a little. "And it's really not so bad. I know I can't take anything personally with her, but when she started in on Grumpy in front of all those people, I wanted to let her have it."

"Oh, trust me." Rose had lived with their mother well into her twenties. Dally didn't have to explain herself.

Her sister glanced in the window and saw that their mother had the store clerk's full attention. "I want to have a good relationship with her. I want the kids to have a good relationship with her. She must be so lonely."

Leave it to Dally to find compassion where Rose only found frustration. "I know." She sighed, watching her mother try on one of the purses. "Now that she's here, we have to figure out how to patch things up between her and Sassy. I think we can make it happen." Their mother needed family. She needed her sister the way Rose needed Dally and Mags.

"You've always been the optimistic one."

"And you've always been the realist." Rose gave Dally a playful nudge.

Her sister grinned. "That's why we make such a good team."

"Exactly." If anyone could figure this out, it was them. And it couldn't be better timing with the grand reopening celebration happening next week.

"Did you see Sassy this morning?" Her sister's grin faded.

"I did. We had a quick breakfast together before she had to run out and be mayor." Rose had carefully watched her aunt for any signs of concern, but… "She seemed great. Full of energy. Happy about her new job. She said a good night's sleep is all she needed." Rose could tell Dally wasn't buying it. "I'll keep watching."

"Great. Thanks." Her sister leaned against the brick wall as though she had no intention of going into the shop. "And I'll keep trying to talk to Mom about Sassy. Maybe I can butter her up a little before we actually bring them together face-to-face."

"That's a good idea." They had to find the right time and the right place. Somewhere her mother couldn't simply walk away…

"Hey, you didn't tell me Colt was selling the hardware store."

"Huh?" Rose replayed her sister's words. Had she said *selling*?

"I saw a *for sale* sign hanging in the window when Mom and I walked past earlier," Dally said. "I thought he would've mentioned it to you yesterday."

"Colt isn't selling." A whoosh of blood seemed to clog her

ears. He couldn't be selling. "I spent the whole day with him, and he didn't say a word about selling the store."

"Oh." Her sister straightened as though taken aback by Rose's reaction. "There's definitely a sign in the window…"

"I'll be right back." Rose marched away from the boutique, from her sister. She didn't know why her heart was pounding this way, why a strange sense of urgency drove her footsteps. She only knew there had to be some mistake. Colt had only just gotten back to Juniper Springs. Why would he be selling the store?

Rose kept her head down all the way to the end of the block and then saw it for herself—the FOR SALE sign hanging in Colt's window. Before she could stop herself, she plowed through the doors at warp speed.

"Rose. Hey." The man himself stepped out from behind the counter.

He couldn't *Rose, hey* her. "You're selling the store?"

"Yep." He walked to meet her, his hands stuffed into his pockets. "It's time to move on. I can't stay here anymore."

"You didn't say anything. Yesterday." A strange anger simmered beneath her politely indifferent tone. They'd talked about a lot of things, but she would've remembered if he'd mentioned selling the store. And what did he mean, he couldn't stay here anymore?

"I made up my mind this morning." He looked around them. "After telling you about the different places Sassy and I traveled, I realized I don't want to be tied down. I don't remember living anywhere else. I was young when we moved here. So I feel like it's time. For new experiences, new places."

For some reason, she took the words as well as she would've taken a punch to the stomach. "Wh-where will you go, though?" Her breathing got all funny.

The man shrugged as though her heart hadn't started to crumble. How could he know she had started to feel something for him when she was trying to deny it even to herself?

"I'm thinking up north somewhere. Maybe in Idaho along the Canadian border. At least for a while."

Rose didn't speak until she was sure her voice would hold. "But what about the resort?" He was part owner...

"You're fully capable." Colt turned away from her and started to straighten the display of gardening gloves next to them. "You don't need me to run the resort."

That was the thing he couldn't see. And that was the thing she didn't even understand herself. She was capable. She didn't need him here.

But she *wanted* him here. In her life. She wanted to fix things with him and laugh with him and amuse him. "It's just... It's irresponsible."

Colt swiveled his head and stared at her as though reminding her she wasn't exactly the authority on responsible choices. "What's irresponsible?"

"Leaving." She was fuming now, and trying to hide her anger only seemed to make it worse. "You're leaving Sassy behind. She's turning seventy, you know." Yes, let him think she was concerned about Sassy. "These next years are the ones she'll need us the most. You're like a son to her."

Colt studied her for a few long silent seconds. Or years. It could have been years. How did he do that? Stare so long without talking? He seemed to be looking for something. Just once she'd like to know what was going on in his head. But then again, she couldn't even figure out what was going on in her own head. Or in her heart. She only knew her chest ached.

"I can come and visit all the time." Colt angled his head to the side as though he was looking at a puzzle. "It's not like I'm going to leave and forget about the woman who raised me, Rose. I will take care of her. I can promise you that."

"I know you will." Because Colt was loyal and faithful and thoughtful.

Oh, no. No, no, no. Her face was flushing. "I have to go." Before he could see the tears in her eyes, she ducked out of the store.

Colt wouldn't move away and forget about the woman who raised him, she knew that. But he might leave and forget all about her.

Chapter Eight

Sassy

S assy had to admit, she'd never dreamed her first day on the job as mayor would be devoted to dealing with porta potties.

"I don't see why we can't place them on the south side of the building," she said to Moe, the town clerk. "Then they'll be out of sight altogether." That seemed to be the simple solution in her book, but after only being in her office for approximately one hour, Sassy had figured out that nothing about running this town was going to be simple.

"That would be nice," Moe agreed. "Except the Whipples, who own the Crazy Moose Pub, said that with the potties on the south side of the town hall, the wind would carry the scent right inside their dining room."

Sassy appreciated the man's patient tone. Moe had been a fixture as the part-time town clerk since he'd moved here from the Bronx eight years ago. He was a jack-of-all-trades—smart as a whip but also highly creative and an incredibly talented musician. With his chunky dreadlocks, he could've passed for a young-looking Bob Marley, if it weren't for his bushel of facial hair. Though Moe preferred to play country music.

"So we can't put the porta potties behind the building because the Whipples are worried about the stench floating across the street and into their restaurant?" She didn't mean to sound disparaging, but really?

"They informed me they are fully prepared to take up the issue with the county if they need to." The roll of his eyes told her what he thought of that threat.

Well, good. At least she and Moe were on the same side here. "Where are we supposed to put them? The roof?" The remodeling project on the town hall was supposed to start in three days—Tony had already started setting up—and the construction workers would need a place to use the restroom.

"If we put them on the roof, you know we're gonna get complaints from the mountainside residents who are obsessed with their views."

"Right." She was beginning to understand why Moe had turned down the mayoral job. From the sound of things, Peg had tried to wrangle him into the role before she'd made a sucker out of Sassy.

Ugh. She glanced at the to-do list she'd scrawled on her notepad when she'd first gotten to the office. "We don't have time for this." She still had to balance the budget— yeah, right—approve the next town newsletter, and edit the proposal for expanding the elementary school. She hadn't had her headache yet that morning, but that didn't mean it wasn't going to ambush her.

"Okay. We're putting those porta potties behind the building. They'll only be there for two weeks." As long as everything went according to schedule. "Tell the Whipples they can have free advertising in the town newsletter as long as the porta potties are there."

"Will do." Moe made some notes on his tablet.

"Great." Sassy refocused on the laptop she'd inherited from Mayor Lund. "Now about this budget…"

"Yeah. About that…" Moe handed her a report. "We're already twenty grand in the hole for this fiscal year."

No wonder Mayor Lund had taken off. Things were a mess. "There is no way we're going to be able to pay a lawyer to challenge Ned's will so we can get that community garden up and running." She was already going to have to cut the budget as it was. She couldn't justify paying their lawyer to do the extra work. With the way the courts moved around here, it could take years.

"I tried telling Peg this wasn't going to work." The man shook his head slowly back and forth. "But that lady's got her own ideas."

"Well, luckily this lady has her own ideas too." They weren't going to get anywhere fighting with the museum. Sassy pushed out of her chair and pulled on the light sweater she'd grabbed when she'd left the house. Had it only been an hour and a half ago? It felt like a year.

"Where are you off to?" Moe stood too. They'd both been seated at the desk in her small office since she'd come in so he could help her acclimate to the computer system, but she needed a walk. Sometimes the best way to handle things was by confronting them in person.

"I'm going to do some research." She retrieved her purse from the coatrack by the door. "You should take an early lunch." Lord knew poor Moe had his hands full with her. "Get out and enjoy the day."

"Don't have to tell me twice." The man collected his binders and notes and tossed them onto his desk on the other side of the room before they walked out of the building together.

When Sassy stepped out onto the street, she swore she could smell the sunshine—the way the tree trunks soaked it in, the way it seemed to enhance the scent of the pine needles on the trees.

"You really think it's a good idea to go talk to Graham?" Moe ambled along beside her as they strolled down the sidewalk.

How did the man seem to know exactly what she was up to? "It's my only idea." The community garden had motivated her to take this job in the first place. It could help so many people in town ... the older residents who were living on a fixed income, the citizens who had a tough time finding regular work. Not only that, but it would bring the community together. She could see the events they would have, planting and weeding and harvesting. "Surely Mr. Wright can be reasonable."

"If anyone can make him see reason, it's you." Moe gave her shoulder a squeeze of solidarity and then stepped off the curb. "I'm going to go break the news to the Whipples over a nice lunch at the Crazy Moose."

"Well, then good luck to you too." Sassy chuckled at the way he saluted her before crossing the street. If the job came with any benefits, Moe might be the biggest one.

And this was the other one. This street. These people. She waved at Barbie Mayhew across the road.

"This town lucked out with you becoming mayor," the woman called.

"Thank y—"

Rose nearly ran Sassy over. "Whoa there, torpedo. Where are you headed in such a fuss?"

It seemed to take her niece a moment to gather her composure. Not that she could hide her emotions from Sassy. She recognized anger when she saw it.

"Did you know Colt is selling the store?" Rose demanded, gesturing wildly to the sign in the window.

Ah. So that's what had her skivvies in a knot. Sassy couldn't say she was surprised. She'd seen something in Colt and Rose's interactions at dinner last night. "I didn't know he'd made the final decision." Her heart sank a little too, but she refused to let Colt's exciting news upset her.

"But you knew he was thinking about selling?" Anger flashed across her niece's face again, but Sassy didn't take her reaction personally. That was the emotion talking. It seemed her niece might have deeper feelings for Colt than she was willing to admit.

"Yes, he did mention wanting an adventure." Their trip had changed him. Sassy had seen a softening, a sort of wonder bloom in Colt that she'd never witnessed before. He'd become more curious and social—striking up conversations with people on the airplanes and the boats and the excursions they'd found themselves on. He'd tried new foods—squid for one. Which he hadn't liked at all, but he'd still tried it. And he'd taken pictures of everything—marveling over the different scenery with an enthusiasm he didn't often show. Instead of being his typical reserved self on their trip, Colt had opened himself up, and she was proud of him.

"I thought he loved it here." Oh, sweet Rosie. That stubborn lift to her chin hid so much.

"He's always been happy here," Sassy said gently. "But I suppose he doesn't necessarily feel anchored to this place." Not after losing his father. Colt liked running the store, but she'd never seen it as his passion in life. It made him a good living, but it wasn't enough to build a life on. He needed more. Adventure. Love. She wanted all of that for him. And for Rose too.

"Why wouldn't he be anchored to this place?" Rose's tone had quieted. "*You're* here."

And Rose was here too. That's what had her niece so upset. She felt like Colt was leaving her behind. "I know he'll visit often." That didn't seem to pry Rose's frown loose. "If you really don't want him to go, you should tell him."

To her knowledge, Colt had never been in a serious relationship before. He'd dated a little in high school, and while he worked on his college degree online, but no one had ever captured his heart. He'd always kept that part of him to himself.

"Oh." Her niece shook her head and raised her hands between them. "No. I'm not suggesting…I mean, it doesn't matter to me if he goes or not."

Mm-hmm. Sassy simply stared at Rose, letting her expression speak for itself.

"It's just, um, well, he's part of your family." Her well-spoken Rosie continued to stumble through the words. "And, uh, he, well, also has part ownership over the resort."

The dear girl. It might be easier if she would admit she has feelings for the man. It seemed to take an awful lot of effort for her to deny it. "I think you should tell him how you feel." She gave her niece a hug. "I don't know what he'll do.

Or if it'll make a difference. But at least he'll have all the facts before he makes a big life decision."

Rose squinted as though she was frustrated, but she didn't try to deny her obvious emotions again.

"Now if you'll excuse me, I have an appointment." Sassy gave her niece's shoulder a loving squeeze and scooted on by. "I'll see you at home later this afternoon."

"See you there," her niece called before walking in the opposite direction. It seemed Rose was not up for another conversation with Colt. And, unless she missed her guess, Colt had no idea Rose felt anything toward him other than friendly.

But she would have to address that problem another day.

Sassy started off in the direction of the museum again, stopping briefly to coo at a sweet baby in a stroller.

After passing the park, she found herself standing in the shadows of the grand Juniper Springs Geology Museum. Housed in the old Episcopal church, the white limestone structure had always been an impressive sight. It had the traditional architecture, complete with a nonworking bell tower and turrets flanking each end. Graham had been meticulous about keeping up the grounds, she'd give him that, though maybe she should really credit the KEEP OFF THE GRASS and NO TRESPASSING signs he'd posted everywhere.

She let herself in through the small iron gate that surrounded the property and followed the stone path, careful not to scuff her foot into the grass, lest she mess something up. That wouldn't start this conversation off on the right foot.

"Can I help you?" Graham stood upright in the middle of the large lush rose garden near the museum's entrance.

"Oh." Sassy paused at the edge of the sidewalk. She'd thought she would have a few more minutes to get her thoughts together, but it appeared the man had been...gardening? Instead of the starched button-up shirts she'd often seen him wear, he had on a casual navy polo shirt and...khaki *shorts?*

"Can I help you, Ms. McGrath?" the man asked again. His voice seemed totally indifferent, much like it had at the meeting yesterday.

"Sassy." She corrected him with a smile meant to offer peace. "Please call me Sassy. No one calls me Ms. McGrath."

"Okay." The man removed his gardening gloves and lined them up on an ornate concrete bench nearby. "How can I help you, Sassy?" This time his tone wasn't quite as formal. That was progress in her book.

Still, she avoided his question. Her father had been an earnest no-nonsense man too, and she'd learned how to ease into important conversations. "This is a beautiful rose garden." For the first time since she stopped, she admired the variety of roses lining the pathway—bright pink hybrid tea roses and orange grandiflora roses and Cherry Parfait floribunda roses that grew in neat little rows. "I used to grow some of these same varieties at the inn." It had been a long time since the rosebushes had flourished around her front porch. Eventually the upkeep of the cabins had consumed her time, and she'd let her own personal garden go.

"They're dying." Graham plucked one of the Cherry Parfaits and walked to her, holding it out. "The leaves have black spots all over them. And they're turning yellow."

Sassy took the stem from him and carefully inspected it. "Rose black spot. It's a fungal disease." She'd dealt with it in her own rose garden a time or two. "All you need to do is get some fungicide from Colt down at the hardware store. And you'll want to prune out all the stem lesions too."

"I'm afraid I don't know much about pruning roses." He did have quite a handsome face when he wasn't frowning. She'd always thought him to be a few years older than her, but now that she focused on his eyes she could see he had to be quite a bit younger.

"I could help if you'd like." It had been years since she'd gotten her hands dirty in a garden, but she knew how to bring roses back to life.

"You want to help?" He shaded his eyes from the sun and seemed to regard her.

"Why not?" The budget could wait. Spending an hour here would only further her cause to find some kind of compromise on Ned's land. She stepped off the path and waded into the rosebushes. "Hand me the gloves."

"Oh." The man seemed to freeze. "You want to work on the roses now?"

"Now's as good a time as any." Thankfully she had opted for casual Friday attire. Or as she liked to think of it, casual everyday attire.

"I'll need the shears, too," she informed him.

Mr. Wright had yet to move, so Sassy walked to the bench and collected the gloves and a small pair of gardening shears herself. "Now, not every stem is going to be affected." She knelt in the soft dirt next to a particularly mature bunch of the tea roses. "See how this one is still green?" She gently tugged it apart from the others so he could get a glimpse. "We want to save those and snip the ones with the black spots."

"Right." Graham nodded, seeming to get his wits back about him. "I have another pair of gloves and shears in the shed. I'll be right back." He seemed to walk the same way he talked—purposefully and precisely.

While he was gone, Sassy got to work pruning the affected stems, setting them in a neat pile next to her. She'd almost forgotten how therapeutic it was to have her hands in the dirt, to smell the earthy and floral scents wafting around her, to feel the sunshine soaking into her from every angle. Yes, a community garden was exactly what the town needed. More time outside. More time together.

"Where should I start?" Mr. Wright asked from behind her.

"Let's work together on these." She patted the ground beside her. "It would appear the tea roses seem to have taken the brunt of the fungus."

The man murmured an acknowledgment and knelt a good few feet away. They worked in silence, clipping and tossing the stems for a few moments before the man spoke. "I hope I didn't offend you at the meeting."

Sassy couldn't help a grin. "You mean when you implied I wasn't qualified to be the mayor?" She had to tease him a little. He made it far too easy.

"It was rude," Mr. Wright acknowledged, his head down as he clipped a stem. "But I didn't intend for it to be. Peg had gotten me all worked up with this threatening email she sent me, and I figured you were part of their plot."

"Ah." Sassy stopped her cutting and waited until he looked at her. "One thing you need to know about me, Mr. Wright—"

"Graham," he interrupted. "Call me Graham."

"Okay, Graham." She set the stem she'd been working on

in the discard pile so she could give him her full attention. "I'm not part of anyone else's plot. I want what's best for this town. That's all that's on my agenda."

"And I want to make sure Ned's wishes are honored." He went back to avoiding her eyes while he worked. "But I don't intend to be rude. I've never been much of a people person."

A snort slipped out before she could stop it, but thankfully it didn't seem to offend the man.

"I know. Some might think I'm in the wrong position, being the face of the museum and all." He meticulously inspected the stems on another tea rose bush. "I'm much better with studying and handling rocks than I am with people. I would rather analyze nephrite and tourmaline and liebigite."

Liebi-what? She couldn't repeat any of those mineral names if her life depended on it. "And I'd much rather deal with people."

"That's why everyone likes you."

Wait just one minute. Was that a smile spreading across his face? Were they experiencing a true miracle right here in the museum's garden?

"Believe it or not, I used to be better." He snipped one of those bright pink roses and held it up as though admiring it. "Before my Betsy passed away. She helped me understand people, I suppose. She helped me understand myself."

Sassy had stopped searching the roses and studied his pensive face instead. "I didn't realize..." That he'd lost someone close to him, that he'd even been married at all. But then, she didn't know this man. She knew the little she'd seen. She knew the little she'd heard. But she hadn't bothered to discover anything about Graham for herself.

"She passed the year before I moved here." A thread of emotion weaved itself into his tone. "Cancer. She had a good few years after the diagnosis, but eventually it spread."

Sassy shifted to sit on the ground so she could relieve her aching knees. "You hardly recognize yourself after they're gone." That's how she'd felt when she'd lost Robert. In some ways, she'd lost him twice. First, when he'd been hauled off to prison, and then again when they called to tell her he passed away.

She'd done her best to hold strong for Colt, but after that call she'd lost a significant piece of herself, and that was when everything at the resort had started to fall apart.

Graham sat back too, setting his shears on the ground. "You were married once?"

"Not officially." Robert hadn't wanted to marry her when he'd been so afraid his past would eventually catch up. "But our souls were intertwined. That kind of love leaves a hole."

"That it do—"

"Graham?" Sharon Zabinski came into view on the stone path. "That is you!" The woman stopped a few feet away. "And Sassy, how nice to see you."

"Nice to see you too." Her knees creaked and groaned as she pushed off the ground to stand up. Sharon was one of the board members at the museum, and another one of Sassy's occasional bridge friends. If she was surprised to see Sassy there with Graham, she didn't let on.

"I know I'm a few minutes early." She cast an apologetic glance at her watch. "But I thought I'd see if you were ready for our meeting."

"Oh. That's right." Graham scrambled to his feet too. "We have a meeting. Sorry. I lost track of time."

"That's no problem." Sharon held out a folder. "I'll go ahead inside and set out the ideas for the new pyrite display so we can go through everything. See you in there." The woman said goodbye to Sassy and disappeared through the museum's heavy wooden door.

After the interruption, Graham seemed at a loss for words again. He stood there staring at Sassy, but somehow seemed far away too.

"Well I guess our work is done for the day." Sassy pulled off her gloves and set them on the bench along with the gardening shears.

"Yes." He stepped closer but then stopped as though he wasn't quite sure what to do. "Thank you," he finally said. "I'm sure I never would've figured out what was wrong with these roses if you hadn't come along." He glanced at the door where Sharon had disappeared. "I'm sure you didn't come here to help with the roses. Was there something else you wanted to discuss with me?"

No, she hadn't come to work on the roses, but working on the roses had given her a whole new perspective. "I did come to talk with you more about the land, but it can wait."

"Until tomorrow?" Graham brushed the dirt off his shorts, reminding Sassy to do the same. "We still have some work to do on these roses if you're free." There went that elusive smile again.

"I can be free." And tomorrow she would come prepared with snacks and some sun-brewed lemon tea. "Same time, same place?"

The man gave her a single firm nod. "I'll look forward to it."

Chapter Nine

Rose

S hh. Marigold, quiet."

Rose peeked out the window of her restored camper to make sure the coast was clear. Colt's truck sat parked next to Tony's, but the man was nowhere to be seen. Good. Hopefully Tony had already put him to work in one of the cabins and she wouldn't have to run into him out on the property somewhere.

She readjusted the curtains she'd made herself and poured another cup of coffee. It had been three days since she'd made a fool out of herself getting all emotional in Colt's hardware store, and she'd managed to avoid him by spending a few nights in Denver with her mother while they shopped for the last of the accessories she needed to give the cabins that perfect homey feel.

She had no idea what had come over her when she'd seen that FOR SALE sign in the hardware store's window, but she refused to overanalyze the situation. "I'm sad for Sassy, that's all," she told her dog.

Speaking of her aunt, she still hadn't mustered up the

courage to set a meeting between Sassy and Lillian. Besides helping her avoid Colt, going to Denver with her mother had ensured that the sisters wouldn't run into each other before Rose was ready to construct the perfect circumstances to bring those two back together. She still had no idea what that would look like. Right now, all she could seem to envision was Lillian turning her back and walking away the second she saw Sassy.

Marigold nosed the curtain to the side again and whined.

Yes, yes, she wanted to go outside. "Give me a minute." Rose took her coffee with her to the tiny bathroom at the back of the camper. It wasn't much—a miniature sink and toilet, and then a showerhead hanging beyond a curtain— but this was home.

When she and her sisters had reunited at the resort last Christmas, they couldn't believe Sassy still had the old camping trailer they used to play in, stocked with all of their toys and books and dress-up clothes. Needing a project to keep her busy, Rose had renovated the inside—painting the walls, sewing new pillows and curtains, and cleaning up every nook and cranny.

As soon as the weather had warmed late in the spring, she'd decided to move into the camper for the summer, and now she wondered what she ever needed three bedrooms and three bathrooms for back in Savannah.

"Simple. That's how I like my life now." She squirted some sunscreen into her hand and smeared it all over her face—a must in the high mountains during the summer. "I don't need things to get all complicated." Specifically in regard to Colt. Not when she had so much on her plate.

Tony and his crew had made good progress on the cabins while she'd been in Denver, but she still had to finish the decorating before the Cleary family checked in tomorrow. So now was not the time to be exploring any feelings. "You want simplicity too, right, Mari?"

The dog whined again, nosing at the curtain from where she sat on the seat of the dinette.

"Good. Glad to see we agree." Rose pulled on a sweatshirt over her tank top and yanked open the door, Marigold leaping up behind her.

Who knew? Maybe Rose would be able to avoid Colt until the store sold, until he left town. Then she wouldn't have to get all weird and emotional about him leaving.

She took the path through the aspen trees, trying to stay out of sight while she made her way to the cabins around the pond. Tony stood on the porch of the Silver Bells cabin talking to one of his crew members. Perfect.

She had about an hour before Dahlia would arrive to help her start putting the finishing touches on the decor—the fun accent pillows she'd found, little Christmassy trinkets to keep the spirit of the season the whole year. "Let's see what we can do to help Tony in the meantime."

Marigold didn't seem all that interested in helping. The dog took off for the pond, likely ready for her early morning dip. "Don't terrorize the geese," Rose called behind her.

She skirted the edge of the trees all the way to where Tony stood. "Good morning." She kept her distance in case Colt was inside the cabin. "Anything I can do to help you out before Dally gets here?"

"Yeah." Tony lumbered down the steps to join her. "Colt

could use some help finishing up the trim in the Reindeer Cabin."

"Oh." Her heart got all squirmy, but she refused to let her smile fade. "Well, I would love to help with that. Of course I would. The problem is…" She couldn't be in the same room as Colt right now. Obviously her body wasn't ready for that, what with the swooshing of her blood and the triple beat of her heart. "I don't really know anything about trim. But I would love to—"

"You don't gotta know anything." Tony stuck a pencil behind his ear and headed for his truck. "Colt knows it all. We need you to hold stuff up, help him measure. Things like that. We got a lot to do today to wrap things up." He didn't wait for a response before he opened the tailgate and started to rummage through his tools.

"Right. Okay. Sure!" Rose did an about-face and blew out a trembling breath. Earlier this week, she and Colt had been joking around about her home improvement ignorance. He'd teased her about how she'd held a hammer. They'd talked about his travels with Sassy. But when she'd found out he was leaving, it was like her heart had gotten away from her, and now she didn't know how to act in front of him.

Case in point—each step that brought her closer to the Reindeer Cabin also seemed to lodge her heart higher into her throat. She didn't have time to stuff it back where it belonged before Colt walked out onto the porch where a big table saw sat.

He noticed her standing at the base of the stairs right away. "There you are."

"Here I am." She tried not to stumble on the first step.

The careful way the man was watching her didn't help with her balance. Colt seemed to see her. All of her. And she wasn't used to a man looking so deeply into her.

"You seemed upset in the hardware store, and—"

"Upset?" She choked out a laugh. "*No*. I wasn't upset. Why would I be upset with you?" If she admitted she had been emotional about him leaving, she would have to explain why, and she couldn't. What would she say? *I don't want you to leave because I'll miss you too much*? She hadn't earned the right to tell him what to do with his life. "I was stressed." Rose found herself nodding slowly. "Yes, very stressed. My mom is in town, and she stresses me out."

"Oh." Colt's gaze dove to the ground between them. "I see."

"Yep. I'm super stressed." Rose took the opportunity to steer the conversation away from how upset she'd been. "She's already had one altercation with Grumpy. She told him she was going to leave a bad review online because he didn't have almond milk."

"Yikes." Eight months ago when they'd met, she'd been lucky to see a shadow of a smile cross Colt's lips, but lately he'd been grinning a whole lot more. Probably because he was looking forward to starting a new life. "Bet that went over well."

"About as well as you would expect." She eyed the saw behind him, ready to move on and find a distraction. "So anyway, that's what was wrong. Sorry I took it all out on you."

"No problem." Colt turned around and lined up a long piece of decorative trim on the saw to make a quick cut. His face changed when he got seriously focused on something. His eyes tapered slightly in the corners and his lips bunched.

He still hadn't trimmed his hair since his vacation...some of it nearly got into his eyes when he bent his head.

She needed to stop noticing the details that made him so appealing. She cleared her throat. "Tony thought you could use help holding things and measuring." Since that about covered the list of her construction qualifications.

"That'd be great." Colt lifted the trim and opened the door. Rose followed him inside.

"What you've done with this place is incredible, Rose."

There went that melting sensation dead center in her chest again. "I didn't really do the work. Tony—"

"But this is all your vision." Colt carried the trim to the opposite side of the living room and leaned it against the wall. "Tony and his crew have done the work, but you're the one who brought this cabin back to life. You've made it into a special place."

The compliment embedded itself deeper than she wanted it to. "We've all made it into a special place. It's the memories we have here." Though she didn't quite remember being with Colt as a kid, her aunt told her they'd spent some time together the year before her family had stopped coming to visit.

"What are your favorite memories?" He seemed to look for something in her eyes.

"Christmas, of course." She stared back at him, a warmth rising through her. "The ice-skating and tree decorating and sledding down the hill." Had Colt done those things with them? He seemed transfixed on her, waiting as though he knew she wasn't done.

Once she got to talking about how much she'd loved

this place as a kid, she might never be done. "Then in the summer...Sassy would create this magical night on our last evening here." She closed her eyes, still seeing the sight. "She would put floating candles on the pond and hang up colorful lanterns on the trees." A laugh snuck out. "She always told us the fairies had come and decorated for us—bringing us into their magic." And when she'd seen that pond all lit up it had felt like walking into another world.

"I was there for that once. The last summer you came."

Rose suddenly felt a heightened awareness of his closeness, his eyes on hers. Her breath caught. "You remember me from back then?"

According to her aunt, Colt had picked her flowers when they were young, and Lillian threw them in the trash, but she hadn't realized Colt had remembered.

"I could never forget you." The tenderness in his voice matched his expression.

Rose couldn't speak. She couldn't breathe. Was he speaking as a friend or...something more?

Before she got her wits about her enough to ask, Colt had turned away and knelt to line up the trim against the wall.

"We should probably get back to work. Can you hold this?" The man gestured to the trim.

Right. She was supposed to be helping him, not standing there struggling to think.

"Sure." Rose knelt on the floor and held the trim against the wall while Colt put nail after precise nail in place. At least watching him work gave her something to look at besides his face.

"You okay?" Colt paused with the nail gun.

"I'm great." She turned her head toward the remaining pieces of trim so he couldn't see too deeply into her eyes. "It's a relief to have this almost done." Let him think she was tired from the long renovation process instead of awkwardly trying to feel her way through certain desires she didn't know what to do with. "I guess my next project will be working on the main house. Sassy mentioned her home was always the last priority and hasn't been updated in years. She said she'd love to see some renovations." Though they'd have to wait until they actually had a positive cash flow. *If* they ever had a positive cash flow...

Colt paused, holding the nail gun against the trim while he focused on her. "What do you want to do with the place?"

"How much time do you have?" she joked. His quick smile drew her in. She could live to see this man smile. "I'd like to completely open up the main level. Take out a few walls. Update the kitchen and flooring. I'd love to do a lot of the work myself so I can save money." She cut herself off before she got carried away. "That'll happen someday. Right now I have to finish this project and get through Sassy's celebration first."

"You'll be ready for a vacation after the party." He popped the last couple of nails into place and stood. "You can always come visit me if you need to get away this fall."

Did he want her to come visit him? She couldn't tell. This fall meant he planned to leave right away. "Have you started looking at places yet?"

"I've found a few houses in Idaho that look interesting. There's some beautiful country up there." Colt selected an-other long section of trim from the collection that leaned against the small island in the kitchen. "I'd better figure it out soon. I might have an offer coming in on the store."

"Already?" Her voice squeaked. Rose followed him outside to the porch and watched him make the cuts on the saw. She'd assumed the sale would take some time.

"My real estate agent is cautiously optimistic." Colt pulled out his measuring tape and checked the length of the trim. "Can't say too much about it yet, but the sale could happen much faster than I thought."

"That's great news." Back when she'd been engaged to marry into a high-profile family, Rose had been good at acting, but she was losing her touch. She tried to infuse more enthusiasm into her tone. "I'm happy for you." The words were true. She'd never realized it was possible to be happy and hurting at the same time for the same reason.

Colt should follow his dreams. He hadn't had an easy life with his mom passing away when he was young and then his dad going to prison when he was a teenager. Even with all that going against him, he'd built a successful business. He'd become a good man. "You deserve this." She held the door open so he could haul the trim back inside.

"I don't know about that. There's a lot I'll miss here." His eyes grazed hers, and then he kneeled down to match up the trim on the wall near the door, all focused and closed off.

Rose knelt right next to him, a tremble in her knees. Would he miss her? She was too afraid to ask. It wasn't like anything could happen between them. She probably wasn't his type. She wasn't outdoorsy enough or tough enough. Or quiet enough...

"Don't worry, though. I won't leave before the big party

for Sassy." Colt picked up the nail gun. "I wouldn't miss that for the world."

"Me neither. It's going to be—"

A tickle skittered across her leg. Rose looked down. "Whaa! Mouse! Mouse!" She leapt for Colt, throwing her arms around his neck and climbing halfway up his body.

"Whoa." He dropped the nail gun, which went off and sent a nail flying straight through the brand-new window across the room.

Rose didn't care. "I feel like it's still on me! Is it on me?" Clinging to the man, she tried to inspect her legs. "I felt it run. Across. My. Thigh." She nearly gagged. "Oh my God! A mouse touched me!"

For a second she couldn't tell if the trembling was coming from her legs or shoulders, but then she realized Colt shook with laughter.

"Where'd it go?" She frantically searched the floor, but there was no sign of the mouse.

"I think you scared it away." The man was laughing so hard he could barely speak.

"It's not funny! It's still here somewhere." The rodent was probably waiting for her to climb out of Colt's lap so it could *touch* her again.

"A little mouse won't hurt you." Colt had stopped laughing but amusement still flickered in his eyes.

Oh mama, those eyes. They were bright and close. *So* close to hers. A new awareness seemed to flood her body. Somehow Colt's arms had ended up around her. He didn't move, didn't push her away. If anything his hold on her seemed to tighten. His eyes were darker now, more intense, and she wondered if he could breathe because she definitely could not.

His lips parted like he wanted to speak. Or maybe he wanted to kiss her the way she wanted to kiss him…

"Rose?" Footsteps pounded the porch steps outside.

She and Colt seemed to move at the same time, both scrambling to stand and back away from each other.

The door opened and Dally strolled in, completely unaware that something had almost happened. *Had* something almost happened? Or had Rose imagined the way Colt's face had tipped toward hers?

"Hey, you two."

"Dally!" Rose had never been so happy to see her sister. "You're here already. Oh, wow." Words were coming out of her mouth, but Rose had little control over them. "Great. We have a ton to do with the decorating. We have to put out the cute pillows and signs I bought." She let her gaze graze over Colt, who had stooped to pick up the nail gun. "You can finish up here? It looks like it's almost done. I'm sure I'm not much help anyway with the holding and the measuring." And the freaking out about mice that led to much bigger problems like her almost kissing him.

"Sure. I can finish up."

Rose was too chicken to bring his face into focus. Was it amusement she detected in his tone? Revulsion? She couldn't hear clearly with the panic rebounding from her heart to her head. No complications! That's what she'd told Marigold earlier. "Okay, great! Then we should get a move on. We want everything to be perfect for the Cleary family. I bought some really cute pillows." She linked her arm with Dally's.

"You mentioned that," her sister said as Rose led her hastily out the door. She moved at full speed, prodding Dally down the steps and along the path that led to the Mistletoe Cabin on the other side of the pond.

"Either you had five cups of coffee this morning, or something weird happened in there before I showed up."

You couldn't get anything past Dahlia. She had a mom's Spidey sense. Rose kept her mouth bolted shut until she and Dally were safely locked inside the Mistletoe Cabin alone.

"What did I miss?" Instead of unpacking the boxes Rose had hauled in here yesterday, her sister parked herself on the brand-new leather sofa. "I obviously missed something good."

Rose couldn't sit. "I don't know what happened. There was this mouse, so I jumped and landed in Colt's arms—"

Dahlia let out a cackle. "You *happened* to jump into his arms? Oh, that's good, Rosie."

"I freaked out!" Obviously she had a minor problem with freaking out. Being level-headed was Dally's job. "Anyway, I was sitting there in his arms. There was definitely staring. Everything around us seemed to stop..."

"And?" Her sister had leaned all the way forward on the couch.

"And then I heard you call me." Rose looked out the window. There was Marigold, sunning herself on a patch of grass next to the pond. Things were not simple anymore. Nope. Not after that moment with Colt. Her dog would be so disappointed in her.

"Damn, I have bad timing." Dahlia laughed. "And here I thought you were only helping him out with the construction work."

"Your timing was perfect." Rose slumped on the couch next to her sister. "It couldn't have been better." At least now she could pretend nothing had happened. They hadn't crossed any lines. She'd gotten a little flustered about the mouse, that was all. But a kiss...a kiss! That was much harder to come back from.

Her sister turned to face her fully, pulling both her knees up on the sofa cushion. "Would it be so terrible if I *hadn't* interrupted?"

"Yes." She let her head rest back against the couch. You could no longer see the damage she'd inflicted on the roof and ceiling earlier that week. Colt had patched the drywall expertly.

"Oh, come on." Dally nudged her shoulder. "You two were flirting like crazy the other night. I can tell you like him."

"And I can tell you like Ike. So why haven't you gone out with him once since you moved to town?" Uh-huh. That was right. She knew how to turn around a question.

"I have two kids," her sister reminded her.

"And a built-in favorite-aunt babysitter." So there. She had no excuses.

A year ago Dally might've shrugged and offered another excuse. But nowadays they didn't hide from each other the way they once had. Her sister sighed. "I don't think Maya is ready for me to date anyone yet."

"Ah." She'd detected a 'tude from her niece when they'd all shared dinner that night, but she hadn't realized it had been directed at Ike. She'd thought it was some hormonal shift. "That's a tough one."

"Yeah." For a second it looked like Dally might say more, but then she grinned. "Don't think I'm going to be easily distracted. If it helps, I think Colt might like you too."

"That doesn't help." Talk about bad timing.

Rose had found her purpose in Juniper Springs, and Colt was getting ready to leave this place behind.

Chapter Ten

Dahlia

T his is absolutely darling."

Dahlia held up the sign she'd unpacked from one of the many boxes she and Rose were working through. "Merry Christ*moose*. I love it." The wooden plaque displayed a metal moose with Christmas lights on its antlers. "You always find the best design elements." It was no wonder Rose had been working toward opening her own interior design business before she left Savannah. "Do you miss doing design work?"

"Yes." Her sister clearly didn't have to think about the question. "But I'm hoping that I'll be able to do some free-lance work when we have things more under control here." She took the sign from Dahlia. "I'm not sure we'll both be able to live off what we make from the resort. Revenue is an unknown right now. So interior design would be a good way to make some extra money."

She'd been thinking the same thing about their salaries. Right now, Jeff was paying some hefty child support, being out of the country and all, but she didn't want to rely on his money. "I can find another job too." She had plenty of bookkeeping skills from the accounting classes she'd taken in college that could be useful to businesses around town.

"I don't want you to have to." Rose held the sign up against the wall near the fireplace. "What about right here?"

"Perfect." Dahlia brought over the hammer and nail set they were using to hang pictures, and they spent a few minutes measuring to make sure the nails were even before they hung the sign.

The MERRY CHRISTMOOSE greeting brought the right amount of fun and charm to the space. "It's incredibly cozy in here." The interior of each cabin had been redone with a small stone fireplace, new hardwood floors, and plush furniture that begged to be curled up on while you drank hot chocolate on those cool summer—or frigid winter—nights.

They'd agreed to keep something of a Christmas theme through the cabins all year round because those were their best memories of this place—Christmases where they gathered and played and ate and found joy in being together.

Rose had selected various rustic accents to remind visitors that they were in the mountains—the moose sign, of course, but also a plaid red and black fleece blanket hanging over the back of the sofa, aspen wood candle holders, beautiful paintings of the peaks outside that were purchased from a local artist. "I wouldn't mind moving in here myself." The house she and the children were renting in town was nice enough, but she hadn't found any time to personalize it or make it theirs.

"I would totally let you if the Cleary family hadn't booked every single cabin." Rose walked around giving everything they'd set up a critical eye. "I'm so sorry there's no other place for Mom to stay."

"It's fine. Having you take her to Denver for two nights really helped give us all a break." The children loved their Gigi, but they didn't appreciate the way she constantly tried to improve their appearance, telling them to stand up straighter or comb their hair or change out of that shirt because it clashed with their shorts. Dahlia had grown up with the nitpicking, and she'd made a conscious effort not to be that mom. So what if Ollie wanted to wear a red shirt with orange shorts? She tried not to let her son's individual sense of style bother her.

"Hopefully Grumpy's coffee shop is still standing when you go pick her up." Rose stashed the hammer and nails back in her hot-pink toolbox.

"There's no guarantee on that." When her mother had told her she wanted to work on her DAR newsletter at the coffee shop, Dahlia had almost refused to drive her there, given what had happened earlier that week. "I wish I could've seen Grumpy's face when she walked in."

"It would've looked something like this." Rose narrowed her eyes into slits and scrunched up her mouth. "Well, look who it is…" she said in her best Grumpy impression. "The almond milk lady."

They both broke out into laughter.

"The woman never backs down from a fight." In some ways, Dahlia wished she'd inherited that fire. Then maybe she wouldn't have let her ex-husband get away with treating her the way he did for so long.

"The woman can be mighty persistent," her sister agreed. "Has she stopped bugging you about Ike yet?"

"Not in the slightest." According to Lillian, Dahlia and Ike should already be married by now. "She thinks I shouldn't coddle Maya." She started to collect the discarded wrappings they'd strewn around unpacking the boxes. "She said the kids need to get used to the idea that I have a life too."

"The woman does have a point." Rose retrieved two bottles of water from the refrigerator and handed one to her.

"I know." Dahlia plopped herself onto the stool at the kitchen island. "But that's my problem. Since they were born, Maya and Ollie have been my life. They've been my whole focus. I don't know any other way. Having kids can be tough on a marriage."

There was no justifying the way Jeff had cheated on her, she knew that. And yet...she also took responsibility for not being fully present in her relationship with her husband. The kids simply made it easier to hide their problems and divert their attention. "Jeff and I were so busy focusing on the kids, we grew apart. What if that happens again, Rosie? The kids need me. I've always been the one who nurtures them, who makes them feel safe."

Jeff had been the quintessential Disneyland dad—fun but not very useful when they were sick or doing their homework or crying about something one of their friends said to them at school.

Rose joined her at the island, leaning into the counter across from Dahlia. Rose looked her in the eyes, and Dahlia let her see everything—the insecurity, the fear, the doubts she harbored about her future.

"I know it's scary to think about giving away your heart," her sister said gently. "But Dally...Ike is *so hot*."

"Ha!" Rose might be the only person who could take her

from being on the verge of tears to hysterical laughter in the matter of a few seconds. "Here I thought you had some sincere words of wisdom for me. Some groundbreaking advice."

Rose giggled too. "Clearly I am not qualified to be giving out relationship advice. I almost married a total snob, and now I'm falling for Colt, just in time for him to leave the state. What does that tell you?"

"It tells me relationships are messy." And she was sure glad she wasn't the only one who couldn't seem to get her love life together. "So you're admitting that you're falling for—"

Her phone rang, letting her sister off the hook. For the moment. Dahlia pulled it out of her pocket and glanced at the screen. "It's Maya and Ollie's day camp." This couldn't be good news. She stood and brought the phone to her ear, already looking for her purse. "Hello?"

"Hi there, this is Misty, the director of the Juniper Springs Elementary day camp. Just wanted to let you know Maya had a fall during our time on the obstacle course a little while ago."

"Okay." Dahlia's heart clutched, but she'd learned to temper the panic until she had all the facts.

"It seems she twisted her ankle," the woman went on calmly. "There is some definite bruising. We're icing it now, but I thought maybe you would want to come pick her up and take her to have it looked at. I've talked with Ollie. He would still like to stay for the day if that's all right with you."

"Yes. Of course." She let out the breath she'd been holding. She'd dealt with plenty of twisted ankles. "Thank you. Ollie can stay. I'll be right there to pick up Maya." She hung up the phone and turned to see her sister already standing at the door. "What is it? Maya or Ollie? Are they okay? Do I need to drive you to the ER?"

"It's Maya's ankle." Dahlia grinned at her sister. "Probably just a sprain, but I appreciate the panic."

"Oh." Rose sighed. "A sprain. Okay. We can handle a sprain."

Dahlia moved out onto the porch. "I'll take her to see Ike just to make sure it's not something more serious."

"Yeah, you will." Rose winked, and Dahlia shook her head at her sister.

"He is a very good-looking man. You can't deny that."

"Why, thank you," Tony called from Gingerbread Cabin's porch next door. "Sorry, ladies. I'm happily married."

"Damn. All the good ones are taken," Rose called back, and the three of them got a good laugh.

"I guess we'll have to become spinster sisters." Dahlia could see it—she and Rose as two crazy old ladies living in the same house. Take about simple. There'd be none of those difficult relationship milestones—figuring out if you're compatible, first fights, arguments over what to watch on TV. It would be all rom-coms all the time.

"That would be perfect." Rose gasped excitedly. "We could be known as the Juniper Spinsters!"

"It's a plan." Dahlia hurried down the steps. "I'll be back to help you finish up here as soon as I can." She dug around her purse for her car keys. "Depending on how long this takes, I might need you to pick up Mom from Grumpy's too."

"I'd love nothing more," Rose said sweetly.

Dahlia shot her a look of gratitude and waved goodbye before climbing into her car. On the drive over to the school, she tried to brace herself for her daughter's wrath. Maya hadn't wanted to go to the camp in the first place, and now she'd gotten hurt. Something told Dahlia this wouldn't be a fun afternoon.

Every time she drove up to the elementary building, she could hardly believe her children got to go to school in such a beautiful location. Two mountain peaks provided the backdrop for the one-story brick building. And talk about a cool playground. The whole area had been built to look like a forest, with trees and logs to climb on, big rocks to explore, and the obstacle course where Maya had likely taken her spill.

Dahlia found her keycard and let herself into the building. She stopped to check in at the office.

Misty was sitting behind a desk while Maya sat in a chair on the other side. Her leg was propped up on another chair.

"Hey, sweetie." Dahlia gave her a hug. "How's the ankle?"

"It hurts really bad." Her daughter still had fresh tear stains on her cheeks.

Dahlia noted the blue tinge on her daughter's lips. "I bet that popsicle you had took the edge off, though."

"Works every time." Misty handed her an incident report. "She was doing awesome on that obstacle course."

"But I lost my balance," her daughter whimpered.

"So did some of the other kids," Misty pointed out gently. "The important thing is that you tried and did your best."

"Exactly," Dahlia agreed. "I'm proud of you. We'll take a quick trip to the doctor to make sure all is well, and then maybe we'll see if the ice cream shop is open."

That put the light back in her daughter's eyes.

Dahlia thanked Misty and signed Maya out, then she helped

her daughter limp to the car. At least it didn't take long to get anywhere in Juniper Springs. Back in Minneapolis it would've taken them almost a half hour to drive to the doctor.

"I was so embarrassed when I fell," Maya said as they pulled up into the medical building's parking lot.

Dahlia cut the engine and turned to her daughter. "Did anyone laugh at you?"

"No. But they probably wanted to." Her daughter's shoulders slumped. "I don't know anyone here. It's really hard."

"I know it is." She reached over to squeeze Maya's hand. "But it's good for us too, honey. Change makes us dig a little deeper inside of ourselves. Change makes us stronger and braver." Dahlia could speak from experience. In the last two years she'd grown more as a person than she had in the ten years before that. "So I'm really proud of you for doing the obstacle course and taking a risk."

Maya's smile seemed to perk up. "I guess I'm a little proud of myself too. It was really hard. And kind of fun until I fell."

"Well, I'm glad you tried something new." Dahlia climbed out of the car and hurried to help her daughter stand. "How about if I give you a piggyback ride inside?"

"Yes!" Maya threw her arms around Dahlia's neck and she crouched so her daughter could climb on.

Whoa. This had been a lot easier a few years ago. She straightened her legs, trying not to let her knees buckle, and moved one careful step at a time.

"This is awesome!"

"It sure is." And a good reminder that she should join a gym as soon as possible.

They made it through the door, somehow knocking Maya's ankle only once, and Dahlia lowered her daughter to a chair.

"Uh-oh." Mrs. Miller stood up behind the reception counter. "Looks like we've got a big owie, huh?"

"I twisted my ankle," Maya informed her gravely. "I can hardly even walk on it."

"Poor thing." Mrs. Miller opened a cabinet and found an icepack. "The doctors stepped out for lunch, but they should be back any minute now."

"Oh." Ike and Dr. Jolly had gone to lunch together? Sure they had. They were colleagues...probably discussing patients. It shouldn't bother her.

Dally reached into her purse to find the incident report. "I'm sure you'll want a copy of this." She handed the paper to the receptionist.

"Yes. I'll put it in her file."

"There's the doctors," Maya said miserably. "They'll probably have to touch it. This is gonna hurt isn't it?"

Dahlia didn't answer. She was too busy watching Ike and Dr. Jolly approach the entrance. They were laughing about something, and she was struck again by how vivacious Dr. Jolly seemed. In comparison, Dahlia felt frayed and tattered.

Just as they stepped through the door, she turned back around to the counter to complete the check-in paperwork.

"Well, well, well. What do we have here?" Ike said behind her. He might as well have pulled her in closer and brushed a kiss on her neck for how her heart skipped. For only a second, she imagined herself walking over to him and greeting him the way she wanted to—with a hug, a hello kiss. What would it feel like to be free to walk into his arms in front of everyone? She might never know.

Dahlia let her daughter explain the injury and how it happened.

"I hurt my ankle when I was about your age too," Dr. Jolly said. "But I was only running. Doing an obstacle course is way cooler."

Dahlia handed the rest of the completed paperwork to Mrs. Miller and finally found the courage to turn around. When she did, Ike was looking at her. She couldn't avoid softening her lips into a smile while she let her gaze linger on him. He looked especially handsome after coming in from the outdoors—his face tanned and his eyes bright.

Before turning to her daughter, Ike smiled back at her— a subtle quirk in the corners of his lips that she'd seen before he'd kissed her last Christmas.

"Don't worry, Maya. We can get you fixed up, no problem." She swore the man had the kindest manner she'd ever seen. "Why don't you come on back right away?" He reached out his hand to help Maya up, but she didn't take it.

"I want Dr. Jolly to look at my ankle."

"Maya." The word came out through a gasp of embarrassment. Not so much at the request, but at the way her daughter delivered it in a sullen, stubborn tone.

"That's a great idea." Ike didn't even seem to flinch. "Dr. Jolly is very good with injuries. She'll take great care of you."

"Oh." The woman hesitated and seemed to get silent reassurance from Ike before smiling. "Yes, I'd love to take a look. Do you think you can walk on it, or should we get a wheelchair?"

Maya scooted to the edge of her seat. "I can walk if you help me."

"Not a problem." Dr. Jolly helped Maya to her feet and encouraged her daughter to lean on her as she led her behind the counter and into the hallway.

"I'm right behind you." Dahlia's face still seemed to be radiating heat. She waited for Ike to come alongside her and then walked into the hallway with him. "I'm so sorry." She still couldn't believe how belligerent her daughter had sounded.

"You have nothing to be sorry about." He laughed a little. "Maya has every right to choose her own medical provider. I'm not offended at all."

Dahlia looked around, making sure they were alone. "She doesn't want to share me with anyone." That had to be why her daughter had turned on Ike so quickly. "I think she's afraid of losing me the way she lost a part of her relationship with her father when he moved."

"That's understandable." He rubbed his hand up and down her arm, and she wanted to lean into him. "You don't have to worry about my feelings. Not when it comes to your kids. They're first. That's the way it should be."

Then why did she feel so bad about it? Dahlia inched closer to him, wanting more. Needing more. "I can't tell you how much I've missed you." She'd forced herself to forget how often he'd filled her thoughts but when she stood this close to him that longing overpowered everything else.

"I could tell you how much I've missed you, but we would need a lot more time than a few minutes in the hallway." His voice had dropped lower and deeper.

"Rose said she would babysit." They could sneak away for a—

"Mom? Are you coming?" her daughter called from the end of the hallway.

She squeezed her eyes shut. "Be right there."

"It's fine." Ike brushed a quick kiss across her lips. "We'll figure out something."

When? How? A sense of hopelessness engulfed her.

"Mom?"

"Coming." Before walking away, Dahlia found Ike's hand and squeezed it. "You are the best man."

"And you're worth the wait." He turned and continued down the hallway, taking her heart with him.

Chapter Eleven

Sassy

If she had to look at one more spreadsheet column, Sassy might very well up and join an online dating website so she could find some motivation to skip town like Mayor Lund had.

"I'm printing out the final budget, then we have to get downstairs for the special council budget meeting." Moe hustled to the other side of their cramped office to where the printer sat, tapping his foot while he waited for the ancient contraption to spit out one piece of paper at a time.

"Think anyone would care if I canceled the meeting?" She was only half joking. She and Moe had been stuck in this office all morning, trimming funds here and there to come up with a recommended budget that wouldn't compromise any of the town's critical operations.

She hadn't even been able to get out for her meeting with Graham today. It was the first rose garden work session she'd missed all week. Though when she texted him to let him know, he'd asked if she could swing by after the council meeting.

The man's text back still made her smile. *I understand. Mayoral duties are of the utmost importance. In lieu of our morning meeting, perhaps you can stop by the rose garden after the budget approval? I would very much like to see you today.*

The words were so formal—so Graham. She could imagine him laboring over them, since she'd come to learn over the last few days he had a difficult time articulating his personal thoughts. Ask him a geological question and the man could recite you an entire dissertation, but when it had come to talking about how he'd managed to pick up the pieces of his life after his wife's death, he'd stumbled and paused and had tried to change the subject at least four times.

She'd kept on him though, asking questions, learning more about him. And she'd come to see Graham Wright through new eyes. She'd looked forward to their midmorning engagements. Though she'd still been getting the headaches regularly, spending time with her new friend had made them seem less pronounced, not so scary.

"What's that smile about?" Moe demanded, standing directly in front of her. Funny, she hadn't even noticed the printer had finished. "Because you surely aren't excited about the meeting. We can't cancel, and you know it. Peg would lose her mind."

"I know. It's best to get it over with anyway." One didn't have to be a genius to know good old Peg would put up a fight when she saw that Sassy had cut funding for the annual Miss Juniper Springs pageant. Seriously, though. It was a new day. Should they really encourage young girls to get all made up and prance around in fancy dresses? In her estimation, the pageant wasn't a critical town function.

"All right. Let's get a move on." She accepted the folder Moe held out. "But I'm cutting this thing off at one hour." Or maybe even less.

"Why?" Moe held open the door for her. "You got a hot date or something?"

Warmth crept into Sassy's cheeks. A blush? That hadn't happened in a good twenty years. She'd almost forgotten how it felt. "No, I don't have a date." Not technically. She didn't know what to call her meetings with Graham. Initially she could've passed them off as business discussions, but they'd taken a turn into more personal matters. She always went to the rose garden with the intention of bringing up the land, but by the time she had to leave to go back to her mayoral duties, she'd forgotten all about her own agenda.

All week that had been her excuse for going back to see him.

"You're smiling again," Moe murmured, pausing on the top step. "Sassy, are you holding out on me? Who's the lucky man?"

"There is no man." Good Lord, she was nearly seventy, for pity's sake. Sassy took the stairs quickly, nearly outrunning Moe all the way to the first floor. "Listen here, mister. I don't need a man to make me smile." She'd been smiling all on her own for over twenty years. Even after Robert had been arrested. Even after he'd passed away in prison, she'd still found reasons to smile. It was nice to have a friend like Graham, that was all. Someone who had experienced a similar loss. Someone who amused her. Someone who always seemed happy to see her.

"I'd still like to know who it is," Moe muttered, then ducked into the meeting room before she could scold him again. Incorrigible man. He was too intuitive for his own good.

Sassy walked into the room and nearly ran right into Peg. "I was just getting ready to come up and find you two," the woman snipped. "Everyone has been here for ten minutes."

"We were finishing up the budget." Sassy pulled a copy out of the folder and handed it to her. "As you know, things were left in quite a mess. I'm not sure anyone has attempted to actually balance the budget in years, and we're not going to operate with a deficit on my watch." She may have originally taken this job because of the community garden, but she intended to be the best mayor Juniper Springs had ever had and leave things in a much better place than they'd been in when she'd walked through the door.

"Wonderful." The woman's smile had a plastic sheen.

Sassy sidestepped her and joined the rest of the council at the table. Moe had already handed everyone else a copy of the budget.

"Let's call this meeting to order." She spent the next half hour quickly and efficiently walking them through the new budget—mainly touching on the changes. "I don't see a way for us to keep funding the pageant," she said before Peg could argue about the missing line item. "But I am sure those who are dedicated to seeing the event continue will step up to raise the necessary funds."

"That's a great idea," Tyra said. "I know the salon would be happy to contribute."

Arnie gave her a short round of applause. "Finally we have a mayor who's willing to be fiscally responsible."

The positive reactions didn't leave Peg much room to contest the change, though her distinctive frown made it clear she didn't approve.

"I noticed you cut the salary line quite a bit." Christine pushed her bifocals farther up on her nose.

Sassy turned to the next page of the printout. "I don't need the income." She had saved over the years, investing wisely in her retirement. And she hadn't even touched the money her aunt and uncle had left her when they'd passed. "So at least for this year, we took out the mayor's salary."

"I see a line item here for the community garden." Peg stared her down from across the table. "Does that mean Mr. Wright has come to see things from our point of view?"

There went the warming trend on her cheeks again. Holy cats, she was way too old to be blushing. "Not yet, but I think we're moving in that direction."

"You've talked to him?" the woman pressed.

"I have." But she couldn't detail their conversations here. In front of everyone. "And I have another meeting set up with him to discuss things further. I may propose a partnership with the museum. They could provide the land, and we could build the garden. I think that's a good compromise." She noticed Moe's eyebrows peak.

"Absolutely not." Peg seemed to channel all of her negative energy into those two words. "Graham Wright can't keep that land. We need to make sure we have control over what happens on that lot, so you'll do whatever you have to do to convince him to sign it over to the town. And if that doesn't work, we'll hire an attorney to contest the will."

It was no use telling her they didn't have a budget for an attorney. "I can talk with Graham again, but—"

"Great," the woman interrupted. "When will you be able to report back to the council?"

"I would say by our regular meeting on Wednesday." That meant she had to talk to Graham about the garden right after this meeting. "Are there any other questions regarding the *budget?*"

Everyone quietly flipped through their packets a few more times.

"I think it's strong work," Arnie said. "Let's move it to a vote."

Murmurs of agreement went around until Peg finally conceded. "Fine. All in favor of passing this year's budget?" When everyone else added their aye, the woman recorded a unanimous result.

"Perfect." Sassy was the first to stand. "Then this meeting is adjourned." The group filed out, waving and offering their thanks, and not a moment too soon. She gathered her things and thanked Moe for all of his hard work. "You've earned yourself an afternoon off, sir."

"Then you'll see me tomorrow." He leaned in and whispered, "Give Graham Wright my best when you see him later."

Was it possible to get hot flashes *after* menopause? "I have no idea what you're talking about."

"Mm-hmm." The man gave her a hug. "Just make sure Peg doesn't find out you're having a secret rendezvous with her nemesis."

"I don't much care what Peg thinks about anything. Even if there were something to find out. Which there isn't." Sassy followed him to the door, and they slipped out into the hallway. Surprise, surprise, Peg had stopped to wait for them at the main entrance.

"We should go have a glass of wine," the woman said, still wearing that same smirk that masqueraded as a smile.

Sassy wouldn't classify the invitation as friendly.

"Unfortunately, I'm not available, ladies." Moe stepped outside. "I have a gig in Salida. But you two enjoy." He winked at Sassy before making a fast escape.

"You and me then." Peg attached herself to Sassy's right side as they walked out of the building. "We can go to the Crazy Moose. We have a lot to discuss."

So she could get an earful about cutting the pageant from the budget? Sassy didn't think so. "I would love to, but I have plans. I'm afraid I have to get going." The woman had best learn now that Sassy wouldn't be bullied into doing whatever Peg told her to do.

"Another time then." The woman gave her a good long glare. "In the future, I would appreciate you notifying me about large changes to the budget before the meeting. I made sure you got this job, and I can just as easily make sure you lose it."

Sassy almost told Peg that she would inform her about changes when she informed everyone else but stopped herself. Would the woman find a way to remove her from office? She couldn't lose this job. Serving this town had helped her rediscover a sense of purpose. She could make a real difference as the mayor.

Instead of retaliating against the threat, Sassy looked directly into the woman's eyes, steeling her gaze. "Understood. Now if you'll excuse me." Sassy left the woman in her dust, taking the long way to the museum so she could walk off her irritation before she saw Graham.

She cut through the expansive park at the edge of Main Street. The late afternoon sun seemed to catch everything in its warm glow, highlighting the leaves on the trees and the petals on the colorful geraniums she passed. A few children laughed and chased each other on the playground with their parents looking on.

One family had spread out a blanket on the lush green grass for a picnic. This place, this town, was worth every bit of stress she had to endure to serve as mayor. For weeks those mysterious headaches had given her a sense of urgency. She was getting older. She didn't have as much time to leave her mark on the world. Had she done enough? Had she given enough? Loved enough?

She couldn't answer yes.

Maybe she had given a part of herself, maybe she'd loved, but she wanted to do something bigger. Whether the headaches were a sign of her fragility or not, she wanted to offer all of her love, all of herself. She wanted to make the world better while she still had time.

She crossed under the shadows of the trees, soaking in the sights and sounds of her town, and by the time she'd made it to Graham's museum, her heart had righted itself. When she stepped onto the stone path that led to the rose garden, a distinct anticipation seemed to bubble up inside her.

Before she rounded the corner, Graham met her, taking long strides, looking dapper in his crisp dark jeans and starched green button-up shirt. Quite the difference from the shorts he'd worn all week.

"Thank you for coming." It was amazing how a change of perspective could alter a person's appearance. How she had always thought him to be so stodgy, she would never know. Now that she'd spent time with the man, the jaw she'd once thought unyielding made him look thoughtful. The eyes she'd once thought to be judgmental were the best pair of listening eyes she'd ever encountered, so focused and intent when she talked.

"I thought we would take a break from working." He offered his arm to escort her and Sassy took it, again smiling at the oddity of his practiced etiquette.

"I suppose we're almost out of work to do in the rose garden anyway." This was her chance—the perfect opening to bring up the real reason she'd come to see him in the first place. But when they rounded the corner, Sassy stopped. A small table with two chairs sat among the roses. Candles flickered in the very center. Candles! And the man had also set out a bottle of wine with two glasses, an assorted platter of cheeses and crackers, and grapes. A picnic in the rose garden…

"I wanted to thank you." Audible nerves made the man's tone stagger. "For helping me save the roses."

Sassy gaped up at him, that post-menopausal heat flashing again. "You drink wine?" was all she could think to say.

Graham had the best laugh. It resonated low and deep, and it didn't come easily, which made the sound that much more meaningful.

"I enjoy wine quite a bit." He took her elbow again and guided her to the table. "I guess I should've thought to ask if you do too."

"I do." She settled into her chair, her stomach flip-flopping. What were all of these strange sensations? They couldn't be signs of attraction. She was almost seventy years old! She'd given up on romantic love after Robert passed away.

And this was Graham Wright. The president of the geology museum who'd always seemed so cantankerous.

"Can I pour you a glass?" he asked, uncorking the bottle.

Unable to find her voice, Sassy nodded. This whole gesture was very sweet, but Graham certainly couldn't be operating under the assumption that they were anything more than friends. If he was under that impression, she had to find a way to set things straight right this very minute.

"Help yourself to the refreshments." He pushed the plate of cheese across the table and poured himself a glass of wine. "How did the budget meeting go?"

"It went fine." How was it that the man seemed to act as naturally as if they sat down for a picnic together every day? "I'm sorry." She couldn't continue pretending this wasn't strange for her. "I have to be honest. I didn't come to see you earlier this week for a date." She gestured to the table and the candles and the wine. "I came because I wanted to talk to you about that land."

"That's what I figured." Graham casually sipped his wine. "But you didn't talk about the land, so neither did I."

Yes, now she realized that had been a mistake. In delaying this conversation she seemed to have misled him into thinking she was interested in something more. "I should have brought it up." Long before he'd gone to the trouble of planning a picnic.

"We can talk about it now." The man set down his glass. "Though I should warn you my position on the matter hasn't changed."

"Neither has mine." Just yesterday she'd found Graham amusing, but now she was downright nervous. She finally took a sip of wine. It was good wine. Velvety and peppery and expensive. "But I am hoping we can come to a compromise."

"What did you have in mind?" His listening eyes had completely focused on her. That expression on his face made her feel seen—not only seen but also valued. Few people in her life had looked at her the way Graham did.

She stared back at him, feeling her world tilt. This was quite the inconvenient time for one of her dizzy spells.

The man continued to wait for her response. Silence didn't bother him, and it wouldn't have bothered her either if she knew what to do with this picnic—with this shift in her heart.

No matter what she felt, she couldn't let it distract her from the reason she had initiated this friendship. "As you know, the town wants the land so we can create a community garden." Now she was the one being overly formal. After all, formality was the best way to hide vulnerability. "But what if we create a partnership?" Forget what Peg wanted. When it came down to it, Ned had left the land to the museum. And she didn't care what she had to do in order to get the community garden going. That might be worth losing her job over. "You provide the land, and the town will provide funds and workers to create a space that will help provide for families in our town." If they were creative enough, they could expand the museum at the same time. "Maybe we can even come up with some outdoor displays that depict the town's mining history."

Graham gazed at her but didn't speak. He seemed to take his time deliberating. What she'd once taken for rudeness she now recognized as a long contemplative pause. "I like the idea of a partnership," he finally said. "Ned wanted the land to be used for a good cause. I think he would've been happy with a garden to help feed people." He paused as though caught up in his thoughts again. "I'll have to take it to my board for a vote."

"Oh." Sassy's shoulders relaxed a touch. She'd expected more questions, more of a debate. "I could go over the numbers of families I believe it would help." She had the statistics for income levels and unemployment in town.

"That won't be necessary." She'd seen him smile at her often over the last week, but she still hadn't gotten used to it. Or, rather, she hadn't gotten used to the way the man's smile lifted her heart.

"We're meeting this Sunday, so I'll have an answer relatively quickly. I don't anticipate running into much opposition." He sipped his wine and swirled the glass. "You don't have to stay. If that's all you wanted to talk to me about. I don't want to keep you."

He didn't say the words with any self-pity. Something told her this wouldn't be the first glass of wine he'd enjoyed alone, but she stayed put. The sun was warm, and she could smell the wine and the roses. It was a beautiful afternoon to share a glass of wine with a friend. Being with Graham made her feel years younger. That couldn't be a bad thing, could it? "The land isn't all I wanted to talk to you about." She sipped from her glass and filled her plate with an assortment of snacks. "I mean, at first it was, but I think we've proven this week that we have far more to discuss."

"Yes. I believe we do." Graham topped off both of their glasses and offered her a smile that seemed to belong to her alone.

Chapter Twelve

Rose

Rose couldn't find a parking spot to save her life.

She slowed her car in front of Grumpy's and scanned the streets. It was just her luck that, at the exact time she was late picking up her mother, the ice cream shop had decided to sell double-scoop cones for a dollar. Crowds flooded the establishment next to the coffee shop, leaving her no place to pull in.

The good news was that Grumpy's coffee shop was still standing, so her mother hadn't burned the place down. Yet.

She guided the car past the antique shop, the clothing boutique, and finally—*finally*—pulled into a spot by Colt's hardware store. As far as she knew, he was still working at the resort, but just in case, she hurried to get out of the car and out of sight, avoiding any potential encounters. It seemed every time she saw him, her heart opened a little more, no matter what her brain said.

But that was a problem for another time. Right now she had to make sure her mother hadn't driven Grumpy to do something crazy. When Dally had sent Rose the text telling her they were going to X-ray Maya's ankle just to be safe, Rose had offered to be on Lillian duty, but she hadn't paid attention to the time, and now she'd better brace for an earful from her mother.

Trying to be polite, Rose worked her way through the ice cream crowd, smiling and greeting a couple of the familiar faces while she edged toward the coffee shop's entrance. She stepped inside, heart engulfed in sudden panic when she didn't see her mother. In fact, no one sat in the coffee shop— not even Grumpy.

"Hello?" Rose rushed to the counter. Where could her mother have gone? She was supposed to wait here for Rose to pick her up. She'd been very clear with her mother that she would be at the coffee shop to pick her up in a half hour.

Voices murmured from the kitchen.

"Mom?" On a normal day she knew better than to invade Grumpy's space behind the counter, but this was an emergency. She couldn't lose her mother in Juniper Springs and risk Lillian running into Sassy before Rose could orchestrate a perfect reunion that would end years of silence and bring the two of them back together.

She peeked into the small kitchen at the back of the shop. "What the hell?"

Her mother stood in front of the counter, where Grumpy sat on a stool, and she was wearing an apron. An apron...

"Rosie! You're just in time." Her mother waved her to an empty stool on the other side of Grumpy. "I was just having Elroy try a vanilla latte, a caramel macchiato, and a mocha all made with *almond* milk."

"I'm sorry..." She didn't bother to contain her shock at

finding her mother in Grumpy's kitchen. First of all, "Who is Elroy?"

"You think my real name's Grumpy?" the man grumbled. He sipped from the first mug her mother set in front of him. "Huh. That ain't half bad."

"See?" her mother sang, pushing a mug in front of Rose. "It's still just as creamy as a regular latte. You can't even tell a difference."

"You really can't." The man took a bigger sip. "Who woulda thought they could make milk from almonds?"

"It's much better for your cholesterol than the whole milk." Lillian toweled off the counter where she'd been working. "And you really need to work on getting that LDL down."

All Rose could do was stare. What was happening here? The last time she'd seen these two together they were ready to strangle each other, and now they were getting cozy in Grumpy's— *Elroy's*—kitchen, talking about his cholesterol problems?

"Try the mocha." Lillian clasped her hands in front of her as though she couldn't wait for his reaction.

The man gave the mug a good sniff before he took a drink. "Delicious," he declared, setting down the cup with a *thunk*. "You were right, Lil. Almond milk brings out the chocolate flavor."

Lil? Rose was gaping at them. You could not walk out onto the street and find two more different people. Underneath the plain black apron, her mother wore a spring-green cashmere cardigan and gray slacks with a pair of shiny gold loafers that had likely cost more than Grumpy's espresso machine. As usual, Lillian's blondish hair had been smoothed and styled, her makeup perfect.

Because of the whole crotchety thing he had going on, Rose had always assumed Grumpy had to be ancient...but now she couldn't be sure. She'd never seen him without his typical scowl, but his mouth had curved into something of a smile. His thinning graying hair had even been smoothed down from its typical disarray. Though he still wore his favorite T-shirt—it said I'M NOT RUDE, I JUST SAY WHAT EVERYONE ELSE IS THINKING—she hardly recognized him.

"The real test is the macchiato though." Her mother set the final mug in front of the man, her eyes dancing with anticipation. "You are not going to believe the roundness the almond milk flavor brings."

Rose finally picked up the latte her mother had set in front of her and took a good gulp to make sure she wasn't dreaming.

"You are a miracle worker." Grumpy sucked down another sip, closing his eyes as though savoring the new flavor. "You ever move to town, you've got a job here."

"Truly?" Her mother lifted a hand to her heart as though the invitation touched her. "No one's ever offered me a job before."

Whoa. Things were getting out of hand now. Talk of her mother moving to Juniper Springs is where Rose drew the line. "We need to go." She walked to the sink and dumped the rest of the latte. "I have to get back to the inn." Preferably before her mother and Grumpy started picking out curtains for his kitchen together.

"Oh, all right." Lillian slipped the apron off over her head and collected her purse and laptop from a desk on the other side of the kitchen.

"Will you be back tomorrow?"

Was it just her or did Grumpy soften the rough edges of his tone when he talked to her mother?

"Of course I will." Lillian sent him a dazzling smile over her shoulder. "Now that you have almond milk on the menu, I'll be here every day."

They said their goodbyes, and Rose led the way outside but stopped abruptly when they reached the curb. "I don't understand." She faced her mother. "Where did he get almond milk?"

"I brought some with me." Her mother linked their arms together. "I could tell the other day that man was all bark and no bite. He needed a little convincing is all."

Rose started off again, walking alongside her mother. She had to laugh. "So you charmed him into adding almond milk to his menu." She shouldn't be surprised. Her mother did have a way with people. She'd forgotten how Lillian always seemed to know what to say to someone to bring them out of their shell or to give them more confidence. It was easy for Rose to discount those qualities in Lillian and focus on what drove her crazy, but the truth was, her mother could be thoughtful and kind.

"We had a wonderful conversation. Elroy is actually quite sweet."

"If you say so." Rose unlocked her car and they both climbed in. Now that the shock of her mother's new friend had started to wear off, the stress crept back in. "I'll run you back to Dally's house on my way back to the inn. Sorry I can't spend more time with you today. I have to finish up decorating the cabins."

"Why do I have to go back to the house?" Her mother

slipped on her sunglasses and glared at Rose. "Why can't I go to the inn and help you? It's like you don't want me there or something."

"Of course I want you there." Rose focused on backing out of the parking spot. She simply didn't want her mother to run into Sassy. Although...her aunt had made herself quite scarce since she'd come home from her trip. Who knew Sassy was a workaholic?

"Then let's go back to the inn," Lillian insisted. "You know where you inherited your sense of style. I'm very good at decorating."

Well, she wouldn't go that far. She and her mother had a different approach. But she could use an extra set of hands. "You know what? I could really use the help." She was too tired and too stressed to argue. Besides, Sassy likely wouldn't be popping into the cabins since Rose had told her she wanted the finished looks to be a surprise. And anyway, maybe this would give her a chance to start the Sassy conversation with her mother. They were running out of time before the big birthday grand reopening celebration, and the sisters reconciling would make the whole event perfect.

"Wonderful." Her mother seemed to beam with satisfaction. "I promise to do whatever you tell me to do."

And likely give her a whole lot of opinions in the process, but Rose didn't have the luxury of being picky. "We mainly have to hang a few pictures and make a few beds." Nothing too glamorous, but she intended to do her very best to make each space welcoming.

When they pulled up at the inn a few minutes later, Dahlia and the kids were climbing out of their car.

"Maya!" Rose cut the engine and jumped out, greeting her niece with a fierce hug. "Oh, I was so worried about you!" She gave the girl kisses all over the top of her head. "You brave, strong, amazing little woman!"

Her niece giggled. "Sheesh, Aunt Rose. It's only a sprained ankle."

"A sprained ankle?" Lillian held her arms open. "Come and let Gigi have a look-see."

Maya obediently limped to her grandmother and held out her splinted foot. "The brace makes it a lot easier to walk. It hardly hurts at all anymore."

"Oh, my poor baby girl." Lillian wrapped her arms around Maya, and Rose shared a look with Dahlia. How come they never used to get that kind of sympathy with an injury when they were growing up?

"Woof!" Marigold came bounding up to the driveway from the direction of the pond in all her wet stinky doggie glory and went straight for Lillian. No surprise there. Her dog was determined to win over her mother.

"No." Lillian backed away, raising her hands out in front of her. "No, no. Sit."

Instead, Marigold wagged her tail and went in for a hug, leaving paw prints on her mother's cardigan.

Lillian huffed and pushed the dog away. "You need to take this animal to a training class."

Right. In all of her spare time. "Mari, come." Rose pulled out one of the dog biscuits she kept in a bag in her purse, and the dog left her mom alone. "Marigold is a mountain dog, aren't you, girl?" She scratched behind the dog's ears. "She wouldn't know what to do in a training class."

"Can we take her for a walk?" Ollie asked, swinging a stick around like a sword.

"Yes!" Maya hugged Mari. "You want to go for a walk?"

"I'm not sure that's a good idea with your ankle." Dahlia smoothed her daughter's hair.

"Dr. Jolly said I can walk as long as it doesn't hurt."

Dr. Jolly? Rose questioned her sister with a long gaze. Why hadn't Maya seen Ike?

"Okay, then." Dally sent her daughter off with a pat. "But don't go too far. And if your ankle gets sore, come right back."

"We will!" The kids and Marigold were already on their way down the hill.

"You shouldn't be letting Maya walk," Lillian said to Dally.

Uh-oh. Rose had seen that look in her sister's eyes before. She'd had a day, and she didn't need their mother to tell her how to parent her children.

"We should get to work right away." Before a full argument could erupt, Rose beckoned them in the direction of the Gingerbread Cabin. Colt's truck was nowhere to be seen, thank the good Lord. The last thing she needed was her mother suspecting Rose had feelings for the boy she'd never liked.

She and Dally and their mother walked the path to the Gingerbread Cabin in silence. Rose was dying to ask her sister why Ike hadn't been the one to take a look at Maya's ankle, but that was not a conversation they could have in front of their mother either. Basically, they wouldn't be talking about anything important for the next couple of hours.

Lillian went inside first, and Dally hung back with Rose. "What if Sassy comes home?" her sister whispered.

She shrugged. "We can't hide them from each other for-ever." If Sassy hadn't become the mayor, they wouldn't have even succeeded this long. "Why didn't Ike check Maya's ankle?" she asked Dally before she lost the opportunity.

Her sister simply shook her head as though she didn't want to talk about it.

"This is quite the *rustic* cabin." Their mother poked her head out the door. "I didn't expect them to be so primitive."

"*Primitive?*" Rose had put everything into redoing these cabins. They were simple but beautiful—they even had marble countertops in the kitchen! What did her mother expect to find in a small mountain town that was off the beaten path? A five-star resort?

"That's the mountain experience people are looking for," Dahlia said cheerfully. She tugged Rose inside the cabin. "The whole point is to provide an escape from the city and the busyness and the technology. People want to reconnect with nature here."

"Well, in that case, I suppose it's perfect." Their mother rolled up her sleeves. "What should I do first?"

Rose looked around, still shaking off the sting of her mother's judgment. "Why don't you unpack this box while Dally and I hang a picture over the fireplace?" She showed her mother the crate on the table that held the candles and trinkets they would use to beautify the space. Then she joined Dally by the fireplace. Before picking up her mother, Rose had already measured and marked where the nails would go, so they quickly got the mountain scene into place with only one minor adjustment.

"That's pretty." Lillian seemed to admire the painting. "I

have to say, I'd forgotten how beautiful it is here in the summer."

Rose widened her eyes at Dally, hoping her sister could read her thoughts. Their mother was reminiscing. This could be their perfect opportunity to bring up Sassy.

"Juniper Springs *is* beautiful." Dahlia went back to the table and pulled out a chair across from their mom. "And we're so happy you came to visit."

Rose tried to swallow all of the doubts that started to well up. They had to have this conversation. "Sassy would be really glad to see you too."

Lillian stopped unwrapping a candle and sharpened her gaze on Rose. "Sassy doesn't care to see me. She's the one who chose that horrible man instead of her family."

Yes, they'd heard all about how Lillian had never trusted Colt's dad, about how she'd asked Sassy not to see him anymore. When Sassy had refused to cut Robert out of her life, their mother had made the decision for all of them. They hadn't talked since.

"She loved him, and he loved her." Rose walked to the table. "Surely you can understand why she couldn't stop seeing him for you."

"The man murdered someone." Their mother went back to unwrapping the candle, her movements furious.

"He didn't murder anyone," Dahlia corrected her patiently. "He was involved in a bank robbery where someone else murdered the guard."

Rose didn't know why her sister tried. They'd explained this to Lillian at least five times.

"And he regretted it. He paid the price." How Dally kept

that steady, calm tone was beyond her. "You have to remember, his wife was dying, and he couldn't afford her treatments. Sassy met him years after it had happened."

"It doesn't matter." Their mother was nothing if not stubborn. "He was a criminal, and she chose him over me."

Rose let out a grunt of frustration. She'd had it—the tiptoeing around, the trying to reason with someone who always chose to be so unreasonable. "What would you do if Sassy walked in that door right now?" Because she could easily make that happen. She could go find Sassy and bring her here, and they could get this done.

"I would leave." Lillian set the candle on the table. "I don't want to see her."

"But she's your sister." Disbelief clouded the words. Sassy and their mother had two brothers who both lived in Florida now, but they each had only one sister. "She's your family." The burn of anger beat through her heart. "You're being selfish and irrational and childish." She'd never spoken to her mother so harshly, and she'd better stop now, or things would only get worse.

"I'm going for a walk." Rose stalked to the door and pulled it open.

"I knew it. I just knew you two would choose your aunt over me eventually." Her mother's voice got weepy. "After everything I've done for you—"

"I didn't choose any of this." The cutting their aunt out of their lives for so long, the refusal to be close to the aunt who loved them. "This was because of your choices." The anger had faded into a heavy sadness. "But you never know how much time you have left to fix the things you've broken."

Leaving her mother with those words, she spun and closed the door, and then stumbled down the steps.

Her niece and nephew were playing with Marigold by the pond, so Rose went the opposite direction, into the woods. She shouldn't have held out any hope that her mother would come around. She should've told her the first day she'd come to Juniper Springs that Sassy was back in town. If she had, Lillian likely would've skipped town and hightailed it back to Savannah.

Maya and Ollie's laughter grew more distant as the trees enveloped her in their sheltered quiet. She followed the creek since she hadn't had much time to explore this part of the property, comforted by the gentle swoosh of the water streaming over the smooth rocks. At least then she'd be able to follow it back to the house.

As much as she tried, it was hard to stay mad in the mountains. And maybe she wasn't mad as much as she was heartbroken for both her mom and her aunt. For what they were missing out on in their golden stage of life. In the last several months, she'd come to rely on Dally and Mags. They were her support. She didn't know what she'd—

A flash of movement up ahead caught her attention. She slowed her pace and tried to see through the trees. It looked like…a person…standing in the middle of the creek? Rose crept closer until she could see.

Colt? The man was fly-fishing. Standing knee-deep in the water with his jeans rolled up.

He hadn't noticed her—he was too focused on flinging his line in the air—so she gave herself a few minutes to simply watch him. The same electrical current that had moved through her when he'd put his arms around her flared again.

He was tall and broad but moved gracefully with the fishing pole, working with the same methodical precision he had used when they'd fixed the roof.

Rose glanced behind her. She could turn around and walk away and he would probably never know she'd been there. But, then again, she had to see him someday, to clear the air after their awkward exchange earlier. And this seemed like the perfect place.

She left the trees and approached the riverbank, her heart pounding harder than it had even when she'd confronted her mother. "Hey."

Colt's arm swung the rod forward and he turned. "Hi." He started to reel in the line as he waded to her.

"I'm sorry to interrupt." She did her best not to sound awkward but wasn't sure if she succeeded. "I didn't know anyone was out here."

"Don't be sorry. I was about done. Not catching much anyway." Colt stepped out of the creek and busied himself with breaking down his fly rod, his movements methodical and focused.

She watched him take apart the pole and stash it into a backpack, but he didn't look at her once. He didn't speak either. In fact, he seemed to completely ignore her.

Rose couldn't stand the silence. "Everything okay?" The last time she'd seen him their faces had been inches apart, and now he seemed to keep his distance.

"I don't know. Is everything okay?" He stood. "Have I done something to offend you?"

"What?" The irritation in his voice made her flinch. That was exactly how he'd sounded when they'd first met last

Christmas. Before they'd gotten to know each other. "No. You haven't offended me at all. Why would you ask me that?"

Colt jammed his feet into a pair of flip-flops sitting next to the backpack. "Because I can't figure out why you keep running away from me like you did at the store and again when we were working on the cabin." His eyes narrowed. She'd seen that look of distrust on his face before too. "I don't get it. It's like all of a sudden you can't wait to get away from me. And I don't even know what I did wrong."

"Nothing." Rose closed her eyes on the threatening tears. "You did nothing wrong." Her voice had weakened but her pulse gained strength. "I didn't mean to make you feel like I was trying to get away from you." She'd been trying to escape her feelings. The same ones that overwhelmed her now.

"Then what were you trying to get away from?" He stepped closer, his gaze searching for something in hers.

"I'm not sure." Conflicted feelings roiled inside of her. Colt was leaving. How could she give him her heart when he'd only take it with him? "I guess I'm a little jealous. You're selling the store, going off on a big adventure." Without her. "And you don't seem the least bit afraid." Or the least bit sad...

Colt's head tilted as his eyes met hers again. "You moved here and renovated an inn. That's a pretty big adventure too." He said the words with something that sounded like admiration. "Were you scared?"

Rose took her time thinking back. Truthfully, she hadn't had much time to be scared. "I was," she finally decided. "But it was a different kind of fear. It was a fear that made me feel more alive." The same way Colt made her feel when she stood this close to him.

"I know what you mean." His eyes seemed fixated on her lips, and there went her heart—dropping like someone had thrown it off a cliff.

Colt didn't speak. He didn't need to because his eyes told her so much. They told her he felt that heat simmering between them. They told her he wanted to touch her, he wanted to pick up where they'd left off. And God help her, she couldn't stop her head from tipping forward with a nod of invitation.

The man took his time leaning in to kiss her, but he wasn't hesitating. He was observing. Her eyes, her lips.

Just when she thought the anticipation might cause her heart to burst, he touched his lips to hers. That was all it took to break apart her resolve. Right away, her knees buckled and she leaned into him, her whole body releasing the earlier tension with a sigh. Colt's lips were firm and insistent as they met hers, but they were somehow tender too. He smelled like the woods—like sunshine and pine. His arms came around her again, stealing her away from time and circumstance and all rationality. And maybe this kiss was worth any potential pain it would bring her…

Colt pulled back and brought his hand to her face, skimming his thumb lightly down her cheek. He was observing her again, looking into her. "I've wanted to do that for nineteen years."

Years? Did he say *years*? She couldn't find the words to respond. She was still too caught up in the hunger, in a desperation she couldn't understand. Rose murmured something unintelligible and urged his lips back to hers. This time the kiss didn't move slowly. It accelerated straight into mouths opening, tongues exploring. She pressed her body to his, wanting less between them—less space, less circumstances, less reality.

"Auntie Rose! Where are yooooouuuu?"

It took Ollie's words a few seconds to register. Her nephew was looking for her. And he couldn't find her kissing Colt.

Gasping, Rose pulled away.

Colt stared at her. She stared back.

"Yoo-hoo! Auntie Rose!" This time the shout came from Maya. They were getting closer.

"I sold the store. It's done." He delivered the words like an apology.

She wanted to ask if he could still break the deal. It couldn't be too late. And yet she knew she had no right to plead with him to stay. She had no right to say anything that might take this opportunity away from him. So instead she stepped out of his reach. "This shouldn't have happened. I'm sorry. I shouldn't have…" She couldn't finish the thought. "I…should get back. I still need to finish the cabins. The Clearys are coming tomorrow."

He nodded, a sad look in his eyes.

Rose tore away from him, jogging to meet her niece and nephew. But no matter how fast she moved, she couldn't seem to outrun the emotions stirred up by that simple kiss.

Chapter Thirteen

Dahlia

W hat do you want to do today?"

Dahlia unlocked the car so she and Maya could climb in. They'd dropped Ollie off at camp, but she hadn't wanted Maya to overdo walking around on her ankle, so they'd planned to have a girls' day out. Which was perfect, since Lillian was still pouting at Dahlia's house. Ever since the confrontation with Rose yesterday, their mother had been playing the martyr card, and she'd had enough of trying to talk her mother out of the poor-me routine.

"I'm hungry," her daughter announced, clicking in her seatbelt. "Let's have breakfast at the Crazy Moose."

"Fabulous idea." Dahlia turned up the radio and headed in that direction, humming along to a Shania Twain classic. This outing was exactly what she and Maya needed—a fun morning away from the unpacking and craziness at home. Plus, she could show her daughter how much fun this town could be. "After breakfast, we can go to that cool boutique and look for a new first day of school outfit."

"Yes!" Her daughter let her head fall back against the seat.

"I don't have anything to wear to school. Kids have different clothes here than they did back home."

Dahlia didn't miss the way Maya kept referring to Minneapolis as their home. They had built a life there, creating so many memories. But she hoped her daughter would come to think of Juniper Springs as her home soon too.

Even just shy of nine o'clock, a line had already formed outside of the small restaurant—a favorite on Main Street. Tourist season might be winding down, but there were plenty of locals who made the lumberjack breakfast at the Crazy Moose a weekly staple in their diets.

Dahlia pulled into the first parking spot she could find, and they got out to take their place in line. She admired her daughter as they stood there. Maya had grown taller over the summer, already up to Dahlia's chin. And instead of having a baby face, she'd started to look more mature, with her pronounced cheekbones and her slender jaw. "You're such a talented, compassionate, brilliant, lovely girl," she said, risking an eye roll.

Instead, her daughter smiled. "I know."

She laughed, wanting to tell her daughter to hold on to that confidence, no matter what else happened in life. No matter if her husband someday cheated on her and left her. "Never forget how amazing you are, how strong."

"Okay, okay." There was the eye roll she knew and loved. "Hey, can I go pet that puppy over there?" She pointed to where an elderly couple stood on the other side of the Crazy Moose's sign. The puppy in question looked to be an adorable white lab mix.

"Sure, honey. I'll hold our place." Dahlia managed to grab

Maya's hand before her daughter bolted away. "Make sure you ask first, though. Right?"

"I know, I know." Maya ran off and stopped a few feet away from the couple, cautiously asking permission. They nodded and invited her right over. The puppy seemed ecstatic to meet a new friend. The second Maya sat down, the little cutie climbed right into her lap and started to lick her face.

Maybe they needed a dog. Marigold was a great substitute, but the kids didn't have to take responsibility for Rose's dog. It would be good for them to—

"Hi there." Dr. Jolly appeared in front of her, somehow looking quite different without her scrubs on. She was as beautiful as ever, maybe even more so in the casual white sundress she wore.

"Hi." Dahlia immediately glanced around to see if Ike was with her but couldn't find him anywhere.

"This place is packed, huh?" The doctor frowned at the line in front of them. "I'm meeting a friend here, but I didn't realize we'd have to come a half hour before we wanted to eat."

"I know. It's always crazy busy." Dahlia checked on Maya with a quick glance before smiling at Dr. Jolly.

"How's Maya's ankle?" The doctor spotted her daughter with the puppy.

"She's doing great." As much as it had embarrassed her when Maya had chosen Dr. Jolly over Ike, she had to admit, the woman had a way with children. She'd been very thorough with instructions for keeping the swelling at a minimum. "We've been icing and keeping the brace on like you said. It doesn't seem to be bothering her much at all."

"Wonderful." Dr. Jolly looked around before facing her

directly. "Hey, I have a question for you." Her tone had quieted. "If you don't mind me asking."

"Oh." A question? What could the doctor possibly want to question her about? "No. Of course I don't mind."

The woman leaned in closer. "Is there anything going on between you and Ike?" She closed her eyes and did a quick shake of her head as though she was embarrassed before she looked at Dahlia again. "I mean, I heard that you two dated last winter, but I wasn't sure if you were still together."

"Uh. Well…" Dahlia struggled to contain her surprise. She glanced to check on Maya again, but the puppy was gone. At some point her daughter had come back and now stood close enough to hear everything they were saying. "No," she finished quickly. "We're not together. We never were, really." She shut her mouth so she didn't keep explaining. Maya had no idea she and Ike had ever even gone on a date.

Her daughter's eyes had narrowed and she crossed her arms.

Dr. Jolly didn't seem to notice Maya. "Sorry if I made you uncomfortable. I really like him, that's all. I know it's not the best idea to have a huge crush on your boss, but who can blame me right?"

"Right." She couldn't seem to find her smile.

"Not that anything will come of it," the doctor went on. "But obviously I didn't want to move that direction if he's seeing someone."

"Well, he's not seeing me." That wasn't a lie. "We're not seeing each other." Because of that scowl on her daughter's face right here.

Dr. Jolly peered over her shoulder. "Oh, hey, Maya. How's the ankle feeling?"

"It's fine," her daughter said with a stiff lower lip.

"Good!" The doctor appeared to detect Maya's sudden attitude. "Your mom said you're doing a great job icing it and wearing the brace."

Maya nodded but kept her eyes cast downward.

"Well, keep it up and you'll be out of the brace in no time," Dr. Jolly told her.

"We have space for a party of two," the hostess called from the doorway.

"Oh, that's you guys." The doctor shooed them forward. "Hope you enjoy your breakfast."

Dahlia thanked her before walking into the restaurant with Maya. The hostess seated them at a table near the window and left them with a promise that the waitress would be by to take their order in a few.

She sat down across from Maya and braced herself for the impending confrontation.

"You went on a date with Ike last Christmas?" her daughter demanded.

Dahlia bought time by situating her purse on the window-sill next to her. She could fib and tell her Dr. Jolly was wrong. Or she could be honest and upset Maya all over again. Neither seemed like a good option. Dahlia hated lying. Even for a good cause. Besides…she did have feelings for Ike. It had caused her physical pain to tell Dr. Jolly there was nothing between them.

She inhaled deeply and trudged on into uncharted territory. "Maya, honey, you know I love you and Ollie very much. You two are my whole world."

Her daughter's glare didn't budge. *And?* it seemed to silently say.

Amazing how a look could rip right through her. "That will never change. No matter what. You two have always come first in my life, and you always will." Yes, she was avoiding the question, but the answer she'd given was the only one that mattered.

"You *dated* Dr. Ike?" Maya leaned halfway across the table. "I heard what Dr. Jolly said. You dated him?"

"Not exactly." She held back an aching sigh. How could she ever put this in terms her daughter would understand? "I went on a date with him. He's a wonderful man. And we enjoyed dinner together one evening while I was here last winter." She didn't want to lie to Maya, but she also didn't need to give her daughter details about her dating life. She didn't need to tell Maya how she'd kissed the man. How he'd kissed her like no one else ever had. She didn't need to tell her daughter how they'd kept in touch on the phone after she'd gone back to Minnesota.

Maya straightened, her shoulders rigid. "You *can't* go on dates with people." She sounded exactly like Dahlia when she forbid her children from doing something dangerous.

The only problem was, Maya didn't get to parent her. "I understand how you feel—"

"No you don't, Mom," her daughter interrupted. "You don't understand how I feel. Did your parents ever get divorced? Did your dad move to a whole other country and you only got to see him like twice a year?"

"No." Her parents had plenty of issues, but they'd stuck it out. Dahlia would've too. She would've stayed unhappily married for her children's sake if Jeff hadn't made the decision for her. She would do anything for her kids.

"You're all me and Ollie have." The tremble in her daughter's voice sliced clean through her heart. "Now we live in a new place, and I don't even have any friends. So I don't want Ike to take you away. I don't want you going on dates. Not with him or anyone else."

What could she do but nod? This wasn't about Maya being difficult. Her daughter was dealing with major uncertainties and fear. And she couldn't ignore that. Being a mom meant putting her own life aside to make sure her children were healthy and secure. "I understand that, honey. I'm not planning to date anyone right now." Maybe when things settled. Maybe when Maya and Ollie had more connections here. When they'd grown up a little. But she couldn't ask Ike to wait for that day. Especially when he had someone as wonderful as Dr. Jolly interested in him. It wasn't fair for her to keep him waiting in the wings when she had no idea how long her children would need. "I know things have been hard, honey. But we'll get through it. And I'm here for you. Anytime you want to talk."

"I know." Her daughter opened the menu that had been sitting on the table. "You're the best mom in the whole world."

The compliment gave Dahlia something to hold on to in the midst of her sadness. Yes, she would give up anything for her children, but it hurt to give up on the hope she'd experienced when Ike touched her.

Over the next hour, she managed to keep her feelings at bay while she chatted with her daughter over a stack of peach-berry crumble pancakes. They talked about the upcoming school year, and even though she was nervous, Maya also seemed ready to have some semblance of a routine again. That was her daughter—structured and routine, just like her.

After they'd finished up, Dahlia paid the bill and they walked out of the restaurant. She checked the time. Ike would be leaving for his lunch break in about an hour, and she wouldn't feel like anything was resolved until she talked to him.

She couldn't seem to stop replaying the conversation she'd had with Dr. Jolly. Dahlia couldn't hold him back.

From their many talks, she happened to know that Ike enjoyed walking through the park to the deli on the days he was at the office and, if she timed things right, she could easily catch up with him there.

"Hey, honey. Do you think we could put off the shopping trip until this afternoon?" Right now she was too distracted to think about much else. "Maybe we could go pick up ingredients for your favorite chocolate chip cookies, and you could show Gigi how to make them?"

"Yes!" Her daughter led the way down the sidewalk, skipping to the car. "That'll make Gigi happy. She seems sad."

Dahlia unlocked the car door and caught herself rolling her eyes. That must be genetic. "Gigi'll be okay. She and Auntie Rose had a little issue, but they'll talk it out soon enough."

"You never let Ollie and me wait to talk things out." Maya climbed into the backseat. "We're usually grounded until we fix the problem."

"You're right. It's always best to solve the issue right away." If she'd learned that earlier in life, maybe she and Jeff wouldn't have skirted around so many of their own problems. "But some issues take a little longer to resolve." Especially when Lillian was involved. Her mother didn't exactly under-stand the taking responsibility for her part thing.

After a quick trip to the grocery store, Dahlia pulled into

the driveway of their new home. The place wasn't nearly as large as their house in Minnesota had been, but it had more charm—at least on the outside. The three-bedroom bungalow had white paint with black shutters and a bright red front door. She'd thought about putting out some fun chairs and decorations on the front porch, but there hadn't been time for that yet. Maybe when things settled down. For the time being, that seemed to be her answer for everything.

She and Maya unloaded the bags and carted them into the house while her daughter chatted about how she wanted to be a baker like Auntie Magnolia someday.

Dahlia had always envied her sister's gift for baking. "I think that would be a great job. You could even start your own business like Auntie Mags."

"I would love that!" Maya opened the front door and paraded through. "Hi, Gigi!"

Lillian sat at the kitchen table, nursing a cup of coffee. In true pouting form, she was still dressed in her bathrobe. Her makeup had been touched up though, so that was something.

"Maya is going to teach you how to make cookies while I run an errand," Dahlia announced, pulling the ingredients out of the bag.

"Yeah, Gigi! My chocolate chip cookies are the best." Her daughter hurried to the pantry and came back wearing an apron. "Everyone says so. Even Auntie Mags loves them, and she's a professional."

"I guess we can bake cookies." Her mother stood and trudged to the kitchen island. "At least *someone* wants to spend time with me."

No eye rolling. No. Eye. Rolling. Dahlia simply smiled at the woman. "Have fun! I'll be back soon." And then maybe she'd drag Rose over here later so the two of them could hash out their feelings and quit wallowing.

If anyone had a right to wallow, it was her.

On the drive to the park, Dahlia allowed herself to feel a degree of self-pity. She was about to tell a man she cared for—a man she was incredibly attracted to—that she couldn't make room for him in her life anytime soon. He might've said he didn't mind waiting, but what would happen when the weeks turned into months and the months to a year or more? The truth was, the timing was all wrong for them.

But that didn't change the fact that it would be very hard to walk away from him.

Before she could change her mind, she hurriedly parked the car and followed the path he usually took, sitting down on a bench to wait. The pancakes seemed to have solidified in her stomach, sitting as heavily as concrete. Three times she almost stood up and left, but then Ike came walking down the sidewalk and she stopped second-guessing. She'd meant what she said to Maya about Ike. He was a wonderful man, and he deserved to have everything.

"Dally?" He quickened his pace when he saw her and joined her on the bench, wearing the grin that lit up his face whenever he saw her. "Why do I get the feeling you were waiting for me?"

She cleared her throat doing her best to strengthen her voice. "I wanted to talk."

"Sure." His smile grew. "I knew this walk would be the best part of my day."

She wished it would be the best part of both of their days. She wished she could wrap her arms around him and kiss him and be free to love him. But she'd lived enough to know that wishes didn't always come true. Right now letting him go was the best thing she could do for both of them.

"I've been thinking a lot and talking to the kids, and I think it's best if we don't see each other. Even as friends." There was no way to make those words any easier to say or to hear.

Ike's smile fell away, turning his expression pensive.

"I know you said you'd wait," she went on before he could speak. "And I really appreciate that, but I can't say where I'll be when the children come around. And I don't think you can really know where you'll be either." Things would keep changing. *They* would keep changing. "Right now, it's too hard. I feel torn. And I can't live like that. I have to choose to be the best mom I can be."

"You're an incredible mom." He held her gaze in his. "Maya and Ollie are lucky."

"Thank you." She couldn't manage more than a whisper without giving in to the threatening tears. "You're going to find someone who's lucky too." Someone who could be fully his. Maybe someone like Dr. Jolly. Dahlia stood, her resolve crumbling. "You are the best man," she said on a sob and then turned to walk away.

He just couldn't be hers.

Chapter Fourteen

Sassy

"Sassy? Did you hear me?"

Moe asked the question from all the way across the room. But how was she supposed to answer when she couldn't see straight?

"Of course I heard you." She hadn't meant to bite the poor man's head off, but there shouldn't be two Moes in front of her right now. There shouldn't be two laptops sitting on her desk and two clocks hanging side by side on the opposite wall. The room shouldn't be spinning as though she'd just gotten on the Seattle Great Wheel again.

Another headache had started early this morning. She'd taken the same over-the-counter meds that had dimmed the pain before, but then the vertigo attacked out of almost nowhere.

"I asked if you wanted to come over here and read this email before I send it." Moe pushed out of the chair behind his desk and stood as though he wanted to get a better view of her.

"I heard." Her hearing wasn't the problem right now. It was her sight. But now the man started to come back into focus as the brief wave of double vision receded.

"All right. What's going on with you?" Moe marched to her side of the office. "You're not yourself today." He parked himself in the chair across from her, a sure sign he wasn't going to budge until he got an answer out of her.

"Nothing's going on." She slipped her bifocals onto her nose and read the first line of the town government's website that she'd pulled up on her computer. The words were clear again, each letter separated instead of blurring together like they had a few seconds ago.

"You're lying." Moe shut her laptop. "And that's not like you."

The man had her there. She hated to lie. "I have a headache. That's all." That's all she wanted these symptoms to be. A simple headache. Something that would go away once she readjusted to the altitude.

"It's not only a headache, Sassy." The man who'd become her friend since she'd taken office cornered with her a long unyielding stare. "I can tell. You didn't want to stand up and walk across the room. Are you dizzy?"

She didn't answer him right away. She hadn't told anyone else about her symptoms. Not Colt. Not Rose or Dahlia. Not Graham...

"I'll call Ike." Moe started to stand, but she reached out her hand to stop him.

"No. Don't call him. Please." She'd thought about this. It was time. She knew that. She knew she had to open the door to what would surely be a lengthy diagnostic process with tests and hospitals, but she didn't want to open that door here. In Juniper Springs.

"If you'd rather I not call Ike, then you'd better go on and tell me what's happening. Before I start freaking out." Moe pulled out his cell phone and threatened to dial.

"I've been getting headaches," Sassy said before he could make the call. "For the last several weeks. Maybe for over a month now. I'm not sure." At first she hadn't paid them much attention. The headaches had been like any other ache associated with growing older—knees, hips, stomach. And she always managed to ignore those pains without a problem. "They started small and more spread out, but now..."

She couldn't ignore them anymore. "They've been coming on more frequently. And I have these awful dizzy spells occasionally too."

"Like I said, we need Ike. Now." Moe fixated on his phone again but she stood and leaned over the desk to snatch it out of his hand.

Not bad reflexes for an old broad. Sassy smiled sweetly at him, lest he forget who he was dealing with, as she sat back down in her chair. "I know I need to get the headaches checked out. And I will. But I don't want to go through all of that here. I want to find a doctor in Denver." She loved Ike like a son, and she didn't want to put him through walking this road with her. "I need to know what I'm dealing with before I tell everyone." Once Colt and her nieces and her friends found out, everything would change. They wouldn't look at her the same. They wouldn't treat her the same. And she wasn't ready to be viewed as an invalid.

Moe seemed to inhale slowly, deeply. "You think it's something serious." Concern glistened in his dark eyes. He wasn't asking a question.

Sassy slid his phone back across the desk. "I've seen these

same symptoms before. My uncle died of a brain tumor." She would never forget how he'd suffered. How her aunt had suffered watching him struggle.

"Even more reason to get checked out now." Moe left his phone where it was. "As soon as possible. We can take you down to the hospital in Salida and get you a CT scan today."

"Not yet. Not today." Her uncle hadn't gotten to make any choices. Everyone else had made them for him. The poor man's voice had dimmed long before he took his final breath, and she didn't want that to be her story too. She wanted to have a plan in place before she had to tell anyone else. "I promise you I will call some doctors in Denver later today." Sassy made sure to add a measure of sternness into her tone. "But until I know what I'm dealing with, I need you to keep this between us."

The man's deep frown told her exactly what he thought about that. "If that's what you want, I will respect it, but I won't like it." His expression softened. "Your family and friends are going to want to be part of this, Sassy. Whatever it is. They're going to want to be there for you the way you've been there for so many others. You shouldn't take that away from them."

The emotion in Moe's voice touched her. "I won't. Once I know more, once I have a plan, I will be an open book. I promise." But she still wanted to be the one writing the story. She wanted to make her own decisions and chart her course before inviting everyone else into the boat.

"I want a full report on what doctors you will be seeing in Denver by tomorrow." Moe held out his hand over the desk like he wanted to shake on it.

That made her giggle, and she took his hand. "I solemnly swear."

He refused to let go of her hand. "And if you have another dizzy spell before the appointment, you have to promise to call nine-one-one. Or I can promise you that *I* will. That's not something you want to mess with."

"Oh, fine." The dizzy spells lasted only a few minutes at the most. She usually just sat and let them have their moment before trying to walk again. "I will be very aware and careful. And I will figure this out." That she could promise.

"Knock-knock."

Graham stepped through the office's open doorway and brought on a different kind of dizzy spell. Sassy popped out of her chair. "What are you doing here?" What if Peg found out he'd stopped by her office?

Panic swarmed her, making her feel the same way she had when her boyfriend had snuck into her parents' house a lifetime ago.

"Well, if it isn't Mr. Wright." Moe rose regally from his chair and met Graham with an outstretched hand. "To what do we owe this impromptu visit?"

"I'm here for Sassy."

"Right. Because we have a meeting." Sassy hastily snatched the sweater off the back of her chair and rushed to the door. She had to get the man out of here before he blew their cover in front of Moe. She shouldn't be caught fraternizing with Peg's sworn enemy before she and Graham made the partnership official. And she certainly wasn't supposed to be getting all swoony at the sight of Graham in a tailored blue suit!

So what if Moe already had an inkling she and Graham

had been spending a lot of extra time together? No one else could know. Not Peg. Not Dahlia and Rose. What would they think about her sneaking around with a man?

"Oh, uh. Yes. Our meeting," the man sputtered behind her. "It was a pleasure seeing you, Moe. I hope you have a wonderful day."

"It was a surprise indeed," Moe said teasingly.

Oh, just listen to him. Moe thought he had everything all figured out. Sassy let go of a sigh. The warmth on her cheeks was not a blush. It was anger, darn it.

Finally—finally—Graham met her in the hallway outside the office.

Sassy didn't waste one second pulling him down the staircase and in the direction of the back door. She cracked it open and peeked out into the alleyway behind the building.

"What's going on? Are you in trouble with the law?" Graham quipped.

But Sassy wasn't in the mood for jokes. She beckoned him out the door and into the alley. "If we go out the front door, word will reach Peg by noon." That woman had spies all over this town. Heck, who was she kidding? This was Juniper Springs. Word about her rendezvous with Graham would reach the Crazy Moose by noon no matter what she did.

"I didn't realize we were on the run from Peg." An edge subdued the man's voice.

"It's not only Peg. We don't want the whole town to get the wrong idea about us." That was the point. If they were seen walking down the street together in the middle of the day for no apparent reason, the rumors would start flying. The town would have them secretly engaged by nightfall.

"You know how fast word travels around here, and—" Sassy looked to her left and then her right, but there was no sign of Graham. She stopped and turned around.

The man stood in the middle of the alley, staring after her. "What, exactly, would the wrong idea be?"

"You know. That there's something going on." She started off again, but then realized she didn't know where they were going. "Why did you come to see me at work anyway?" Their meetings had been confined to the rose garden, which was safely tucked out of sight from the street...

"I wanted to show you something." Graham had caught up to her, but he didn't look at her. Instead he stared straight ahead with a blank look in his eyes. "But don't worry. We can take the alleys all the way there so no one will see us together."

Oh, dear. She'd hurt him. "I didn't mean..." She wasn't sure how to finish. How could she explain the panic and the fear and the uncertainty and the irrational reactions this man stirred up in her when she didn't understand them herself?

Graham didn't wait for an explanation anyway. He kept walking—outstriding her by a good two feet as they passed behind the antique store and the gallery and the jewelry shop before continuing behind the museum until they reached the empty lot next door.

The empty lot that had started this whole mess in the first place.

Sassy followed Graham through the bramble of weeds and grasses that had grown tall on the property until he came to an abrupt stop.

She almost went to apologize again, but before she could get any words out, she saw it. The sign.

JUNIPER SPRINGS COMMUNITY GARDEN had been hand-carved on a large wooden plaque. A deep jagged line formed the mountainous horizon above the words, and juniper trees completed the frame below them.

Sassy approached the sign, which leaned up against a tree trunk on the property. "It's a work of art." She ran her fingers along the words, marveling at how smooth the finish was. Graham had mentioned he enjoyed woodworking, but she had no idea he could produce something so beautiful. "You made this?" She whirled to look at this man who had been so full of surprises.

He nodded, his mouth still set in a solemn frown. "I've talked to each board member. They love the idea of a partnership that would incorporate plaques and different displays depicting the town's mining history." He walked to where the dirt met the sidewalk. "I thought the sign could go here, along with maybe a few benches where people could sit and rest." Graham moved along the west side of the property. "And over here we could plant a few apple trees. I've been doing a lot of research, and dwarf red delicious apple trees grow very well in Colorado."

Sassy watched him stroll across the property, tears misting her eyes. He must have spent every waking minute contacting his board members, working on the sign. And the partnership…he'd given up on expanding the museum for her. Some thanks she'd offered him by basically showing him how embarrassed she was to be seen with him.

"On this side, we could build raised garden beds to cut down on weeds. We could plant all varieties of vegetables and add an irrigation system connected to the museum's water line…" He suddenly seemed to realize she hadn't said anything and hurried back to her, stopping a good few feet away. "Those were my thoughts. But of course you are welcome to do whatever you'd like for the garden. I don't have to be involved—"

"I'm sorry." Sassy crossed the distance between them. This might be the nicest thing anyone had ever done for her, and she had treated the man so poorly. She took both of his hands in hers, holding on to them tightly. "Oh, Graham, I absolutely love this. All of it. The partnership, the sign."

A pure unfiltered hopefulness widened his eyes only a touch, but she saw it. She recognized it. She had spent a great deal of time looking into his eyes.

"I'm sorry. I didn't meant to imply that I'm embarrassed to be seen with you." She let go of his hands, needing to move, to walk, to pace while she worked out her feelings. "It's not that I'm embarrassed at all." Though she would love to blame simple chagrin. "I'm afraid." She might never have acknowledged the truth if it hadn't been for his kindness and selflessness. But now she owed him honesty. "Because if other people see us, they might recognize what I'm trying hard not to. That there *is* something between us." She wasn't sure what yet. But physically—emotionally—something changed in her when Graham came around.

She risked a glance at him, almost afraid of what she'd see.

But there was no judgment in the man's steady, wise eyes.

"I have been alone for almost twenty years," she continued. "I had given up on—"

What exactly? What part of her heart had shut down without her knowing when Robert passed away?

"I had given up on any notion of romantic love." To even say those words out loud! She was almost seventy years old. She might have a brain tumor. What could she possibly offer this man?

Honesty. That was all she could give him.

"All I know is that when I see you, my heart lifts. And it startles me every time." When Graham came near, she didn't feel old anymore. She didn't feel any of the aches and pains and limitations her body was slowly succumbing to. "You make me feel a happiness I thought was long dead. And I don't know what to do with it. Not now. Not in this stage of my life." Not when she had been on her own, keeping her heart all to herself, for so many years.

Graham said nothing. He held her gaze locked in his for so long, she wasn't sure if he was still breathing...if *she* was breathing.

Then his expression changed again. The same way it had changed at the meeting the first night she had spoken to him. Within two brisk steps he was there, right in front of her, pulling her into his arms. "Can I kiss you, Sassy McGrath?"

The passion simmering in his low voice sent her world spinning again, but there was no pain, no headache, no unpleasant vertigo because Graham was holding on to her and he was going to kiss her and none of this made any sense at all, but maybe that was the best thing about a kiss. It didn't have to make sense.

Instead of answering, Sassy did the work for him, bringing their lips together, because she couldn't wait one more second to be senseless with this man.

A kiss. It held so much power. With Graham's lips moving over hers, nothing else in the entire world mattered. He already seemed to know how to hold her, how to show her all the things they hadn't yet talked about. There was nothing formal or awkward about the man's kiss. The brush of his lips across hers was soft, almost teasing before becoming urgent and deliciously passionate.

Sassy couldn't seem to let go of him. She couldn't seem to slow the kiss, even though her heart galloped and her lungs gasped. She might very well have a heart attack right here in this open lot, but she would still say this kiss was worth it.

"What on earth?"

Peg's haughty tone might've been the only thing in the world that could bring Sassy back to that empty lot. She broke off the kiss but couldn't bring herself to pull away from the man, no matter what kind of trouble this might land her in.

"Just what do you think you're doing, *Mayor* McGrath?" The woman stood on the sidewalk across from them with two of her friends. All three of them were clad in yoga gear and must have walked out of the studio across the street.

Sassy almost laughed. Showing up here around the same time the yoga class ended sounded about right for her luck.

"Someone in class mentioned there was a sign for the community garden over here, so I thought I would come and see for myself, and this is what I find?" With all the wild hand gesturing she was doing, Peg nearly dropped her rolled-up mat. "This is unbelievable! He's nearly ten years younger than you!"

This time Sassy did laugh. "Is that true?" she asked

Graham in mock outrage. She already happened to know he was sixty-three, which would put him at not quite seven years younger.

The man smiled back at her as though they were the only two standing there. "I might be a smidge younger, but you, my dear, are much lovelier."

Why, he'd just earned himself another kiss, the Romeo.

"I have to say, I thought more of you, Sassy. This is shocking. Simply shocking." Peg continued her tirade. "We will most assuredly be discussing this irresponsible behavior at the town council meeting on Wednesday night," she added before stomping away.

After she'd gone, Graham's smile fell away and concern took over his expression. "I'm sorry. This is exactly what you'd worried about. I'll tell them all it was my fault. That I just got carried away and kissed you."

"No, you will not." Sassy gave him another smooch. "I might've been a little afraid of you, but I am definitely not afraid of Peg or her town council."

Chapter Fifteen

Rose

W elcome back to the Juniper Inn, Mr. and Mrs. Cleary."
No, no, no. That didn't sound right. Rose cleared
her throat and tried again. "Mr. and Mrs. Cleary, it's so wonderful to *finally* welcome you back to the Juniper Inn!"
Hmmm…that might be a tad overenthusiastic. Plus, she
didn't want to imply it was their fault they hadn't visited for
so long.

"Ugh." She straightened the vases of wildflowers she'd
picked earlier in an effort to spruce up the new check-in counter.
It might be silly to be nervous, but the Clearys were their first
guests at the inn. The guests who would test out their new
cabins. The guests who would give them either stellar five-
star reviews online or a critical one-star condemnation.

"What do you think, Mari?" she asked the dog, who lay
on her large fluffy pillow a few feet away. "Are we ready
for this?"

The dog raised her head and whined a little like she was
nervous too.

"We have to be ready." Rose said the words mainly to remind

herself. "Because the Clearys will be here any minute." She looked around again to make sure everything was perfect.

Back in the day, Sassy had always welcomed the guests to the inn by greeting them at their reserved cabin—taking cash or check only and giving them the key. Times had changed though, and if they wanted to be competitive in the resort market, Rose knew they had to create a more modern process and facility. So she'd had Tony convert the old barn on the property into a guest welcome center and gathering place.

The check-in counter would be the first thing people saw when they walked in. It had a computer and a variety of brochures for area attractions and points of interest. Beyond the counter, the space really sparkled, if she did say so herself.

One corner of the barn had been dedicated to several round tables that could each sit six people comfortably. A small drink station along the wall offered hot and cold water along with a variety of teas, hot chocolates, and instant coffees as well as a mini fridge stocked with sodas. A huge bookshelf on the other wall housed all varieties of board games and puzzles.

In the other corner of the huge space, she'd had the crews build a massive stone fireplace as a focal point, and Rose had carefully chosen the most comfortable sofas and overstuffed chairs she could find to position around the hearth. In keeping with the rustic mountain theme, she'd decorated the space with a variety of homey cabin-like accents, including antler chandeliers and paintings of local wildlife she'd purchased at the Juniper Springs gallery.

This room had eaten up nearly half of their renovation budget alone, but looking at the space now, she had no regrets.

Rose sighed happily, thinking about all of the Christmas singalongs that could happen right there in front of the fireplace this winter. It would be the perfect spot to—

"Hello?" The door creaked open, and she quickly jolted back into position behind the counter.

Marigold immediately scrambled to her paws and took her place as Rose's sidekick, sitting dutifully to her right, that fluffy tail sweeping back and forth over the hardwood floor.

"Welcome back to the Juniper Inn!" She greeted the elderly couple who walked in with her brightest smile, not caring that her voice had gone about five octaves too high and her volume about three notches too loud. This was happening! After all the work and the headaches and the growing pains and the surprises, they were welcoming their first guests to the new and improved Juniper Springs Inn!

And Mr. and Mrs. Cleary happened to be adorable. There was no other word to describe them. They were both on the shorter end of average height with white hair—though Mr. Cleary's had thinned considerably. Mrs. Cleary had round pink cheeks and blue eyes that seemed to shine, thanks to the genuine smile on her face.

"Why, thank you." The woman lugged her large purse up onto the counter. "I can't tell you how thrilled we are to be back."

"I almost didn't recognize the place," Mr. Cleary added, taking a good long look around the room. "We always thought it was beautiful, but this is beyond our expectations."

Pride swelled inside of her, making her chest feel as though it could burst. "I'm so glad. I'm Rose, Sassy's niece."

"Rose!" Mrs. Cleary hurriedly dug a pair of glasses out of her purse and slipped them on. "My, it's been years since we've seen you. You had to be ten years old the last time we crossed paths with you here at the inn."

"That's right." According to Sassy, the Clearys had stayed at the inn one summer when Rose was visiting with her family. Rose didn't remember meeting them, but then again, she'd likely been too busy wandering in the woods and swimming in the pond to pay much attention to the adults.

"You're beautiful." The woman nudged her husband. "Isn't she beautiful, Gerald?"

"She is." The man gave his wife a tender smile. "But no one is as beautiful as you, love."

Aww. That would be why these two were celebrating their fiftieth anniversary this week. Instead of gushing over the two of them, Rose tried to remain professional. "Your cabins are all ready for the week. You'll be the first group we've welcomed since the remodel."

"That's just what we were hoping for." Mrs. Cleary grabbed her husband's hand. "We couldn't think of a more special way to celebrate this big milestone than coming back to this place that holds so many wonderful memories for our family."

"Speaking of family..." Mr. Cleary lumbered to the door. "Hey, everyone, come on in. Wait until you see what they've done in here."

The doors opened wide and people of all ages started to spill in to the barn—children and moms holding babies and men ranging from early twenties to fifties.

Marigold could no longer handle behaving. The dog barked and yipped with excitement, bolting over to greet all of her new friends.

"All right, pups." Rose gently took hold of the dog's collar and urged her out the door. "We'll introduce you later. Right now you can go find the squirrels." At the sound of that key word, Marigold took off for the trees.

Rose stepped back inside, maneuvering around all the people to get back to the check-in counter. She had known the reservation had included nearly thirty family members, but she still shook her head in awe. "What an amazing group you have." Earlier that morning at breakfast Sassy had walked her through the Clearys' family tree. Mr. and Mrs. Cleary had three kids, who were all married and in their fifties now. Each of their kids had three kids, and now Gerald and Nadine also had three great grandchildren and one on the way.

"Our family is our whole life." Mr. Cleary draped his arm around his wife's shoulders.

The young children in the group dispersed, immediately gravitating toward the game area, while the adults stood around chatting.

"We enjoy every minute we get to spend with them."

"I can see why." Rose had always wondered what it would be like to be part of a large, close-knit family. Her parents had never made aunts, uncles, and cousins a priority. Well, after her mother's falling-out with Sassy, that was. "Your reservation is all paid for and taken care of." She selected the cabin key cards and placed them in the welcome folders she'd designed. "I've assigned everyone as you requested. There's a map on the back showing where each cabin is located."

"Wonderful." Mrs. Cleary took the stack of folders and leaned in closer. "Say, you don't remember my grandson, Nolan, do you?"

Rose thought back, but she couldn't even place the Clearys in her memory. "I'm afraid not. Have I met him before?"

"Yes, that last summer we were here." Even the woman's laugh seemed to twinkle. "He had quite the crush on you that week. He's only a few years older, you know."

"Oh, I guess I'd forgotten." Rose scanned the group behind the elderly couple, looking for a familiar face.

"Nolan, darling," Mrs. Cleary called. "Come and say hello to Rose."

The man strode over from where the children had been playing. Rose had been too distracted to have seen him earlier, or she surely would've noticed him.

No, she would've done more than notice him. She might've smiled the way she had to be smiling now.

To say Nolan Cleary was handsome wouldn't quite cover it. The man had a magnetism about him—tall enough to be noticed in a large, crowded room, dark hair with just the right amount of wave and styled like he cared, and eyes she could tell were a deep blue even with the distance between them.

He didn't move with an overly confident swagger like most men that good-looking would have. He had more of a laid-back gait that seemed neither too hurried nor too leisurely.

"He thought you were the prettiest girl he'd ever seen," the woman gushed while her grandson made his way over. "You remember Sassy's niece Rose, don't you?" she asked when he approached the counter.

The man stopped abruptly, seeming to take Rose in. "Rose? Of course I remember Rose." Two long strides brought him the rest of the way to the counter.

"Hi." Rose suddenly realized all eyes—including Nolan's

smoldering pair—were focused on her. "It's nice to see you again." She tried to think of something else to say, something clever or charming, but before anything came to her, Sassy waltzed into the barn, setting off a new round of chaos.

"I hope I didn't miss the party." She hugged her way through the Cleary family until she made it to the counter, where Rose still stood tongue-tied and smiling awkwardly.

"You didn't miss anything," Rose told her aunt. She sure didn't seem to have any problem talking to Sassy. "In fact, the Clearys just arrived." And her aunt hadn't shown up a moment too soon, rescuing her from making a fool out of herself in front of Nolan Cleary. Sheesh, a good-looking man had never flustered her back in Savannah.

"I was just reintroducing Rose to Nolan." Mrs. Cleary tugged on her grandson's hand, presenting him to Sassy.

"Nolan!" Sassy hugged him like he was a part of the family. "That's right. You two have met before."

"We have indeed," the man confirmed, quirking his lips at Rose as if to say he remembered her well. "It's great to be back here. I couldn't believe how many memories flooded me on the drive in."

"We're thrilled you all could come back to celebrate such a special occasion with us." There. Rose had finally broken her uncertain silence. And she'd sounded quite professional, to boot.

"We are too." Mr. Cleary shared a long, loving glance with his missus before placing a hand on his grandson's shoulder. "Nolan here was talking about wanting a tour of the place. Since it's been so many years and all."

"Oh, I'm sure Rose would be happy to take him." Mrs.

Cleary gathered up her purse. "They can walk around and meet us over at the cabin in a little while."

"What a fabulous idea," Sassy agreed with a wink at Rose. "She'd be happy to take him for a walking tour. Rose can tell him all about the upgrades she's made around here too."

"Oh. Uh." Rose peeked at the man again.

He caught her glance and grinned. "I'd love it, if you could spare the time."

"He could bring his camera and take some pictures while you're out," Mrs. Cleary offered. "Nolan is a famous photographer."

The man's chuckle held the perfect blend of humility and amusement. "Don't listen to her. That's not true."

"It is so," Mr. Cleary argued stubbornly. "He's sold his photographs to all the big magazines—*National Geographic*, *Time*, the *New York Times*. We've got them all framed and hanging on our walls at home."

"That's amazing." Sassy gasped and turned to Rose. "You just said the other day that we need to get updated pictures for the website and brochures now that all of the projects are finished."

"That's true." But why did she feel like this was a setup? Maybe because both Mrs. Cleary and Sassy had that spark of mischief in their eyes. But they really did need some professional photographs of the inn. And it wasn't like she was attracted to Nolan. Sure, the man had that Disney prince vibe going on, but her heart was already occupied at the moment.

As much as she wanted to forget about kissing Colt, the memory seemed to sneak up on her at the most inconvenient times—when she was trying to fall asleep at night or when she was supposed to be focusing on something else…like right now.

"I'm happy to take him on a tour." Rose shut out the thundering in her heart brought on by thoughts of Colt. "And please feel free to call me anytime if you need anything at all during your stay," she said to Mr. and Mrs. Cleary. "My number is right on those folders I gave you." She almost reminded them about the party for Sassy, but quickly bit her tongue before she ruined the surprise.

"I'm sure everything will be lovely." Mrs. Cleary squeezed her hand. "Sassy, if you have time, I would love to catch up over some tea. Everyone seems happy here for now anyway." The woman gestured to where the children had all spread out and were playing games.

"What a marvelous idea." Her aunt linked her arms with Mr. and Mrs. Cleary and led them to the drink station, leaving Rose and Nolan alone.

"You sure you don't mind doing this?" the man asked, serving up a grin with a side of repentance in his eyes. "Because I can wander around alone if you're busy."

"I don't mind at all." She would do whatever she could to keep her customers happy. "It'll be fun for me to show off all the work we put in over the last several months."

"Perfect." Nolan walked to the door and held it open for her. "I'll let you lead the way."

They stepped outside and were instantly greeted by the late afternoon sunshine filtering through the aspen leaves. A warm breeze seemed to make the light dance across the green grass.

"I need to grab my camera." Nolan stopped at a dark SUV and retrieved a surprisingly compact camera with a massive lens. "I don't go anywhere without this." He slipped the neck strap over his head. "When you love what you do, it never feels like work."

"I couldn't agree more." Rose strolled alongside him, deciding they would visit the pond first. She could already see Marigold down there, staring intently at the water as though searching for a critter.

"So when did you come back to the Juniper Inn?" Nolan asked, adjusting something on his camera.

"Last Christmas. Sassy invited my sisters and me to come." A nostalgic sigh rose up in her chest. How beautiful it had been here then with the soft mounds of snow frosting everything over. It was still beautiful, of course, but there was no more magical time than Christmas.

"My grandparents mentioned you were engaged on the drive in." The man left the sentence open-ended.

"Yes. I was." She wasn't surprised they'd heard. Though she hadn't been in close touch with Sassy before last year, her aunt had kept tabs from afar, making sure all of her friends stayed up to date on news regarding her beloved nieces.

Rose stepped around a large log and led the way down to the water's edge, grateful she'd opted to wear her casual tennis shoes with a nice pair of leggings and tunic today.

Marigold bounded over to meet them, bombarding poor Nolan with one of her signature hugs.

He simply laughed and hugged the dog back.

Once her dog calmed, Rose answered his earlier question. "The engagement wasn't the right thing for me. I think I knew it before I came to Juniper Springs, but when I got here, I couldn't pretend anymore. I knew this is where I belonged." And her fiancé hadn't wanted anything to do with the small town. "We were looking for different things in life."

"I can relate." Nolan raised the camera and seemed to test the lighting with a few shots, checking the screen on the back after each one. "My divorce was final six months ago."

"I'm sorry." His words weren't particularly melancholy or anything, but she still knew how hard it was to walk away from a significant relationship. She could sympathize.

"Like you said, we wanted different things." Nolan knelt down and angled the camera up to take another picture that likely captured the peaks in the distance. "She wanted luxury and city life. And I'm more of a wanderer." The man stood back up and faced her. "I took a clue after she cheated on me with someone at work."

Rose winced for him, but he shook his head. "I don't blame her for the problems we had. We were young when we got married. Neither of us really knew who we were."

"Sometimes it can take a while to figure out who you are." She turned a slow circle, gazing around the property. "Coming back to this place helped me figure it out. I love it. The harsh changes in the weather, the stunning landscape, the small community that sticks together and gives everyone a place to belong. It's not the perfect place to live, but it has made me stronger and tougher and open and more resourceful—" She stopped suddenly, catching a glimpse of someone farther up the hill.

It was Colt, and he seemed to be watching them.

"That's exactly how I feel anytime I'm not in the city."

Nolan raised the camera in her direction. "Let me get a shot of you. The inn owner in her natural habitat."

Rose nodded, but she kept peeking up the hill. Colt still stood a few feet away from his truck, his gaze aimed right at the pond.

How long had he been standing there? Should she go talk to him?

"All right, give me your best smile," Nolan coaxed.

Rose tried, but her heart had started to drum again.

Nolan lowered his camera. "I said smile. You're giving me the same look my grandmother gives me when she thinks I'm insulting her cooking."

Rose laughed. "You should never insult your grandmother's cooking."

The man raised his arms in a dramatic surrender. "I added salt *one time*, and I'll be doing penance forever."

"I know all about penance," she said through another laugh.

"That's it. There we go. Turn to the side and look at the camera," the man directed. "I promise I won't insult your cooking."

She did as she was told, finding it easier to smile and striking a few more poses before telling Nolan she was sure he had enough shots to thoroughly embarrass her.

As they moved away from the water's edge she looked back up the hill again, but both Colt and his truck were gone. What was he thinking? Why did she never seem to know? The questions distracted her while she finished Nolan's tour.

"I'm impressed," Nolan said as they walked back to the welcome lodge. "I'd love to hear more about the process over a cup of coffee."

Rose glanced at her watch. It had been a half hour since Colt had taken off, and she wouldn't be able to think about anything else until she talked to him. "I'll have to take a rain check on the coffee," she told Nolan, already heading for her car. "I have something to take care of in town."

"Sure." He gave her a wave and then disappeared into the barn.

Rose wasted no time peeling out of the driveway. She sped through town and parked in front of Colt's store. The man himself was right outside the door, stacking firewood bundles on a shelf.

He must've seen her pull up, but he didn't look at her.

"Hey." Rose approached him slowly, her heart flooding with every emotion that had threatened to carry her away when he'd kissed her.

"Hey." Still, the man didn't turn around. He kept right on working, methodically stocking the shelf.

He certainly didn't seem happy to see her, but with Colt it could be hard to tell. She cleared her throat. "That man I was with at the resort…that's Nolan Cleary. He's an old family friend."

Colt snatched another bundle of firewood out of the crate and shoved it onto the shelf. "Why would I care who he is?"

That tone…it was the same one he'd used when they'd first gotten reacquainted last Christmas. Back when he'd thought she was a snob. Rose shuffled her feet, trying to get him to look at her. If he would just look at her. "I didn't want…I mean, nothing is happening between Nolan and me. He was only taking pictures for the website."

Colt stepped around her to the other side of the shelf.

"Like I said, why would it matter to me who you spend your time with?"

What did he mean why would it matter? "We kissed, and it was—" Amazing. Meaningful. Impactful…

"Pointless." He finally stopped stacking the wood and faced her.

The indifference on his face pushed her back a step.

"Like you said, the kiss shouldn't have happened." His tone had a razor-sharp edge. "I've never been good enough for anyone in this town. After all, I'm the son of a felon. Now that I'm leaving, I can finally put all of that behind and start over in a place where no one knows about my past."

This. This is why he'd said he couldn't stay in Juniper Springs anymore. "Colt…" She wanted to let him know his past had never mattered to her. But what did she know about how he'd felt growing up here, where everyone knew what his dad had done? He needed to start over. She had to let him go.

"I have to check on my customers." The man left her standing there and pulled open the door, ready to walk away.

But she had one more thing to say. "You're good enough for me." That was all she wanted him to know.

He paused like he was going to turn around but, after a few seconds, Colt stepped inside the store without looking back.

Chapter Sixteen

Dahlia

Dahlia filled up a vase with water and arranged the bouquet of daisies she'd picked up at the store on her way home from dropping Maya and Ollie off at camp.

There. That ought to bring a cheerful vibe to the table she'd set for lunch with Rose and their mother. Nothing said *behave yourselves* like a cluster of perky white daisies sitting between adversaries.

Instead of pouring their iced tea into real glasses, she found her stylish heavy-duty plastic outdoor ware. You couldn't be too careful when Lillian and Rose both had their hackles up. They hadn't spoken since their fight earlier that week, and Dahlia didn't want any glass shattered on the floor of her kitchen.

"What can I do to help?" Lillian shuffled into the kitchen, holding her shoulders in a sulky posture. At least she'd gotten dressed in something other than her velour tracksuit. The lovely coral-colored button-up blouse and pristine white slacks were a sure sign her pouting was almost over.

"Thanks, but I've got everything under control." Dahlia

brought the bowl of chicken salad she'd made earlier to the table and then took the butter lettuce leaves she'd washed from the colander and arranged them on a platter. "Remember, you promised to be civil to Rose during lunch."

"I am always civil." Her mother sat at the table in a huff. "She's the one who attacked me."

"She only wants you and Sassy to have the chance to be a family again." Dahlia set the iced tea pitcher next to the chicken salad. They might be sitting here a while, and they'd need refills. "She wants what's best for you both. We all do."

She didn't give her mother the chance to launch into a defense for why she could never reconcile with Sassy. Dahlia had already heard every excuse. "I think I heard Rose's car pull up. I'll be right back."

She rushed out of the kitchen and through the living room, picking up Ollie's soccer ball, pogo stick, and lightsaber on the way. After stashing her son's treasures into the front closet, she stepped out onto the porch to warn her sister. "Mom is still pouting." She tried to keep it down so her voice wouldn't carry through the open window. "Try to be patient. Okay? I know it's not easy, but we have to try."

"I'm always patient," Rose grumbled, stomping up the steps.

Great. Her sister already seemed to be in a mood. "What's wrong?" Dahlia moved to block the door. If Rose went in there with a scowl already in place, a full-on war would break out.

"What's *wrong*?" Her sister posted her hands on her hips. "I'll tell you what's wrong. The Clearys have an extra-hot grandson named Nolan, and Mrs. Cleary and Sassy talked me into taking him for a tour of the property."

"Nolan came?" Dahlia couldn't help a giggle. "He had the hugest crush on you."

"So I've heard." Rose's eyes darkened. "Anyway, there we were wandering around the property while he took pictures of me for the website, and who do I catch watching us from the main house?"

That was an easy one. "Colt?"

"Yes, Colt." Rose leaned against the door and sighed. "The man I kissed yesterday."

"You *kissed* him?" Forget about keeping her voice down. This was huge! "I thought he sold the store?"

"He did," her sister said miserably.

"Then why do you care if he saw you with Nolan?" Seriously, her sister had to be the only person who would lament having two wonderful, good-looking guys prowling around her. "Sounds like it might not be a bad thing for you to hang out with Nolan if Colt is skipping town anyway."

Rose stood upright again and frowned at Dahlia. "Would you want to hang out with anyone besides Ike right now?"

The reminder of what she was missing stung. "No."

"That's how I feel," Rose murmured. "I went to see Colt at the store after he saw me with Nolan, and he was upset. He said he couldn't wait to leave this place behind. I know I won't see him anymore. But I lo—"

Her sister snapped her mouth shut with a surprised look that made Dahlia gasp.

"You *what?*" she demanded. "*Love?* Were you going to say you're in love with Colt?" Because that's sure as heck what it sounded like she'd been about to say.

"I don't—"

"Dahlia?" Lillian peered through the window. "The oven timer went off," she said without acknowledging Rose.

"Right." She had a tray of scones in the oven. "We'll finish this discussion later," she whispered to her sister before opening the door for her.

Rose trudged inside the house with an air of irritation that made Dahlia regret calling this little meeting. Maybe she should've let them continue giving each other the silent treatment. That would've made her life a lot easier.

When they walked back into the kitchen, Lillian had retreated to her seat again. Rose sat directly across from her.

"Hello, Mom." It sounded like her sister had already gritted her teeth.

"Rose." Lillian carefully smoothed her napkin over her lap. Shaking her head, Dahlia sat next to her sister. Since they all knew why they were there, they might as well jump right into the discussion. "You two need to apologize to each other," she announced, selecting a few lettuce leaves before she passed the platter to Rose. "So we can all move on and enjoy being together." Maybe *enjoy* was a stretch. She should've gone with *tolerate*…

"Apologize?" Their mother snatched the platter of lettuce leaves out of Rose's hands. "Okay. Fine. I'm sorry you think I'm such a horrible person, Rose. I'm sorry you hate me."

"Oh, please," her sister fired back. "You know I don't hate you. I simply can't understand why you choose to punish your sister for falling in love."

Dahlia relaxed a little. At least Rose was controlling her tone.

"Of course you don't understand." Their mother scooped

some chicken salad onto her lettuce with frantic movements. "You don't understand anything."

Dahlia shared a look with Rose, silently admonishing her to breathe, to think first instead of retaliating right away. *Patience*, she mouthed.

Her sister closed her eyes for a few seconds, as though it took everything in her to hold back. "Then please tell me." Her tone had quieted. "Please tell me why you were so angry that Aunt Sassy chose to let Robert and his son stay when it hardly affected us at all."

"That's a good point," Dahlia added gently. "We lived thousands of miles away from Juniper Springs. We only came out here to visit once in the summer and once in the winter. You might not have liked Robert, but we wouldn't have been spending much time with him."

Seeing her mother's shoulders rise and fall with furious breaths, she decided to stop there. Lillian's face had reddened too.

Here we go…

"We have a right to know." Rose had never had a problem pushing their mother. "There must be another reason you cut her out of your life."

"*I* needed her, damn it!" Their mother slammed her palms down to the surface of the table, making the dishes tremble. "I needed her, and she chose him instead."

Dahlia cautiously moved the chicken salad and platter out of Lillian's reach. This was getting ugly fast.

"Why did you need her?" Rose pushed again.

Tears started to stream down their mother's cheeks, and she pushed her plate away, leaving her food untouched. "I was going to bring you girls out for a whole summer that year so I could have some space, a break from my life." A sob wobbled out. "Sassy knew I needed that. She knew what I was going through. And she still wouldn't kick that criminal out. I didn't feel safe staying at the inn with him there, but she didn't care."

Dahlia stared at her mother in complete shock. The anger seemed to have receded, but the tears gained momentum. "Why did you need a break?"

Lillian's chin lifted stubbornly, and she stared over their heads for a few long silent seconds.

"Mom, what was going on?" This time Dahlia was the one to push. She had to. Memories had started to come back to her. She remembered that summer. Something had shifted in their house. Their dad had spent a lot of time away, traveling for work, staying at the office late. "Did it have to do with why you and Dad had been arguing so much?"

Lillian continued to stare over them, as though she could see the past playing out on the wall behind them. "He had an affair," she finally said.

Something inside of Dahlia clicked—a missing puzzle piece. Rose gasped in horror.

"Daddy?" Her sister's head shook. "No. He wouldn't have—"

"He cheated on me with one of his patients." Lillian's voice steadied.

"I don't believe you." Rose turned to Dahlia as though looking for an agreement, but she couldn't offer one.

She believed what their mother said. On some level she knew. Because she remembered more. She remembered the wedge that seemed to drive her parents apart that year. She'd simply thought her parents were busier, consumed with their own lives, but there had been much more to their unhappiness.

"I wanted to leave him and move out here for the summer so I could figure out what to do," their mother went on. "Sassy said we could come and stay, but she refused to tell Robert to leave."

That's why Lillian had been so angry. Because everything had to be on her terms, and Sassy had stood up to her. "She didn't tell us that part of the story." Likely because their aunt hadn't wanted to ruin their image of their father.

"I needed a break," their mother said, getting weepy again. "And I didn't get one. I had nowhere to go. So I stayed with him. I moved forward. And every day I lived with the reminders of his betrayal."

Rose was quiet, staring at her hands.

Dahlia couldn't seem to find any words to fill the silence either. She thought about all those years her parents had been distant and cold with each other. She'd noticed. Especially when she would go to a friend's house and see a married couple who actually smiled and laughed and went on dates together. On some level she'd been aware that her parents were pretending. Maybe that was why Lillian had always obsessed over making everything look perfect—to hide the mess that hid underneath.

But what had ignoring the problems offered any of them?

At breakfast with Maya earlier that week, her daughter had asked her if Dahlia knew what it was like to survive a divorce. She didn't. But she'd known what it was like to live with two people who didn't love each other.

When she met Jeff, she didn't know how to love him, how he should love her. So she'd basically built the same façade her parents had. And maybe...just maybe her kids would be better off having seen their parents acknowledge the lie—showing them that was not how things were supposed to be.

"Why have you never said anything?" Rose finally asked their mother. "All this time. I don't even know what to think."

"What does it matter now?" Lillian used her napkin to blot the tears from her cheeks as though it were that easy to move on. "He's gone. Everyone I care about is gone. You girls left and moved away. I have no one."

"I'm sorry, Mom. I didn't know." She genuinely meant the apology. She might've offered her more grace if she'd understood where her bitterness had come from. "But Sassy didn't abandon you." Dahlia gentled her voice. The years of her mother's bitterness all made sense now. She wasn't angry at Sassy for abandoning her. She was angry at their father. "We could've come to spend that summer here. There was plenty of room at the inn. Robert wasn't a horrible person. Sassy would never kick out anyone who needed a place, no matter what the ultimatum."

"There you go defending her again." Lillian stood. "I've lost you. I've lost my family."

That seemed to snap Rose out of her stupor. "Mom—"

"Forget it." Their mother pushed in her chair and crossed the room. "I'm going for a walk."

That was what Lillian had always done—she'd walked away from honest conversations. And Dahlia had always tried to go after her. This time was no different. She caught up to her mother at the front door. "Where are you going?"

"Into town. I know the way." She stepped outside. "Let me be. Please." The tears seemed to have dried up, and now Lillian's face hardened into a look of indifference.

She'd shut down her emotions. They wouldn't get anywhere with her right now. "Fine. Do you have your phone?" The last thing they needed was for their mother to go missing.

"Of course." Lillian turned and walked away from her, crossing the yard and continuing on down the sidewalk.

Well, that did not exactly go how she'd planned. Dahlia wandered back into the kitchen in a fog and joined Rose at the table again.

Her sister glanced across the table, wide-eyed and pale. "Do you believe her? I mean, do you think Dad really—"

"Yeah. I do." Dahlia started to clear the plates. It was obvious no one was going to eat anything. "I know they put on a good front, but they never seemed happy. They were comfortable and compatible most of the time but never overly affectionate."

"I guess that's true." Her sister walked to the sink and started to clean the dishes while Dahlia stashed the food in the refrigerator. "Geez. We can't let her wander around Juniper Springs all afternoon." Rose shut off the water.

"No, I suppose you're right." Their mother had never had a stellar sense of direction. "We can drive down to Main Street and meet her. That way we'll be able to give her a ride home when she's ready."

"Perfect." Rose grabbed her purse off the counter. "I have to run some errands for the party tomorrow anyway."

They got into Dahlia's car and talked through what they'd

learned while Dahlia drove to Main Street and found a parking spot.

"It's so unbelievable," Rose said for at least the tenth time.

Rose continued to talk about her shock, but Dahlia had stopped listening. Ike stood across the street—in line at the Crazy Moose. And Dr. Jolly was with him. Both of them had traded in their scrubs for casual summer attire, and they were chatting with the ease of old friends.

"Do you think she forgave him before he died?" Rose asked.

"Mm-hmm. I would guess she did," she answered halfheartedly. She couldn't seem to force her gaze away from Ike and Dr. Jolly.

"Dally, what's—" Rose followed her gaze across the street. "Oh."

"I'm sorry. I'm paying attention. Really." She cut the engine and withdrew the keys, holding them tightly in her fist. "I'm sure Dad and Mom came to terms with everything before he passed away. They did go on a few vacations together after we all moved out." She hoped they'd had at least a few happy years together.

Now Rose was the one who wasn't paying attention. She stared at Ike and Dr. Jolly. "You think they're on a date?"

Dahlia didn't want to know. "Dr. Jolly is amazing. I would be happy for them both if they ended up together." She climbed out of the car determined to make those words true. Living in Juniper Springs, she'd likely run into the two of them a lot. It was something she'd have to get used to.

"Sometimes love really sucks," Rose muttered. She came around the car. "Maybe pretending is the better way to go. Then you don't have to feel the agony of all the emotions."

"But then you don't get to feel the passion either." Dahlia

linked her arm through Rose's and pulled her to the sidewalk, walking in the opposite direction of the Crazy Moose. "I think the passion has to be worth the agony once you find something real. Don't you?"

"I guess." Her sister rolled her eyes. "At least according to the Hallmark Channel."

Despite the ache beneath her breastbone, Dahlia laughed. "At least we have each other in the midst of the agony." That seemed to make it more bearable. At least for her.

"And at least we have each other to deal with our mother," Rose added. "Speaking of…where do you think she's gone off to?"

"Only God knows." Dahlia scanned the streets. A few people were window-shopping at the storefronts, but the whole downtown area seemed pretty deserted. Given that it was still the lunch hour, most people were probably seated in the restaurants along Main Street. She gave in to temptation and snuck a peek over her shoulder.

Ike and Dr. Jolly must've gone inside.

"Call me crazy, but maybe we should check Grumpy's." Rose veered off the sidewalk, and Dahlia followed her across the street.

"I guess that would make sense." Well, it wouldn't make sense, exactly. Rose had told her all about their mother's kitchen rendezvous with Grumpy, but Dahlia still had a hard time picturing the man calling her mom Lil. "I really hope they're not making out in the kitchen or something."

Rose visibly shuddered. "There are no guarantees, I'm afraid. I swear Grumpy was making eyes at her that day when I caught them in the kitchen."

"Dear God." Dahlia braced herself and opened the coffee shop's door, prepared for the worst. A few patrons sat at tables sipping coffee. One woman had a laptop open on a table near the window, and two elderly men were playing chess.

"At least they wouldn't be here alone," Rose whispered on their way to the counter. "I don't even want to—"

Dahlia shushed her so she could hear the voices coming from the kitchen.

"They don't seem to appreciate me at all, Elroy. I don't understand how my own daughters could be so ungrateful."

Yep, they'd found her.

"Knowing Rose and Dahlia like I do, they appreciate you more than they let on." Grumpy's voice had taken a soothing tone. "They're good eggs, those two. You raised them right, Lil."

Dahlia shared a look with her sister and prayed that they wouldn't find their mother lip-locked with the coffee shop owner when they went back there.

Rose edged her back against the wall and eased behind the counter like some secret agent.

Dahlia had to hold her hand over her mouth so she wouldn't laugh. Following her sister's lead, she got close enough to peek into the kitchen.

Holy guacamole with chips and salsa. The man had his arms around their mother, hugging her while he ran a calming hand up and down her back.

"There now. Your girls love you. I know they do."

Dahlia didn't want to interrupt, but this was also the perfect opening. She stepped fully into the room. "It's true. We love you, Mom."

"And we're sorry you had to struggle for so many years," Rose added. "That had to be incredibly hard."

Lillian lifted her head, her eyes still bright with tears. "It was. It really was."

Grumpy stepped away. "Look now. Your girls came to find you. I told you they were good eggs." He smiled at her and Rose. A real smile. Dahlia was almost too shocked to smile back.

"I'll make us all an almond milk latte," Grumpy offered. "And we can sit and have a chat together."

"That would be wonderful. Thank you, Elroy." Lillian squeezed his hand with obvious affection, and Dahlia didn't miss the way their eyes met.

What in the world?

Never in a million years would Dahlia have dreamed Grumpy would be the one to catch their mother's eye.

Chapter Seventeen

Sassy

"Well look at you, Miss Talk of the Town."

Moe blew into the office with the force of a tornado and dumped his satchel on his desk before walking to hers. "I knew there was something going on between you and Graham. Kissing in public in broad daylight?" The man clapped his hand over his heart. "It's downright scandalous."

Sassy continued to focus on her notes for the town council meeting, but she couldn't hide a smile. "Well, how could I resist him?" It was a good thing she was sitting down, because thoughts of kissing Graham tended to make her knees buckle.

There were a hundred reasons why she shouldn't be kissing him, but none of them changed the fact that she'd like to kiss him again sometime. "And you know how much I like to give people in this town something to talk about."

It had been years since she'd been the one churning the gossip mill. "I figure making people talk simply means I'm living my life." Maybe living more than she had for the last several years. "Or at least what I have left of my life." She hadn't had another headache episode since Moe had witnessed her dizzy spell, but even with no headaches she hadn't felt quite right. Lately, she'd been having trouble sleeping, and she found it difficult to focus on anything for too long.

"Did you call a doctor in Denver?" Moe sat in the chair across from her, his expression a mixture of sternness and concern. "When is your appointment?"

As much as she would've liked to forget about calling the doctor, she knew the man wouldn't leave it alone. "I've made plans to drive to Denver on Monday. The appointment is that afternoon." Well, the first appointment anyway. She assumed there would be labs and maybe an MRI or a CT scan to schedule. "I booked a hotel so I can spend a few nights there in case they need to run additional tests."

"Do you want me to go with you?" He didn't hesitate before asking.

"Thank you for the offer, but no." Sassy gave his hand a tender squeeze. "This is something I want to do on my own." Once she knew what she was dealing with, she would lean on her friends and her family.

"All right then. I'm available if you change your mind." Moe stood and walked to his own desk. That was one of the best things about him. He knew when to let something go. "Have you prepared a strategy for the meeting?" he asked, shifting into business mode. "Because I have a feeling half the town is going to be there to see how this scandal shakes out between you and Peg. And we still need the council to approve the partnership with the museum, all drama aside."

"My strategy is always to tell the truth and to do what's best for this town." If that wasn't enough for the council and whatever spectators came to witness the drama, then she didn't want to be mayor anyway. "Peg should be happy I was smooching Graham. I know she said it wouldn't work for the museum to keep the land, but Graham and his board are fully committed to the garden. He's not going to change his mind. So she'll have to come around to the idea of a partnership whether she likes it or not."

Moe laughed and took a seat behind his desk. "I like your style."

"Sassy?" Rose's voice drifted through the doorway.

Oh goody! She felt like she'd hardly seen Rose at all lately. "Yes, we're right in here." She scrambled out from behind her desk to go meet her niece in the hallway.

Rose and Dahlia were all the way at the other end, wandering.

"What a treat!" Sassy met them each with a hug. "Getting to see both of you at once is such a rarity these days." Dahlia had especially been absent from the inn lately. Not that Sassy could say much about being too busy.

"We wanted to come to the meeting." Rose had never been good at glaring, but she seemed to be trying awfully hard to come across steely and tough. "You know, the meeting we had to hear about from Tony, whose wife told him that Peg freaked out when she caught you and some Graham fellow kissing."

Ah, yes. The old rumor mill had been hard at work. Sassy glanced around the hallway. It seemed deserted, but around here you never knew. "Why don't we go into the office?" She waved them through the door.

"Glad to see there are reinforcements," Moe commented from behind his computer. "I hope you two are staying for the meeting."

"We wouldn't miss it." Dally pulled some chairs up to the desk, and they all sat down.

"So, tell us all about Graham." Rose leaned over the desk, her eyes bright with excitement. "This is so exciting!"

"Yes, do tell," Moe taunted from the other side of the room.

"You hush." Sassy pointed at him but she couldn't hide her smile. "I was going to tell you girls about Graham, but the truth is I didn't even know how I felt about him until he kissed me yesterday." How strange to say those words— and blush like this—at her age. She hadn't seen Dally for even a minute, and Rose had been quite occupied with making sure the Clearys had everything they needed last night. "It all started the day I went to meet with him about that plot of land next to the museum. We wanted to put a community—"

"Yes, Tony told us all about it," Rose interrupted with an air of impatience. "A garden is great, by the way, but I want to hear about you kissing Graham."

What could she say? "The meeting I had with him that first day turned into working on the museum's rose garden with him. We got to know each other." She was pretty sure she'd had this goofy smile on her face since the kiss. "He's a different man than I thought he was. He's kind and thoughtful and very smart, but also open to new ideas. And he is the best listener I have ever met." He made her feel like she was the only one who had anything worth saying.

"That's wonderful." Dahlia shared a happy look with Rose.

"You deserve to find love," Rose chimed in.

"Hear, hear," Moe called.

"I'm not sure it's love." After all, it hadn't even been a

week. "But it does feel like something wonderful." Her heart hadn't been this light in years. "I wasn't trying to hide my time with Graham from you girls. I would have told you. I simply haven't seen as much of you as I'd like."

Dahlia and Rose shared a look Sassy recognized from her own past—a message traveling between sisters.

"We've had a lot going on too." Dally bit lightly into her lower lip—something she did every time she was nervous.

"Mom is here," Rose blurted as though she'd been dying to say those words for a long time.

Sassy wasn't sure she'd heard them right. "Lillian? Here in Juniper Springs?" Saying her sister's name instantly choked her up. She'd been six years old by the time her mom finally gave her a baby sister, and they had been nearly inseparable until Lillian cast her out of her life, leaving a wound on her heart that had never fully healed.

"She's been here for nearly a week." Dahlia's voice bore an apologetic tone. "We didn't want to hide her from you. We were only trying to figure out how we could get you two together so you could finally patch things up."

"I would love nothing more." They made it sound like all she and Lillian had to do was tie up a few loose threads, but in reality their relationship had unraveled a long time ago. She'd given up hope for reconciling with her sister. Lillian had always been stubborn.

"I don't even know why we tried," Rose grumbled. "She's impossible."

Sassy tried to smile past a stab of pain. "She doesn't want to see me." It wasn't a question. Lillian's silence over the last eighteen years told her everything she needed to know. At first, Sassy had tried. She'd called and written letters. All of which had gone unanswered.

Remembering they weren't alone, she glanced across the room. Moe had focused on his computer and was obviously pretending not to listen. It didn't matter anyway. The man was a vault. He'd never spill her secrets.

Dahlia's shoulders slumped. "We still haven't told her you're in town. I was afraid she would leave. But we've been pushing her on why she won't see you, and..." She looked at Rose as though passing the baton.

"She told us about the affair," Rose said. "About how she wanted to come up here for the summer to figure out what to do, but you wouldn't ask Robert to leave."

"And we totally don't blame you, by the way," Dally said quickly. "He shouldn't have had to move out so we could stay. That would have been ridiculous."

Sassy glanced at the time and shut her laptop. Across the room, Moe had started to gather his things for the meeting. "I can't believe she told you." Maybe it wasn't too soon to give up hope that Lillian would come around. She had told them about the affair. That meant she was acknowledging the past. Thinking about it. "Your mother feels like I abandoned her." And maybe that was Sassy's fault. She'd always spoiled her sister. Sassy had loved her so much, she'd always let her have her way. Lillian had been the youngest—the baby—and Sassy had treated her like a princess.

"Harrumph," Rose grumbled. "As if Mom has the right to feel that way."

"Of course she has the right." She knew how humiliated her sister had been when she found out that husband of hers was cheating on her. "It was never my intention to hurt her, but her feelings are valid." At the time it had felt like an impossible choice to make. "I struggled with the decision. And I almost asked Robert to leave. But he had Colt. They had nowhere to go. I loved him, and I couldn't turn him out when he needed a place for his son." As difficult as it had been, she'd made the right decision. When the police had eventually come for Robert, she had been there for Colt. He'd become a son to her. Raising him had been the most important thing she'd done in her life.

"We tried to tell Mom you couldn't just kick Robert and Colt out," Rose said. "But she's so stubborn."

The same could be said about Sassy. Pigheadedness happened to be a McGrath family trait, but Rose likely already knew that. She'd been cut from the same cloth. "I'm very thankful you tried. And I would like to see her when you think the time is right." Maybe it was the doctor appointments she had hanging over her head that had sparked her hope again.

Lillian was in Juniper Springs, and this might be her only chance to see her sister before her health declined. "Even if she decides to walk away and leave. I would still like to see her so I can tell her how much I love her." She needed her little sister back in her life.

"Then we'll make it happen," Rose promised, as determined as she'd been when she took over the inn. "I don't know how, but we'll find a way."

"I hate to break up the party, but the meeting is supposed to start in five minutes." Moe scooted past them, holding his laptop under his arm. "I'll head down and tell everyone you're on your way."

"Thank you, Moe." Sassy started to collect her notes but

then thought better of it. She didn't need a script for this meeting. She needed to speak from the heart.

She and her nieces filed out the door and made their way down the steps.

"Are you ready to face the town?" Dahlia asked when they paused outside of the meeting room.

Sassy evaluated her current state. Unlike the last time she'd walked into this room, she didn't seem to have any nerves at all. In fact, she felt more settled than she had in a long while. "Yes. I think I am ready."

"The real question is, are they ready for her?" Rose grinned and Sassy couldn't believe how much her niece still looked like the little girl she'd danced around the living room with. Her nieces were so grown up now. If only time could stop moving. If only she could pause her life right here instead of facing an uncertain future…

"They're ready for you." Moe appeared at the door, reminding her that time didn't stop. It marched on whether you wanted it to or not.

The three of them walked in together, and she had to stop so she could properly gape at the number of people sitting and standing in the audience area chatting away. The town council had taken their places at the table, and nearly every chair in the other half of the room had been filled.

"Wow, we should've saved ourselves a seat," Rose murmured.

"There's a few over there." Dahlia pointed to two empty chairs at the far edge of the front row.

"Let's go before someone steals them." Rose gave Sassy a hug and the girls drifted away while she made her way to the center of the table.

For the most part, people hadn't even seemed to realize she'd arrived. The talking continued in a loud buzz as if people had come mostly for a social hour.

"Nice of you to join us," Peg commented from the next chair over. The look in her eyes could've given Sassy frostbite.

She chose to ignore the woman and took her seat, searching the crowd for...

Graham. He sat in the very center of the front row, and she could see the encouragement in his kind eyes all the way from here. She smiled back at him and waved, not caring who saw or how they felt about it.

"All right, everyone." Moe's loud whistle silenced the room. People scrambled to their seats and turned their full attention to the table at the front of the room.

Sassy stared at all of the familiar faces—the people she'd chatted with in town or played bridge with or had welcomed to the annual Christmas extravaganza at the Juniper Inn year after year. She loved them. She loved this town. And she loved that this moment belonged to her. It might be her only moment to express her heart, since Peg would likely oust her after this, so she would revel in this opportunity. She would make the most of it.

"Let's call this meeting to order." She spoke with the same steadiness she felt inside. "I can't tell you all how delighted I am to see you here. We appreciate you taking the time to learn more about the community garden we hope to launch soon." Never mind that the majority had most likely come to see a show. "Today, our largest agenda item is to discuss the community garden we would like to build on the land next door to the museum."

She went on to talk about the plans she and Graham had discussed—the different types of produce they would grow and the events that would help bring the community together. "We feel this garden will not only offer food assistance but will also bring our community closer together." She found her gaze wandering to find Graham's again, and the man gave her a thumbs-up.

Peg cleared her throat, a sure sign she had prepared a soliloquy for this very moment. "It is the town council's feeling that a *partnership* is not acceptable or appropriate for the community garden."

Sassy took a look around the table. No one else seemed to look directly back at her. Surely the other members weren't going to sit by and let Peg have all the say.

"The original intention was that the town should own the land in order to have the rights to do whatever we deem is in the best interest of Juniper Springs as a whole." Peg folded her hands on the table and gave a practiced smile, mainly addressing the audience.

Oh, gracious. She couldn't let this continue. "And as mayor, I feel very comfortable about the agreement we have made with the museum. We've initiated the contract process with a local attorney—"

"I would imagine you feel *more* than comfortable, given the conflict of interest you have with the museum's president," Peg interrupted.

A murmur went around the room, but it didn't fluster Sassy. This was exactly what she'd expected from the woman. "You are the only person I know who would call caring about someone a conflict of interest."

A few people in the audience laughed.

Sassy didn't give Peg a chance to respond. "I have lived in this town for almost fifty years now. Juniper Springs is my home. It's the place I love. All I want to do is to bring people in this community together. It doesn't matter how that happens—if we own the land or if the museum owns the land—it really belongs to all of us."

Applause broke out, and Rose and Dahlia both whistled. Sassy found Graham's face again, and that intense and tender gaze told her everything she needed to know. This would be all right. No matter what happened, he would be there at the end of it.

"That's a beautiful sentiment." Peg's voice was hollow. "But when it comes down to it, whoever *owns* the land can dictate what happens with it. What if the museum decides to sell it in a few years?" She didn't pause long enough for Sassy to inform her that wouldn't happen. "The fact is, Ned originally wanted that land to go to the town before Mr. Wright got hold of him and coerced him to change his mind. That lot rightfully belongs to Juniper Springs."

"Or maybe Ned knew *you* would have a conflict of interest, Peg." Those were the first words Moe had spoken since the meeting started. The man stood from his place at the end of the table and handed out a sheet of paper to the council members. "As you'll see, I did some digging. It seems that you were planning to get the council to agree to sell off subsections of the land, and the bank has already promised financing to certain business owners to develop them."

"What?" Sassy studied the paper, her heart starting to race, a headache starting in at her temples. Moe's handout featured two email exchanges. One regarding a new restaurant building and the other a dentist office. Both were to be built next to the museum, and the bank would be the main investor.

All of the pieces seemed to click into place at once, and she stared at Peg in shock. "You lied." All along, the woman and her bank president husband had been planning to profit off businesses that they'd planned to put on that lot.

"How did you get that information?" the woman seethed, hastily moving around the table and trying to gather the papers. "That's illegal! You can't steal private emails and spread them around!"

"I didn't steal them." Moe pulled another stack of paper out of his satchel and started to hand them out to the audience. "They were given to me by an unnamed source voluntarily."

Sassy had a hard time containing her laughter. That sly fox! When he'd asked her if she had a strategy he'd known she wouldn't need one. He'd been working on all of this behind her back.

Peg watched helplessly as the rest of the town read through her deceptions. "We were still planning to move forward with the community garden." Desperation laced her voice. "It's a very large plot of land, and there's plenty of room for both buildings as well as a garden. I was only thinking of what's best for this town. We can subdivide the property and fill the coffers with the proceeds."

No. She didn't care about the money the town would make from selling off subsections of the lot. "You only care about how much the bank is going to profit from financing two new businesses in town." Sassy couldn't listen to the woman speak another word. "I wish I could say this is unbelievable, but I should've known when you asked me to take over as mayor. You were looking for a pawn. You wanted someone who would give you exactly what you wanted." She'd been an easy target. All Peg had to do was mention a community garden, and Sassy had let down her guard.

"No." The woman vigorously shook her head. "That's not true at all."

The sound of voices rose as the spectators read the emails. "A fast-food restaurant?" someone called. "You're trying to ruin this town!"

And Sassy had almost helped her. "You expected me to simply let you and the council subdivide that land however you wanted." With their money and clout, Peg and her dear husband would've likely convinced everyone on the council the new businesses were in the best interests of the town.

That was not going to happen on her watch.

"We're moving this to a vote. Now." Sassy glanced around the table. "All in favor of moving forward with the community garden partnership with the museum, say aye."

The unanimous response came in one by one. "And all in favor of firing our head council member?" She didn't even know if she had the authority to do that, but she sure as heck was going to try.

Another round of ayes went around the table.

"You can't fire me!" Peg shouted. "I do everything for this town! You don't have the authority!"

"Actually she does." Moe produced a copy of the town bylaws and read section 5.1b out loud, finishing to another round of applause.

And that was that. "Thank you for your service," Sassy said, dismissing the woman. "But it will no longer be needed."

Chapter Eighteen

Rose

W hat do you think?"

Rose stood back and evaluated the colorful paper lanterns she and Dahlia had hung from the lower branches of the juniper and aspen trees around the pond.

"It's beautiful." Her sister reached up to touch a bright pink one. "I can't wait to see them all lit up after sunset."

"I know. It's going to be absolutely magical." Rose admired the space they'd decorated. At first she'd thought they could have Sassy's surprise party in the barn, but the outdoors was the heart of the Juniper Springs Inn.

To dress the place up for the party, Rose had placed four banquet tables in one long line right near the pond's sandy shoreline. She'd decorated them with linens and glass lanterns and fairy lights. Eventually they would set the food there—she checked her watch—if the catering staff from the Crazy Moose ever arrived.

"Everything is going to be perfect," Dahlia told her, as if sensing her stress level had started to rise again.

"It has to be perfect." This wasn't simply a surprise birthday party. This was a tribute to their aunt.

Rose walked to the opposite side of the table, where she'd set up picture boards on easels. It had taken hours of poring through the old boxes and filing cabinets in Sassy's attic, but she'd managed to document her aunt's history at the inn, and thanks to Nolan, she'd even been able to add pictures of the Clearys enjoying the new and improved spaces.

"I don't even want to know how much time this took you." Her sister studied the black-and-white pictures displaying the inn's earliest days.

"The Juniper Springs Inn has a history of giving people a refuge from the chaos. I don't want to forget that. I'm planning to hang these in the barn after the party." That way everyone who came to stay could see the history and become part of the legacy.

Rose focused in on one of the pictures from their last summer at the inn when they were young. Their mother and Sassy stood behind her and Dahlia and Mags with their arms around each other. "You're still okay with going to pick Mom up before the party starts?"

"Yes. I told her I would pick her and the kids up at four o'clock so we could do something fun." Her sister winced. "I hope this works, Rose. She's not going to be happy when she finds out Sassy has been here the whole time."

"And she's also too concerned with appearances to make a scene." This was their last chance to bring Lillian and Sassy together. Their mother was supposed to leave on Monday. "We promised Sassy she would have a chance to talk to her. And at least with other people around, Mom won't get nasty."

Commotion broke out up the hill as the Cleary family

returned from their hiking excursion and parked all six of their SUVs near the cabins.

Nolan climbed out of one and waved at Rose. She felt her sister watching while she waved back.

"So Nolan seems nice," Dahlia commented slyly.

"Yes, he's nice." Rose started to rearrange the glass lanterns on the table, moving her way down while avoiding that smirk on Dally's face.

"I know how you feel about Colt, but he's leaving." Dally kept the statement gentle, but it still nicked her.

"I'm fully aware he's leaving." Her voice was not nearly as tame as her sister's. She couldn't help it. Thinking about Colt made her insides knot up, and the tension had to find a way out.

She couldn't forget him turning his back on her when she told him he was good enough for her. It was like he didn't believe her—like he thought he assumed she was too good for him too. Last night Colt had sent her a benign text informing her that he wouldn't be around this morning but that he would still take Sassy out for lunch in Salida so he could bring her to the surprise party. That was it. No *Hi*. No *You're good enough for me too*. No *Are you thinking about me as much as I'm thinking about you? Because not seeing you is killing me*.

"Do you remember what you said to me last winter when Ike started coming around?" Dahlia nudged her shoulder to get Rose to turn around.

"Nope." Yes, she was being stubborn, but that's what thinking about Colt leaving did to her. It made her sad, and she would much rather be mad. "I don't remember what I said to you at all."

Uh-huh, her sister seemed to say with a raise of her eyebrows. "You said it was okay to have a little fun, that it was good to put myself out there. And it really was." Her eyes held a motherly concern. "You and Gregory broke up eight months ago. Colt is leaving. What would be the harm in having a little fun with Nolan while he's staying here?"

She'd said almost those same words to Dally about Ike. She remembered every bit of advice she'd given Dahlia last Christmas, how she'd encouraged her sister to let herself have fun, to let herself live. But the problem was that Rose felt ready for more than a little fun. Maybe because her feelings for Colt ran deeper.

Rose went back to rearranging the flowers on the table, but her sister tugged on her arm. "Have you told Colt you love him?"

"I couldn't." He'd walked away from her and he hadn't even looked back. If he'd turned, she would've tried to tell him how she really felt. But he hadn't. "I don't think telling him would make much of a difference."

"Then maybe you should move on—"

"Hey, ladies." Nolan interrupted their chat, and Rose immediately put her smile back on. She couldn't let paying customers see her mope.

"I thought you could use some help setting up." He had his camera around his neck as usual.

"That would be great!" Dally answered before Rose could tell him they were nearly done. "We still have to hang the birthday banner and a few more lanterns."

Rose shot her sister a look. They could easily handle the final touches themselves.

Dahlia didn't look in her direction, smiling at Nolan instead. "In fact, I have to call the restaurant to make sure the food will be here on time." She started to walk away. "So if you could help Rose, that would be great."

"Not a problem." The man removed his camera from around his neck and set it on the table. "The picture boards look awesome." He seemed to take time to study each one. "What an amazing history this place has."

Rose softened a bit. It wasn't his fault Dahlia was giving her paybacks for her matchmaking antics with Ike last Christmas. "And thanks to you, we have a good record of the inn's present too." She pointed out the pictures he'd taken. "I had to rush the printing, but they turned out beautiful."

"It's hard to take a bad picture of this place." He shot her a sideways glance. "And of you. You're quite photogenic."

And he was quite the charmer. Rose waited for a spark or glimmer or even a flicker of something, but nothing came.

"I can't believe how you captured the reflection of the peaks in the pond. It looks like a painting." She pointed out the picture in the middle. "This one is my favorite. The one with the canoe pulled up on the shoreline."

Nolan turned and glanced at that place where the canoe still sat. "I've never been canoeing, believe it or not. I've been skydiving and bungee jumping and whitewater rafting, but never canoeing."

"That's crazy." What kind of person had never been in a canoe? "It's pretty peaceful. Especially in the mountains. I can take you out a little later. I mean, not that you couldn't figure out how to take it out yourself or anything, but—"

His laugh interrupted her. "It sounds to me like canoeing

is more fun with someone else. I'd love it if you took me out there later."

"Sure." Except…would spending time with him give him the wrong idea? "Um, Nolan…there's something I should—"

"Rose!" Dally came sprinting back down the path. "Look who's here!" Her calm, mature older sister jumped up and down and squealed and pointed at a car that was slowly making its way down the drive.

She squinted. Was that…"Mags! Oh my God!" Rose took off up the hill, somehow managing to stay on her feet even wearing her wedge sandals.

She and Dahlia both made it to the car at the same time. Eric hadn't even cut the engine, and they were already crowded around the window and peering into the backseat at their brand-new nephew.

"I get to hold him first!" Rose tried the door handle. Locked, damn it.

"No, I get to hold him first. I'm the oldest." Dally playfully nudged her out of the way.

Mags got out of the car laughing. "Come on now, you two. We're going to be here for a week, so there'll be plenty of time to get your baby fix."

Eric climbed out of the driver's seat and carefully removed the baby carrier from the back while Rose and Dally hugged Mags and squealed some more.

"You two are going to scare him," their brother-in-law teased. He pulled back the covering so they could get their first in-person glimpse at little Luca's face.

"He looks so much like both of you," Rose marveled. She'd

seen the baby on video calls, of course, but those few minutes hadn't been enough. "Look at those darling eyelashes."

"And all that dark hair," Dahlia gushed beside her.

Somehow Luca was still asleep, even with all the noise.

"I didn't think you would come." Rose couldn't even tear her gaze away from Luca to look up at her sister.

"We weren't going to," Mags said. "But then we decided we couldn't miss it. We had to be here to celebrate Sassy."

"I'm so glad." Rose went to work on all the buckles to free her nephew so she could hold him. "It wouldn't have been the same without you." Ha! Finally, she lifted Luca into her arms while Dally pouted.

"He is the most precious thing in the entire world." Rose held the tiny bundle against her chest and inhaled his sweetness.

"We sure think so." Eric eased an arm around Mags, pulling his wife to his side with an expression of pride and love so obvious it brought tears to Rose's eyes.

"Okay. My turn." Dally butted in and stole the baby from her arms. "I don't think Maya and Ollie were ever this small."

"What do you think about hanging the banner here?" Nolan called from a pair of trees by the pond.

Oops. She'd forgotten all about Nolan. "That looks great! Thanks."

Mags gave her a quizzical look. "And who might that be?" she whispered.

"Nolan." Thankfully he seemed too busy working to notice they were all staring at him. "He's staying here with the Cleary family and wanted to help us decorate."

Mags looked to Dally as though unsatisfied with Rose's answer.

"He seems to have a little crush on Rose." Dahlia had always been the informant. "But Rose is quite enamored with someone else at the moment."

"Who?" their sister demanded. "Darn it! I knew I was missing all the good stuff not being here."

Rose tried to glare at both of them to signal to keep it down but ended up smiling instead. Mags was here! "We have a lot to catch up on." She turned to Eric. "We're going to borrow your wife and son for a while. You can bring all your things to the second-floor bedroom in the main house."

"Will do." He planted a kiss first on his wife's lips, then on his son's forehead. "After I unload our year's worth of gear from the car, I can help Nolan finish up down there."

"Thank you," Rose called sweetly, already dragging her sisters away. On the way to her little camper home, Mags must've asked fifty questions, but she didn't answer any of them until they were seated at her small dinette.

"You've been hogging the baby," Rose informed Dally. "It's my turn."

"I'm going to have to set a timer for you girls." Mags's threat was a throwback to one of Lillian's favorites from their childhood.

"Fine." Dally kissed Luca's head and passed him across the table.

Rose snuggled him in her arms again. Oh, that baby smell. There was nothing better.

"So tell me…what's wrong with Nolan?" Mags resumed her interrogation.

"Nothing's wrong," Rose said in a baby voice. "Isn't that right, Luca? Do you recognize my voice from the video calls? I bet you do. Your Auntie Rose loves you soooo much."

The baby fluttered his eyes open but then closed them again.

"Rose has a thing for Colt," Dally announced in her authoritative way.

"*Colt?*" Mags's loud voice startled the baby. "As in Mr. Grumpy?"

"It's not my fault." Rose bounced Luca lightly until he drifted back to sleep. "You don't get to choose who you lo—" She stopped abruptly. That sneaky L word almost slipped out *again.*

"*Love?*" Mags pressed her hands into the table and leaned halfway across. "You're in *love* with Colt?"

"I don't know." But her heart had never hurt as much as it did when she thought about Colt leaving. She'd never felt more despair than when he'd left her standing outside the store. "It doesn't matter anyway. He's moving away from Juniper Springs. He sold the hardware store. And he told me he wanted to leave everything behind. That includes me." She snuggled the baby in closer. This. This little bundle of swaddled joy is what she wanted. Part her and part the person she loved most.

A hollowness seemed to surround her heart.

"I'm sorry, sis." Mags squeezed her arm. "I didn't know he was moving. Or that you cared about him so much. You haven't said anything."

"We've had a few other things going on." She readjusted Luca in her arms so she could get a better look at his face. She could stare at that miniature button nose all day.

"Yes, we've had a few other things going on," Dally added with a chuckle.

"How are things going with Lillian?" The skepticism in Mags's tone said she already knew.

"We told Sassy that Mom was in town and she desperately wants to see her." Dahlia held out her arms as though reminding Rose it was her turn to hold the baby.

"That was only five minutes," Rose whined.

Mags shook her head at them. "It's my turn anyway. He'll want to eat soon enough, and neither of you can help him with that."

"Okay." Rose sulked while she got up to pour them each a glass of the lavender honey sweet tea she kept stocked in the fridge.

"So you're still planning to bring Lillian to the party?" Mags unwrapped her son from the nest of blankets and kissed his chubby cheeks.

"It's now or never." She set the glasses of tea in front of her sisters and sat back down.

"I still can't believe Dad had an affair." Luca had started to fuss, so Mags unbuttoned her shirt and nestled him in, silencing his cries within seconds. "I mean, I know he worked a lot, but he was a good dad. He seemed like a good husband..."

"I don't think I've processed that information yet." Rose would likely need a few more months. After their mother told them about the affair, she and Dally had video called Mags, and they'd had a long talk. But Rose still couldn't see her father as someone who would betray his wife.

"Enough about the hard stuff." Dally seemed to dismiss the conversation with a wave of her hand. "How are you and Eric and Luca settling in?"

Mags's happy sigh spoke for her. "This whole last eight months has been wonderful and weird and miraculous and exhausting." She smoothed her hand over Luca's tuft of dark hair. "Eric and I have never been closer. Even with all the hormones and the mood swings and the sleepless nights. We have loved each other through it all."

A pang of longing seemed to resound in Rose's heart. Yes, yes, yes. She wanted to love someone through everything too. Good. Bad. Pain. Joy. That is what she wanted to build, no matter what it took. And there was only one man she wanted to build it with.

Mags talked more about the baby, telling them again about her seventeen hours of labor and what it was like to bring Luca home after all the many losses she and Eric had experienced over the years.

"Restoration." That was the word that kept coming to Rose's mind lately. She'd restored the inn. Mags and Eric had restored their hopes by bringing a baby home. Dally had restored her life after her ex-husband's betrayal. Sassy had found a restored purpose in her new role as the mayor.

"Yes." Mags nodded slowly, shifting Luca and buttoning her shirt back up. "It does feel like restoration. Things were really tough after the miscarriages, but they didn't stay that way, and now we appreciate every cry and cuddle and sigh from Luca even more."

"I hope we can help Mom and Sassy restore what they had once." Rose took her sisters' hands. "Because I could not live without you two."

"Same," Dally and Mags said in unison.

They talked a few more minutes about the impending

reunion between their aunt and mother, but when Rose glanced at her phone, she jumped up. "We still have so much to do, and Sassy will be here in less than an hour."

"No problem." Dally stood up.

"We've got this." Mags shuffled out of her seat with the baby, and Rose followed them toward the door. Before she could step out, Mags paused and held her back.

"If you do love Colt, you have to tell him, Rose. Love doesn't come easily or often." Her tone held the gravity of experience. Last winter, she and Eric had been on the verge of a divorce, but they'd found their way back to each other. "Sometimes you have to fight for love. Trust me. It's worth being vulnerable. It's worth risking potential heartbreak. If your feelings for him run that deep, he has a right to know. Even if he doesn't feel the same way. Even if he still chooses to go. He should know."

"He should." But she may have lost her chance to tell him.

Chapter Nineteen

Dahlia

I never thought I would call a grown man adorable, but look at Eric."

Dahlia paused from folding the glittery paper napkins Rose had chosen for the party and snapped a picture of her brother-in-law, who was setting up chairs with Luca wrapped in one of those swaddle things around his broad chest. Every once in a while, Eric would bow his head as though talking to his son.

"It melts my heart." Mags leaned in. "Along with other parts of my body." Her sister's eyebrows shot up. "There is nothing sexier than seeing Eric change a diaper. Oh! And sometimes he'll fall asleep with Luca on the couch, and it's the best thing I've ever seen, this big strong man holding a tiny baby." She scrolled through about fifty pictures, showing Dahlia every single one.

What would it be like to have a baby again? Her uterus cramped with longing just thinking about it. Nothing about childbirth or what came after was easy, but Maya and Ollie were the best things she'd ever spent her time and energy on.

They consumed her heart. "I do love a man who's good with kids," she admitted, and then instantly regretted the words when she saw the sparkle in her sister's eyes.

"Speaking of a man who's good with kids, how's Ike? You've hardly talked about him on the phone at all lately."

After escaping the camper conversation unscathed, Dahlia thought she would be able to avoid this conversation. Unfortunately, her sister continued to stare at her, waiting for an answer.

"He's fine. I'm pretty sure he's dating someone else." She did her best to say the words with an air of indifference, but her voice cracked on the last syllable.

"No." Her sister put away her phone and gave Dahlia her full attention. "No way is he dating someone else. I saw how he looked at you last Christmas."

Last Christmas felt like a hundred years ago. She decided to give Mags the short version. "I told him I couldn't be in a relationship right now. Maya is struggling too much with the thought of me dating again, and Ike hired this gorgeous new doctor as his partner anyway." That about summed up their current predicament.

"That doesn't mean he's attracted to her." Her sister went back to folding the napkins, her grin undeterred.

"I don't know who wouldn't be attracted to Dr. Jolly." Try as she might, Dahlia hadn't been able to find one flaw in the woman. "I've met her a few times. She's wonderful with the kids and seems like a kind person. And did I mention she's gorgeous?"

"So are you, you know." Mags hit her with a napkin. "I don't understand what's happening around here. I leave for eight months, and you kick Ike out of your life, and Rose falls in love with Colt." Her sister threw up her hands. "It's like you two are lost without me."

It was true...out of the three of them, Mags was the only one who currently had her life together. "You could always move here."

"No, I can't." Mags looked horrified. "Visiting is one thing, but being subjected to snow seven months out of the year?" Her sister shuddered. "No, thank you. Besides, I can't leave the beach."

"Maybe I should move to the beach." She wasn't sure how she was supposed to live in Juniper Springs and run into Ike and Dr. Jolly all the time.

"You can't give up on Ike." Mags folded the last napkin and put it in the basket. "And you said you loved it here."

"I do," she said, through a sigh. She would love it more if she could give in to her feelings.

"Ike! Thanks for coming!" Rose's happy greeting drew Dahlia's attention away from Mags. She frantically looked around until she spotted him walking toward the table.

Mags hummed happily. "Well, look who it is. I wonder why he's here."

"We invited him to the party," she whispered, smoothing down her hair before she had to turn around and face him.

"Was he supposed to be a half hour early?"

"Hush, you." She pointed at her sister sternly and went to meet Ike so he wouldn't get near Magnolia. She didn't need her sister offering either of them her two cents about their lack of a relationship.

Ike had come dressed for a party in casual dark jeans and a royal blue polo.

"Hey." It was incredibly difficult to sound casual when her heart got all wound up like this. "How are you?"

"I'm okay." He wasn't smiling. "I came early because I was hoping we would have a chance to talk before the party starts."

"Oh. Um." Dahlia stalled by looking at her phone. As selfish as it was, she didn't want to hear him say he was going to pursue a relationship with someone else, even though she'd basically told him that's what he should do. "I have to go pick up my mom and the kids soon…"

"This won't take long." Ike seemed to glance at Mags and Rose before he nodded toward a path that disappeared into the woods. "Can we go for a quick walk?"

"Sure." She purposely avoided looking at her sisters. "A walk would be nice." Or painful, depending on what he had to say.

The man gestured for her to go first, and suddenly she was hyperaware of every movement she made. Did her butt look good in these jeans?

"You and Rose have really made this place shine." When the path widened, he fell in stride next to her. "I can't believe the changes that have taken place in only a year."

He'd lived in one of the cabins last year while he was having a house built on the edge of town, and the place had basically been falling apart.

"It was mostly Rose," she admitted, continuing down the path. "I tried to help as much as I could but…I didn't anticipate how difficult things would be with the move."

Getting married right out of college, she'd never moved on her own. It was humbling to admit it, but Rose really stepped up and did the work. As much as she hated taking a backseat when it came to the work, she was proud of her sister too.

Ike stopped and faced her. "I feel like the upgrades reflect both of you. And Sassy too. It's a beautiful way to honor what she started here."

"I agree." Just when she thought maybe they could be friends, she looked into his eyes and felt the fireworks in her chest, the telltale weakness in her knees. It didn't matter what she said, she couldn't be trusted alone with this man. "I should probably get going…"

"I saw you in town yesterday," Ike interrupted before she could walk away.

"Oh?" She played dumb even though she knew what he was talking about. He must've seen her and Rose pull up in the car when he was standing in line with Dr. Jolly.

"You and Rose were parked in front of the coffee shop." His head tilted slightly as if he was trying to look past her façade. "I was in line for the Crazy Moose." He'd caught her looking at him, she could see it in his eyes.

"Right. That's right." She laughed a little but it came out awkwardly. "We were looking for our mother. She'd gotten upset and run off. We found her in Grumpy's kitchen, if you can believe that…" Why did she have to babble when she got nervous? "Anyway, did you have a nice lunch with Dr. Jolly?" Her shoulders braced for his answer, but hopefully he didn't notice.

Ike seemed to consider the question. "It was a good lunch."

"That's great! She seems amazing. The kids love her, I know that." She couldn't seem to stop the words from gushing out. "And she's so pretty too. Really lovely." And young and unburdened and free from the worry lines Dahlia had noticed taking root in her forehead the last few months.

"Sure. Dr. Jolly is great." She didn't miss how he hadn't called the woman by her first name. "Here's the thing though…She's not the one I think about when I wake up in the morning." His voice had dropped lower. He eased a step closer, still holding her gaze. "She's not the one I want to hold in my arms when I'm sitting on the couch watching a movie."

Dahlia couldn't seem to breathe or swallow. Unshed tears heated her eyes.

"She's not the last person I want to see before I fall asleep." Ike didn't touch her, but he didn't need to. She felt the sincerity of his words.

"She's not?" The hoarse whisper was barely audible to her but he seemed to hear.

"No." A smile spread across his face. "You're the one I want to be with. Only you. And the last thing I want to do is make you feel torn. But I also have to be honest. With you. With myself. And with Dr. Jolly."

"Honesty is good." She reached for his hand. She didn't have nearly as much willpower as he seemed to.

Ike weaved his fingers through hers. "I told Dr. Jolly I consider her a great friend while we were at lunch, but I also told her I'm not available. My heart is not available."

A couple of tears broke free, and she didn't try to wipe them away. "How come?"

His gaze gently chastised her. "You know why. I'm not in a hurry, Dally. I've waited thirty-four years to feel like this about someone, and I would wait thirty-four more." He ran his thumb over her knuckles and then let go of her hand. "It's okay if you're not ready, if your kids aren't ready. I'm fine. I wouldn't trade something real for something pretty or lovely, when I already see the most beautiful person in the world standing right in front of me."

Ike shoved his hands into his pockets. "That's all I wanted to say." He started to walk away, but Dahlia couldn't let him.

"I think about you first thing in the morning too." And she typically shed a few tears, knowing she couldn't do a damn thing with those thoughts. "And all I want right now—*all I want*—is for you to sit and hold me on the couch while we watch a movie." She had never experienced the feeling of full contentment like she did every time Ike had wrapped her in his arms.

"I'm in love with you. I have been since last Christmas." The words coaxed out more tears. "Sometimes those feelings makes me want to hide. Sometimes they make me want to sing in the shower." As with any kind of love there were moments of joy and moments of pain, fear and courage. "I *am* in a hurry, and yet I can't do anything but wait." Well, maybe there was a little something she could do. Only this once. Dahlia stood on her tiptoes and brushed her lips over his.

"What are you *doing*?"

It took a few seconds for her daughter's voice to register. "Maya?"

Dahlia looked to the left, her breathing still shallow.

Her daughter stood there glaring, hands on her hips. Lillian wasn't far behind.

"You said you weren't going to date anyone! And you were *kissing* him!" Maya took off running in the direction of the pond.

"I have to go after her," she called over her shoulder, already running away from the man minutes after she told him she loved him.

"Dear heavens, I'm sorry." Lillian hurried to keep up with Dahlia. "I didn't realize you would be with Ike out here. We didn't mean to interrupt anything."

Whether they'd meant to or not, they had. They had caught her in a moment of weakness that her daughter would likely make her regret. "What're you doing here?" she asked, moving quickly along the path.

"The kids wanted to play at the pond." Her mother's voice got short. "I asked Elroy to give us a ride over here. I had no idea there was a party. What's it for?"

"Oh. Well...uh. It's kind of a grand reopening thing." If she told her mother the whole truth before Sassy arrived, Lillian would leave. "We can talk about it later. Right now I have to go find Maya." She moved faster, leaving her mother behind, and broke free from the trees.

Her daughter had made it all the way to the banquet tables, and she was crying on Rose's shoulder.

Dahlia rushed over before everyone heard what had happened. "Honey..." She gently tugged her away from Rose. "Nothing has changed. I meant what I said to you. Ike and I aren't dating."

"Leave me alone." Her daughter turned away.

"Look at me, Maya." Dahlia had always been painfully honest with her kids. She'd always made it a point to apologize to them when she was wrong, and this moment wouldn't be any different. "I'm sorry. I'm so sorry that what you saw upset you. It shouldn't have happened. You have to understand that

I care about Ike very much. And he cares about me. But we have talked about it a lot, and we both want what's best for you and Ollie. That's the most important thing to us. So we're not dating. And you have my word that I will not kiss him again unless you feel ready to let him into our lives."

"You promise?" Maya's bottom lip trembled.

"I promise." She would give it time and find a way to be patient.

"Okay." Mistrust still lingered in her daughter's eyes, but at least she wasn't crying anymore.

"Come on, sweet girl," Lillian cooed, reaching for her granddaughter's hand. "I'll walk you up to the house, and we can get you cleaned up before the mystery party."

Dahlia almost followed them, but she still had to help Rose finish up the decorations.

Before she could do anything, Ike walked out of the woods and approached her. "I'm so sorry. I never intended—" He stopped and shook his head. "Maybe I should go."

"No. Don't leave." That wasn't fair to him. "Maya will be fine. And Sassy will want you here. You're her friend and you should be able to celebrate with us."

She would simply have to keep her distance.

No matter how much she felt for Ike, she wouldn't break her promise to Maya.

Chapter Twenty

Rose

R ose watched Lillian lead Maya up the hill.

Wasn't this peachy? Her mother had shown up early and unannounced—two things a Southern woman never did. Now Rose wouldn't be able to control the situation when Sassy arrived in forty minutes, give or take. Maybe she should text Colt to ask him to meet her at the barn. Or maybe she should hide her mother somewhere for a while...

"What do you think happened with Dally, Ike, and Maya?" Mags rushed over from the makeshift bar they'd made out of wooden pallets. There was plenty of wine and beer, but Mags's drink smelled like a ginger ale, complete with a pink umbrella sticking out of a lime on the rim of the glass.

"My guess is Maya interrupted something." At least based on what she'd caught between her niece's sobs. Ike and Dahlia were still talking at the edge of the trees, and neither of them was smiling. "I doubt it was anything more than a kiss though, since Dally is determined to honor her daughter's wishes that she doesn't date."

She could see how much Dahlia loved the man, and how

much he loved her sister back. It had to be torture for them to see each other all the time while ignoring the chemistry between them. "Maya tends to have a dramatic streak."

"Kind of like someone else I know." Mags winked at her.

Yes, there might be a slight resemblance between her and her favorite niece. "She's got moxie. Nothing wrong with that." Maya would learn how to harness her emotions just like Rose had. For the most part.

"Think Dahlia will ever be allowed to date?" Mags set her drink on the table and seemed to do a visual check on Eric and Luca, who were hanging out with Ollie near the pond.

"Give it six months." Rose spread out the yellow and coral-colored rose petals she'd scattered across the white tablecloth earlier. "By then, Maya will have a ton of friends. She'll be in school. I think in time she'll feel a lot more secure." Rose would help her in any way she could.

"Auntie Rose," Ollie called. "Can we go swimming?" He pointed to a few of his new best friends—kids from the Cleary family. Everyone had started to gather in the area, anticipating the moment Sassy arrived. Rose looked at her watch again. Which should happen in just thirty-four minutes.

"I already put my swimsuit on," the boy informed her showing off his Star Wars swimming trunks.

She smiled, remembering how much she'd loved to swim in the pond. "Sure, honey. But you know the rules. An adult has to be out in the canoe with you so we can make sure everyone stays safe."

"I would love to chaperone the swimming, but I have to feed the baby in a few." Mags drifted in the direction of her husband.

With Dally otherwise occupied and the Cleary adults all enjoying themselves around the bar, she was about the only option left.

"Pleeeaaase, Auntie Rose?" her nephew begged. "I love you! You're the best aunt in the whole world!"

"Never forget that, kiddo." Rose glanced at her watch again. She had roughly half an hour. Lillian hadn't come back down from the house. Maybe she and Maya would hang out up there for a while, and Rose wouldn't have to worry about a confrontation between the sisters until she could get Ollie out of the pond.

"Fine." Cue the dramatic sigh. "I'll go out in the canoe to watch you swim. But only for twenty minutes, then you all need to get out and dry off so we can get ready to surprise Sassy. Capisce?"

"Yes, ma'am!" Ollie kicked off his flip-flops and started to wade into the water.

"I'll go out with you." Nolan seemed to appear out of nowhere. Last she'd seen him, he'd been taking pictures of the picture boards. "This might be a good time for you to teach me how to paddle."

"It's really easy." Rose couldn't help a smile. "I'm sure you could figure it out all on your own."

"I probably could, but it wouldn't be as fun." She wished that glimmer in his eye would do something for her. Anything. He had nice eyes. But she didn't see into them the way she saw into Colt's.

"All right. We'd better get out there then." She knelt to unbuckle her wedge sandals.

Nolan kicked off his shoes too, and together they slid the boat into the water. "Climb in nice and easy," Rose instructed.

She remembered all too well how quickly this old canoe could tip. She stepped into the boat and wobbled to the seat at the back, while Nolan took the one in the front.

Eight kids—including Ollie—were already splashing in the water, safely secured in their life vests.

Rose picked up her paddle and maneuvered the boat to avoid getting drenched. "So I'll paddle on the left side if you paddle on the right."

"Sounds like a plan." The man dipped his paddle into the water like an expert.

"You're a natural," Rose told him.

"So I am." Nolan laughed. "You're right. It's pretty easy." He glanced over his shoulder at her. "Maybe I just wanted to spend some time with you. I enjoyed our photo shoot yesterday."

"Oh. Uh-huh. I enjoyed it too." But not exactly in the same way he seemed to. Rose could feel her smile fading. This was the conversation she should've had with him earlier. "Nolan—"

"Auntie Rose! Watch this!" Ollie doggie paddled up next to the boat. "I've been taking swimming lessons, and I'm getting really good!"

"You certainly are." She splashed him with the paddle, making him giggle.

"Better watch out I'll get you back," the boy threatened, sending a spray of water in her direction. "Ahh!" she squealed. Mountain water was so much colder than she remembered.

"You seem to have a great relationship with your sister's kids." Nolan snapped a few pictures of Ollie.

"I do. I'm so thankful they moved here." Rose paddled the

canoe along, following Ollie to the middle of the pond. "It was harder to stay close when we all lived so far away from each other." Really, Sassy had brought her and Mags and Dahlia back together. And now they made sure to talk as much as possible, and she would get to be part of Maya's and Ollie's growing up. She couldn't imagine anything better.

"I love living close to my family too, being part of everyone's life." Nolan secured the camera strap back around his neck.

"It must be fun to have such a big family."

"It is," Nolan agreed. "Though I'd still like to have my own family someday too." He hadn't said the words with any undertones of an innuendo, but they still made Rose squirm. She'd already learned that superficial attraction wasn't enough. Gregory had been charming and handsome and thoughtful. But after she broke off the engagement, Rose had realized she'd never felt that deeper stirring for him. That intensity. She hadn't known what she was supposed to feel until Colt had rescued her on the roof. Now that she knew, she couldn't settle for anything less, even if Colt was moving. "Nolan—"

"Surprise, Sassy!"

Whaaaa? Rose turned her head toward the sudden chorus of *happy birthday*s coming from the Cleary family.

Her aunt was walking down the hill!

"Wow!" Sassy hurried the rest of the way to the table. "A party for me? I can't believe this!"

"Oh no!" This wasn't how the surprise was supposed to go. Rose furiously started to paddle. She hadn't even heard Colt's truck. The kids had been too loud. "Don't be early! I specifically told him not to be early!" In her haste to get them back to shore, she lost her grip on the paddle and the thing sank beneath the water's surface. "Shoot!"

Sassy and Colt had arrived at the table, where Dahlia was giving her aunt a great big hug.

"I can paddle us back," Nolan offered calmly.

Rose nodded, but she was too busy looking at Colt to respond. Colt, who was staring at her and Nolan in the canoe together. Colt, who made her pulse race and her body ache with longing. Colt, who was now walking away, retreating back up the hill. Leaving like he had when he saw her with Nolan the other day.

"Wait!" Rose scrambled to her feet, the canoe rocking beneath her. She couldn't let him go. She couldn't let him think there was anything going on between her and Nolan.

"Whoa." Nolan stopped paddling. "Easy. I've got my camera with me."

"I'm sorry." But she couldn't make herself sit down. Colt was still moving. He hadn't even turned around. "Colt!"

Now everyone had gone silent and they were all staring at her—the Clearys, Dahlia and Ike, Mags and Eric. She didn't care. Dahlia had been right. Colt had a right to know how she felt about him. Rose couldn't bear to let him walk away upset.

"I don't want to paddle until you sit down," Nolan said slowly, as though suddenly concerned about her.

Damn it, Colt was still walking up that hill. "Paddle," she instructed Nolan. "Hurry. Please."

The man mumbled something inaudible and dipped the paddle into the water again. The sudden movement knocked her off balance. Rose scrambled to find her footing, but pitched to the left and couldn't steady herself before she toppled into the pond.

"Auntie Rose! I'll save you!" Ollie swam to her, but she managed to get her feet underneath her, able to stand on her very tiptoes and keep her head above the surface. Cold! So freaking cold!

"Rose!" Sassy cried. "Dear God! Are you all right?"

Finally—*finally*—Colt seemed to notice the commotion. He turned around and immediately started to jog back to the pond.

She flailed and moved, half running in slow motion and half swimming until she dashed out of the water and met him, soggy and gasping.

"What happened?" The man hastily looked her over. "Are you okay?"

Everyone standing around the table and the bar seemed to wait for an answer. They were all staring at her—Sassy and her sisters and the Clearys and the kids who'd been swimming…

"No." Her lungs seized with lack of oxygen and emotion. "I'm not okay. I know how it looks with Nolan and I out in the canoe together. I know how it looked the other day when we were doing the photo shoot." She tried to slow down the words, to speak clearly, but her chattering teeth made that difficult. "You're the one I can't stop thinking about though. You're the one who makes my heart beat faster. You're the one I'm falling in love with. So don't leave the party. Please."

Colt's eyes were as wide as a deer's that had run in front of a car. "I … *wasn't* going to leave. I was going to get Sassy's present out of my truck."

"Oh." The burn of humiliation took care of the chill in her body. "Right." Rose backed up a step, feeling the weight of every stare aimed in her direction. It seemed she'd gotten a little carried away, as per usual. "Well, good then. Whew. That's a relief." She laughed awkwardly, unable to control the sounds coming out of her mouth. "You know, I should go change." Her bare feet moved clumsily over the ground. She had to get up to the house so she could hide in the closet where she kept her vast wardrobe. No one would ever find her there.

"Rose," Colt called behind her.

"I'll be back in a few!" She couldn't stop, couldn't turn around. There were too many eyes focused on her. "I'm pretty wet! And cold!" And mortified. Nope, that didn't quite cover it. Disgraced. Yes, disgraced and insane. What had she been thinking, practically leaping out of a canoe to ruin Sassy's party by making a scene in front of everyone?

Footsteps scuffled behind her, but they only drove her to move faster. Get away. She had to get away.

"Will you wait up?" Mags wheezed behind her. "I'm not used to the altitude and I just gave birth."

"I have no excuse." Dahlia panted as she fell in step with her. "Other than I'm out of shape and have a serious chocolate addiction."

Rose couldn't even muster a smile to indulge her sisters' attempts to pretend nothing had happened back there.

"Come on, Rosie." Mags tugged on her arm until she slowed her footsteps. "Are you okay?"

"I'm great! Fantastic!" There went the maniacal laugh again. "I just made a complete fool out of myself by professing my undying love for a man who doesn't love me back in front of at least forty people. I have never been better!"

Dally snuck in front of her. "You don't know he doesn't love you back."

"Yeah," Mags added. "You didn't even give him a chance to talk after professing your undying love."

Rose sidestepped her sisters and stomped up the porch steps. "He could've followed me. He could've chased me down the way I chased him down—nearly drowning myself in the process, thank you very much—but he didn't. I think it's pretty clear how he feels."

Everyone had seen how Colt felt.

"You basically told him not to follow you," Dally pointed out, ever and always the voice of logic. "I'm sure he would've followed you if we hadn't."

She appreciated them trying to encourage her, but the fact remained that she was up here and Colt was down there. "It's fine." This wasn't the first time she'd been humiliated, and with the way her passion tended to take over, it likely wouldn't be the last either. "I don't want this to ruin Sassy's party." They had to get this shindig back on track right now. "I'm going to change. And then we need to find Mom so we can give those two a little privacy when they're reunited."

Yes, they had to make a plan and stick to the plan. No running on emotion anymore today. "I'm not sure this party could handle another scene."

"It wasn't *that* big of a scene." Dally peeked through the living room window. "Mom and Maya are inside. It looks like they're reading a book."

"Perfect." Rose opened the screen door. "You two go back down the hill and get Sassy. Tell her we need her up here for a few minutes." She stepped inside the house. "I'll get changed and start to prep Mom for what's coming."

That ought to be enough to get her mind off Colt.

Chapter Twenty-One

Sassy

I f there was one thing Sassy had learned how to do it was to make sure the show went on.

Years ago, they'd hosted weddings and receptions at the inn, and glitches never failed to come up—an impromptu mountain storm in the middle of a wedding ceremony, a swarm of mosquitos during an outdoor cake cutting.

In all those years at all those events, she'd never dealt with quite the amount of awkwardness dear Rose had left in her wake. She'd desperately wanted to follow her poor sweet niece up the hill to console her, but with Dally and Mags both gone, someone had to get this party back on track. Starting with some music.

"Colt?" She waited for him to come out of his fog. He clearly had no idea what to do in this current situation, so he needed a job. "Why don't you connect to the Bluetooth speaker at the bar and play some good music?"

Nothing broke the ice like Dolly singing about islands in the stream.

"Right. Music." Colt still hadn't seemed to come back fully, but she would have to deal with him in a few minutes. Right now she was going to get Mr. and Mrs. Cleary a drink.

Thankfully Eric had positioned himself behind the bar, which gave her the perfect excuse to steal her great-nephew. "It's so good to see you two offscreen." She held out her arms and accepted the baby, cuddling him in her arms.

"Good to see you too. We wouldn't have missed your party for anything." Eric slung a towel over his shoulder. "What can I get you?"

"Two glasses of chardonnay and one cab, please." She waved Mr. and Mrs. Cleary over. The talking had picked up again, but there were still some hushed conversations going on. Lord only knew what people thought of Rose's theatrics. Though she had to admit…she was proud of her niece. It took more courage than most people had to stand up and reveal your heart in front of everyone. If her complete vulnerability hadn't convinced Colt that her feelings for him were real, nothing would.

"Meet my new great-nephew." She presented the baby to her old friends, and Luca worked his magic right away.

"He's darling!" Mrs. Cleary cooed at Luca. "Oh my goodness. Look at those bright eyes!"

"Quite the handsome fella," Mr. Cleary added.

"He takes after his father." Eric handed a chardonnay to Mrs. Cleary and Sassy and the cab to Mr. Cleary.

"Meet Magnolia's wonderful husband." Sassy readjusted little Luca so that his miniature chin rested on her shoulder. In her estimation, babies liked to see what was going on in the world.

"Little Magnolia." Mrs. Cleary shook her head. "I can

hardly believe all the kids are grown up and having babies of their own." The woman glanced at Nolan, who was still near the shoreline of the pond playing with the kids. "Nolan had so hoped things would work out with Beth."

"I was sorry to hear about his divorce." She felt for the man—especially because he did seem to be harboring a crush on Rose, but her niece had already given her heart away to someone else. "He won't have a problem finding a wonderful woman. With his success and kind heart? When the right one comes along he'll know."

"I suppose you're right." The woman leaned closer. "But I do have to admit, I love Rose. She obviously cares for Colt very much."

"Yes, she does. Though she hadn't been willing to admit it to herself or anyone else until today." Sassy could see the shock still on Colt's face. The man had started talking to Ike, but he only seemed to be half listening to what the doctor was saying. "One's heart can only contain love so long before it has to burst out." She'd experienced that phenomenon recently herself.

"Eric…" Sassy turned back to the bar. "Why don't you tell Mr. and Mrs. Cleary about your home in Florida. They own a condo not too far away, I think."

"Oh, you live in Florida?" Mr. Cleary moved right on to talking about golf, and Sassy snuck away from the conversation, still hogging Luca.

"Happy birthday, Sassy." Ike greeted her with a hug and kiss on the cheek. "This is quite the party."

"Maybe I should go talk to her?" Colt ran his hand through his hair, leaving the top in a tufted mess. He looked at Ike. "Is that what you would do?"

The doctor shook his head. "I don't know, man. I'm not any better off than you at the moment. You both missed quite the scene earlier when Maya caught Dally and me...uh...*talking* alone in the woods. She was pretty upset."

Talking. Right. "Maya will be fine," Sassy told Ike firmly. "And Rose..." She peered up at Colt. "Rose let her heart guide her when she fell out of that boat and came after you. I suggest you do the same, my dear. Before it's too late." That was the only advice she could offer him. "Your heart will know what to do."

"Sassy..." Graham waved from the path near the parking lot.

Speaking of acting on the heart...She held the baby out to Colt. "Hold little Luca for me, will you?" She passed the baby off and floated to meet the man of her dreams. Not caring who saw, Sassy walked into his arms.

He held her for a few seconds before stepping back so he could get a good look at her. "I didn't think you'd be here yet."

"We arrived early." But not a moment too soon. If Rose had been prepared for them, she likely never would've told Colt the truth about her feelings, and then where would they be? "But it's already been quite the party."

The man's expression fell. "I can't believe I missed your grand entrance. I was working on the planter boxes for the garden and lost track of time." He reached out for her hands. "I wanted to be here when you arrived so I could be the first to wish you the happiest of birthdays."

"You're here now. That's what matters." He was here, and Rose loved Colt, and Dally and Ike had shared a kiss. All at her big surprise birthday celebration. This day couldn't get any more perfect. "I can't wait to introduce you to everyone. There are so many people for you to meet." She wrapped her arm through his and led him in the direction of the bar so she could show him off to the Clearys.

"Um, Aunt Sassy?" Dally called from somewhere behind her.

"We're sorry, but we need to borrow you up at the house for a few minutes," Mags added.

An aunt's work was never done, it seemed. And, oh how she loved this. Loved being needed. The years before her girls had come back to her were too quiet and too lonely. Now that Mags and Dally and Rose were all back, she would drop anything and everything when they called on her.

She faced Graham, ready to apologize, but knew at once he wanted her to go be with her nieces. "I'm happy to introduce myself to everyone." Confidence shone through his smile.

She'd like to think she had something to do with drawing him out of his shell the way he'd drawn her out of her loneliness, but perhaps he'd always been friendlier than she'd given him credit for.

"I'll be right back," she promised already following her nieces up the hill.

"I'll be waiting for you."

She had come to love the sound of Graham's voice, that comforting low baritone. And those words... *I'll be waiting for you.* No one had ever been waiting for her. It had always been her waiting on those she loved.

"We're really sorry to pull you away from the party." Mags fell in step with her. "But you should probably know what you're walking into."

Dally moved to her other side. "Mom is up at the house."

Sassy ground to a halt. "Lillian is here?" Hope swelled beneath her ribs. "For the party?"

The two sisters shared a long look that told her what she needed to know. Lillian hadn't come to celebrate her.

"She doesn't know you're here," Dally admitted.

"But Rose is telling her now, so hopefully by the time we get up there…" Mags let her sentence trail off.

Hopefully what? There would be a lightning strike and Lillian wouldn't walk out on her the second she saw her? Sassy found it hard to move. Because once she reached the house and saw the sister she still loved every bit as much as she had when they had been girls playing dress-up, she would have to watch Lillian walk away again, and she didn't know if she could bear it.

"She can't get far." Dally had always had such intuition in knowing what people were thinking. "Even if she tries to walk away. It's not like she has a car."

Yes, Lillian might be forced to stay, but that wasn't how Sassy wanted things. "If she wants to leave when she sees me, one of you girls needs to drive her back to your place." She gently squeezed Dally's arm. "I don't want to keep her here against her will. I have been waiting to see her for a long time, and when I do, I will say my piece." This might be the last opportunity she had to tell her sister how much she loved her. Those doctor appointments on Monday were looming ever closer. "But if Lillian wants to leave, I will let her go." The same way she had years ago.

"Oh, Sassy." Mags hugged her tight. "I just have this feeling everything will work out this time. I don't know why, but I believe it."

"Then I will believe it too." Standing side by side with her nieces gave her the courage to move again, to face the possibility of a crushing disappointment. "At least I have you three." She would hold on to her girls, no matter what happened with Lillian.

They remained silent for the rest of the walk up to the house. Sweet Mags and Dally seemed almost as nervous as she was. When she started up the steps to the porch, a wave of dizziness seemed to crash over her from nowhere, but she couldn't tell if it was the anxiety mounting inside of her or another headache on the horizon.

Not now. She didn't have time to deal with a headache. She had to be fully present for this. What if she never saw her sister again?

"Here we go." Dally opened the door and gestured for Sassy to go first. She teetered her way into the house, pressing her hand against the wall as she walked down the hall and into the living room.

Lillian sat on the couch with Maya. Rose was standing in front of her mother, arms crossed, face red.

A hundred tears seemed to gather in her eyes all at once, nearly blocking her vision. She had waited years to be in the same room as Lillian, and she didn't care if her sister was happy about this meeting or not, she intended to make the most of it.

"My God, Lil. You're still every bit as beautiful as you were in your thirties."

Lillian merely stared at her, her face an expressionless mask.

"Maya, honey, why don't you run back down to the pond and play with Ollie and the other kids?" Dally coaxed gently. "Uncle Eric is down there. We'll be right behind you."

"Okay." Maya scooted off the couch, her eyes wide, as though she felt the gravity of this situation. "Happy birthday, Auntie Sassy." The girl gave her a hug on her way out of the room, and Sassy savored the show of affection. Would she find the same warmth from her sister?

"I don't want to talk to you." Lillian spoke first after the front door had opened and closed. "I didn't even know you were in town." She stared at the wall, so Sassy moved right in front of her.

"You don't have to talk. You don't even have to look at me." All she needed was for Lillian to hear her. "But I will ask you to listen."

Mags and Rose and Dally drifted to the outskirts of the living room but didn't leave them alone, which was just as well. They should be a part of this conversation.

"I'm turning seventy today, Lil." That was the first time she'd said her new age out loud, and it sounded strange and formidable. Seventy. So close to eighty. Nearing the end of her life. But in so many ways, her life was really just beginning. With Graham. With her beautiful nieces and great-niece and great-nephews. Maybe with her sister too. "I am so sorry I hurt you all those years ago." She paused to let the words have the space they deserved. "But I wasn't choosing Robert over you. Regardless of what you might think, I have always loved you, and I considered you my very best friend."

Those years seemed to come rushing back through her— the memories of her and Lillian lying out by the pond in the summer and singing Christmas carols around the tree with the girls when they would come to visit in the winter.

"I thought you were my friend too." The coolness in her

sister's voice seemed to match the ice in her eyes. "But you weren't there for me when I needed you the most. And I can't forget that."

"I'm not asking you to forget it. I'm telling you I'm sorry. Choosing between you and Robert seemed impossible. So I didn't ask him to leave. I couldn't." She hadn't wanted to lose either one of them, but she had no doubt Lillian had been in pain after learning her husband had cheated on her. "I understand why you felt I abandoned you, but I am asking you to move past it. Finally. After all these years. We could be a family. All of us. Together." It didn't matter if Sassy had two years left or twenty-five, she wanted the rest of her life to be about love and family. "I love you so much, Lil. If you could only forgive me—"

"Forgive you?" Lillian rose from the couch. "What was it about Robert that made you choose him?" Her hip kicked out the same way it had when she had been a feisty teenager. "Was it his felony record? His lack of a job? I was your *sister*." The first trace of emotion wavered through her words. "I had always been there for you, Sassy. I brought my girls out to visit you and gave you a family. And then you turned your back on us."

"Mom!" Rose marched into the fray. "Enough. That all happened years ago. The only thing that matters now is the future. It's past time for you to stop being so bitter and cruel."

Lillian seemed to wilt right in front of them, and Rose squeezed her eyes shut. "I'm sorry. I didn't mean—"

"I'm going for a walk." She stalked out of the room, and Sassy didn't try to follow her. That would only chase her farther away.

Dahlia was the first one to move, following in her mother's

footsteps, but Rose held her sister back. "I'll go after her. That was my fault." She turned to Sassy. "I'm sorry. I lost my temper and ran her off. But I will bring her back to the party. I promise I'll find a way."

"I said what I needed to say." And she had no regrets. Not anymore. She'd voiced her apology. She'd told Lillian she loved her. There wasn't anything else to be done.

Sassy comforted her niece with a loving squeeze of her hand. "Now the rest is up to her."

Rose nodded, but the slump in her shoulders hinted at her pessimism. She hurried from the room and disappeared out the door.

"Why don't we go back to the party?" Mags suggested. "I'm dying to meet this Graham fellow. He sure sounds like a charmer from what Dally and Rose said."

"Oh, he is, though." Sassy followed her nieces outside, giving her temples a quick squeeze while they weren't looking at her. The headache was coming—starting in the shadows, but it wouldn't be long before it gained momentum. Maybe not until after the party though. Then she could lie down...

"Rose and Dally said you and Graham bonded over roses?" Mags asked.

On the way down the hill, Sassy told them about how she'd walked into that garden prepared to negotiate with a miser, and she'd walked out with a growing affection for the man. "And it seems to grow every time I'm with him," she finished, watching Graham chat with Mr. and Mrs. Cleary as though he'd known them forever.

"We're thrilled for you." Dally punctuated the words with a happy sigh.

"I'm thrilled for me too." Sassy brought them to Graham and made the necessary introductions.

Mrs. Cleary's wink told her that her old friend approved.

Just as she and Graham were walking to the bar to get a drink, Maya and Ollie came running out of the woods. "Auntie Sassy! Auntie Sassy! We made you a present! You have to come see!"

She gave Graham an apologetic look, but he simply smiled and waved her away. "I'll get our drinks and see you in a few."

"I can't wait." She took Ollie's and Maya's hands and let them lead her toward their surprise.

It seemed a great-aunt's work was never done either. But it didn't matter how many times she walked away, she knew Graham would be there waiting on her when she came back.

Chapter Twenty-Two

Dahlia

Y ou look like you could use a drink." Colt handed Dahlia a glass of chardonnay over the bar.

It seemed he'd taken over as bartender while Eric and Mags were busy changing a diaper.

"I could say the same about you." She gladly accepted the wine and leaned in. "Are you doing okay?" On a normal day, Colt didn't seem to enjoy being the center of anyone's attention—especially people he didn't know all that well. Though everyone seemed to have forgotten what had transpired earlier. The party was in full swing. A few more people from town had shown up, and the Cleary family seemed to have started up a lively conversation with Ike.

"I'm . . . fine." The man's long pause wasn't all that convincing. "Is Rose still around?" He almost seemed to wince as he said the words.

"She's around here somewhere." Dahlia had been scanning the property on and off since she and Mags and Sassy had come down here twenty minutes ago. "She's off talking with our mother somewhere." Hopefully they would both be in one piece. She was still kicking herself for not insisting that she go after Lillian with Rose. Her sister likely could've used the backup.

"Why? Did you want to talk to her about something?" She didn't mean to tease Colt, but she was dying to know what he was thinking. She'd never been able to read the man. Was he in love with Rose too?

"Yeah." His half smile told her nothing. "I suppose we have some things to talk about, she and I." *And not you*, his expression seemed to add.

But she was Rose's sister. She couldn't help but meddle some. "That was sure something how she jumped out of the canoe for you, huh?" She propped her chin on her fist. "I mean, she really put herself out there."

"Yup." Colt gazed at the pond. He had one of the best poker faces she'd ever seen.

"You know, if you need help figuring out what to say to her when she comes back, I'm really good at talking through things." She sipped her wine. "Nobody knows Rose better than me."

"I don't need help, but thanks." The man pulled a bottle of beer out of the ice trough and handed it to Nolan a few feet away.

Poor Nolan. Since she obviously wasn't going to get anything out of Colt, she moved on to the Clearys' grandson. "Great party, huh?" she asked casually.

The man gave her a deadpan look. "Don't worry about me. I'm good. I already knew Rose wasn't into me."

"You did?" She set down her glass.

"Sure. I could tell. She liked me, but she also friendzoned

me the first few minutes we met." He glanced at Colt with a grin. "I figured there had to be a reason, and I was right."

"I know she thinks you're a great guy." But as Rose had said before, she didn't get to choose who captured her heart.

"She's pretty great too." He grinned. "Impulsive, but pretty great."

Dahlia had to laugh.

"Uncle Nolan! Come take my picture." One of his nieces called him away.

"Duty calls," he said, adjusting his camera before hurrying to the pond.

With no one else to talk to, Dahlia's gaze wandered to Ike again. Now he was holding little Luca against his chest while he talked to Eric and Mags. Just when she thought her heart couldn't hold any more love for him...

"He looks like a natural." Colt leaned into the bar next to her. "I'm pretty good at figuring out what to say too. If you need advice."

Dahlia sent him a sideways glance. "Any advice on how to get a tween girl to be fine with her mother dating someone? Because that's all I need help with at the moment."

"Not a clue." Colt pulled out a beer and popped the top before taking a sip. "According to Sassy if you give things time, they tend to work out."

She couldn't resist the opening. "But you don't want to take too much time." She raised her eyebrows so he wouldn't miss her meaning. "You especially don't want to wait too long before discussing your real feelings for someone." Hint, hint. Rose was already sure Colt didn't care for her the way she cared for him. He needed to change her mind fast.

"Don't worry." Colt walked around the bar and stood by her. "I won't wait too long. If you see Rose, tell her I'm looking for her."

She was about to ask what he planned to say, but the man seemed too wise to continue standing by her any longer. He walked to a nearby table and started to collect empty glasses.

Dahlia checked her watch and again scanned the area for Rose and her mother, but there was still no sign of them.

"Everything okay?" Ike wandered near the bar.

"I don't know yet." She told him about the confrontation between Lillian and Sassy. "I'm about ready to send out a search party." She couldn't imagine why they'd been gone so long.

"Maybe they're just somewhere talking." Ike somehow always managed to put her at ease.

"I hope so." She peeked up at him, her cheeks getting all warm and tingly like they had when she'd kissed him. "I think Maya is okay, by the way. At least, she seemed to bounce back when she came down here to play." Her daughter had sure been excited about whatever it was she and Ollie had wanted to show Sassy.

"I'm sorry she saw us though." He blew out a sigh. "It's my fault. I should've waited to talk to you until we were really alone."

"No." Dahlia almost reached for his hand, but then thought better of it. "I'm glad we got to talk. And…" She smiled a little. "And, well, I'm glad we got to kiss too. I've really missed that." Really, really, really missed it. She'd forgotten how wonderful it felt to have Ike touch his lips to hers.

"I've missed it too." A gravelly quality lowered his voice.

"I hate that we can't kiss more right now." Sheesh. Just *talking* about kissing him made her breathless.

"Me too." Ike never seemed to look away from her when they were talking. "But let's look at it this way. Waiting a little longer will build more anticipation."

"I already have quite a bit of anticipation." Just ask her heart. It seemed to find a different rhythm when Ike came close. "Every minute will be—"

"Ike! Dr. Ike!" Maya's terrified scream pierced the party's cheerful volume. Her daughter came sprinting out of the woods, and Dahlia's heart dropped.

Everyone went silent, gathering around the bar with looks of concern.

Ike ran to meet Maya. He took a knee in front of her. "What is it? What's wrong?"

"It's...Auntie Sassy..." Her daughter wheezed as though she couldn't catch her breath.

"Where is she?" Ike was back on his feet, already running to the woods.

Dahlia started to clumsily jog, catching up to her daughter.

"She's...she fell." Maya started to cry. "She fell and now she won't open her eyes!"

"Where?" Ike had stopped to wait for them by the trees, and now Colt and Graham had joined them too.

Dahlia took Maya's hand. "Can you show us?"

"I think so." Her daughter started to run again.

"Call nine-one-one," Ike instructed Colt. "Tell them we need an ambulance here now."

Colt was on the phone talking before Ike even finished the sentence.

God. Dear God. Tears blinded Dahlia's eyes too. Not Sassy. They couldn't lose Sassy. She tried to find strength, but nothing could've prepared her for what she saw when Maya stopped running and pointed.

Her beloved aunt lay sprawled on her side in the tall grasses, her eyes closed, her body still.

Ollie was crying over her while some of the Cleary children stood back, looking stricken.

"Sassy?" Ike knelt and immediately grabbed her aunt's wrist, his fingers checking for a pulse.

Dahlia forced herself to keep looking in his eyes. He gave a slight nod as though trying to put her at ease. Her aunt's heart was still beating. She was alive.

Moving in closer, Dahlia pulled Ollie into her arms, holding him tight while he cried on her shoulder.

"Sassy? Wake up. We need you to wake up." The doctor seemed to do a visual inspection of her body and then shifted, placing both hands on either side of her head. He looked at Colt. "Help me roll her gently onto her back."

Together, the two men carefully moved Sassy, and Ike leaned over her. He was listening for breath.

Please. Please. Dahlia's hands pulled into fists.

He nodded at her again, and the relief nearly forced her to her knees.

"What's wrong with her?" Maya wailed, throwing herself down next to Sassy. "Is she dead?"

She was about to pull her daughter away, but Ike turned fully to Maya. "She's okay," he murmured in a soothing tone. "Thanks to you, we can help her." He reached his hand to Maya's face and wiped away some of her daughter's tears.

"We will help her. I promise. You did good, honey. You did real good."

Her daughter nodded, her lips still trembling.

"Hold on." Colt smoothed Sassy's beautiful red hair away from her face. "The ambulance said they were only ten minutes out. We're getting you help. You have to hold on."

The terror in his normally strong voice nearly tore Dahlia's heart in two.

"What does she need?" Graham approached them at a jog. "What can I do?"

Ike was holding Sassy's wrist again. "Just let her know you're here." He gestured to Sassy's other side, and Graham sat beside her, taking her free hand in his.

"Her pulse is stable, so that's good news." Ike took his time examining Sassy's head. "I don't see any obvious wounds."

"Right before she fell, she said she had to sit down," Maya told them, whimpering. "She said she was dizzy and she needed to rest." The tears started to fall again. "We shouldn't have made her walk out here with us…"

"It's not your fault." Ike lifted Maya's chin. "This is not your fault. Okay? You were brave. You did everything right."

Still holding on to Ollie, Dahlia lowered herself next to Maya and held both of her children. "It'll be okay," she murmured over and over.

"Sassy." Ike spoke authoritatively. "Open your eyes. We're all here. We want to see you open your eyes."

Her aunt groaned in response.

"That's it." Ike checked her pulse again. "Wake up, Sassy. Come back to us."

Dahlia studied her aunt's face. She swore her aunt's eyelids fluttered. "Aunt Sassy? Where do you hurt? What do you need?" There had to be something they could do for her...

"Graham?" Her aunt opened her eyes. "Oh, Graham."

"What is it?" The older man stroked Sassy's face with tenderness. "What do you need, sweetheart?"

"I'm sorry." Her eyes closed again, and it was all Dahlia could do to not shake her back awake. Thankfully Ollie was still hugging her as though he was afraid to look at anything else, so she clung to him too.

"There's nothing to be sorry for," the man insisted. "You rest. We have help coming. Everything will be—"

"Headaches," her aunt interrupted. "I've had terrible headaches."

"For how long?" Ike's expression noticeably tensed.

"Over a month." Sassy's eyes filled with tears. "Sometimes dizzy too. I..." She cleared her throat. "I have some appointments in Denver on Monday..."

She'd been having headaches for over a month and hadn't said anything? Dahlia rested a hand on her aunt's shoulder but kept the questions to herself. All that mattered now was that Sassy got the help she needed before it was too late.

"Do you remember what happened?" Ike seemed to be taking mental notes.

Her aunt smiled weakly. "The children made a heart out of flowers. And I loved it." Her eyes found Maya's, and Dahlia's daughter planted a light kiss on her great-aunt's cheek. "We were going to walk back when the dizzy spell hit. And then...everything slowly faded away."

"Good. That's good that you remember." Ike appeared to check her eyes. "Do you know what day it is?"

"It's my birthday." Sassy squeezed Graham's hand. "I should've said something about the headaches." Her eyes found Dahlia's. "To all of you. I was going to as soon as I knew what I was dealing with." Her aunt's eyes closed again. "I didn't want to worry everyone."

"How's your headache now?" Ike asked. "Do you still feel pain anywhere?"

"It's not as bad now," she murmured too weakly for Dahlia's comfort. "I still feel the headache, but I'm not as dizzy." Her aunt started to sit up, but Ike gently guided her to lie down.

"Not so fast." The doctor was smiling, but Dahlia could read the concern in his eyes. He suspected something, she could tell.

"We need you to be real still," Ike told Sassy with the perfect blend of sternness and compassion. "We're going to send you to the hospital in an ambulance to make sure everything is all right."

For the first time, Ollie pulled his head off Dahlia's shoulder. "An ambulance?" The prospect of first responders seemed to pique her son's interest.

"Ambulances are cool," he told Sassy solemnly.

"Maybe you can ride with me then." Her aunt reached up to pat the boy's cheek. "You and your mom, of course."

"Can we, Mom?" Light had found her son's eyes again. "Will they let us ride in the ambulance?"

"I sure hope so." Because she didn't want to leave Sassy's side.

Chapter Twenty-Three

Rose

W ill you stop running away from me?" Rose followed her mother down the shoulder of the road, hoping Lillian wouldn't make good on her threats to walk all the way back to town.

That would eat up the rest of the afternoon, and they really needed to get back to the party.

"Seriously, Mom." She teetered along the gravel in her wedge sandals. If she'd known she was going to have to chase her mother all the way to Juniper Springs, she would've put on her running shoes.

"Why are you following me anyway?" Lillian whirled. "Why don't you follow Sassy? You like her more."

Engaging in this argument had been like spinning on a merry-go-round, but Rose couldn't seem to find a way off. "We aren't choosing Sassy over you." She carefully controlled her tone so her voice wouldn't rise. She had been trying to talk her mother down, but any minute now her temper might take over again, and they would be right back where they'd started.

"We want to be a family. That's *all* we want. For you and Sassy to be sisters again so we can enjoy being together." Rose approached her mother before Lillian decided to turn and walk away again. "Don't you remember what it was like when we would visit here all those years ago? Don't you remember the fun we had together?" There had been laughter and silliness. Much more so than there ever had been at their home in Savannah.

While they visited Sassy in Juniper Springs, Lillian used to act like a different person—she hadn't cared so much what people around her thought. "Life could be like that again."

"No. It can't." Her mother spun away from her and started walking again. Thankfully there'd been enough pauses that Rose could still see the turnoff for the resort's driveway. But not for long, if they kept walking.

"You don't understand what it was like." Her mother's shiny loafers scuffed through the dirt faster. "You have no idea."

"Then tell me." Rose caught her hand and pulled her to a stop again. "I *want* to understand." More than anything she wanted to find a connection with Lillian, a way for them to relate so this didn't have to be so hard. The fighting. The dancing around their issues. "Please, Mom. I'm listening."

"I was terrified." Lillian yanked her hand away. "I had three young daughters, and I thought your father was going to leave me." A few tears trickled down her cheeks, but she angrily wiped them away. "I had never had a well-paying job. I was a mother. And a wife. What was I supposed to do?" she nearly yelled.

Rose stared at her mother, at the tear stains on her cheeks, at the redness in her eyes. This woman looked nothing like the put-together picture of Southern elegance Rose remembered. But the outburst of emotion was good. Maybe they were finally getting somewhere. "That must've been so hard."

The firmness in her mother's jaw seemed to soften. "I was too humiliated to tell my parents about the affair. But I thought at least I could come and stay with Sassy for a while. I could've brought you girls and started over here. I could've built a whole different life, if only Sassy had listened to me."

But where would that have left her father? Rose didn't voice the question. Now—years after his death—the question didn't matter. Lillian had stayed. Her family had stayed together. But she couldn't decide if that was better or worse than the alternative.

She never would've called her parents happy. In her memories, they seemed to function well together. But they hadn't laughed and teased each other. They hadn't spent any time alone together that she had been aware of. Her father worked as much as he could—even going into the office on weekends.

Maybe her parents loved each other. Maybe they had to pretend. Maybe marriage had to be a little bit of both. The point was, the problems in Lillian's marriage couldn't be blamed on Sassy. "We still could've moved to the inn. Even with Robert and Colt living here." She had no doubt that Sassy would've welcomed them.

Her mother blew out a sigh of obvious frustration. "I didn't trust him. You don't have children, so you can't understand. My whole life, all I've wanted to do is protect you girls. I knew something was off with that man. So I stayed in Savannah. I stayed in the marriage and had to face your father's betrayal every day for the rest of his life."

Ah. Rose let the words simmer a minute. That's where it all came from. The bitterness. The resentment. Instead of placing the blame where it belonged, Lillian had shifted the responsibility for years of unhappiness to Sassy. It made sense. Lillian had dumped her anger on someone she didn't have to see, someone she didn't have to live with. "Are you sure it's not Dad you're still angry with?" she asked quietly. "He's the one who really hurt you. Not Sassy. You heard what she said. She loves you. She apologized. All she's wanted over the years is to see you again, to talk to you."

"I…" Her mother hesitated as though suddenly unsure what to say. Tears started to trickle down her cheeks. "I don't know. I don't know who I'm mad at anymore. Maybe myself. But I'm so tired. I'm tired of being angry."

"Dad is gone," she reminded Lillian gently. "Sassy's Robert is gone. But you two aren't. You could still have each other." She paused as her mother seemed to consider the words. Maybe they were getting through. At least Lillian had started to show some real emotion. "It might take time to put the past to rest for good," she went on. "I get that. But today could be a start. Today we can go back to the party and be there for your sister. It's one step." Though she knew that the first one could be the most difficult.

"It's too late." Lillian's hand started to shake as she wiped away her tears. "I was so horrible to her. All these years." She stared at Rose, her face crumpling with remorse. "How could she ever forgive me? How can I forgive myself for how I've treated her?"

"Mom…" Rose wrapped her arms around Lillian, pulling her into a hug. "None of that matters now. The important thing is what you do—"

A loud noise interrupted. A siren?

She turned in the direction of the noise and watched an ambulance barrel around the corner before turning into the inn's driveway. It sure seemed to be in a hurry.

"What's happened?" Her mother gaped at the flashing lights. "Why is there an ambulance here?"

"I don't know." But someone had obviously called them. "It can't be good. Come on." Rose grabbed Lillian's hand and moved as quickly as she could, given her wedge sandals and her mother's sleek loafers.

Nightmares raced through her mind as they traveled along the road's uneven shoulder. What if one of the children had been hurt swimming?

Lillian squeezed her hand back. "It's not Maya or Ollie," she murmured. "My God, it can't be Maya or Ollie."

Just when Rose opened her mouth to assure her mother it wasn't the children, Dally's car drove out onto the highway and sped past them. But it was Ike, not Dally, in the driver's seat.

"He's in an awful hurry." Lillian held on to her tighter. "Where's Dally?"

"I don't know." Rose wished her voice would stop wobbling. "Everything's going to be fine."

By the time they reached the driveway, they were both struggling to jog, with Rose half stumbling on the uneven gravel. Fear gripped her as she remembered her aunt's episode after she'd first returned home from her trip. "What if it's Sassy? What if—"

Her heel caught on a larger rock and slipped out from under her, rolling her ankle with a hard crunch in the bone. Pain shot all the way up her leg, forcing her to the ground.

"Rosie?" Her mother crouched next to her. "Honey…are you okay?"

"No." The throbbing had already started on the outside of her ankle and she could feel the instant tightness and swelling. A sharp pain radiated from her ankle and set her teeth on edge. "I don't think I can walk."

"It's okay." Lillian jolted to her feet and ran away as fast as her loafers would take her. "You'll be okay, sweetie! I'll get you help!"

Rose helplessly watched her mom disappear, but she couldn't sit here and do nothing. There was already some other emergency happening. She didn't need to add to the drama. Again.

Gagging back nausea, Rose staggered to her good foot and tried to put some weight on the damaged ankle. "Come on," Rose whispered to herself. She could do this. She could get to the bottom of the hill on a bum ankle. Slowly, she limped along, battling the overwhelming urge to stop and fall to her knees so she could throw up. After a few steps she had to pause and breathe, closing her eyes, shutting out the pain.

"Rose?"

At the sound of Colt's voice she raised her head.

The man was sprinting toward her. "Your mom said you were hurt?"

"My ankle." She eased in a slow, settling breath. No throwing up. She couldn't throw up all over Colt's shoes. "I think it might be broken."

"We need to get you to the hospital." Colt easily lifted her into his arms and started off down the hill, moving slowly and carefully. "Maybe they can make room in the ambulance."

"No. I refuse to ride in an ambulance when there's obviously a real emergency. I don't want anyone to worry about me right now." She looked into Colt's eyes, seeing all of the concern and worry he hid there. "Who's hurt?"

He hesitated, watching the ground instead of looking back at her.

"Please tell me." Rose touched his cheek with her hand, guiding his gaze to hers. "I have to know."

He stopped moving briefly, readjusting her as though trying to make her more comfortable. "Sassy collapsed in the woods."

She tried to swallow but it felt like someone had jammed their fist into her throat. "Is she——?"

"She's stable right now." His tone held a remarkable calmness. "The paramedics are just getting her into the ambulance. Dahlia and the kids are riding with her. Ike already left to head to the hospital."

Rose looked ahead of them. She could see now. The ambulance sat near the pond. They were pushing a gurney inside. Oh, Sassy. "What happened? Why did she collapse?"

"We don't know. Maya came running out to find us." Colt slowed his steps on the last steep part of the hill. "It sounds like she fainted. Your mom is pretty upset. When I ran up here, she was trying to talk to Sassy but the paramedics kept sending her away."

Rose took in the scene in front of her. The Cleary family had respectfully gathered near one of the cabins as though wanting to give everyone else space. Graham had started up his Jeep and was waiting next to the ambulance. Mags and Eric were standing outside the ambulance's open doors with Lillian, who was crying.

"Sassy! I'm so sorry! This is my fault," their mother wailed. "I was awful earlier. Just awful!"

The doors to the ambulance shut with a horrible thud, and Rose couldn't help but cry. She'd wanted to see her aunt. To kiss her cheek. To tell her everything would be okay.

"She'll come through," Colt murmured. "Ike doesn't think it's her heart."

Then what was it? She couldn't bring a voice to the question. What would've made her aunt faint? What would've given her that dizzy spell in the kitchen after she'd come home from her trip? She wasn't sure she was ready to know.

"Oh my God. Rose." Lillian trudged up to meet them. "I can't believe—I don't think she heard me tell her I was sorry. What if she never knows? We've lost so many years together."

Rose grabbed her mom's hand again, squeezing it tightly in hers.

The sirens started up and Colt moved to the side of the driveway, pulling Lillian along with them as the rig rolled past.

"Sassy," Lillian yelled again. "I'm so sorry! I'm sorry!" Her mother followed for a few steps and then hunched over with her hands on her knees. "She didn't hear me. What if she doesn't make it? What if I don't get to see her again?"

"We can't think like that." Colt carried Rose to his truck a few feet away. "I'll give you two a ride to the hospital."

He opened the door and settled Rose in the passenger's seat before opening the back door for her mother. "Sassy's tough. She's a fighter. She'll pull through okay."

The man climbed into the truck next to Rose with a strength and confidence she wished she could find for herself.

"Let's prop your foot here." Colt patted the console between them. "Try to keep it elevated."

Rose shifted her body so she could get her foot up.

"I'll try to go slow." He carefully removed her sandal and gave the outside of her ankle a good look. "Definitely looks broken. But it doesn't seem displaced." He started the engine and put the truck into gear. "Looks like you and Sassy will get to be patients together."

"No." Rose crossed her arms and looked out the window. "I refuse to get treated until I can check on her." Who cared about an ankle when her aunt might be dying?

"I don't understand." Her mother whimpered in the backseat. "What could've happened? Why did Sassy faint? What could be wrong with her?"

While he drove, Colt relayed the little he knew to Lillian. Rose sat back, focusing on fighting the pain in her ankle, the fear in her heart.

Eventually silence took over for the rest of the drive, which seemed to take a good five hours instead of twenty minutes. Colt pulled the truck into a spot in the ER parking lot and was opening her door before Rose could move.

"I can try to walk," she offered.

"I don't mind carrying you." The curve at the corners of his mouth reminded her of those few seconds before he'd kissed her. That seemed like years ago now.

"Okay." Rose wrapped her arms around his neck as he lifted her off the seat.

"Hurry up, you two." Lillian waved them to the doors. "We have to find her right away. I have to see my sister." Her mother sped in ahead of them, but Colt seemed to go through the doors extra slowly.

"We have things to talk about." His gaze found hers. "When we get Sassy through this. I have a few things to say to you."

Her heart held on to the promise. When they got Sassy through this. And they would get her through. All of them together.

When they walked into the waiting room, Ike was already talking to Lillian, but he stopped when he caught sight of Rose. "I heard we've got a broken bone." He carefully took her bare foot in his hand and examined her ankle. "We should get you back into a room so we can get some X-rays."

She didn't give a damn about her broken bone. "What's going on with Sassy?" Rose demanded. "We want to see her."

"They're taking her back for a CT scan right now." Ike smiled a plastic, vague, doctor's smile that didn't suit him at all.

"But why?" Lillian's voice got weepy again. "What are they looking for?"

"They want to rule some things out." He slipped a supportive arm around Lillian and guided her to a nearby chair. "I promise I'll keep you posted as soon as I know anything. Dahlia and the kids will be out in a few minutes. Ollie needed to find a bathroom."

Colt started toward the row of chairs where Lillian sat,

but Rose gave him a look silently nodding toward Ike. She had more questions her mother didn't need to hear.

Ike was moving toward the doors that led to the exam rooms, but Colt caught him.

"Please tell me what they're looking for," Rose said quietly. Because she was a master at drumming up worst-case scenarios.

Ike quickly looked around before leading them to a corner. "They're concerned about a possible tumor. Or a stroke. Those are the biggest worries right now." His grim expression told her just how worried he was.

Rose nodded, biting into her lower lip so she wouldn't sob.

"I'll keep you all posted. The second I find out more, I'll let you know." Ike squeezed her forearm. "In the meantime, I want you to get that ankle looked at. You have to take care of yourself if you want to take care of Sassy." The man hurried away and disappeared through the doors.

The ache in her chest swelled, making it hard to breathe. The sob worked its way out of her, along with the tears.

"Don't cry, Rosie." Colt pressed his lips against her cheek in a tender kiss. "No matter what Sassy has to go through, we'll all face it together."

Chapter Twenty-Four

Sassy

I don't suppose you can keep my door locked."

Sassy tried to bat her eyelashes at the dashing young nurse who had wheeled her all over creation for tests since she'd arrived at the hospital. Theo, his name was. He had thick dark hair and a quick smile with lady-killing dimples.

"Someone might accuse me of imprisonment if I locked your door." Flashing that charm, the nurse wheeled her gurney into its place in front of a whole bunch of awful-looking machines and gadgets attached to the wall. Add those tubes and wires to the dim lighting and the tiny little window that hardly let in enough light to create any shadows on the floor, and you had a dungeon.

Lord have mercy, it looked exactly like some Elizabethan torture chamber in here. See? This was why she didn't do hospitals.

"I wouldn't mind being imprisoned if it buys me some time before I have to face my family." She was only half teasing. Her headache had gone on past, but now knots of tension and worry seemed to have embedded themselves into the very fabric of her stomach, all prickly and sharp.

She hated this. Hated worrying everyone, hated seeing them all make such a fuss. "I'm not used to it," she told Theo, smoothing the thin bedcovers over her legs. "I'm not used to having a whole family to answer to." For years her decisions and struggles and complications had been hers alone, and this whole mess only proved she wasn't good at sharing them with anyone else.

"Miss Sassy…" The young man's impish look scolded her. "Accepting hugs and love from your family doesn't seem all that difficult."

She harrumphed. "It is when you've been hiding headaches and dizziness from them for the better part of two months." Guilt. That's what had cloaked her heart in its heavy darkness. She wasn't a liar, but she'd justified keeping things from Rose and Dally and Colt. And Graham too. Sweet, thoughtful Graham. What had he thought when he'd heard her telling the paramedics she'd been having all of these symptoms?

She knew exactly how she'd feel if it had been her. Betrayed. Hurt. Left out.

Theo pulled down the rails on the sides of the gurney and locked the wheels into place. "Well, from the sound of things, there are a whole group of them out in that waiting room ready to see you. I heard rumors about nieces and nephews and even a little newborn. If I lock this door, they'll likely come charging in to break it down anyway." He leaned over her. "That's a mess I don't want to have to clean up."

"You're no help." She crossed her arms and slumped her shoulders against the pillows. She had no right to pout. She knew that. And yet she couldn't stop that lower lip of hers from trembling. It wasn't that she didn't want to see any of them. She was worried about how they would look at her lying in this bed—like she was weak and old and...well...possibly dying?

All those tests and they still had no results yet. Lying in that tube for the CT scan had been torture—knowing they could see inside her body, that some nameless technician behind the wall was looking at exactly what was wrong with her but wouldn't tell her until the doctor could come down and explain it all.

"How about this?" Theo pulled the curtains open a bit more and an actual ray of sunshine landed on the floor a few feet away. "I'll tell them they have to come visit in small groups. That way it won't be quite as overwhelming." The man typed a few things into a tablet that sat on the counter near the sink. "Now who would you like to see in here first?"

She nearly said Graham, but he happened to have more patience than some of the others who were likely sitting out in that waiting room. "I need my nieces." They likely weren't too happy with her right now. "And my sister...if she's here." Lillian had been trying to talk to her when the paramedics had loaded Sassy up in the ambulance, but she hadn't been able to hear much with all the noise.

"Coming right up." Theo left her with that charming smile.

Sassy sat up in the bed and rearranged the pillows. Not much could be done about her hair at this point, but she combed it into place with her fingers as best she could.

"Sassy? My dear Sassy." Lillian rushed into the room first, her arms outstretched, her voice almost melodic.

Her sister had always known how to make a dramatic entrance.

"I'm sorry." Lillian grabbed both of her hands. "You have to forgive me. I was being stubborn and single-minded, but when I saw you lying on that gurney…" She shook her head and closed her eyes as though she couldn't continue. "Things are changing," she said after a long pause. "Starting right now. I'm going to be here for you. Whatever you need. I'll do anything to help you."

So much for doing her best to look healthy and not sickly. Lillian definitely thought she was dying. But still, if this was what it took to bring her sister back to her, she'd gladly accept her sister's look of pity. "I'm glad you're here, Lil."

"We're all here." Dahlia and Magnolia walked into the room together. And Rose… what on earth was she doing in a wheelchair? "What happened to you, darling girl?" Now that her niece had fully rolled herself into the room, she could see quite the complicated wrap on Rose's right ankle.

Her niece groaned. "It's a long story involving wedge sandals and the driveway." She rolled her eyes. "Minor fracture, according to the doctor, but they're making me drive around here in this dumb thing." Her niece pushed herself alongside the bed. "Enough about me though. Why didn't you tell us? Why didn't you tell us you were having headaches? I knew you got dizzy that night at dinner, but I didn't think much of it. You seemed fine…"

Sassy opened her mouth to spout off the answer she'd formulated—the one she'd convinced herself was true, but the hurt on all three of her niece's faces stopped her. She'd thought she kept the headaches from them because she wanted to protect them, but that wasn't it at all.

"I don't think I wanted the headaches to be real." That was the plain truth. "I didn't want them to mean anything or to be part of a bigger problem. Not now. Not when you're all here and the inn is reopening and I'm starting this whole new life." She hadn't wanted anything to threaten her happiness. "Not telling anyone made them feel less scary, I suppose."

Denial allowed her to protect herself from the possibility that everything would be taken from her. "It's not that I didn't trust you or want you all to be part of my life." She made sure to make eye contact with Rose and then Dally and then Mags. And Lillian. She still couldn't believe her sister was here. Talking with her. "I simply didn't want to acknowledge that something was truly wrong."

"We can understand that." Mags took her hand. "But don't hide anything else from us. You've given each of us so much. Now it's time for us to give back to you."

"Have the doctors said anything?" Out of the four of them, Dahlia seemed to be hiding her concern the best. She had practice being a mom and all.

"I don't have any test results yet." But relief still settled her. The tests were done. She'd taken the first step in finding out what was to come. "Ike is running around trying to harass them into finding some answers as soon as possible, so it shouldn't be too long before we hear something."

Yet another person she would have to apologize to when the time was right. Ike hadn't demanded to know why she hadn't come to him in the first place—he was too kind to ask—but he wondered. She could see the questions in his subdued expression whenever he talked to her.

"Whatever they find out, you know you're not alone." Rose pushed herself out of the wheelchair and stood on her good foot. "You have so many people in your corner."

"Exactly." Lillian prodded her daughter to sit back down in the chair with a motherly look. "I was talking to Elroy about your symptoms, and—"

"Who's Elroy?" Sassy couldn't seem to remember anyone by that name around these parts.

Rose and Dahlia laughed.

"That's Grumpy's real name," Rose said.

"No!" Sassy laughed too. "How in the world did you find that out?"

All eyes turned on Lillian.

Her sister's perfect, creamy, moisturized skin turned a bright shade of red. "He told me. I couldn't very well call him Grumpy. That's not a proper name."

"And they are on a proper-name basis," Rose informed her, teasing Lillian with a bounce of her eyebrows.

A few weeks ago, news of Grumpy and Lillian would've shocked her, but after spending time with Graham, she knew love could come out of nowhere and hit you right between the eyes.

"*Anyway,*" Lillian went on. "Elroy said his son knows a fantastic neurosurgeon in Denver. So if we're dealing with a tumor or anything at all with your brain, we're going to find you the absolute best care and get you all fixed up."

Magnolia's weary expression revealed she feared it wouldn't be that easy. Sassy could see the concern in all of their expressions, as much as Dahlia was trying to hide it.

"Whatever it is, I'm going to fight it. I can promise you that." She wasn't going to let anything steal this time from her. Her nieces gave her courage. Her sister gave her courage. She was stronger here with them.

"We'll fight it together." Dahlia hugged her and then moved out of the way so the others could follow, but a knock on the door broke up the party.

Theo poked his head in. "Time's up," he announced. "We have to keep on schedule people. Sassy is in demand."

Rose squeezed her hand. "Send Ike out to see us the second you hear anything," she instructed.

"I promise." Sassy blew her nieces kisses as they filed out of the room. "No more secrets."

Even though the girls had gone, Lillian lingered by the bed. "I know it was ridiculous of me to resent you all these years." The mask of indifference had fallen away from her sister's face. "I was angry and hurt, and I directed all of my pain at you. I was scared to confront the real problems in my marriage."

"I know how it feels to be scared." Fear had made her do something she never would've done—hide, lie. But that was over now. The fear. She would hold on to the hope instead. She would hold on to the strength her family brought. "You always have a place in Juniper Springs. With me. With your daughters. They love you so much, Lil."

"I love them too." Tears glistened in her sister's bright blue eyes. "And you. I love you, Sassafras. You can't leave me. Not now. I have a lot of years to make up for."

"*We* have a lot of years to make up for." Another gust of courage blew through her. "And we'll have the time. We'll make the time to build some new memories."

"Knock-knock." Graham sauntered into the cramped hospital room with his calm manner and steady sureness.

"I'll see you very soon." Lillian slipped past the man with a smile.

Sassy was smiling too—ear to ear—at the sight of this man while tears leaked from the corners of her eyes. "I suppose I owe you an explanation." Even with the guilt weighing down her heart, she found it easy to look into his eyes. They were home.

"No." He eased onto the bed next to her, slipping his arm around her shoulders. "You don't owe me anything. That's not why I'm here." He seemed to study the details of her face with his meticulous powers of observation. "I'm here to sit with you. I'm here to make sure you have everything you need. I'm here to make you smile. That's all."

Darn those tears. She couldn't seem to shut them off. Graham was so kind. So good. But this wasn't fair to him. "We just started to spend time together, and this is a lot." She couldn't stand the thought of him feeling obligated to bear her burdens. Especially when she hadn't been up front with him from the beginning. "I don't expect you to take on any of my problems. I don't know if I'm sick or if I have cancer. This could be a hard road, and I don't want you to feel like you have to walk it with me." She held her breath. Seeing him walk away now might very well tear her heart in two, but she had to give him the choice.

Graham pulled his arm away and shifted to face her fully. "If you only had a week left on this earth, I would want to spend every minute of it with you." There wasn't one note of uncertainty in his voice. "You brought me back to life with your kindness and your grace." He leaned forward and kissed her softly, taking her away from the hospital, from so many unknowns. "You helped me feel a purpose again," he murmured, still lingering close enough that she could feel his breath against her skin. "I don't know what the future holds for either of us. But I do know that love has come back into my life, and it is a gift."

He held her cheek in his palm. "*You* are a gift, dear Sassy. So I will hold on to you as long as I can. I'll hold on to you as long as you'll let me."

Chapter Twenty-Five

Dahlia

I don't like it here." Maya pulled her feet up onto the waiting room chair and hugged her knees to her chest.

"Me neither." Ollie mimicked exactly what his older sister did down to the sulking expression on her face.

"I'm not sure anyone *likes* hospitals." Dahlia halfheartedly flipped to the next page in the travel magazine she was pretending to read, but she couldn't seem to focus on any of the words or even the beautiful pictures.

They'd been waiting at least an hour to hear anything from Ike, but he hadn't come out to see them. Did the long absence mean bad news?

She shouldn't think like that, but thinking was all she seemed to be able to do. Earlier, the waiting room had been crowded and loud and comforting, but now it had gotten too quiet. Mags and Eric had left to go get the baby down for a nap, promising to be back later, and Colt had said he had something to take care of. Rose had been too restless to sit still, so she'd wheeled herself off in the direction of the cafeteria with Lillian following close behind, admonishing her to be careful, and Graham seemed to have earned himself a permanent spot in Sassy's room.

"I'm hungry." Ollie spun himself around in the chair so that his legs were sticking up in the air. "I could eat five whole pepperoni pizzas and a chocolate cake right now."

"I couldn't." Maya still seemed a bit pale from the shock of the afternoon. "I'm not hungry. Do you think Sassy's gonna be okay, Mom?" She had asked the same question at least twenty times in the last hour. Sweet girl. She was such a worrier.

Dahlia set down the magazine and gathered her daughter into her arms planting a kiss on the top of her head. "Yes, honey. I believe she will be okay." Sometimes thinking and believing were two different things. She always tended to be too practical, but in this case she wanted to rely on her heart. "They're taking very good care of her. You saw her in the ambulance. She was wide awake and smiling and still the same Aunt Sassy."

"That's how she was before she fainted too," her daughter muttered.

Dahlia held her. No matter how much she wanted to, she couldn't erase the images of Sassy lying on the ground unconscious from her daughter's memory. Trauma like that took time to get over. Time and love, and right now she had plenty of both to offer.

"Hey, you two!" Rose wheeled herself out from a hallway on the other side of the room. "Anyone want to go for a ride?"

"That wheelchair is not a toy." Lillian stalked along behind Rose with her hands on her hips. "You can't take them for a ride. All we need right now is someone else getting hurt."

"They need a little fun." Rose ignored their mother and waved the kids over.

"I wanna ride!" Ollie leapt out of his chair and sprinted to Rose, jumping into her lap.

Her sister winced but laughed at the same time and turned them in a circle. "See? Totally safe and fun." She spun them around again, making Ollie giggle.

"Well, I refuse to watch you injure yourself anymore." Their mother marched to the chair next to Dahlia and plopped down. "Really, Rose. You're a grown woman tearing around here in that thing like a child."

"You're a grown-up?" Ollie wrinkled his nose like he couldn't quite believe it.

"Sometimes." Rose shrugged. "Today—right now—I feel like being a kid." She did a few more 360s.

"Woo-hoo!" Ollie raised his arms in the air. "Look! No hands!"

"Good Lord," Lillian huffed.

Dahlia let the two of them carry on. They could all use a little fun right now.

"Maya, why don't you drive?" Rose pointed to the handles behind her. "I'll bet we could really get up some speed with a good driver."

Her daughter remained firmly enclosed in Dahlia's arms. "That's okay. I don't really feel like it right now."

"What would you like to—"

The door to the hallway opened, and Rose fell silent. Ike stepped through, wearing the best smile Dahlia had ever seen. With a smile like that, he must have good news.

"Dr. Ike…" Maya rose slowly, cautiously.

No one else said anything, but they all crowded around him.

"I have great news to report." He seemed to especially address her daughter. "Sassy's scans are clear. They've ruled out a stroke and any tumors."

"She's going to be okay?" her daughter asked in disbelief.

Dahlia shared a long look with Rose along with some tears. She couldn't hold them back.

Ike knelt in front of Maya. "They're still doing some tests, but yes. It looks like Sassy will be okay."

"So what was it then?" Lillian asked before Dahlia could. "There must be something causing the headaches and dizziness."

The man nodded, staying right where he was at Maya's level, as though he could tell she needed the most reassurance. "Right now they're conducting some hearing and balance tests. Sassy mentioned she's had ringing in her ears too, so this could be related to some type of inner ear problem that's causing her vertigo."

"That's it?" Rose laughed. "An inner ear problem?"

"That's awesome!" Ollie cried, and Rose spun them in a few more circles.

"Thank God." Lillian sniffled a little, and Dahlia put her arm around her mother.

"There's no definitive diagnosis yet." Again, Ike seemed to be speaking to Maya. "But that's the way they're leaning right now. And that's really good news, because inner ear problems are treatable."

"So she really will be okay?" Her daughter's voice was small, still unsure. "I thought she was dead..."

"I know." The man gazed into Maya's eyes with such

kindness. "I know how scary it was, but you were very strong. You did exactly the right thing, and we're all grateful to you."

"Thank you." Her daughter threw her arms around Ike, nearly knocking him off balance. "Thank you for helping her. I'm so glad you were there."

"Me too." Ike brought his arms around her, carefully hugging her while she cried.

After a few seconds, Maya lifted her head and gazed at him. "I think I want to be a doctor someday. Like you and Dr. Jolly."

"You would make an amazing doctor." He stood. "Anyone who can stay so calm and know just what to do in an emergency definitely has what it takes."

"You really think so?" The hope in her daughter's eyes lifted Dahlia's heart.

Ollie hopped out of Rose's lap. "Since Sassy's feeling all better now, can we have pizza for dinner? My belly is talking."

"Yes. Of course, sweetie." It had been hours since any of them had eaten. Ollie's five thirty dinner hour had long since passed them by. And now that they knew more about Sassy's condition, even she could eat. "I have some pizzas in the freezer from the last time we ordered." Seeing as how she had to drive two towns away to get the kids' favorite pizza, she always stocked up. "Let's go home and have some dinner."

"Do you want to come with us, Dr. Ike?"

Dahlia was sure Maya's question had stopped her heart.

For a second the man looked too stunned to speak, but he seemed to recover quickly. "I would love to come with you. If you're sure it's okay."

"*I'm* sure." Maya glanced up at Dahlia.

She tried to keep her response casual, but she was having a hard time pulling back her emotion. "It's okay with me too." She knew it was only dinner, but she wanted to laugh and cry at the same time. Inviting Ike over was a big step for Maya. "What do you say, Ollie?"

"Yes!" The boy's face got skeptical. "As long as you like pepperoni pizza. That's my favorite."

"It's my favorite too." Ike high-fived her son, and then his gaze lingered on Dahlia. "I'll check in on Sassy one more time and be right back."

"Sure." Sheesh. That high breathless quality in her voice made her sound like she was under some kind of spell. "Okay. We'll be waiting right here."

Ike's very kissable lips smiled at her before he walked away, and it was all she could do to not fan her face.

"Sounds like it's going to be quite the dinner at your house." Rose's smirk was so subtle the kids didn't seem to notice it.

"Um, yeah." She'd almost forgotten her sister and mother were standing there. "Do you want to come and have some pizza too?"

"No." Lillian still seemed to be sniffling. "I'm staying with Sassy. All night, if that's how long she's here. I refuse to leave her alone."

"I want to stay for a while too," Rose said. "Colt said he'd come back and get me later. But you guys have fun." The singsongy tone made it clear she knew they would have fun.

"Colt's coming to pick you up later, huh?" Rose wasn't the only one who could tease.

"I must say…" Their mother looked back and forth between the two of them. "You girls sure have some wonderful men in your lives."

Dahlia could hardly believe her ears. Lillian used to be able to find a flaw with everyone and had no problem pointing it out. And she'd never liked Colt.

"You seem to have a pretty great man in your life right now too," Dahlia reminded her.

Their mother blushed.

"Grumpy is never as nice to other people as he is to you," Rose added. "I didn't even know he had it in him."

"Love brings out the best in people," Dahlia told their mother. That's what Sassy had taught her.

"Love, pshaw." Lillian waved off the thought, but her cheeks got even redder.

"I'm ready." Ike hustled through the doorway again. "Sassy is going to stay overnight for observation, but they've detected a slight loss of hearing and are leaning toward a Ménière's disease diagnosis."

Maya stopped chasing her brother. "That sounds scary."

"It only means there's a problem very deep inside of her ear," he explained patiently. "But there are a lot of ways to treat it so she doesn't get the headaches and dizziness."

"Oh good." Maya took the doctor's hand. "Then we don't have to worry about her anymore. We can go have some dinner."

"Exactly." The man looked almost bewildered by her daughter's sudden affection for him, but Dahlia could see…Maya had a new hero.

"Finally! Pizza!" Ollie grabbed Ike's other hand and they said their goodbyes.

She followed the three of them out to the parking lot, her heart melting at the sight of her children walking alongside the man she loved.

"Is it hard to be a doctor?" Maya asked Ike as they all climbed into the car.

"Not when you really love it." He started the engine and waited until they'd all clicked in their seatbelts before backing out of the spot. "I think it's the best job ever. I get to spend the day talking to people, helping them."

"You also give them shots," Ollie reminded him a little crossly.

Ike laughed. "Yes, sometimes I have to do that too. That's not my favorite."

"Mine either," her son mumbled.

"What is your favorite part?" her daughter asked.

Dahlia gazed at the man next to her, anticipating his answer. She wanted to know everything about him.

He seemed to take his time thinking. "My favorite is when I call a patient who was sick or hurt to check in and they tell me they're feeling all better."

"That would be my favorite part too," Maya agreed. "Like when you said Sassy was going to be okay, I got this really happy feeling inside."

"Me too." The man smiled and looked in the rearview mirror. "That feeling is the best part of being a doctor."

The rest of the drive home, they played a competitive game of I spy to help Ollie forget about his growling tummy.

Finally, Ike parked on the street in front of her little bungalow, and they all piled out of the car.

Ollie led the way into the house. "Dr. Ike! You have to

see the spaceships I have. I built one out of LEGOs all by myself."

"*Almost* by yourself," her daughter corrected. "I helped with some of the steps."

"Not very much though," the boy whispered.

Dahlia gave the kids a warning look so they wouldn't start a fight. "Maya, why don't you get out some plates and set the table for me?"

Her daughter bounded away, always excited to help in the kitchen.

"Come on, Dr. Ike." Ollie pulled the man's sleeve in the opposite direction. "I have to show you the spaceship."

"I'd love to see it." He paused. "But do you need any help in the kitchen?"

"Nope." Dahlia flicked on the oven. "All I have to do is unwrap the pizzas and heat them up." Back when she had a supermom complex, she used to make her pizza dough from scratch. But after the divorce she'd discovered the miracle of frozen food. God was she glad she didn't hold herself to unattainable standards anymore.

"Come on, Dr. Ike! I want you to see my room!" Ollie wouldn't be put off anymore.

"Coming." The man sneakily gave her hand a squeeze before following her son down the hall.

That touch. That simple small touch seemed to warm her all the way through.

While Maya set the table, Dahlia threw together a quick salad, humming the whole time. She didn't even realize her daughter was watching her until she spoke.

"You seem really happy, Mom."

"I am." She set the salad bowl on the table and sat beside her daughter. "I'm happy because Sassy isn't sick. And because I have the best two kids any mom could ask for."

"And you're happy because Dr. Ike is here," Maya prompted.

"Yes." There was no denying it. "I'm happy because we get to share dinner with Dr. Ike. Together."

"I'm happy about that too." Her daughter took her time folding the napkins into flower shapes—something she must've learned from her aunt Rose.

When the timer dinged, Ollie and Ike rushed to the table like they couldn't wait to eat any longer. They all sat down chatting and laughing as though it were the most natural thing in the world.

After dinner, Ike rinsed the plates, enlisting Ollie's help to load them into the dishwasher, and Dahlia served them each a heaping bowl of ice cream. After the day they'd all had, they deserved it.

"Let's watch a movie!" Ollie jumped up and down on the couch. "How about *The Empire Strikes Back*? That's my favoritest of all the Star Wars ever."

"I think that might be my favorite too." Ike launched into an imitation of Darth Vader that made Ollie run to grab his light saber. After a quick chase around the room, they all settled in together on the saggy old couch—Dahlia on the end, then Maya, then Ike, then Ollie.

Between Ike and Ollie, they quoted at least half the movie.

When the credits started to roll, Dahlia stood and beckoned the kids off the couch. "All right, you two. It's time to get ready for bed."

Miracles of miracles, they actually listened, standing up

with big yawns. They seemed too tired to even try and stay up later.

"Goodnight, Dr. Ike." Maya gave him another hug. "Thanks for having dinner with us. I hope we can do it again soon."

"Me too!" Ollie picked up his lightsaber, slashing it through the air. "Now we have to watch the rest of the Star Wars movies together."

"I think that can be arranged." The man fist-bumped her son and told him goodnight.

Dahlia followed her children down the hallway to their bedrooms, glancing over her shoulder. "I'll be right back." He'd better not go anywhere.

Ike took all of their ice cream bowls to the kitchen like a saint. "I'll be here."

She did her best not to rush through their bedtime routine. Usually Ollie stalled as much as possible, but the sweet boy's eyes closed almost as soon as his head hit the pillow. Dahlia walked into her daughter's room, where Maya was already snuggled in her bed.

"Ike is really nice," she said, setting her book aside.

"He is." Dahlia sat next to her and pulled the covers up, smoothing them in around her shoulders the way she liked.

"Do you love him?" her daughter asked through a yawn.

"I'm not sure yet." She happened to be of the opinion that love was more than a feeling. Love was a commitment. "But I think I could love him someday." She leaned down to kiss her daughter's forehead. "It's still true what I told you before, honey. I can wait to love him. I can wait to go on dates with him."

"You shouldn't have to wait if he makes you happy." Her

daughter's smile turned sleepy. "I liked having him here tonight. And at the party. It's nice to have a doctor around."

"It sure is." During that whole scene with Sassy, Ike had kept his composure. He'd kept everyone around them calm, monitoring Sassy and offering reassurance where needed. She looked down to tell her daughter again how proud she was, but Maya's eyes were closed.

"Goodnight, sweetness," she whispered, giving her one more kiss. Quietly, Dahlia left her daughter's room and crept back down the hall.

Ike stood at the kitchen island, holding up two glasses of the nice bottle of pinot noir she had been saving for a special occasion. "Wine?"

"Yes, please." She took the glass from him, lingering close, looking into his eyes. "Let's go sit on the deck."

It happened to be the perfect night—clear and still. There was always a chill in the mountains during the evening, but tonight Dahlia felt warm and full.

She led him to the small wicker couch she'd found at a garage sale and turned on the gas fire pit Rose had given her as a housewarming gift.

Then she sat next to Ike and let herself sigh deeply, exhaling the stress of the day and inhaling him.

The man moved his arm around her and made her life perfect. It wouldn't be perfect all the time, but right now, in this moment, she had everything. "Maya said she really enjoyed having you here tonight."

Ike set down his wineglass and turned fully to her. "Does that mean it can happen again?"

"I think it does." If it were up to her, he'd be camping out here. But that didn't exactly work with the kids. "I suppose we'll still have to take things somewhat slow." She played with the collar of his shirt.

"I can do slow." He lowered his lips to hers and proved that slow and sensual was his specialty.

Chapter Twenty-Six

Rose

This wasn't exactly the birthday party she planned for her aunt, but Rose had to admit...a picnic in Sassy's hospital room wasn't a bad way to end this crazy day.

"This is the first birthday I've spent in the hospital in seventy years." Sassy bit into a chocolate explosion cupcake Graham had found them at a nearby deli.

That man had been such a dear. He'd managed to scrounge up some of the best food she'd ever eaten. And then he'd offered to drive all the way back to the inn to pick up a change of clothes for Sassy, leaving Rose and Lillian and Sassy to have a little much-needed girl time.

"Hopefully this will be the last birthday you spend in the hospital." Rose shifted in her chair next to the bed, readjusting her casted ankle on the pillows next to Sassy's legs.

The doctor had allowed her to ditch the wheelchair as long as she promised to not put weight on it for two weeks and to use the crutches. "Next year we'll have to plan something really wild. Maybe a girls' trip to Vegas or something." That she'd like to see—her mother and Sassy parading around the Strip.

"We could do Vegas." Sassy dabbed at her mouth with a napkin.

"We certainly could." Lillian was sitting propped up on the bed next to Sassy, and Rose couldn't believe how much the two sisters looked alike. She wouldn't have realized it if they weren't side by side, but they had the same nose and mouth. "We used to get pretty wild in our day."

Rose laughed, nearly spraying chocolate cupcake crumbs all over the both of them. "Right. Okay. You were the two most scandalous sisters in the South." She couldn't seem to stop laughing. From the accounts she'd heard from her grandparents, Lillian and Sassy were perfect angels, and why couldn't Rose and her sisters be more like them?

"It's not a joke." Her mother tossed a pillow at her. "Why, back in Savannah, we used to go skinny-dipping in the neighbor's pond all the time."

"You're damn right we did," Sassy said proudly. "We'd sneak over there after Mother and Daddy were asleep so we could go swimming to cool off. It was innocent enough until that time you invited half the school's basketball team to join us. You were twelve years old going on twenty back then." She jabbed a playful elbow into Lillian's ribs.

"The basketball team?" Rose gasped in mock horror. "You swam naked with the basketball team? Mother! I'm shocked!"

Lillian and Sassy's giggles took fifty years off them easily.

"That might've been one of the best nights of my life, if you want the truth." Lillian reached for another cupcake, and Rose tried not to stare. Her careful, calorie-conscious mother was actually enjoying herself.

"We lured those basketball boys right into the pond and then snuck out the other side." Her mother hooted with laughter. "They had no idea where we'd gone to."

"That is my new favorite story." Rose sat up in the chair a little so she could see them better. "I can't imagine the stories you have." The stories she'd never heard while they were estranged. They had so much to catch up on.

"Actually, your father was one of those basketball boys," Sassy told her.

"He was?"

Her mother's expression didn't darken the way she'd expected it to.

"Yes. He was." Lillian stared at the wall across the room as though remembering. "He came over that night. I had a crush on him even then."

It was easy to forget her parents had been high school sweethearts. In her memories they didn't talk about their younger days much. "Did you love Dad?" She'd been wondering since her mother had told them about the affair. "I mean, I know you had your problems. But did you love him? Even after you found out he was cheating on you?"

"I must've loved him, because I hated him so much." She hugged a pillow to her chest. "If I hadn't loved him, the cheating wouldn't have mattered, would it? It wouldn't have hurt me so deeply."

"I guess not." Love was wonderful, but she was learning it could be painful too. She snuck a quick glance at her watch. Before he left the hospital, Colt had said he would come back to pick her up around six, but he still wasn't back, and she'd heard nothing from him.

"I knew your father was sorry. He begged me to forgive him. And, over the years, I guess I did in a way." Lillian leaned her head onto Sassy's shoulder. "Like so many other relationships, we started out strong, but we lost each other. Life got in the way." Her mother pointed at Rose. "That's why I'm so glad you moved here. Away from Gregory. Away from that life."

Okay, now Lillian was just talking crazy. "You're *glad*?" All she'd heard from her mother for months after her broken engagement was how she'd ruined her life.

"It was difficult for me at the time," Lillian admitted. "I wanted you to have everything. But yes. If you would've stayed in Savannah and married Gregory, you wouldn't be glowing the way you do here. This place suits you, honey."

"This is where I belong." Life in Juniper Springs had been a struggle. It would likely continue to be a struggle on and off— with reservations and income at the inn constantly going up and down. There would be complications and blizzards and more unexpected roof leaks, no doubt. But the struggles had only made her stronger and smarter and more determined.

"What about you, Lil?" Sassy asked. "Where do you fit now?"

"I'm still figuring it out, I think." She shot Rose a questioning gaze. "I may have to rent one of the cabins for a few months. To see if I can make a place for myself here."

A month ago, those words would've terrified her, but now she couldn't imagine anything better. Rose had changed a lot in the last year, but it appeared her mother had too. "You don't have to make a place for yourself. We'll make a place for you, if this is where you want to be."

Her mother glanced out the window. "I'm not sure how I'll manage with all of the dirt. And the snow."

"You get used to it after a while." Heck, if she could get used to the dirt and snow anyone could. Besides that, her mother had nothing tying her down. "You can always have a winter home in Savannah—a place to escape to when you need a break from the snow."

Lillian seemed to consider the idea. "I have been thinking about downsizing anyway. And with all of you here…that's an idea, Rosie."

"With all of us here and with *Elroy* here," she teased.

"Elroy." Sassy shook her head with amusement. "I still can't believe Grumpy's real name is Elroy. I figured he came out of the womb wearing that scowl."

"You should see him smile when Mom's around." She nudged Lillian's foot with her cast. "I didn't know he had it in him."

"Hello?" The door creaked open, and Mags stepped into the room with her bundle of joy strapped to her chest. Eric hovered in the doorway behind her.

"What are you two doing here?" Rose pulled her foot off the bed so she could try to stand with the crutches.

"We wanted to come and see all the good news for ourselves." Mags walked to Sassy and kissed her cheek, letting their aunt get another good look at the baby. "And Colt asked if we could bring you home."

"Oh." The happiness that had just been bubbling inside of her seemed to all drain away. Colt had sent them to get her? Clearly he didn't want to have that talk he'd promised her. Maybe she'd been wrong to think it would be good news.

There was a possibility he'd simply wanted to let her down gently. "Great." She cleared her throat. "Good. I'll get to ride with little Luca then."

Rose sat back down in her chair while Mags and Eric visited with Sassy and Lillian for a few more minutes.

She was fine. More than fine. Her heart wasn't aching. Nope. She refused to let it feel the weight of disappointment.

When the conversation started to wind down, she and Mags and Eric finally filed out of Sassy's cramped hospital room. Rose made sure to keep a smile on her face as she hobbled out to the parking lot with Eric spotting her like he was afraid she might fall over.

When they reached their rental car, Mags faced her. "We offered to come and pick you up, if it helps. I wanted to see Sassy again and tell her goodnight."

It didn't help. Earlier Colt had told her they had a lot to discuss, and now he didn't even want to suffer through the half-hour drive back to the resort with her. Fine. It was fine. She could take a hint. "I'm not sure what you're talking about," she said to her sister. "I'm great." Before Mags could see through the lie, she opened the door and slid onto the backseat next to the car seat, wrangling the crutches onto the floor.

"Okey-dokey then." Mags got Luca all strapped in and kissed his button nose. "Keep an eye on my little darling."

"Not a problem." Rose couldn't resist giving the baby a kiss too.

Silence seemed to sit heavy in the car as Eric drove them toward the highway, but Rose didn't feel up to breaking it for once. So she focused on her little perfect nephew, hoping his contented little breaths could take the edge off her heartache.

"Anything you want to talk about?" Mags finally asked.

"No." It would be better not to talk. Oh, who was she kidding? She was a total talker. "Maybe. I mean, come on. You guys were there. You saw what I did. I left nothing on the table. I told him exactly how I feel about him, and I thought the drive back would be a good chance for us to talk. I thought he *wanted* to talk. But no. He sent you. So I have no idea what he's thinking. Or if he's even thinking about me at all." She finally took a breath, but once she got going it was hard to stop. "I mean, I really put myself out there."

"In front of *everyone*," her sister offered.

"Thanks for that." As if she needed to be reminded of one of the most humiliating moments of her life. "But yes, I made a complete fool out of myself, and all I'm getting in return is this horrible silence. I hate silence. I'd take anything right now. Even if Colt told me I'm not his type. Or that I disgust him. Knowing that is better than knowing nothing. Right?"

"For sure." Strangely, Mags didn't turn around to look at her. In fact, her sister remained weirdly quiet on the subject.

"You want me to kick his ass for you?" Eric offered.

"No." That answer might've been too hasty. "Maybe. You want to know what I think? I think he's already left this place mentally behind." And her along with it. "He couldn't wait to sell the store so he could move on with a whole new life, and then I come along and complicate things for him. He probably wishes I'd kissed Nolan in the canoe. Then there wouldn't be any decision to make. I'd be with Nolan, and Colt would be free to move on without another thought."

"Why didn't you kiss Nolan?" This time her sister did peek back at her, but she turned around so fast Rose hardly caught a glimpse of her face.

"Because he's not Colt." The words sounded every bit as pathetic as they felt. "I don't understand anything about how love works. I only know you can't force it." She hadn't been able to force it with Gregory, and maybe she'd actually learned something from her whole engagement debacle. She didn't want to force love. Especially with someone who didn't love her back. Rose let her shoulders slump against the back of her seat and watched the lights in town pass by out the window.

Thank God. They were almost home, and she could hole herself up in her trailer, turn on some music, and snuggle up with Marigold and the emergency supply of brownie batter ice cream she kept in the freezer for occasions exactly like this one.

Eric turned into the driveway, but instead of parking in front of the house, he continued on down the road.

"Uh..." Rose gazed at her trailer sitting up on the hill behind them. "I'm not sure I'm going to be able to make it up the hill on my crutches. There're plenty of places to park in front of the house."

"We are under strict instructions to bring you to the pond," Eric informed her with a mysterious grin.

"Instructions?" That sat her upright. She started to look around, out the side windows and then through the windshield.

"Oh Mylanta." The whole surface of the pond was glowing. There had to be a hundred floating candles dancing on the water. White lights were draped from the trees right at the edge, creating a canopy over a freestanding bench swing that had to have been brought over from one of the cabin's front porches.

And there was Colt. Walking away from the pond and toward the car.

Rose shook the back of her sister's seat. "How could you do this to me? How could you let me sit back here the whole ride home thinking he wanted nothing to do with me? You're my sister!" She should've known something was going on when Mags wouldn't look back at her. The woman had always been a terrible liar.

"He made us swear." Her sister held up her hands, shirking responsibility for any of it. "It might've been the most difficult hour of my entire life, but I did it! I kept a secret."

Rose didn't have time to congratulate her before Colt opened the back door. He reached in and carefully lifted her into his strong arms.

"I can use my crutches," she said weakly. Everything seemed to have gone weak—her knees, her heart. Right now it was very possible she wouldn't be able to move.

"I'd rather carry you." He ducked his head and looked into the car. "You two have my thanks."

"We were more than happy to help." Mags squealed a little and clasped her hands in front of her chest. "You two have a *wonderful* date."

"We will," he assured everyone. Including Rose. It was already wonderful. Being held by him. Being taken care of.

She put her arms around his neck, and he eased them down to the pond.

"It looks beautiful," she whispered. Light seemed to flicker and sparkle all around her—transporting her back into the fairy world Sassy had once created for them. "There are so many candles. And the lights . . . this must've taken you forever."

"Now you know why I was running late." Colt leaned over to set her on the swing and then sat next to her. "But I wanted to make this night memorable. I wanted to create a clear picture you can always hold on to. The same way I can still clearly see the moment I first met you."

She pulled her legs up so she could shift to face him. "You still remember the moment we met?" She'd been younger, and she couldn't see the picture. She couldn't recall any details . . .

"You were standing right there." He pointed to a sandy spot on the shoreline. "Your hair was braided, and you were wearing a red dress with polka dots."

A laugh snuck out, but also a couple of tears. "I loved that dress." But she didn't remember wearing it that day. She didn't remember anything about the day she'd met Colt.

"I walked down to the pond from the cabin my dad and I were renting." He pointed at Mistletoe Cabin, dimly lit up the hill. "You asked me if I wanted to play." His eyes stared deeply into hers, saying so many wonderful things between the lines, that he trusted her, that he felt something for her too. "I wasn't good at playing pretend. But I wanted to make you happy, so I said yes." He brought his hand to her face, skimming his thumb down her cheek. "Right then and there, you made me a prince. And you were the princess. I couldn't believe you thought I even had the right to pretend to be royalty."

He was still smiling, but there was something sad in the words. Something heavy. Rose snuck her hand into his, weaving their fingers together, feeling that small touch raise up a longing she hadn't known she was capable of.

"The way I grew up—moving around a lot, my dad struggling to find work—I always felt like I was less than everyone else. It got to the point where I accepted it. Being less important and less cool and less worthy of good things."

Those words opened the shutters on his soul, and now she could see. She could understand why he didn't speak much, why he'd shut her out, why he'd been so caught off guard when she'd told him how she felt earlier. Oh, Colt. If only he could touch her feelings for him, test out their strength...

"I fell in love with you that day because you saw me differently than other people did." His hand trembled in hers. "You saw me as someone who could maybe be a prince, and I never forgot that."

For the first time he looked away from her, staring at the ground next to them. "When you moved here permanently, I knew I couldn't stay. I knew I might see you every day, still loving you after all this time but not being able to tell you. Not being able to show you. That's why I wanted to move away. I never thought you would love me back."

The tears were flowing now. There was no stopping them. No controlling her emotions. "But I do." She held her hands on either side of his face, keeping him right there, willing him to see how much. "I do," she said again, drawing his lips to hers.

With the light and candles flickering around them, she kissed him with all the intensity the last couple of weeks had built into her, with all the strength and hope she could offer him.

And still it wasn't enough.

"I'm not moving," Colt murmured when she pulled back to breathe for a minute. "I sold the store, but I'm not moving."

"Good." Rose kissed him again, smiling against his lips. "Because I might need a handyman to help me out around here, and I think you've got exactly the kind of skills I'm looking for."

"I have skills," Colt confirmed. His hands moved to her lower back and she maneuvered her casted foot so she could straddle his lap. "Just wait."

"Oh, no," Rose whispered in his ear. "I'm done waiting."

Chapter Twenty-Seven

Sassy

Sassy put the coffee on, anticipating Lillian's impending arrival in her kitchen.

She paused in front of the window while she could, enjoying the view of the early morning sun waking up the trees while she sorted through the craziness of the last two weeks.

When she'd first started to talk about the community garden, she never dreamed it would all come together so quickly, but nearly everyone in town had gotten behind the project, helping to clear the lot and build planters and seating, and they were already breaking ground today.

"Good morning!" Lillian came in through the back door like she had every morning since Sassy had been released from the hospital. "How are we feeling today?"

She asked that same question every morning too. But it made Sassy smile. "Feeling great. Better than ever." The combination of physical therapy and antihistamines had done wonders for the headaches and dizziness. She handed her sister a full, steaming mug. "What about you? How are you this morning?"

"Wonderful. I'm telling you...this fresh mountain air is very invigorating. I feel years younger here." Lillian sat at the table.

"Are you sure it's the fresh mountain air making you feel younger?" She sat across from her sister. "Because I've noticed Grumpy has been coming around quite a bit." The man's car had been parked at Lillian's cabin after ten more than once this week.

"I've been teaching Elroy how to cook." Her sister wasn't very forthcoming about their budding relationship, but her face got rosier every time she brought him up. Not that she was one to talk.

"Is this attire really appropriate for a ribbon-cutting ceremony?" Lillian looked down at the T-shirt and jeans Sassy had lent her, changing the subject yet again.

Sassy let it slide. "We're going to a ribbon-cutting ceremony and community garden work day. Trust me. You're going to want jeans."

Lillian frowned and raised her leg, giving the denim a skeptical eye. "I don't know why anyone wants jeans."

"You get used to them after a while." Sassy finished off her coffee and carted the mug to the sink. "You never know, you might even like them eventually." After years of wearing her favorite jeans, she couldn't even think about putting on a pair of slacks.

Another argument rose in her sister's expression, but the door opened again.

Rose and Colt walked in, hand in hand. "I'm out of coffee." Her niece couldn't even pry her eyes off the man long enough to glance at Sassy. "Mind if we have some of yours?"

"I always make extra." And she loved this—having her door open for anyone who wanted to walk through. Sassy poured them each a mug, and they all sat down at the table together.

"You can have one of the cabins, you know," she told Rose. "You don't have to stay in the trailer." It was such a tiny space, though she'd fixed it up to be so homey. "It's starting to get colder overnight."

"But I love the trailer." Her niece hardly looked at her with Colt right there. That man held all of Rose's attention.

"What about you?" Sassy gave Colt a questioning glance. How he even fit in that short bed was beyond her. Though they likely wanted their own space, and Colt's apartment above the store had been included in the sale.

"Don't look at me." The man slipped his arm around Rose. "I love being wherever she is."

"Oh, leave them alone, Sassy." Lillian got up from her chair and started to wash the dishes. "I think a trailer is romantic."

This from the woman who'd once tried to drag Rose home to Savannah so she could marry another man.

"I know it'll get colder," Rose said dreamily. "In another month or so maybe we'll move into a cabin for the winter, but don't worry about me. I'm staying warm." The smile she shared with Colt melted Sassy's heart. "What about you, Mom? Are you liking staying here? How's Gingerbread Cabin treating you?"

"It's been wonderful." Lillian wiped her hands on a towel. "Every morning there are two young fawns grazing right outside of my window. And the chipmunks that live under the porch are darling."

"That's great." Rose's mouth pulled into a grimace. "As

long as they're not living in the walls. I'd prefer to not have to do any more remodeling for at least another year."

"There will be no need." Sassy collected her purse from the hook behind the door. "Everything around here is perfect. You've both done a marvelous job." She waved Lillian along. "We need to get going. I promised Graham I would meet him at eight."

"Right behind you."

She and her sister hurried out the door and got into Sassy's car.

"What a beautiful day to plant a garden." Lillian glanced up at the sky. "Not one cloud. I'm so happy I get to be here with you."

Sassy stopped the car before turning out onto the highway. "Having you here makes everything feel complete." For years she'd lived with a piece of herself missing, and now she had her sister back. They had so much to do together. "Hey, remember how we always talked about taking a trip to Europe when we were younger?" As girls, they'd had all of these romantic notions about riding gondolas in Venice and posing in front of the Eiffel Tower in Paris.

"We had big dreams." Lillian smiled as though remembering.

"And I want the rest of my life to be about fulfilling dreams." Sassy pulled the car out onto the highway. "So I was thinking…maybe we do it. Maybe we take a trip to Europe next spring, just the two of us."

"Yes!" Her sister gasped. "Can you imagine the fun we'll have? We'll drink wine and eat cheese and pastries."

"And we'll shop and go to fancy restaurants and visit all

of the museums." Sassy found a parking spot in front of the empty lot. "We'll have the time of our lives."

"We certainly will." Lillian pulled out her phone. "I'm going to text my travel agent right now."

Sassy chuckled. With Lillian in charge, that trip would be planned by noon.

After Lil shoved her phone back into her purse, they climbed out of the car.

Quite the crowd had already gathered with their gardening tools and sun hats.

Lillian spotted Grumpy and quickly hurried away, leaving Sassy to walk around and check that all of the plants they'd purchased had been delivered.

"Fancy meeting you here."

Sassy spun so she could throw her arms around the man who had given her a second wind. "I can't believe we're planting already. I can't believe this is happening."

"It's remarkable." Graham took a quick glance behind him before giving her a secretive kiss. "You're remarkable."

Sassy looked at all the people again, still stunned. "This town is remarkable."

"There you are." Moe rushed over with a photographer trailing behind him. "The newspaper wants a picture for the front page."

Sassy obediently put her arm around Graham and smiled while the woman snapped a couple of pictures.

"I need to check in with the sprinkler guy to make sure the lines are all in," Graham said, as soon as they were done. "But I'll see you in about ten minutes for the big ribbon cutting."

"Ten minutes!" Already? She peeked at her watch. Lordy, he

was right. "We'll meet by the podium," she told him sternly. Earlier, he'd insisted that she cut the ribbon, but she'd politely told him heck no, they were cutting that ribbon together.

"I'll be there." Graham stole one more kiss and ran off while Sassy wandered to the beds they'd already installed for the berry patches.

"Look at all you've managed to do during your two-week tenure." Dahlia met her near the sidewalk along with Ike and the children.

"If it's only been two weeks since you've become mayor, I can't wait to see what's in store next year." The doctor gave her an overly gentle hug. "Still keeping up with your PT during all the busyness, I hope."

"I most certainly am." Sassy winked at Ollie. "I need to be able to run as fast as my great-nephew, after all."

"Look at my shovel." Ollie held up a gardening spade. "I've got gloves too." He pulled a pair of heavy-duty work gloves out of his back pocket.

"Then you and I will plant the green beans together," she teased.

"Ew. I hate green beans." Ollie made a face.

"I'll help you with the green beans." Maya held up her pink shovel. "I love them."

"Perfect." She gave them both a squeeze. "You two are going to be such great helpers."

"I can't believe how many people are here." Rose and Colt joined their little group, and with Lillian not too far away, their family was complete.

"It's amazing how you've brought people together," Colt said.

"It's not me, dears. It's all of us. Together. That's the real beauty of this moment." It was Graham giving up the land. And Moe faithfully working so hard for this town. And Grumpy providing the bottomless coffee for everyone who had shown up today. It was the many local businesses that had donated money to purchase the new plants and fruit trees. And it was them. Her family. "It's incredible what we can accomplish when we are all together."

"I still want to accomplish a Star Wars holiday," her great-nephew informed her. "That would be the best holiday ever."

"I'll get it on the next agenda," she promised.

"Sassy, it's time!" Moe called her to the podium.

"Oh, this is so exciting!" Rose gave her a hug.

"I'll take lots of pictures," Dahlia promised.

Her family hurried away with their little group, looking as proud as punch. Sassy was proud of them too. Especially for following their hearts. And it had paid off. Rose and Dally had never looked happier.

"Are you ready, Madam Mayor?" Graham always seemed to appear right when she needed him.

"I am." She took the man's arm and walked with him up the steps of the small stage Moe had set up.

The crowd had gathered around, and what a beautiful sight it was to see all of these people unified in one common cause.

Moe gave a brief introduction and waved off their applause for him, humble man that he was. Then he turned the mic over to Sassy. She stepped forward, feeling the love coming at her from all directions. "I want to thank you all for coming out to celebrate the opening of our first community garden in Juniper Springs."

The applause went on a little too long for her comfort level. She raised her hand for quiet. "As you can see, we have quite a bit of work to do in this space. But we are thrilled that so many people have turned out to be a part of making this community a better, more welcoming, more compassionate place."

"Woo-hoo!" Rose and Dally were carrying on near the front of the crowd.

Sassy sweetly shushed them. "This garden represents our commitment to taking care of one another. And we are so excited to see it grow into a place where we can gather and provide for anyone in need."

She rushed to continue before the applause got out of hand again. "I think we are ready to officially welcome you all to the Juniper Springs Community Garden."

Moe handed her the scissors, but Graham suddenly moved in front of the mic.

"If I may take one more moment, I have something to say."

That was funny. Graham had insisted he didn't want to speak. He should, though. They were partners in this. Sassy started to step back to give him space, but he took her hand and guided her to stand facing him.

Then he lowered himself to one knee.

Murmurs and cries came from the crowd, but Sassy shut them all out. Every single one of them. She had waited seventy years to see the man she loved on his knee in front of her, and Graham was all she wanted to focus on.

"Sassy McGrath, I was sure my heart had died before you

walked into the rose garden that day. I was sure I would never feel it beat with anticipation again. But you breathed new life into me with your vibrance and your strength. You gave me hope."

"Aww!" Rose and Dahlia were closer. Sassy could hear them, but she couldn't look. She couldn't take her eyes off this man.

"Life is too short to wait when you've found the love of your life." Graham took her hand in his. "So I'm asking you here, in front of our community, to be my wife." He held up a ring. A beautiful ring with the diamond embedded in the center of delicate golden rose petals.

"You could get married in the garden," Ollie cried.

A few people laughed.

Sassy cried. And then laughed with tears running down her face. "That is a mighty fine idea."

"Is that a yes?" Graham's poor knee had to be aching by now.

"Yes, my darling." Sassy tugged on his hand so he would stand and kiss her. Right now. Here on the stage in front of the whole town. "That is my wholehearted yes."

Chapter Twenty-Eight

Rose

I t's snowing!"

Rose rushed into the kitchen in a full-blown panic. "It can't snow in September! It's too early!"

"Honey, in Colorado it can snow whenever it wants to." Sassy sat perfectly still in the kitchen chair while Mags and Dally fussed over her hair and Lillian sat in front of her, touching up her makeup. Maya was busy walking around, taking pictures from all different angles.

"No talking," Lillian reminded Sassy. "I'm almost done outlining your lips. We don't want you looking like a clown for your wedding now, do we?"

"Your wedding!" Rose ran to the window. There had to be six inches of snow on the ground. "It's snowing on your wedding day. We're supposed to have the ceremony outdoors in the garden." This was going to be a disaster. "I don't understand. Yesterday, it was seventy degrees."

"We could always call the church to see if it's available," Mags suggested, adding another curl to Sassy's hair.

"Absolutely not." Their aunt pushed the lip liner away

from her mouth. "Graham and I are getting married in that garden come hell, high water, or a foot of snow. That is where I want my wedding, and that's where it will be."

"Snow makes everything pretty," Maya insisted, fluffing her beautiful orange flower girl dress.

"Right. Okay." At least the nine-year-old could be the voice of reason. "Everything will be okay." Rose flipped through the notebook she'd put together while she'd planned Sassy and Graham's shotgun wedding. After their engagement, they had no time to lose, her aunt had said. So they'd managed to plan the entire thing in just over a month. "I'll send out a text alert telling all of the guests to bundle up and wear their boots." Ugh! Snow boots at a wedding. "We won't need the chairs from the museum." Everyone would have to stand for the ceremony. "And since Colt is helping set up at the garden, I'll text him and let him know to stop by Graham's house to grab your coat on his way to pick us up."

Sassy had moved in with Graham a couple of weeks ago, but she'd spent the night once more at her old house with Rose and Mags and Dally and their mother since it was bad luck for the groom to see the bride before the wedding. They'd made the most of Sassy's last night as a bachelorette by reminiscing and watching old home videos while they overdosed on ice cream. It had been the perfect way to send their aunt off into married life.

"Now that everything's decided, I'm going to finish your makeup," Lillian informed Sassy. She added a few swipes of the blush brush and smiled. "It certainly didn't take much. You've always had radiant skin."

"You look beautiful." Dally stood back and admired the bride.

Rose joined her sister and snapped a picture on her phone. "You're the most stunning bride I've ever seen." Sassy positively glowed with happiness.

"Oops, one more minor adjustment." Mags smoothed out one of the natural-looking curls she'd put into Sassy's long red hair and added another squirt of hairspray. "There. Now you won't have to worry about your hair getting in the way of the kiss."

"Honey, nothing is getting in the way of that kiss." Sassy held up the hand mirror and turned her head side to side as though admiring their work on her hair and makeup. "I've been waiting for this day for fifty years. Twice I thought I had found the man I would marry, and I lost them both. But Graham...he was worth the wait."

She set down the mirror and stood, smoothing out her lovely dress, which happened to be the same color blue as a clear Colorado sky. As maid of honor, Lillian wore a honey-yellow gown, while Rose, Dally, and Mags all wore varying shades of green. Her aunt was adamant that her wedding would be full of colors, just like the garden. Not that it would matter now. They were all going to have to wear coats. Rose cringed. And probably hats and gloves too. But this was Sassy's wedding, and they would make the best out of whatever happened.

"Okay, people, we need to get moving." She glanced at the clock on the oven. "Colt will be here to pick us up in approximately ten minutes."

"He's already here," Maya informed her. "I saw him outside."

Rose's heart lifted. He was there. It had only been twenty-four hours since she'd seen him, but it could've been a year for

how much she'd missed him. "Start getting your coats on."
She waved everyone out of the kitchen and led the way down
the hall into the foyer, where she hastily pulled on her coat
and hat so she could get a few minutes alone with her man.

She stepped outside before anyone else and found Colt
shoveling a path for them to the Suburban he'd borrowed to
bring them all to the ceremony. Because of course the man
was shoveling. Even though they'd been dating for a month,
his thoughtfulness continued to surprise her.

"Morning." He leaned the shovel against the porch and
met her on the stairs, giving her a good once-over. "You're
looking sexy today."

"I'm wearing a down coat." Rose could never hide her smile
from him. He seemed to draw it out with his very presence.

"And you make a down coat look real good." He leaned in
to kiss her, moving his hands to her hips and then around to
her lower back, holding her close.

"Gross." Maya stepped out onto the porch, followed by
Lillian, Mags, Dally, and then Sassy. "You're not the ones
getting married today," her niece reminded them.

No, sadly they were not.

Colt said nothing, but his smile seemed to hide a secret.
After kissing her once more, he released Rose and hurried to
the SUV to retrieve Sassy's coat.

Yet again his thoughtfulness had come through. She hadn't
needed to worry about texting him. He knew Sassy would
need her coat.

Colt slipped past Rose and helped her aunt get the jacket
on before offering his arm to her aunt. "Madam Mayor, you
look beautiful."

"You clean up pretty well yourself," Sassy teased peering up at Colt. "I can't remember the last time I saw you in a suit."

Rose had never seen him in a suit, but yes, it fit him quite nicely, accentuating his broad shoulders and trim physique. His hair still had that seductive unruliness about it, but he'd styled it with gel. Desire rolled low through her belly and heated her right up.

But Sassy. They were focusing on Sassy right now. And their mission was to pull off the perfect snowy fairy-tale wedding. "Let's get going. We don't want to be late." She marched to the SUV with Colt escorting Sassy behind her. They all piled into the car, trying to keep their dresses and makeup and hair intact, even with all the warm-weather gear on.

"I think snow on your wedding day is good luck," Lillian said, peering out the window.

Rose stared at the frozen landscape as they drove onto the highway. "It does give the world a magical look." With everything frosted over and sparkling, it wasn't exactly what she'd envisioned when she'd planned the perfect fall wedding, but the snow would only make this celebration more memorable.

"It will the best day of my life," Sassy said dreamily.

"Yes, it will be." Rose would make sure of that.

Guests had already arrived and were standing in a cluster in front of the arbor and podium Colt had helped Graham set up the day before.

They parked on the other side of the museum, out of sight of the garden, and then piled out of the car, lining up in their assigned order for the walk down the sidewalk aisle. Rose handed Maya the lipstick she'd stashed in her coat pocket. "Want some?"

"Heck yes!" The girl glanced at her mom. "Is it okay?"

"Sure, honey." Dahlia helped her apply the lipstick and then refreshed her own before handing it back to Rose.

"This is so much fun!" her niece bubbled, nearly spilling her basket of rose petals.

Rose felt giddy too. Everyone she loved was here. Sassy was about to start a new life with the man she adored. There was nothing better than a wedding.

Music from Moe's band started to float toward them—giving them their cue.

"This is it, everyone." She took her place in line behind Mags. "Maya, you're leading the way. We'll follow you." She double-checked to make sure they were in the right order—Maya, Lillian, Dally, Mags, her. And then Colt would walk Sassy down the aisle. "Okay, sweet girl." She gave her niece the signal.

The processional started in front of the museum, and then her niece turned down the sidewalk that led into the garden, just like they'd practiced. Graham was waiting underneath the arbor joined by his two adult sons, Ike, and Grumpy. Eric stood in the center, ready to preside over the ceremony with little Luca strapped to his chest, the baby's face barely visible from under his coat.

Rose walked slowly down the aisle, smiling at everyone who'd braved the elements to be there.

Ollie waved like crazy from the front row. "Hi, Maya! Hi, Mom! Hi, Auntie Mags and Rose!"

"Hi, buddy." She gave him a wink before taking her place under the arbor and facing the crowd.

Moe started a violin solo, creating the perfect serenade for Sassy as she walked toward them. Her aunt's face beamed, and Colt grinned like a proud son.

Tears started to roll freely down Rose's cheeks and didn't stop once through the entire ceremony. Graham and Sassy said their vows with love and conviction, not taking their eyes off each other once, even when Ollie asked loudly how much longer this was going to take.

When Eric pronounced them husband and wife, Graham kissed Sassy with a heartfelt tenderness to the chorus of cheers and whoops.

The ceremony ended with hugs and well-wishes, and then they all crowded into the museum's main hall, where they ate and danced and toasted in a whirlwind celebration before sending the happy couple off on their honeymoon.

With the town council on cleanup duty, Rose walked out of the museum hand in hand with Colt. "That was the best wedding I've ever been to, but I'm ready to go home."

"I'm ready too." He pulled her in closer against his side. The snow had stopped, and the sun was peeking out from behind the gauzy clouds, making everything sparkle.

Colt opened the passenger's door for her and helped her climb into his truck before sliding into the driver's seat next to her. "I've known Sassy a long time, and she's never looked happier," he commented as they drove through town. He shot her a sideways glance. "I've never been happier either."

"I feel the same way." Rose held his hand while they drove back to the inn—to the place they were making theirs.

He parked close to the porch and then hurried around to her door, opening it and lifting her into his arms.

Rose laughed while he carried her up the stairs and then across the threshold into the house, kissing her the whole way.

Marigold came bounding to them, jumping and yipping as though she wanted in on their game.

"It's okay, girl." Colt gave her a good scrub behind the ears, and she calmed right down.

He set Rose's feet on the floor, and they shed their coats and boots, kissing their way into the living room with Marigold at their feet. Rose would've kept moving all the way to their bedroom upstairs, but Colt stopped. "Remember how you said you wanted to do some work on the house?" he murmured, his lips still close to hers. "We should start now."

"Um…" She worked her hands up his chest. Talking about renovations wasn't exactly what she'd had in mind for tonight. "Maybe we can talk about that tomorrow…"

The man seemed to ignore the suggestion, breaking away from her and walking to the wall that separated the living room from the kitchen. "Let's do it. Let's take out this entire wall and open up the kitchen to the living room."

The prospect of a design project momentarily distracted her from her urgency to get him into bed. "That's exactly what I've been thinking." It would be beautiful—all of the light coming in from the living room windows…

"We should start now." Colt went to the closet and brought back a sledgehammer, offering it to her. "Go ahead, whack the wall."

Seemingly bored with all of the chitchat, the dog retreated back to the couch and curled up.

Rose laughed, but it quickly became apparent he wasn't

joking. "Really? You want me to whack the wall? Right now?"

"Really." He bounced his eyebrows with a look of entice-ment. "It's fun. You'll love it."

"But I'm still in my dress." She looked down at the simple fitted gown she wore. "These aren't exactly work clothes."

"That's no problem. Just take a swing." He nudged her to the wall. "Trust me. Hit it right here."

"Okaaaayyyy." Rose lifted the sledgehammer and swung it into the wall, cracking the drywall.

"You have to hit it harder than that." Colt snuck behind her, reaching his arms around so they were both holding on to the sledgehammer. He helped her raise it up, and they swung it together, this time breaking all the way through.

"There we go." He released her and stood back.

"What's that?" Rose moved closer to the hole they'd made. There was a box hidden inside, taped to one of the studs. And it had her name on it. Eyeing Colt, she pulled it out and opened it, finding a smaller box. A ring box. "Colt?" Her knees started to buckle.

"I didn't want to steal Graham and Sassy's thunder before the wedding." He took the smaller box and got down on his knee. "But I couldn't wait much longer."

"You hid a box in the wall?" Rose laughed while a few tears escaped. How had she missed that? "When? Where was I?"

"You've been a little busy with Sassy's wedding plans." The man opened the box, revealing a diamond solitaire ring, and gazed up at her with tears in his eyes too. "I knew the second you walked out of that pond, all dripping wet and passionate, that I couldn't wait anymore. I've waited for you all these years while I built a life for myself. But now I want to rebuild everything with you. Not just this house. I want to build a family and a life with you. Marry me, Rose. I don't want to rush you—"

"This is perfect." Rose cut him off and sank to the floor with him. "The perfect time. The perfect moment." With only the two of them—and Marigold—dreaming about what was to come at the place they both loved. "Yes. Yes, yes, yes." She kissed him. "Yes." There were no reservations, no hesitations. She may not have known it, but she'd been waiting for Colt her whole life too.

READING GROUP GUIDE

YOUR BOOK CLUB RESOURCE

The
Summer
Sisters

A LETTER FROM
THE AUTHOR

Dear friends,

Thank you for reading *The Summer Sisters*! When I finished writing *Home for the Holidays*, I just knew I had to continue with Sassy, Rose, and Dahlia's stories in another book. Each of these characters has touched my heart in a different way, and I hope they've touched your heart too.

One of the things I love the most about this story is the courage these three women display as they step into something new and unknown. Rose left behind her life in Savannah to renovate an inn. Dahlia moved her children to a new state so she could pursue her dream of working with her sister. And Sassy determined that she wouldn't let her age or her health concerns stop her from taking on an exciting new role in the town she loves. Their journeys aren't without questions and doubts and heartaches, but they don't let those things stop them from going after what they truly want in life—meaning, purpose, love, and faith in themselves and in each other.

I have always believed that the most growth comes when we step outside of our comfort zones and embrace something new. But in order to do that, we all need someone cheering us on—supporting, inspiring, and encouraging us. It is the bonds between Sassy, Rose, and Dahlia that make them each brave. The truth is, we need each other. Our connections are where we find hope and happiness and strength. Spending time with Sassy and Dahlia and Rose made me treasure the connections I have with my family and friends even more. I hope their story inspires us all to pursue our dreams while holding on to what is most important.

All the best,
Sara

QUESTIONS FOR READERS

1. Sassy, Rose, and Dahlia are at very different places in their lives. Did you find yourself relating to one of their situations more than the others? Which character would you most want to spend some time with at Grumpy's coffee shop?

2. Rose has taken on most of the work at the Juniper Inn and is reluctant to ask for help, even though she's overwhelmed. Why does she feel the need to prove herself to her sisters and Sassy? Has there ever been a time when you've taken on too much to prove something to someone else?

3. At the beginning of the story, Sassy is harboring a secret about her health. Why do you think she wants to hide her symptoms from her family? What would you have done in her situation?

4. Though Dahlia and Ike had a whirlwind romance the Christmas before, she later realized how difficult it would be to juggle a romantic relationship with being a single mom.

How did you feel about Dahlia's decision to focus solely on her children and keep her distance from Ike? What other issues do you think might have played into her decision?

5. Sassy, Dahlia, and Rose are each in the process of reinventing themselves and building new lives. Who do you think struggled with this the most? How did each character handle the new situations they found themselves in?

6. How did you feel about Lillian as a character? Did learning more about her past change your impression of her throughout the story?

7. Sassy, Dahlia, Rose, and Lillian are all navigating the joys and difficulties of romantic love. Which romance captured your heart the most and why?

8. Rose's feelings for Colt caught her off guard. Why do you think she didn't see her love for him coming? How did you feel about Colt's revelation of why he had been planning to move away at the end of the story?

9. What was your initial impression of Graham? Did your feelings change as the story went on? How is love at a later stage in life different than it would be for a younger couple?

10. How did Ike's patience eventually win over Maya and Dahlia? What challenges do parents face as they seek to balance their kids' needs with their own?

11. What do you think is at the root of Lillian's bitterness toward Sassy? Why do you think she is able to have a change of heart all these years later?

12. As Sassy celebrates her seventieth birthday, she is thinking about the kind of legacy she wants to leave. After reading this story, what legacy did Sassy leave you with? What about Rose and Dahlia? What kind of legacy do you want to leave for the people in your life?

About the Author

National bestselling author Sara Richardson composes uplifting stories that illustrate the rocky roads of love, friendship, and family relationships. Her characters are strong women journeying to define their lives and pursue their dreams. Her books have received numerous award nominations and critical acclaim, with *Publishers Weekly* recognizing her stories as "emotionally rich, charmingly funny, and sensitive."

After graduating with a master's degree in journalism, Sarah realized she was too empathetic to be a reporter and started writing her first novel. When not writing, Sara can be found promoting women's health and empowerment by teaching Pilates or hiking the trails near her house. A lifelong Colorado girl, Sara lives and plays near the mountains with her husband, two sons, two fur babies, and a tortoise named Leo.